THE FALLS OF DOOM

Under the blazing sun, the path climbed steeply toward the top of the cliff. The rags on Wallie's feet were blood-soaked, and the pain and heat seemed unendurable. Then they were at the top. The prisoners were unchained and allowed to collapse.

Peering over the edge, Wallie saw white fury and rocks. No man could come through that alive. Nor did it seem possible to leap far enough to soar beyond to the still water at the base of the falls. He shook his head, raging at the injustice and cruelty.

A guard called time. The first prisoner went limp. Slaves carried him to the edge and swung. One by one, the prisoners went over the edge, to be torn apart by the rocks and fury below.

Then it was Wallie's turn, and he started hobbling down the slope. He increased his speed to a run, reached the edge, threw his arms out, and sailed off into space in a ragged dive.

There was wind and spray in his face, and then nothing.

By Dave Duncan
Published by Ballantine Books:

A ROSE-RED CITY

SHADOW

The Seventh Sword
THE RELUCTANT SWORDSMAN
*THE COMING OF WISDOM
*THE DESTINY OF THE SWORD

*Forthcoming

THE RELUCTANT SWORDSMAN

Book One of *The Seventh Sword*

DAVE DUNCAN

A Del Rey Book

BALLANTINE BOOKS • NEW YORK

The Seventh Sword
is fondly dedicated to
JENNI and JUDY
who had patience, love, and understanding
for a father with such strange unworldly ideas.

CONTENTS

BOOK ONE: HOW THE SWORDSMAN WAS
SUMMONED 3

BOOK TWO: HOW THE SWORDSMAN
RECEIVED THE SWORD 67

BOOK THREE: HOW THE SWORD WAS NAMED 129

BOOK FOUR: HOW THE SWORDSMAN WAS
ENSNARED 195

BOOK FIVE: HOW THE SWORDSMAN
FOUND HIS BROTHER 267

APPENDIX: LIST OF SWORDSMEN

SMITH—Walter Charles Smith, aged 36 years, passed away on April 8th, at Sanderson Memorial Hospital, after a brief illness. He is survived by his sister, Mrs. Cecily Smith Paddon, of Auckland, New Zealand, and an uncle, Mr. Clyde Franks, of Pasadena, California. Born in Weyback, Saskatchewan, Walter attended high school in Binghamton, New York. He obtained his Bachelor of Engineering degree from the University of Waterloo, Ontario, and an MBA from Harvard. During the past three years he was manager of the local AKL petrochemical plant. He will be greatly mourned by the many friends he made during his short stay in our community, and his willing and generous contributions to it will be sadly missed. Walter was active in the United Way, Uncles at Large, and the Historical Society, and at the time of his passing was president of Avenue Tennis Club. In accordance with his wishes, his body has been donated to medical research. Memorial service will be held at Parkdale Unitarian Church on Tuesday, April 12th, at 2 P.M. In lieu of flowers, contributions may be sent to Uncles at Large, 1215 River Road.

BOOK ONE:

HOW THE SWORDSMAN WAS SUMMONED

†

"Keep my heart true to Your laws," Honakura warbled, laying a shaky left hand on the smooth brilliance of the tiled floor.

"Let me serve Your will with all my strength," he wailed, cracking on the high note as usual, and placing his equally frail right hand beside the left.

"And show my eyes Your purposes." This was the tricky part—the ritual called for him to touch his forehead to the mosaic, but he had not achieved that maneuver these last fifteen years. He curled forward as far as he could. If the Goddess chose to stiffen his ancient joints, then She would have to settle for the best he could manage... and of course She would.

He strained there for a moment, hearing the quiet chanting of other priests and priestesses nearby as they also made their way through the morning dedication. Then, with a quiet and unscheduled "Ooof!" of relief he pushed himself back to sit on his heels, place his palms together, and look up adoringly at Her. Now he was permitted a silent and private prayer, a personal appeal. He had no doubt what it would be, this day as many before it. *Most High Goddess, do something about the swordsmen of Your guard!*

She did not reply. He did not expect Her to. This was not the Goddess Herself, but merely an image to assist

3

humble mortals in visualizing Her greatness. Who should know that better than a priest of the seventh rank? But She would hear his prayer and one day She would answer.

"Amen!" he quavered.

Now he could start to plan his day, but he remained for a moment sitting on his heels, hands still together, reflecting, gazing up lovingly at the majesty of the Most High and the vast stone trelliswork above Her, the roof of Her temple, the holiest of all the holy places in the World.

He had many meetings planned—with the Keeper of the Coffers, with the Master of Discipline for Acolytes, with many others, almost all holders of offices that Honakura himself had held at one time or another. Now he was merely Third Deputy Chairman of the Council of Venerables. That innocent-sounding title concealed much more than it revealed. Power, he had long since discovered, is best exercised in secret.

Around him the morning dedications were ending. Already the first of the day's many pilgrims were being led in to make their offerings and supplications. Money was clinking into the bowls; prayers being mumbled under the quiet prompting of priests. He would begin, Honakura decided, by guiding a few pilgrims himself. It was a worthy service to the Most Holy; it was a task he enjoyed; it was a good example for the juniors. He lowered his hands and glanced around in the hope that there might be someone handy to help him rise—not the easiest of movements for him now.

At once a brown robe was at his side and strong hands assisted him. With a quiet mutter of thanks, Honakura reached his feet. He was about to turn away when the man spoke.

"I am Jannarlu, priest of the third rank..." He was making the salute to a superior, words and hand gestures and bowings. For a moment Honakura reacted with shock and disapproval. Surely this young man did not think that so trifling a service could justify him in forcing himself on a lord of the Seventh? This place, before the dais and the idol, was the holy of holies, and while there was no law against conversation or formal saluting here, custom forbade it. Then he recalled this Jannarlu. He was old Hangafau's grandson, said to have promise. He must know better, and therefore must have good reason for the impropriety.

So Honakura waited until the salute was completed and then made the ritual response: "I am Honakura, priest of the seventh rank..." One of Jannarlu's face-marks was still slightly inflamed, so he was a very new Third. He was tall—much taller than the diminutive Honakura—with a bony, ungainly presence and a hook nose. He seemed absurdly young, but then they all did these days.

Close by, an ancient crone dropped a gold in the bowl and began entreating the Goddess to cure the agony in her bowels. Beyond her a young couple were praying that She not send them any more children, for a few years at least.

As soon as Honakura had finished, the words spurted from Jannarlu: "My lord, there is a swordsman... a Seventh!"

She had answered!

"You left him out there?" Honakura demanded furiously, keeping his voice down with difficulty, struggling not to show emotion to anyone who might be watching.

The Third flinched, but nodded. "He is a Nameless One, my lord."

Honakura hissed in astonishment. Incredible! With forehead covered and wearing only black, like a beggar, anyone could become a Nameless One. By law, such persons could bear no goods and must be on the service of the Goddess. Many regarded it as a special penance, so the practice was not uncommon among pilgrims coming to the temple. But for a lord of the Seventh to reduce his standing in such a way was highly unusual. For a swordsman of any rank it was almost unthinkable. For a swordsman of the seventh rank... incredible!

It did explain how he had arrived alive.

Could he be kept alive?

"I told him to cover again, my lord," Jannarlu said diffidently. "He . . . he seemed quite pleased to do so."

There was a hint of levity there, and Honakura shot him a warning glance while he pondered. Jannarlu's ugly brown face seemed slightly flushed.

"You did not hurry, I hope?"

The Third shook his head. "No, my lord. I followed . . ." He gestured toward the sick old crone, who was now being helped up by her attendant priestess.

"Well done, priest!" said Honakura, mollified. "Let us go and see this wonder of yours. We shall walk slowly, conversing of holy matters . . . and not in quite the right direction, if you please."

The young man blushed with pleasure at the praise and fell into step beside him.

The great temple of the Goddess at Hann was not only the richest and oldest building in the World, it was certainly the largest. As Honakura turned from the dais, he was faced with a seemingly endless expanse of gleaming, multicolored floor, stretching off to the seven great arches that formed the façade. Many people were walking there, coming or going—pilgrims and their guides of the priesthood—but so vast was the space that mere human beings seemed hardly larger than mouse droppings. Beyond the arches, out in the brilliant sunlight, lay a view of the canyon and the River and the Judgment, whose rumbling roar had filled the temple for all its many millennia. Along the sides of the wide nave stood the shrines of lesser gods and goddesses, and above them the fretted windows blazed in hues of ruby, emerald, amethyst, and gold.

Honakura's prayer had been answered. No . . . the prayers of many. He was certainly not the only one of Her servants here to make that prayer each day, yet it was to him that the news had been brought. He must move with caution and courage and determination, but he felt warm satisfaction that he had been chosen.

It took a long time for him to reach the arches, with the young Third fidgeting at his side. They made an odd pair, Honakura knew, in their priestly gowns, Jannarlu in the brown of a Third and he in the blue of a Seventh. The younger man was tall, but Honakura had never been tall and now he was shrunken and stooped, toothless and hairless. The juniors referred to him behind his back as the Wise Monkey, and the term amused him. Old age had few amusements. In the unkind silent hours of night he would feel his bones rubbing against the sheets and quietly wish that She would soon rescue him from it and let him start anew. Yet perhaps She was reserving him in this life for one last service, and if so, then this was surely it. A swordsman of the seventh rank! They were rare, as the priests had discovered—rare, and very precious when needed.

As he walked, he decided that young Jannarlu had shown great discretion in coming to him, and not to some blabbermouth middlerank. He should be rewarded. And kept quiet.

"Who is your mentor now?" he asked. "Yes, I know him. A worthy and holy man. But the Honorable Londossinu is in need of another protégé to assist him in some new duties. They are sensitive matters, and he needs a man of reticence and discretion."

He glanced sideways at the youngster beside him and saw a flush of pleasure and excitement. "I should be greatly honored, my lord."

So he should be, a Third being offered a Sixth as mentor, but he seemed to be hearing the message. "Then I shall speak to your mentor and the holy one, and see if a transfer can be arranged. It will have to wait until after this matter of the swordsman, of course...until after that has been successfully concluded."

"Of course, my lord." Young Jannarlu was staring straight ahead, but could not quite suppress a smile.

"And where are you in your inurement?"

"I am due to start the fifth silence in another week," said the lad, adding helpfully, "I am eager to begin."

"You will begin as soon as I have met this marvel of yours," Honakura stated, with a silent chuckle. "I shall send word to your mentor." An astute young man! The fifth silence lasted two weeks—the matter would certainly be settled by then.

At last they had reached the arches. Beyond them the great steps fell away like a hillside to the temple court. The top was already cluttered with rows of pilgrims patiently kneeling in the shadow. Later in the day, when the tropic sun discovered them, they would find the waiting harder.

Out of habit the priest glanced over the faces of the closest. As his eyes met theirs they bowed their heads respectfully to him, but from long experience he had already read the rank and craft marks of their brows and made a preliminary diagnosis—a potter of the Third, probably a health problem; a spinster of the Second, perhaps a sterility case; a goldsmith of the Fifth, good for a fair offering.

Few of the heads were bound. Honakura could make an easy guess as to the swordsman. The man had chosen to approach one of the side arches, which was fortunate because the token guard stood only at the center arch, but it was a curious choice for one of his rank. Something must be seriously awry for him.

"The big one, I assume? Very well. And there, I believe, is the Honorable Londossinu himself. Let us speak to him right away." That was convenient, for Honakura disliked overloading his memory these days, and it was surely the handiwork of the Holiest. The whole affair was then disposed of in a dozen words—plus a few meaningful glances, nuances, hints, and insinuations. The transfer of mentors would be arranged, and Londossinu would get the committee appointments he had been seeking for two other protégés, plus promotion for another. And young Jannarlu would be kept quiet. Honakura waited until he saw the young man head back into the temple to begin the ritual of silence, quite unaware of most of the dealings that had just been completed around him. There was no hurry; the Nameless could bring no offerings and hence were low priority for the attendants.

Yes, the handiwork of the Goddess! His prayers had been answered by a highrank swordsman, the man had come—*incredibly!*—incognito and hence safely, and he had even avoided the two bored swordsmen posturing by the center arch, who might just possibly have guessed from his long hair that he was a swordsman. Praise to the Goddess!

Honakura began to amble in the right direction, nodding his head to the bows he received. By law, a Nameless One could only be questioned by priests or searched by swordsmen, but it was not unknown for junior swordsmen to torment such for sport. The little priest wondered what the reaction would be if some were to try that and discover that they were dealing with a swordsman of the Seventh. It would be an entertaining incident to watch. Fortunately, in the present case, the man's rank had not yet been revealed.

At last he reached his objective.

The man was very large indeed—even kneeling, he carried his eyes not much beneath Honakura's. Swordsmen were rarely large, for speed was more important to them than strength. If this man also had agility he would be formidable, but then he was, reputedly, a Seventh, and there could be none more formidable. Apart from the black rag around his head, he wore only a dirty scrap of black loincloth. He was filthy and sweat-streaked, yet his size and youth made him impressive still. His hair was also black, hanging to his shoulders, and his eyes were utterly black, the pupils lost in the iris. Forceful eyes...bearing anger they would strike dread. Looking into them now, Honakura saw other things: pain and fear and despondency. Those came often to the Goddess in the eyes of supplicants—the sick, the dying, the bereaved, the lost—but rarely had he seen them so intense, and their presence in the eyes of this huge and healthy youngster was a staggering shock to him. Awry indeed!

"Let us go over to a more private place," he said quickly. "My lord?"

The young man rose effortlessly, rising over the little priest as dawn climbs the sky. He was very big and when he moved he rippled. Even for a swordsman he was young to be a Seventh, probably younger than Priest Jannarlu of the Third.

They walked to the end of the façade, and Honakura motioned to the plinth of a badly corroded statue. The swordsman sat without argument. His apathy was astonishing.

"Let us dispense with formalities for the moment," Honakura said quietly, remaining on his feet, "for we are not unobserved. I am Honakura, priest of the seventh rank."

"I am Shonsu, swordsman, and also of the Seventh." His voice was in keeping with the rest of him, massive. Distant thunder. He raised a hand to remove the rag, and Honakura shook his head.

"You seek help from the Goddess?"

"I am haunted by a demon, holiness."

That explained the eyes. "Demons can be exorcised, but they rarely ravage those of high rank," Honakura said. "Pray tell me of it."

The fearsome young man shuddered. "It is the color of sour milk. It has yellow hair on its belly and its limbs and its face, but none on top of its head, as though its head were put on upside down."

Honakura shuddered, also, and made the sign of the Goddess.

The swordsman continued, "It has no foreskin."

"Do you know its name?"

"Oh yes," Shonsu sighed. "It babbles at me from dusk until dawn, and lately even by day. Little it says makes sense, but its name is Walliesmith."

"Walliesmith?" Honakura echoed doubtfully.

"Walliesmith," the swordsman repeated in a voice that could not be doubted.

That was not the name of any of the seven hundred

and seventy-seven demons—but a demon would naturally not tell the truth unless properly invoked. And, while the sutras catalogued demons of the most hideous and grotesque aspect, Honakura had never heard of one so perverse as to grow hair on its face.

"The Goddess will know it, and it can be expelled," he said. "What offering will you make to Her in return?"

Sadly the young man dropped his gaze. "My lord, I have nothing left to offer, except my strength and my skill."

A swordsman, and he did not mention honor?

"Perhaps a year or two of service in our temple guard?" Honakura suggested, watching closely. "The reeve is the valorous Lord Hardduju of the Seventh."

The swordsman's was a hard face, and now he gave the priest a hard look. "How many Sevenths do you need in a temple guard?" he asked warily. "And by what oath would I be sworn?"

Honakura edged a little closer to his meaning. "I am not familiar with all your swordsman oaths, my lord. Now that you mention it, I never remember more than one Seventh in the guard at a time, and I have worked here more than sixty years."

They studied each other in silence for a moment. The swordsman frowned. While his kind had few scruples at eradicating each other, they did not often appreciate advice on the subject from civilians. Honakura decided to reveal a little more.

"It is rare for highrank swordsmen to visit the temple," he said. "None at all for at least two years. Curiously, though, I have heard of several who arrived at Hann and stated that to be their intention—at least one Seventh and a couple of Sixths."

The swordsman's huge fists clenched. "Implying?"

"I imply nothing!" Honakura said hastily. "Pure hearsay. They were reported to be planning to take the ferry, and then that long trail through the trees. Probably they changed their minds. One did make as near as a pilgrims' hostelry, but was unfortunate enough to partake there of some tainted meat. You are all the more welcome for your rarity, my lord."

Muscles did not necessarily imply stupidity—the young man understood. A dark flush of fury crept over his cheekbones.

He glanced around, looking at the grandiose façade of the temple and at the great court below, flanked by the shingle beach and the still pool, beyond that to the River frothing and foaming as it emerged from the canyon, and along the canyon to the mist-shrouded splendor of the Judgment. Then he turned his head to survey the wooded park of the temple grounds with the big houses of the senior officials. One of those would certainly go with the office of reeve. "To be a swordsman in Her temple guard would be a great honor," he said.

"It seems to be even better rewarded these days than it used to be," Honakura remarked helpfully.

The hard face became menacing. "A man could borrow a sword, I expect?"

"That could be arranged."

The young man nodded. "My service is always to the Goddess."

Now that, Honakura thought happily, was how a deal should be made. Murder had not even been mentioned.

"But first the exorcism?" the swordsman said.

"Certainly, my lord." Honakura could not remember an exorcism in the last five years, but he was familiar with the ritual. "Fortunately, it does not require that your craft or even rank be mentioned. And your present garb will be adequate."

The swordsman sighed with relief. "And it will succeed?"

One did not become or prevail as Third Deputy Chairman of the Council of Venerables without learning to cover one's hindquarters. "It will succeed, my lord, unless..."

"Unless?" echoed the swordsman, his broad face darkening with suspicion...

Or was it guilt? Carefully Honakura said, "Unless the

demon has been sent by the Most High Herself. Only you know whether you have committed some grievous transgression against Her."

An expression of great agony and sorrow fell over the swordsman's face. He dropped his eyes and was silent for a while. Then he looked up defiantly and growled, "It was sent by the sorcerers."

Sorcerers! The little priest staggered back a step. "Sorcerers!" he blurted. "My lord, in all my years in this temple, I have never heard a pilgrim mention sorcerers. I had hardly thought that such truly existed any more."

Now the swordsman's eyes became as terrible as the priest had guessed they might. "Oh, they exist!" he rumbled. "I have come very far, holy one, very far. But sorcerers exist, believe me."

Honakura pulled himself together. "Sorcerers cannot prevail against the Holiest," he said confidently. "Certainly not in Her own temple. If they are the origin of your distress, then the exorcism will succeed. Shall we see to it?"

Honakura beckoned over an orange-gowned Fourth and gave orders. Then he led the swordsman through the nearest arch and along the length of the nave to the statue of the Goddess.

The big man sauntered at Honakura's side, taking one stride to his three, but his head twisted and turned as he gaped around at the splendor, as all visitors must on their first glimpse of this most holy sanctuary—seeing the great blue statue itself, the silver dais before it loaded with heaps of glittering offerings, the multicolored flaming of the stained-glass windows along both sides, the miraculous fan vaulting of the ceiling hanging like distant sky above. The temple was busy, with many priests, priestesses, pilgrims, and other worshipers moving over the shining mosaics of the pavement, yet their tiny figures were dwindled to dust specks by its immensity, and the vast space seemed filled with a still peace.

Inevitably, as he drew near, the swordsman became conscious only of the majesty of the statue, the Goddess Herself, the shape of a robed woman sitting cross-legged with Her hands on Her knees and Her long hair spilling down. Huge and ominous and majestic, She loomed more and more enormous as he approached. At last he reached the edge of the dais and threw himself on the ground in reverence.

An exorcism called for many priests and priestesses, for chanting, dancing, gesturing, ritual, and solemn ceremony. Honakura stood to one side and allowed Perandoro of the Sixth to officiate, for it was a rare opportunity. He himself had led an exorcism only once. The swordsman crouched on his knees within the circle, head down and arms outstretched as he had been instructed—put a tablecloth on that back, and it would hold a dinner for three. Other priests and priestesses watched covertly as they went about their business. Pilgrims were shunted tactfully to the sides. It was very impressive.

Honakura paid little attention to the preliminaries. He was busy planning his next move against the unspeakable Hardduju. A sword was easy—he could get one from Athinalani in the armory. A blue kilt for a Seventh was no problem, either, and a hairclip was a trivial detail. But swordsmen sported distinctive boots, and to send for a pair of those, especially in the size required, would certainly provoke suspicion. Furthermore, he was fairly sure that the rituals of dueling required that his new champion obtain a second, and that could make things complicated. It might be that he would have to spirit this dangerous young man out of sight for a day or two while the preparations were put in hand, but so far his presence was a secret. Honakura felt great satisfaction that the Goddess had not only answered the priests' prayers in this fashion, but had also entrusted him with the subcontracting. He felt sure that Her confidence was not misplaced. He would see that there were no mistakes.

Then the chant rose to its climax, and a chorus of, "Avaunt!" The swordsman's head came up, first looking wildly around, and then up at the Goddess.

Honakura frowned. The dolt had been told to keep his head down.

"Avaunt!" proclaimed the chanters once more, their rhythm just a fraction off perfection. The swordsman jerked upright on his knees, head back and eyes so wide that the whites were showing all around. The drummers went ragged on their beat, and a trumpeter flubbed a note.

"Avaunt!" cried the chorus a third time. Perandoro raised a silver goblet full of holy water from the River and cast the contents over the swordsman's head.

He spasmed incredibly, leaping straight from his knees into the air and coming down on his feet. The dirty loincloth fluttered to the floor, and he stood there naked, with his arms raised, his head back, water dribbling down his face and chest. He shrieked the loudest noise that Honakura had ever heard uttered by a human throat. For perhaps the first time in the age-old history of the temple, one voice drowned out the chorus, the lutes and flutes, and the distant roar of the Judgment. It was discordant, bestial, horrifying, and full of soul-destroying despair. It reverberated back from the roof. It went on for an incredible, inhuman, unbelievable minute, while the singers and musicians became hopelessly tangled, the dancers stumbled and collided, and every eye went wide. Then the ceremony ended in a chaotic, clattering roll of drums, and the swordsman swayed over backward.

He fell like a marble pillar. In the sudden silence his head hit the tiles with an audible crack.

He lay still, huge and newborn-naked. The rag had fallen off his forehead, revealing for all to see the craftmarks on his forehead, the seven swords.

††

The temple was a building whose origins lay hidden back in the Neolithic. Many times it had been enlarged, and most of the fabric had been replaced from time to time as it had weathered or decayed—not once, but often.

Yet the temple was also people. They aged and were replaced much faster. Each fresh-faced acolyte would look in wonder at an ancient sage of the Seventh and marvel that the old man had probably known so-and-so in his youth, little thinking that the old man himself as a neophyte had studied that same so-and-so and mused that he was old enough to have known such-and-such. Thus, like stones in an arch, the men and women of the temple reached from the darkness of the past into the unviewable glare of the future. They nurtured the ancient traditions and holy ways and they worshiped the Goddess in solemnity and veneration...

But none of them had ever known a day like that one. Elderly priestesses of the Sixth were seen running; questions and answers were shouted across the very face of the Goddess, violating all tradition; slaves and bearers and healers milled around in the most holy places; and pilgrims wandered unattended before the dais itself. Four of the largest male juniors were led into back rooms by venerable seniors of unquestioned moral probity, then ordered to take off their clothing and lie down. Three respected Sevenths had heart attacks before lunch.

The spider at the center of the web of confusion was Honakura. It was he who poked the stick in the ant hill and stirred. He summoned all his authority, his unspoken power, his unparalleled knowledge of the workings of the temple, and his undoubted wits—and he used them to muddle, confuse, confound, and disorder. He used them with expertise and finesse. He issued a torrent of commands—peremptory, obscure, convoluted, misleading, and contradictory.

By the time the valiant Lord Hardduju, reeve of the temple guard, had confirmed that truly there was another swordsman of the Seventh within the precincts, the man had totally vanished, and no amount of cajolery, bribery, interrogation, or menace could establish where he had gone.

Which was, of course, the whole idea.

Even a day like that one must end. As the sun god began to grow tired of his glory and dip toward his exit, the venerable Lord Honakura sought rest and peace in a small room high in one of the minor wings of the temple. He had not visited those parts for years. They were even more labyrinthine than the rest of the complex, but ideal for his purpose. Trouble, he knew, was seeking him out—it might as well be given as long a search as possible.

The room was a small, bare chamber, higher than it was wide, with walls of sandstone blocks and a scarred floor of planks bearing one small, threadbare rug. There were two doors, for which even giants need not have stooped, and a single window of diamond panes, whorled and dusty, blurring the light to green and blue blotches. The window frame had warped so that it would not open, making the room stuffy, smelling of dust. The only furniture was a pair of oaken settles. Honakura was perched on one of those, dangling his feet, trying to catch his breath, wondering if there was any small detail he might have overlooked.

Knuckles tapped, a familiar face peered in and blinked at him. He sighed and rose as his nephew Dinartura entered, closed the door, and advanced to make the salute to a superior.

"I am Dinartura," *right hand to heart,* "healer of the third rank," *left hand to forehead,* "and it is my deepest and most humble wish," *palms together at the waist,* "that the Goddess Herself," *ripple motion with right hand,* "will see fit to grant you long life and happiness," *eyes up, hands at the sides,* "and to induce you to accept my modest and willing service," *eyes down,* "in any way in which I may advance any of your noble purposes," *hands over face, bow.*

Honakura responded with the equally flowery acknowledgment, then waved him to the other settle.

"How is your dear mother?" he asked.

Dinartura was a stooped young man with thinning light-brown hair and the start of a potbelly. He had lately abandoned the kilt of youth for the sleeveless gown of middle age, a cotton robe in the brown color of his rank, and he tended now to hold things very close to his nose when he wanted to see them. He was the youngest of Honakura's sister's children and, in Honakura's opinion, an inexcusably prosaic dullard, boringly reliable.

After the formalities had been given a respectable hearing, Honakura said, "And how is the patient?" He smiled, but he waited anxiously for the reply.

"Still out cold when I left." Dinartura was presuming on his nephewship to be informal. "He has a bump on his head this big, but there are no morbid signs. Eyes and ears are fine. I expect he will awaken in time, and be as good as new in a day or two."

Honakura sighed with relief, so the healer added hastily, "If She wills, of course. Head injuries are not predictable. If I did not know you, my lord uncle, I would be more cautious."

"We must be patient, then. You think two days?"

"Three might be safer," the healer said. "If you have any strenuous exercise in mind for him," he added, being uncharacteristically perceptive. "When you need to tie him down would be about right, I think." After a pause he said, "And may I inquire what all this is about? There are many rumors, not one of which seems credible."

Honakura chuckled, slavering slightly. "Find the least credible and you will be closest to the truth. Under the nightingale, then?"

"Of course, my lord."

Honakura smiled to himself at the memory. "Your patient is one of five young men injured in the temple today."

"Five!" Dinartura peered closer to see if his uncle was serious.

For a moment Honakura wondered how much power he had expended during the day. He had very few IOUs left to call now; he had amassed debts. "Very sad, you will agree? All lying prone, covered by sheets, and not speaking or moving. All have been rushed to safe places —in litters, in sedan chairs, in carriages. In some case the litters were borne by priests, too! At least twenty-two healers have been running around, and a few dozen other people. A couple of the victims were taken right out of the temple grounds, into the town, but others went from room to room, in one door and out the other... There are eight or nine sickrooms like this"—he gestured toward the other great oaken door —"presently being guarded."

That door led out into another corridor, but he saw no reason to mention the fact.

"Guarded by priests," the younger man said. "Then you do not trust the swordsmen? Of course I saw my patient. Do swordsmen really act as you obviously fear?"

The priest nodded sadly. "In this case, nephew, perhaps."

The temple had a guard to maintain order, to protect the pilgrims, and to punish crime... but who watched the watchers?

"I have heard stories," Dinartura muttered, "of pilgrims molested on the trail, especially. Are you saying that the swordsmen do this?"

"Ah, well!" Honakura replied cautiously. "Not directly. The gang or gangs on the trail are not swordsmen —but they are not tracked down as they should be, so there is bribery."

"But surely most are men of honor?" protested his nephew. "Are there none you can trust?"

The old man sighed. "Run down to the courtyard, then," he suggested. "Pick out a swordsman—a Third, say, or a Fourth—and ask him if he is a man of honor. If he says—"

The healer paled and made the sign of the Goddess. "I had rather not, my lord!"

His uncle chuckled. "You are sure?"

"Quite sure, thank you, my lord!"

Pity! Honakura found the thought entertaining. "You are right, in a way, nephew. Most, I am sure, are honorable, but every one is sworn to a mentor, who in turn is sworn to his own mentor or, ultimately, to the reeve himself. He alone has given an oath to the temple. Now, if he does not order a patrol on the trail, who is to suggest it to him? The rest obey orders—and say nothing. Indeed, they must guard their tongues even more carefully than the rest of us. Their danger is greater."

Then he noticed the look he was being given and knew exactly what thought accompanied it: *The old boy is wonderful for his age* ... He found that very irritating and patronizing. He was still better at almost anything than this ninny would ever be.

"So what are you doing about it, my lord uncle?"

Typically stupid question, Honakura thought. "Praying, of course! Today She answered our prayers by sending a Seventh. She summoned a demon to drive him here."

"Are your exorcisms always so violent?" Dinartura asked and flinched at the frown he received.

"Exorcisms are rare, but the sutras warn that there may be extreme reaction." Honakura fell silent, and there was a pause.

The settle creaked as Dinartura leaned back and regarded his uncle with some curiosity. "This Seventh?" he asked. "Why insult him with those quarters, with a single slave instead of a flock of attendants?"

Honakura recovered his good spirits and chuckled.

"It was the most unlikely place I could think to put him—a lowly pilgrim cottage. It opens directly onto a busy road, and he has no clothes, so he isn't going anywhere if he wakes up. But tell me," he added with interest. "The slave? Kikarani promised a pretty one. How did she look?"

His nephew frowned, thinking. "Just a slave girl," he said. "I told her to wash him. She was tall . . . and large. Yes, quite pretty, I suppose." He thought some more and added, "A certain animal sensuality, if a man wanted that."

That was typical! At least Honakura still noticed pretty girls. He knew very well what duties Priestess Kikarani assigned to her slaves. She fought fang and claw to keep her position as hospitaler, so he could guess what sort of girls she had. "Nephew! Did you not notice?"

The younger man's face turned pink. "I think that she will suffice, uncle, if the swordsman wakes up and wants something to do . . . and finds that he has no clothes."

The old priest cackled. He would have said more, but at that moment the door flew open, and loud voices could be heard shouting in the anteroom. Then the reeve marched in. Honakura scrambled to his feet and scurried over to the other exit. He turned his back on the door and the blandest expression he could manage on the newcomer.

Hardduju of the Seventh was a large man, although not the size of Shonsu. He was around forty, starting to run to fat. His beefiness bulged over the top of a kilt of blue brocade shot through with gold thread; it bulged also between the tooled leather straps of his harness. He had no neck. The sword hilt behind his right ear glittered and flashed with many small rubies set in gold filigree. The hairclip holding his thinning ponytail shone in matching gold and ruby fires, as did the gold and ruby band on one fleshy arm. His boots were of kidskin beaded with garnets. His heavy face was inflamed and furious.

"Hah!" he said on seeing Honakura. For a moment the two stood in silent confrontation—neither the priests' craft nor the swordsmen's could ever admit that the other had higher status. But Hardduju was obviously the younger, and the visitor. Moreover, he was impatient, so he yielded precedence, whipping out his sword. The healer flinched, but it was merely the start of the swordsmen's version of the greeting to an equal. "I am Hardduju, swordsman of the seventh rank . . ."

When it was finished, Honakura gave his most impeccable response in his thin, slurred voice, waving his twisted old hands in the gestures.

Behind the reeve appeared a muscular young swordsman of the Fourth in an orange kilt, and a weedy slave in the usual black loincloth. The slave carried a large bundle wrapped in a cloak. He was ignored, but after a hesitation, Hardduju proceeded to present Adept Gorramini.

Honakura in turn offered Healer Dinartura.

Then the swordsman stepped very close, folded his thick arms, and glared down at the little priest. "You have a swordsman of the Seventh?" he barked, without waiting for further niceties.

"You refer to the formidable Lord Shonsu, I presume?" Honakura said, as though there might be some doubt. "I did have the honor of being of assistance to the dread lord this morning, yes." He studied Hardduju's harness with interest, it being at eye level for him.

"An exorcism, I understand?" The swordsman was having trouble keeping his voice within polite limits, the priest noted—and made a vow to irritate him much more before he was done. He raised an invisible eyebrow at the harness and mumbled some nonsense about professional ethics.

"It would have been proper for the valiant lord to have paid his respects to me upon arrival," Hardduju snarled, "but then I understand that he was not suitably dressed. I have come, therefore, to wait upon him and wish him a speedy recovery."

"You are most gracious, my lord." Honakura beamed.

"I shall certainly see that your good offices are reported to him."

The swordsman scowled. "I have brought a sword and other trappings for him."

That was unexpected good fortune. Honakura wondered how reliable the sword might be. "Your kindness is beyond belief! If you would be so good as to have your slave leave them here, then I shall see that he gets them and is informed of your benevolence."

A low growl escaped from the beefy chest. "I beg leave to pay him my respects in person. *Now!*"

The old man shook his head sadly. "He is resting, and indeed is in the care of the resourceful healer."

Hardduju turned to regard Dinartura like something scraped off the sole of his boot. "A Third, to care for a Seventh? I shall bring a more cunning and a better."

"The knowledgeable healer is a nephew of mine," Honakura remarked brightly.

"Aha!" Hardduju bared teeth in satisfaction. "So I have found the real one at last! Well, I shall not disturb the doughty lord unduly. But I *shall* pay my respects." He reached to open the door, and Honakura spread his arms to block him. He was not seriously worried about overt violence, for priests were sacrosanct, but he knew that he might be laying himself open to dark deeds in the future. Hopefully Shonsu would take care of that possibility for him in a day or two.

For a moment the two faced off. The reeve started to raise his sword hand.

"Go ahead, my lord," Honakura baited. Even the gorilla of the Fourth was looking startled at the move.

But the reeve was not quite rash enough to draw on a priest of the Seventh. Instead he just picked him up like a child and set him aside. Then he flung open the door and marched through it.

The younger swordsman grinned triumphantly at the priest and moved to follow. He was almost knocked over as Hardduju came storming back into the room.

Honakura winked at his nephew.

Then he turned politely back to the reeve. "You will have to be patient, my lord, as I said." He paused and then added very deliberately, "But the implacable lord has assured me that he will call upon you in the near future."

The swordsman glared furiously... apprehensively? Then he barked at the slave to lay down the bundle and led Gorramini away. The slave closed the door silently. Honakura looked at his nephew and chuckled, rubbing his hands.

He tottered off wearily then toward his own quarters, thinking he had earned a warm soak and a good repast. By the time he arrived, however, he had reluctantly concluded that his normally lackluster nephew had made an astute observation for once. No lord of the seventh rank would be pleased to awaken in a sleazy pilgrim hut. An important ally must not be alienated. He issued more orders.

Shortly thereafter, no less than six sedan chairs began to circulate around the temple grounds, all with curtains drawn. One by one they eventually passed out through the gate into the town and circulated some more. They dropped passengers and then picked up others...

Having changed sedan chairs twice, and being satisfied that he had sufficiently confused any possible followers, Honakura ordered his bearers to proceed out of town. There was only one road, and it angled steeply up the valley wall. A few centuries earlier some enterprising builder had constructed a line of cottages along the side of this road, and these were available for pilgrims—not the wealthy, but not the poorest either, for the poor slept under trees.

He had not come this way for many years and he peered with almost childish excitement through a gap in the curtain at the tangle of roofs and treetops below him. Beyond the town, of course, towered the massive pile of the temple itself, its golden spires gleaming in the warm rays of the sun god, who was now nearing the horizon by the pillar of spray that stood always above the Judgment. The worst part of old age, Honakura decided then, was boredom. He had not enjoyed a day so much for longer than he could recall.

The chair stopped, and he clambered out as nimbly as he could, dodging then through the bead curtain that hung over the cottage door before him.

The place was even smaller and more dingy than he had expected, merely four walls of greasy stone blocks and a low thatch ceiling that stank abominably after a day of tropic sun. He noted the one window and a bed whose sag and tilt were obvious even from the doorway; uneven stone flags on the floor; two ramshackle wood chairs and a rough table; a small bronze mirror fastened to the wall. After a couple of breaths he could smell the acrid traces of urine and bodies under the stink of the thatch. The fleas and bedbugs could be taken for granted.

Evening sunlight streamed through the window onto the wall beside the bed, where the swordsman lay flat on his back. He looked even larger than Honakura remembered, wearing nothing but a cloth laid over his loins, sleeping as babies should but so seldom do.

A girl was sitting on one of the chairs at his side, patiently waving a fly whisk. She slid swiftly to her knees when she saw the rank of her visitor. Honakura waved at her to rise, then turned as his bearers followed him in with a large hamper and the bundle contributed by the nefarious Hardduju. Quietly he ordered them to return in an hour.

The swordsman was obviously alive, but not conscious, and hence no immediate problem. Because he had teased his nephew on the subject, the old man took the time to study the girl's appearance more carefully than he might otherwise have done. She wore only a brief black wrap, of course, and her hair was roughly hacked short, but she was clearly of good peasant stock —tall and strongly built, her features broad but attractive, marred by the black slave line that ran down the middle of her face from hairline to mouth. Yet her skin was free of pockmarks, her breasts were splendidly rounded under the wrap, her limbs well formed. The wide, full lips looked enticing. Honakura was impressed. She was probably worth five or six golds on the open market. He wondered how much Kikarani made off her in a week and how many more like her the old witch ran in her stable. Yes, had the swordsman required entertainment, he would certainly have found this one adequate.

"Has he awakened at all?"

She shook her head, nervous at his high rank. "No, my lord." She had a pleasantly tuneful contralto voice. "I thought he was going to, my lord, for he was groaning. Then he quieted. He seems to be just sleeping a normal sort of sleep now, my lord."

That seemed a reasonable guess, and it was a perceptive comment from a slave.

Obviously she had obeyed Dinartura's instructions and washed the swordsman. He looked quite respectable. She had even combed out his long black hair.

Honakura hesitated, but if there was truly danger, as he feared, then every visit he made would increase that danger. The potential victim must be warned. "Waken him!" he ordered.

The girl cringed. Probably she had never met a Seventh before and now she was alone with two of them. "Go on," he said, more gently. "I won't let him eat you."

Gingerly she reached down and gave the sleeper's shoulder a gentle shake.

The swordsman sat up.

The movement was so sudden that the girl leaped back with a gasp, and even Honakura retreated a pace from the foot of the bed. The man glared wildly around, heavy black eyebrows lowered in a scowl. He took in Honakura and the woman and the room in one lightning scrutiny. Then he seemed to relax a fraction. He looked them all over once more, sitting upright and not saying a word. He lingered his gaze appreciatively over the girl and finally brought it back to the man facing him.

"Who the hell are you?" he demanded.

Honakura recoiled another pace at this unexpected vulgarity. Then he recalled that they had not observed the proprieties of formal salutes at their earlier meeting and so, although he was the elder, he proceeded with the greeting to an equal: "I am Honakura, priest of the seventh rank, Third Deputy Chairman of the Council of Venerables, and I give thanks to the Most High for granting me this opportunity to assure your beneficence that your prosperity and happiness will always be my desire and the subject of my prayers."

The swordsman raised an eyebrow incredulously at the recital and the elaborate gestures. He glanced at the girl to see her reaction. There was a long pause.

Then he nodded solemnly to Honakura and said, "Likewise, I'm sure. My name is Wallie Smith."

†††

Jja leaped forward and assisted the old man to a chair. His face had turned gray and he was gasping for breath. She had been surprised to hear his name, for her mistress Kikarani had returned from a summons to the temple that morning in a storm of alternating terror and fury, breathing plagues and disaster against this same holy Honakura—Jja had envisioned an enormous, dreadful ogre, not a quiet and kindly old man. She hovered over him for a moment, worrying: should she run for a healer? But that would be for the swordsman to decide. She heard a creak from the bed and turned to see that he had pulled himself back so that he could lean against the wall. He was modestly adjusting the cloth over himself. She was going to kneel beside the priest, but the swordsman smiled at her and pointed to the chair at his side. He had a very kindly smile.

"And what is your name?" he asked, as she obediently went over.

"Jja, my lord."

"Jja?" he echoed, sounding it. "Jja! How do you . . ." He frowned and tried again: "How do you . . . Damn!" he muttered. He tried once more: "How do you make-marks-to-see for that?"

She did not understand. He was looking puzzled himself.

The old man had recovered some of his breath. "My lord," he said faintly. "This morning you told me that your name was Shonsu."

The big man stared at him menacingly for a moment. "I don't remember that." He frowned, looking puzzled again. "In fact I don't remember anything for . . . well, it feels like quite a long time."

"You said," the priest repeated, "that your name was Shonsu and you were being haunted by a demon named Walliesmith. Now you say that you are Walliesmith . . ."

"Demon?" The swordsman uttered a deep, rumbling chuckle. "Demon? Shonsu?" He thought for a moment and repeated, "Shonsu?" as though the name had a vague familiarity. "Well, Wallie Smith is my name, but I'm no demon." He grinned an astonishingly friendly grin at Jja and whispered: "Honest!"

"Certainly it is not the name of any of the known demons," the old man muttered. "There is a demon of the seventh circle named Shaasu, but I'm sure that wasn't what you said."

The swordsman looked questioningly at Jja, as though asking her if the old man often raved like this. Then he slapped at a mosquito on his leg.

He stared at the leg. He peered at his arm, turning it over. He raised a hand to his face. Now it was he who went pale.

Again he moved with incredible speed. He jumped off the bed, holding the cloth about himself, and took two fast strides across the room to the mirror—and recoiled from what he saw there. "*Oh, God!*" He stooped once more to peer at his face, stroked his chin, rubbed a finger over his facemarks, tugged a strand of his long black hair. He found the lump on the back of his head and fingered that.

Time passed. A party of young women returning from the fields went by on the road. The hot little cottage was full of their giggling and the baiting calls of the boys following, jesting and shouting at the girls and one another. Both groups faded away down the hill toward the town, and still the swordsman stood by the mirror, looking himself over, even peering under his wrap. Finally he turned and came back, very slowly, with his face tightly closed. He sat on the edge of the bed and seemed to sag.

"Shonsu, you said?" he asked.

The old man nodded. "You got a bump on the head, my lord. Sometimes that can cause confusion . . . with all respect, my lord."

"Tell me the whole thing—from the beginning!"

Honakura looked at Jja. "Leave us," he said.

The swordsman did not appear to have moved, but his hand was on Jja's arm. "Stay," he said without looking at her.

It was a large and a strong hand, and a tremor ran through her at his touch. He felt it. She blushed as his eyes swiveled to study her. Then he smiled gently and took his hand away. "Sorry," he murmured. A Seventh apologizing to a slave? She was astounded and confused. She hardly heard the start of the priest's story.

Yet when he described the demon she was horrified— hair on its face and its belly? It must have looked like an ape.

"I came," Honakura said, his voice still shaky, "to explain why a noble lord like yourself had been put in such obnoxious quarters with inadequate ministration . . ."

The swordsman glanced at Jja and winked, then said, "I have no complaint about the ministration." Her heart turned over.

"You are gracious, my lord," the priest continued, not

paying much attention. "But the fact remains that your life may be in danger. Not that I doubt your prowess, my lord," he added quickly. "I am sure that in a matter of honor you will dispose of Hardduju without the least problem. He is the only Seventh in the valley. He gives you fifteen years and is seasoned in debauchery. It is the thought of treachery that haunts me."

The swordsman was shaking his head gently and frowning, as though he could not believe any of this.

"No, I do not fear swordsmen coming themselves," Honakura explained. His color was returning, his voice stronger. "Rather the brigands who depend on the corruption of the guard for their protection. But no one will look for you here, my lord."

Jja drew a breath and then fell silent, hoping that they had not noticed; but evidently little escaped the swordsman, for his fearsome deep eyes were on her again. "You were going to say?" he asked.

She gulped. "About noontime, my lord..."

"Yes?" He nodded encouragingly.

"I stepped outside, my lord...just for a moment, my lord. But I had to relieve myself. I was only gone a moment."

"That's fine." He was terrifyingly attentive and patient. "What did you see?"

So she told how she had seen a priestess of the Fifth, a round, middle-aged woman, coming up the road and looking in all the cottages. It was a sight she had never seen before, and she had remembered how her mistress Kikarani had stressed that no one was to know that the noble lord was there.

Honakura hissed. "As I feared, the subornation has penetrated even the priesthood! You are discovered, my lord!"

"Wait a minute, though," the swordsman rumbled, still watching Jja and smiling slightly once more. "Did she get in and see me?"

Jja felt her face flame. "No, my lord."

"But the fact that she was not admitted will tell them what they want to know," the priest said angrily.

The swordsman ignored him. "What did you do, Jja?"

She bent her head and whispered how she had removed her dress and concealed him with her body, pretending that they were making joy together. The woman had not come in and could not have seen him properly.

Then there was a silence until she tremulously looked up and saw that he was smiling—no, grinning—at her, a cheeky, little-boy grin, very surprising on so strong a face.

"I wish I had been here!" he said. He turned to the priest. "I repeat that I have no complaint about the service."

Honakura was beaming. "It is the handiwork of the Goddess! Truly I was right to believe that She guided you here! Not one slave in a million would have had the wit to protect you in such fashion, my lord, or have wanted to."

"*Slave?*" She had thought his smiles frightening and had given no thought to what his anger might be. "Is that what that line on your face means, that you are a *slave?*" She nodded timidly and the rage was whirled round toward the priest. "And who owns this slave?"

"The temple, I suppose, or Priestess Kikarani." The priest was not cowed, merely puzzled. "Why, my lord?"

The swordsman did not answer. He scowled blankly across the room for a moment and muttered, "What cesspool did I drag that from?" Then he shrugged and spoke to the priest again.

"So I am supposed to kill this . . . Hardduju . . . person, am I? What about his friends?"

The old man seemed surprised. "If you mean the swordsmen, my lord, then they will respect the outcome of a formal challenge. Most of them, I am sure, are men of honor. Then, when you have been invested as reeve, you can punish the recreants, provide proper protection for the pilgrims, and hunt down the brigands."

"I see." He fell silent and sat staring at the floor. A

mule train came clattering by, hooves staccato on the cobbles, the riders making relieved noises at seeing their destination so close at last. A single horse trotted up the roadway. The Sun God was very low, the patch of light on the wall fading to pink. Flies buzzed. The swordsman waved them away idly, once in a while snatching one out of the air and killing it.

Then he frowned back at the priest. "All right, where is this?"

"This is a cottage for the use of pilgrims," Honakura said.

"Where?"

"Just outside the town."

"What town?" The swordsman's voice was growing deeper and dangerous.

Patiently the priest answered. "The town by the temple, my lord. The temple of the Goddess at Hann."

"Hann? Thank you," said the swordsman. "Never heard of it. What . . . Which . . ." He growled in frustration and then said with an effort and in a sudden rush, "What large-body-of-land-surrounded-by-salt-water are we on?" He seemed as surprised as they were.

"Salt water?" Honakura blurted. He looked at Jja, as if even a slave might give him support. "We are on an island, my lord, between the River itself and a small branch of it. But the water is not salt." Then he added hurriedly, to forestall any more questions, "The small branch has no name of its own, although it is sometimes called the River of the Judgment."

"And what is the big branch called?"

In a despairing voice the old man said, "Just the River. There is no other, so why should it have a name?" After a moment's silence he added, *The River is the Goddess and the Goddess is the River.*

"Is she, though?" The huge young man rubbed his chin for a moment, thinking. Then he demanded, "What day is this?"

"It is Teachers' Day, my lord," the priest said. He

frowned at the look he received and snapped, "The third day of the twenty-second week in the year 27,355 from the founding of the temple!"

The swordsman groaned and said nothing more for a while.

The patch of light faded out and the cottage grew dim. He rose and walked over to rest his elbows on the windowsill, staring out at the road. His bulk made the gloom deeper. Jja could see the passersby faintly through the beads over the door—workers heading home from the fields, a few pilgrims being led along to cottages by her fellow slaves. Then a horseman went by, and the big man jerked back with an oath.

He turned and leaned against the wall between the door and the window, so that his face was in shadow. He folded his arms—arms thick as most men's legs—and spoke to the priest again.

"It's an interesting tale," he said, his deep voice very quiet. "There is one small problem—I am no swordsman. I wouldn't know which end of a sword was the handle."

"My lord," Honakura bleated, "you are still disturbed from the exorcism and the blow on the head. I will send a healer to you again . . . after a few days' rest you will be restored."

"Or dead, according to you."

"It is true," the old man replied in a sad voice. "The danger is greater now, for if the reeve finds you in a vulnerable state, then he will certainly challenge. It would be his only hope."

"No, it wouldn't." The big, deep voice was still strangely soft. "Let me explain. You do not exist, Lord —is that right?—Lord Honakura. Nor, I regret to say, do you, beautiful Jja. You are inventions of a sick mind, both of you. Truly I am Wallie Smith. I've been ill. I had . . . oh, hell! Words again! I got an insect in the brain . . ."

He looked at their expressions and uttered a deep

bass laugh. "That wasn't right, was it? A bug? That means small insect, too, doesn't it? I did get bitten by an insect, and it gave me a fever in the brain. It made me sleep a lot and have strange...dreams." He rubbed his chin again, pondering. "I think that name 'Shonsu' came into them. Anyway, I was very ill. Obviously I still am. That's why you don't exist. I'm imagining all this."

He frowned at the expression on the priest's face. "I think I'm not expected to live, because my sister flew in from...Oh, never mind that bit!"

In diplomatic tones Lord Honakura said, "You have had a bang on the head, my lord. Just like a fever, a head injury may cause strange dreams, or even allow minor demons to penetrate. We can try another exorcism in the morning."

"In the morning," the swordsman said, "I shall wake up back in the...house of healing. Or perhaps I shall die before that. I am still very ill. But no more exorcisms. No duels. No swordsmen."

There was a long silence.

"I wonder..." The holy man wiped his lips. "When I was a boy, about two lifetimes ago...One day a swordsman came around looking for a recruit. Of course we lads all wanted to be sworn as swordsmen." He chuckled. "So he tested us. You know the test he gave us, my lord?"

"No," the big man growled. His face was shadowed.

"He made us try to catch flies."

"Flies? With a sword?"

The old man chuckled again and glanced at Jja to see if she had noticed also. "By hand, my lord. Very few people can catch a fly. But you have been sitting there doing it, without even seeming to look at them."

Then the big man chuckled very slightly also, in the shadow. "Whereas you, I think, could talk them down out of the trees, Lord Honakura. Let us discuss it again tomorrow, then—if you still exist."

The priest rose, looking even older and more shriveled than he had before. He bowed and muttered a formal farewell to the swordsman, then pushed out through the curtain and wandered off down the hill.

And Jja was alone with the swordsman.

†† ††

"Flies!" the swordsman snorted. "Are you hungry, Jja?"

She was starving. She had not eaten all day. "I could fetch food from the kitchen, my lord. It isn't very good —for one of your rank, my lord."

He swept up the hamper and laid it on the bed, where he still had some light. "I'm hoping this may help," he said. "Yes!" Then he started to lift out great silver dishes wrapped in linen cloths, muttering in astonishment as he laid them on the wobbly little table. "Ruddy fortune in bullion! If we do get invaded by brigands, we'll throw these at them, right? And enough forks and spoons for a whole gang of them. Can you fight off the brigands with a fork while I run for help, Jja?"

She was perplexed and uncertain. She ought to be setting out the food for him, not the other way around, but she had never seen such dishes or smelled such savory scents as those that now drifted through the cottage. And he had asked a question, obviously a joke, and jokes were difficult for a slave to handle. "I could try, my lord, if you were quick."

He grinned, white teeth flashing in his faintly visible brown face. "Here's a candle," he said. "Do you know how to light it? I don't."

She fetched a flint from the shelf and lit the candle, and the whole table sparkled with many little flames.

"Candlelit dinner for two," he said. "Pardon my informal dress. Now you sit there and tell me what you think we should start with."

"My lord . . ." she protested. She must not sit at table with a free man.

He paused, standing by the table with a bottle in his hand, his face and chest shining in darkness, lit strangely from below by the flickering light and its myriad reflections. "When your mistress, this . . . Kikarani? When she gave you orders about me, did she say what you were to do when I awoke?"

"Yes, my lord." She looked down at her hands.

"And what were those orders?" She could hear amusement, but no anger or threat.

"I was to do anything you said, my lord."

"Mmm? Anything?"

She nodded to the floor. "There are a few things I don't have to do for the pilgrims, my lord, even if they ask. But she said . . . she said, 'In this case do anything at all, anything, just keep him there.' My lord."

The man cleared his throat harshly. "Right. Well, here are my orders. First, stop 'my lording' me and call me Wallie. Second, forget you are a slave and pretend that you are a beautiful gentlewoman. I expect most swordsmen with seven swords have a beautiful lady at home in a castle somewhere?"

"I don't know, my . . ." It made her forehead prickle with sweat, but she managed to say, "Wallie."

"Neither do I," he said. "But let's pretend that I'm a great swordsman and you are a great lady. Now, tell me what you think of this wine, Lady Jja."

She had never tasted wine before. She had never eaten off silver dishes. She had never sat with a lord. But she was ravenous, and the food was the best she had ever tasted—meat in rich sauce and tender vegetables and fluffy white bread that she knew only by hearsay.

He did most of the talking, sensing perhaps the strain she was under and knowing that conversation was beyond her means. "You are very lovely, you know," he said. "You should have long hair, but of course this is a hot climate. Laundry work, I expect? Yes, your hands . . .

"Black is not your color," he said later. "Blue, I think. I did a very good job of imagining beauty, but I should have imagined you in a long blue dress...no sleeves, shiny light-blue silk, cut low in the front and clinging...You would look like a goddess...

"This wine isn't too bad, is it? And this looks like a fruit pie for dessert. There was a jar of cream somewhere. And here's a cake! Eat up, there's lots..."

It was a dream, she was certain, sitting in the warm dark with a single candle flaring off silver and shining on a great lord smiling at her, teasing a little. Not a rasp-handed old stonemason of the Third making a pilgrimage to beg the Goddess to cure his cough, or a toothless gray shepherd of the Fourth wanting his herds to prosper, but a very large and very handsome young lord, flashing white teeth in that big smile and sparkling at her.

A dream that might come in a dream.

And he cared. She knew men—she could see the man-interest in his eyes when he looked at her. For once, she was enjoying that. She tried very hard to be a good slave, to make amends to the Goddess by doing her duty conscientiously, but sometimes it was not easy. Tonight she thought it would be quite easy, although it was strange that he had not even handled her yet.

At last they had both finished eating, and her head was spinning from the wine. Now, surely, he would give her the usual orders. She waited for them with a strange excitement that she had never known before, but they did not come. He just sat, holding a goblet, gazing sadly into the candle as moths crazed wildly around it.

Then he seemed to remember her. He jerked out of his sadness. "We could dance," he said. "If I could just imagine up some musicians! Do you dance, Jja?"

She shook her head. "I don't know how...Lord Wallie." Not wanting to disappoint him, or perhaps because of the wine, she added rashly, "I can sing a little."

He was pleased. "Sing me a song, then."

And even more rashly, she sang a little slave song.

"In my dreams I hear me calling,
  Hear me calling here to me,
  From a life I've left behind me,
  Or a world I've yet to see.

"Someday when the Goddess calls me,
  I will find that other me:
  Handsome lord or lovely lady,
  Once again I shall be free."

He asked her to sing it again, listening to the words
carefully. "That's your explanation, is it?" he asked.
"You think Shonsu lived in one world, and Wallie Smith
in another, but they were the same person? The same
soul? And somehow they got mixed up?"

She nodded. "That is what they say dreams are, my
... Wallie. Your other lives."

He considered the idea carefully, not dismissing it as
slave nonsense. "Reincarnations? I can see why you
would like the idea. But surely one enters a world by
birth and leaves by death?" Then he smiled, but as
though it were an effort. "If I'm a newborn baby, Jja,
how big am I going to be when I grow up?"

"I ... don't know, my lord."

"Sorry! I shouldn't make fun of ... I know you're trying to help, and I'm grateful. Why are you a slave?"

"I was very wicked, my lord."

"In what way?"

"I don't know, my lord."

"In a previous life?"

She nodded, perplexed. Why even ask such things?

He scowled. "So the priests tell you to be a good
slave in this life? Bah!"

He fell silent again, brooding. Greatly daring, she
said, "The Goddess will care for them."

"Who?"

She had been wrong, she sensed. "Your womenfolk
... sons ..."

For a moment the sparkle of man-interest was back in his eye. He shook his head. "None of those! No one special...Were you wondering?" Then his mood went bitter. "And why only mention sons? If I had daughters, would I not care for them also?"

She stammered. "I thought...a swordsman..."

He sighed. "I'm no swordsman, Jja. Not in this world nor any other. And I never will be!"

"The Goddess can do anything, my lord."

He smiled again, ruefully. "I doubt if She could make me into a swordsman! Fencing must take years of practice. Jja..." he paused. "Please listen carefully. I don't want to make...joy...with you tonight, although I'm sure you expect me to. But you mustn't think it's because you're not desirable—the sight of you makes me shiver and makes my flesh rise. It isn't that, you're gorgeous."

She must not let her disappointment show.

He was looking down at the candle again. "And it isn't because I know that you have to do it with a lot of men. I can guess that that's what happens, isn't it?"

Perhaps he had sworn an oath? "Yes, my lord... Wallie. If they pay my mistress."

He bared his teeth at the candle. "So you have no choice, and therefore I do not think less of you because of it. So it isn't that, either, you see... This may be hard for you to understand. Where I come from we despise people who own slaves. If I said *lie down*, you would have to lie down, and that isn't the way it should be. A man and a woman should do that thing because they love each other and they both want to do it. So I'm not going to."

"I do want to, my lord!" Oh, no! Where had she found the courage to say that? But of course, this was only a dream.

"Because it is your duty! No, Jja."

It must be the wine...she had to fight down a desire to explain how she fetched the highest price, how Kikarani therefore saved her for the older men, the ones to have the most money, how it was the older, uglier women who got the young men. Could he not guess why she had thought to hide him from the spying priestess in the way she had? Or even guess that she had wanted to weep with frustration because he was not able to respond, while at the same time she had been terrified that he might wake up and find a slave lying on top of him?

She said, "My lord," bowing her head.

"You sleep on that side of the bed, then." He rose, not looking at her. "And I'll sleep this side. Now, where do I go to . . ."

"Outside, my lord," she said in surprise.

He grinned around at her—that strangely boyish grin that came and went very suddenly, making him look very young and happy. "I wasn't planning to do it inside! Anywhere's okay, huh?"

He stepped out through the curtain into the warm tropic night. She tidied the table. There was plenty of food to be saved for tomorrow, so she fished out a few moths that had fallen in, covered the dishes, wrapped them again, and packed the hamper. Finally she pinched out the candle and the cottage was dark, only a trace of a silver glimmer from the Dream God glistening through the window.

Then she heard him, and went out to see.

He was leaning against the wall by the door, his head on his arms. His whole body was shaking with sobs. A swordsman weeping? That seemed very strange, but already she knew that this was no ordinary swordsman.

Again, it must have been the wine that gave her the courage to put an arm around him, to lead him inside and over to the bed. He said nothing. The bed creaked loudly as he lay down. He buried his face and continued to sob. She took off her wrap and went around to lie on the other side of the bed as she had been told. She waited.

Finally he choked off his sobs and said in a whisper, "That light in the sky? What is it?"

"It is the Dream God, my lord."

He did not reply. She waited, but she knew he was not asleep.

It was the wine . . . "The god of sorrows and the god of joy are brothers, my lord."

After a moment he rolled over and said, "Tell me, then."

So she told him, as she had been told once, long ago, by another slave, a young man she would never see again. "The god of sorrows and the god of joy are brothers. At the time of the unrolling of the World, they both courted the goddess of youth. It was the god of joy she chose, and they loved greatly. In time she bore him a son, the most beautiful baby that even the gods had ever seen, and the father delivered the baby himself and held him up for his mother and the gods to look at.

"But the god of sorrows was jealous and greatly enraged at the sight of the child—and he hurled his wrath and killed him.

"Then the god of sorrows was terrified at what he had done and fled away, but all the other gods wept. They went to the Goddess Herself and besought justice. And so She decreed that ever after the god of joy might deliver from the goddess of youth the most beautiful of the gods, but he would always be a baby, and he would only live a few moments. But although he would be only a baby, he would be stronger than his father, and the god of sorrows, the most terrible of the gods, would not stand against him and would flee from him always. That is why only this smallest god, of all the gods, can put to flight the god of sorrows."

"And what is the name of this smallest god?" asked the man in the darkness.

"He is the god of ecstasy, my lord," she said.

He turned to her and took her in his arms. "Then let us seek this little god of yours together," he said.

She had thought a swordsman might be brutal, but he was the most gentle of men. He was patient and strong and untiring and considerate in a way no man had ever been to her. Together they summoned the little god many times, and the god of sorrows was driven away.

†† † ††

A fly buzzed in his ear, waking him. He opened his eyes and then closed them again quickly. Thatch?

It had not gone away.

There had been hospital, with its grave-faced doctors in white coats and tired-looking nurses with needles . . . familiar faces faking cheerfulness . . . flowers sent by the staff at the plant . . . smells of disinfectant and the sound of floor-polishers . . . IV bottles . . . pain and confusion and the damp heat of fever.

There had been dreams and delirium . . . fog and a giant of a man with brown skin and long black hair and a brutal face—a wide face, high cheekbones, broad jaw; barbarian tattoos on his forehead. He had seen that monstrous naked figure shouting at him, threatening.

He had seen that face again last night in the mirror.

Under the damp sheet he felt one arm with the hand of another. That body was still there. Wallie Smith had never had arms like that.

So it had not disappeared as he had hoped it would.

A bird was calling an idiotic two-note refrain not far away, and he could hear voices, more distant, and a rooster, ever hopeful.

"Ferry mule train!" That must be from near the bottom of the hill. Then a very faint bugle . . . and under it all was the deep rumble from the waterfall, most distant of all. The sound of hooves echoed into the little room. "Ferry mule train!" He wondered if mules looked like that absurd horse he had seen, camel face and basset-hound body.

It had not gone away. Encephalitis often produced

strange mental effects, they had said. He had thought the delirium was over, the strange visions and the pain and confusion. Now it had become more real, more terrifying.

It did not feel like delirium.

He must remember that it was all hallucination. They would cure him, somehow, and drag him back to the real world, the world of hospital sounds and hospital smells; away from this madness of stink and mule hooves and roosters.

Reluctantly he opened his eyes again and sat up. Only the woman had gone. Now if *she* had been real . . .

She had felt real, deliciously, wonderfully real. Of course sexual hallucinations would be the most vivid, wouldn't they? That would make sense. Nothing else did. What sort of Oedipal garbage was he fantasizing with this super-jock body he had conjured up? And what subconscious nastiness was he revealing when his delusions invented slave girls? A little insecure, are we, Wallie-boy? Ugh!

He rose and stretched. He felt good, enormously good. He strode over to the mirror and studied that cruel, barbaric face with its tattoos of the seven swords. Was this how he fantasized himself, his subconscious desires exposed by delirium? Did he see himself as an inadequate wimp and want to be a big, strong, fantasy hero?

The foreskin bothered him more than anything else. If he pinched it, it hurt. How could he feel pain in something that had been cut off when he was a baby? There was no trace of his appendectomy, but he did have a red birthmark on his left knee and a conspicuous scar on his right shoulder and some faint little marks on his ribs, mostly on the right side. So he wasn't quite a perfect specimen, and somehow that was odd.

The mule train clattered closer and then stopped nearby. Again he heard the skinner make his call. He went over to the window and peered out, keeping back from sight. Two men were paying the skinner and climbing on mules, and there were half a dozen people mounted already. The mules were even more grotesque than the horse—long ears and camel faces. Then he remembered the rings he had seen in the night sky. It had been the rings that had finally cracked his precarious self-control. It was not only an imaginary country he was conjuring up in his madness; it was a whole imaginary world, a ringed planet.

And the people surprised him a bit—smallish, although that might be just because he seemed to be much larger than average. They had brown skins, all of them, with hair of light or dark brown. One of the women on the mules showed a reddish tinge, perhaps dyed. A neat, compact people, mostly slim and agile, they seemed to laugh and chatter a lot...features vaguely Amerindian to Caucasian. They might have stepped out of a documentary on the South American jungles, or perhaps southeast Asia. Beardless—he rubbed his chin and there was no trace of stubble, no hair on his chest or legs.

There were other people walking up and down the roadway—men in loincloths, and women in simple wraps that tied under their arms and hung to their knees, like bath towels. Jja's had been shorter, but then she was a whore. The muleskinner wore leather breeches. The old man had worn a robe that covered all of him except his head and hands. Then he saw a middle-aged couple going over to the mule train, and they were wearing robes, but sleeveless, so the amount of cover must be related to age. Not a bad idea; show off the good-looking youngsters and hide the old. Some of the men and women in his world could learn a thing or two here.

Wallie reminded himself sternly that this was an illusion.

Yet he felt so good! And curious! He wanted to explore this fantasy world...but he had no clothes. Could that be his subconscious mind telling him to stay in his hospital room?

He had nothing at all—he could not even see the wrap he had used the previous evening. Newborn naked!

He had never been a great collector of possessions, for he had been too much of a wanderer. His childhood had been a continual bouncing from parent to parent, from aunt to uncle; then college; then a succession of jobs. Roots were something he had never had, and worldly goods likewise. But to have nothing but a bed sheet to cover himself . . .

Illusion! Delirium!

The mule train moved off. He watched the pedestrians for a while and then turned away. He thought of a test, and began by feeling his pulse carefully. It was slow, of course, an athlete's heartbeat, although he could not clock it. He dropped to the grubby, smelly flagstones and did fifty fast push-ups. Kneeling, he tried his pulse again. It seemed very little faster. Wallie Smith might have managed ten or fifteen, never fifty, and his heart would have gone into fits.

That did not prove much.

A fly buzzed at him, and he snatched it out of the air to see if he really could. He could, but that proved nothing, either.

A small boy walked in through the bead curtain and grinned at him. He was naked, nut brown, and skinny. He had curly brown hair and an impish face and a tooth missing. He looked about eight or nine and he was carrying a leafy green twig.

"Good morning, Mr. Smith!" His grin grew wider.

Wallie felt a twinge of relief—no more "my lord" stuff! He stayed on his knees, because that made their eyes more or less level.

"Good morning. Who are you?"

"I'm a messenger."

"Oh? To me you look like a small, naked boy. What should you look like?"

The boy laughed. "A small, naked boy." He pushed himself up on one of the chairs.

"I was hoping that you might be a doctor." But Wallie was unhappily aware of the dirt, the insects, the smells. Hospital?

The boy shook his head. "No more doctors. They call them healers here, and you're wise to stay away from them."

Wallie sat down and crossed his legs. The stone was cold and gritty on his buttocks. "Well, you did call me 'mister,' so maybe I'm starting to come out of it a little bit."

The boy shook his head. "Last night you were speaking the language of the People. You had Shonsu's vocabulary, which is why you couldn't say some words that you wanted to. He was a fine swordsman, but no intellectual."

Wallie's heart sank. "If you were really a small, naked boy you wouldn't know these things, nor talk like that."

The boy grinned again. He started swinging his legs, leaning forward on his hands and hunching tiny shoulders. "I did not say that that was what I was. I said that was what I was supposed to look like! I need to convince you that this is a real world and that you were brought here for a purpose."

His grin was infectious. Wallie found himself returning it. "You're not doing very well so far."

The boy raised a mischievous eyebrow. "The woman did not convince you? I should have thought that she was very convincing."

Peeping Tom? Wallie pushed down a surge of anger. This boy was merely one more figment of his deranged mind, so of course he knew what had happened in the night. "That was the most unreal of all," he said. "Every man has ambitions, sonny, but there are practical limitations. That was *much* too good to be true."

The boy sighed. "The men of the World are even lustier than the men of Earth, Mr. Smith, hard as that may be to believe. Walter Smith is dead. Encephalitis, meningitis...they're only names. There is no going back, Mr. Smith."

They all wanted to convince him that he was dead! And if he were? Who would care? *No one special*, he had told Jja, and that was a depressing thought. He had no roots, anywhere. No loved ones left except a sister he had not seen in ten years. If he were indeed dead, it would hardly matter to anyone. The plant would run as well without him—he had built a good team there, able to operate with no supervision. Harry would move into the corner office, and business would go on as before.

Neddy would mourn. But Neddy's mother had already taken him and moved back east. It had been on a farewell camping trip with Neddy that Wallie had been bitten by the damned encephalitis-carrying mosquito... in an area where mosquitoes had never been known to carry encephalitis before. Neddy would mourn him but would survive. Wally had to admit that he had done a good job on Neddy. The boy was in much better emotional shape to stand the loss than he would have been three years ago, when Wallie first became surrogate father to him. Neddy was already reconciled to their parting...

No! Start thinking like that and he would indeed be dead. The start of recovery was always the will to live. Remember that it was still delirium! It had to be.

He looked up and saw the little boy watching him with a mocking expression.

"This is heaven?" Wallie scoffed. "It doesn't smell the way I expected."

The little boy's eyes flickered. They were extraordinarily bright eyes. "This is the World, the World of the Goddess. The People are preliterate, Mr. Smith. You should know from Earth that before the Age of Writing comes the Age of Legends. I am a legend myself."

"I'll believe that."

The boy nodded rather sadly and paused. "Let's try it from the other end, then. Shonsu was a swordsman, a remarkable swordsman. The Goddess had need of a swordsman. She chose Shonsu. He screwed up. He failed, and failed disastrously."

"What does that mean?" Despite his skepticism, Wallie was intrigued.

"Never mind! He was punished for his failure, by

death. He died yesterday of a fractured skull." He smiled once more as Wallie's fingers reached for the lump on his head. "Never mind that, either—it was cured. That body is in perfect working order, a remarkable specimen of the adult male. As you doubtless noted?"

"Let's leave that part of my fantasies out of this, shall we?"

"As you please." The boy waved his twig idly. "Shonsu is dead, then, but the task remains undone. You were available, Mr. Smith. Never mind how. You have been given that remarkable body, you have been given the language, and you have been given the highest possible rank in one of the two top-ranking crafts in the World. All crafts have their patron gods, but the priests and the swordsmen belong to the Goddess Herself... and they don't let anyone else forget it, believe me! Those are exceptional gifts you have received."

"And I am supposed to undertake the mission?"

The gap-tooth grin flashed briefly. "Exactly."

"Dangerous, I assume?"

The boy nodded. "Moderately, yes. So the body is at risk—but it was a free gift, remember! If you are successful, then you will be rewarded with long life and satisfaction and happiness. There are almost no limits on a swordsman of the Seventh, Mr. Smith—wealth, power, women. Anything you want, really. Any woman will accept you. No man will ever argue with you."

Wallie shook his head. "Who are you?"

"I am a god," the boy said simply. "A demigod, to be exact."

The big man looked around the squalid little cabin, smiled, and shook his head. "I think the asylum must be very full. They are doubling up the inmates."

The boy scowled angrily. The flies did not seem to buzz around him the way they did around Wallie. It was an insane conversation, yet Wallie had nothing better to do with his time.

"A swordsman is a soldier, is he?"

The boy nodded. "And policeman. And judge. And other things."

"I know absolutely nothing about soldiering."

"You can be taught, very painlessly. And taught to use a sword, too, if that is worrying you."

"That is not something I yearn for breathlessly. Let me guess, though. The mission was to kill this Hardduju character. Am I right?"

"No!" the boy snapped. "You are wrong! However, you should do that also. As an honorable swordsman, you should regard it as your duty to uphold the honor of your craft. Hardduju is venal."

Wallie rose and wandered over to sit on the bed. "He certainly seems to have more enemies than friends. It is none of my business, and no one has proved anything to me, anyway."

The boy twisted round on the chair to face him, looking furious. "You don't need a trial in his case, for he is a swordsman. All you need do is challenge. You need give no reason, and he cannot refuse. I assure you that he is no match for Shonsu."

Wallie laughed. "He would be for me! Except perhaps at tennis. Can I choose the weapons?"

The boy bared his teeth in anger. "You were given Shonsu's language, Mr. Smith—you can be given his skill as easily. The task is important! Much more important than shaving a few mils off the unit cost of polypropylene, say, or evaluating consultants' reports on alternative catalytic systems for hydrogenation."

"You've been going through my IN basket, haven't you, figment? Well, prove it! Tell me what this so-important task is."

"Gods do not beg!"

Wallie shrugged. "And I do not believe in gods."

"Ah! Now we have it, don't we?"

"Do a miracle," Wallie suggested, grinning. "Turn that chair into a throne."

The boy's face was shadowed, but the bright eyes seemed almost to flash. "Miracles are crude! And they are not done upon demand!" Then he returned to his grin again. "Besides, if I performed a miracle, it would hardly help you to believe that the World is real, would it?"

Wallie chuckled and agreed. He wondered when breakfast would be served. The boy leaned back in the chair. It was too big for him, and he bent like a banana, stared at Wallie with his chin on his chest. "Where does faith come from?"

He could bang the boy's ear and throw him out, but what would he do with the rest of his day? "Faith? It comes from upbringing."

The boy sneered at him. "That just pushes the problem back one generation, doesn't it?"

"True," Wallie agreed, amused. "Well, define faith as an attempt to attribute your own values to an omnipotent being. How's that?"

"Lousy," the boy said. "Why should you want to attribute et cetera, et cetera?"

Wallie felt that he was being nudged toward saying something he didn't want do, but he wasn't sure what. "To find a happy ending? To explain suffering by postulating a deeper meaning?"

It was growing hot already, although the sun was still low and the day young. Wallie could feel perspiration running down his ribs. The skinny boy seemed unaffected.

"Better," he said. "Now, how can we give you faith in the World? You had a taste of its joys. Would a taste of its suffering do any more—a taste of hell work better than a taste of heaven?"

"No." That was not an attractive prospect.

The dark eyes flickered again. "So you refuse the edict of the Goddess, do you?"

If it were not absurd, that small boy might be thought to be threatening . . .

"Tell your goddess to blow it out her ear," Wallie said firmly. "I have absolutely no intention of being a swordsman, in this or any other world."

The boy stared at him coldly. "I'm only a demigod—I

shall tell Her no such thing. Why don't you come down to the temple and tell Her yourself?"

"Me? Bow to an idol? A clay idol—or stone?"

"Stone."

"Never!"

"Why not?" the boy asked. "You honored a cloth flag often enough."

Wallie felt he had lost a point somewhere. "But I believed in what the flag stood for."

Then the boy laughed and jumped off the chair. "There it is again! But we must move—there are assassins on their way here, so you should leave."

Wallie sprang to his feet also. "Kind of you to mention it. I need some pants."

The boy pointed to the bundle on the floor. "You haven't opened your present."

How had he missed that earlier? Wallie lifted the bundle onto the bed and unwrapped it.

"Put on the kilt first," the boy said, watching him. "A little short, perhaps, but it will do. Now the harness. The boots won't fit."

"No, they don't," Wallie agreed, struggling. He needed about a size thirty, he concluded.

"Cut the ends with the sword, then." The boy sniggered. "You can't be a swordsman with bare feet."

Wallie drew the sword. It was fearsome. "What do they use this for?" he asked. "Elephant hunting?" Holding the blade near its end with his fingertips, he used the point to slit the toes of the boots. Then he could get them on, but they pinched and his toes stuck out the ends. The boy giggled once more.

"Why don't I just leave the sword for now?" Wallie said.

The boy shook his head. "A swordsman without a sword would be a public scandal."

The scabbard was attached to the harness and hung down his back. When he tried to lift the sword high enough to insert the point, his hand hit the roof. He tried to sit on the bed and found he was sitting on the scabbard. He began to lose his temper, for the boy was grinning widely.

"You could kneel," he suggested. "Or bend over. Of course the scabbard will tilt to the side."

So it would, sliding on the straps across his back. Wallie could pull the top of the scabbard to one side and the bottom to the other and, with much cursing and almost losing an ear, he sheathed the sword.

"Not bad," the boy said, regarding him. "You have the guard on the wrong side. Shonsu is ambidextrous, so it doesn't matter, I suppose. Remember to take it with your left hand when you want to kill someone."

"I've no intention of trying to draw this!" But Wallie did draw it, then replaced it the other way round.

"Now straighten it up with the hilt beside your ear," the boy said. He picked up a small leather thong, the only thing left on the cloak. "Hairclip," he explained.

"I never went for the leather scene," Wallie muttered, pulling his hair back and tying the thong around it— thick, heavy hair, not Wallie Smith's hair. "I really have to go out in public in this rig? I'll be arrested." He scowled into the foggy, spotted mirror.

The boy laughed. "Only swordsmen arrest people, and you're a high-orbit swordsman. No, you're fine. The girls would whistle at you if they dared. Let's go."

Wallie hesitated, seeing the cloak on the bed and the hamper with the fortune in silver dishes inside it. "What happens to this stuff?" he asked.

"It will be stolen," the boy answered. "Does it matter?"

Wallie detected an odd note in the question, saw a gleam in the sharp eyes. It was a trick question—if he admitted that it mattered, then he was admitting that the things had value and hence that they were in some way real. Once he took that hook, he would be as good as landed.

"Not to me."

"Then let's go," the boy repeated, dancing over to the door.

"Hold it, Shorty!" Wallie said. "How do I know that you aren't leading me into a trap?"

The mischievous pixie face grinned again, showing the missing tooth. "I am."

The same question hung in the air, this time unspoken: *Does it matter?*

Wallie shrugged and smiled. "Lead on, then!" He followed the boy out of the cottage.

††† †††

It was a beautiful morning, languorously tropical, even if it did smell too much of horses and people. As soon as he cleared the shadow of the cottage, the sun struck hot on his back—the sort of morning that made him think of summer vacations, of beaches and suntanned girls, of hiking in forests or beating tennis balls. The boy skipped across the road, jumped up on the low parapet, and started trotting down it, arms outspread to keep his balance, wobbling. Wallie marched over to join him and noticed the long drop to trees below. But any comment from him would draw the same question again.

There were only a few people coming up the roadway. As he approached they made gestures and bowed. He nodded to them and kept on marching.

"How do I respond to the salutes?" he demanded of his guide.

"A nod is fine," the boy said, now walking more steadily on a broader stretch of wall. His face was almost level with Wallie's. "Ignore the blacks and whites, of course. Yellows, too, if you like. Greens and blues you should acknowledge—clenched fist on the heart. That means you're not going to draw, you see, just like a handshake means you don't have a weapon hidden." He spread his arms again for a crumbling, narrow section. "Don't smile—it would be out of character."

"Not even at pretty girls?"

The boy glanced a warning at him. "From a swordsman of your rank it would be almost an order."

Wallie took a closer look at the next few groups he passed. Orange garments went with four facemarks, brown with three. White meant one, obviously the very junior. He had seen no black garments yet, but he knew what that meant—slave. Preadolescents, male and female both, went naked like his companion.

"That's for civilians," the boy continued. "With swordsmen it's a lot more complicated. One type of salute for just passing in the street, another for serious talk. Depends on whose rank is higher and so on." He jumped a gap and landed as surely as a goat on the other side. "Replies are different from salutes."

Wallie said nothing to that. The road angled down the side of the valley into a crowded huddle of buildings, beyond which towered an immense cathedral-like edifice, surmounted by seven golden spires . . . the temple of the Goddess at Hann. Certainly that was their destination. Beyond the temple, the far wall of the valley, steep and bare and rocky, was split by a canyon. From the window of the cottage he had been able to see along that canyon to the falls from which rose the great plume of spray; from his present position only the cloud was visible.

The rutted road was foul with mule droppings and other filth—he was having trouble keeping his toes clean, and he eventually gave up and let the chips lie where they may. The boots pinched, and the boy was keeping up a fearsome pace, even for legs as long as Shonsu's.

Then they reached level ground, and the boy had to walk on the road beside him, and they slowed. The town engulfed them at once in rank, narrow squalor between high wooden buildings that covered almost every level inch. Between them snaked mean little streets full of scrambling throngs of people, carrying bundles or pushing carts or just hurrying. Yet somehow there was always room for a swordsman of the Seventh, and he was not jostled, although the saluting became perfunctory. The smell was much worse than it had been on the hill.

"Browns are the commonest?" Wallie asked.

The boy was having to do more dodging to keep up with him, but Wallie kept moving—let him worry.

"Thirds. That's craftsman level." He disappeared around a hawker's cart and rejoined Wallie at the other end. "Qualified artisan. Whites and yellows are apprentices. Above that you're into postgraduate." He grinned up briefly.

There were many stray curs grubbing around the refuse, and the high walls shut out the sun. The air was a garbage of insects and smells, human and animal and stale cooking and decay, except where a spice shop or a bakery wafted its fragrance into the street like an oasis.

Wallie had it worked out now: white, yellow, brown, orange, and red. Green and blue must be at the top, but he had seen none of those. Apparently purely arbitrary.

"Why that sequence?" he asked.

"This way," the boy said, turning down another winding alley, which was just as foul and dark and crowded. "No reason. Because it's always been done that way. That's the standard explanation for anything."

Beggars wore black, usually just a grubby rag. Many of them had rags around their heads, too . . . to avoid disgrace to their crafts? He could guess at some of the facemarks. A loud clanging noise ahead proved to be a smithy, and of course the smith's marks were horseshoes. A man pushing a cart of boots and shoes had three boot shapes. Many of them were ideograms, though, and he could not guess their significance: diamonds, semicircles, chevrons?

"They ought to burn this place down and start over," Wallie grumbled.

"They do, every fifty years or so," the boy said.

The ground floor of most buildings held a shop, with a sign above the door and sometimes a display table, carefully guarded, and those restricted the traffic even more. A few establishments, like the smithy, had people working in full view, weaving or sewing or turning pots. Jugs meant potter.

Wallie noted the signs of disease, too—blindness and emaciation and ugly rashes. The poverty was overwhelming, old women bent beneath bundles of wood and children working just as hard as adults. He did not like it. He had seen poverty before—in Tijuana, for example —but Tijuana had the excuse of being new, temporary. This town seemed ancient, and permanent, and therefore somehow worse.

The boy was continually dodging up alleys, avoiding the main streets, although those were barely wider and perhaps more crowded because they carried more wagons and carts. "Are you trying to confuse me, or are we avoiding someone?" Wallie demanded.

"Yes," the boy said.

It was a shantytown with a glandular condition— some of the buildings were four stories high. Now he noticed that many of what he had thought were stray dogs were lanky pigs, rooting for their living in the gutters. Pigs would eat anything, even feces, and their presence explained some of the smell.

"I suppose a river goddess wouldn't approve of flush toilets?" Wallie asked.

The boy stopped and looked at him furiously. "You will not make jokes like that!"

Wallie clipped his ear—and missed. He could catch flies but this urchin could dodge him? "Not too real there," Wallie said, and laughed.

They were standing in one of the alleys, pedestrians edging nervously around both sides of the dangerous swordsman.

"Come here!" The boy stepped over to a display in a narrow doorway, a vertical board with strings of beads hung on it. A wrinkled old crone in brown crouched on a stool at the side, holding her toes in. The boy reached up and pulled off a string of beads. The woman scrambled up in surprise to fawn at the noble lord and be ignored.

"Look, now!" The boy waved the string of beads on

one finger—green clay beads on a thread without a
clasp. "Every one is the same yet slightly different; it has
no beginning and no end; it runs the same in both directions; and the string goes all the way through. Okay?
Let's go!"

He started to walk. Wallie grabbed his shoulder and
this time connected. "Those aren't yours, Shorty!"

"Does it matter?" the boy asked, showing his tooth
gap.

"Yes, it does. Worlds may differ, or minds may get
sick, but morals don't change." Wallie glared down at
him, holding the puny shoulder firmly in his big hand.
The old woman fretted and chewed her knuckles and
was silent.

"That's something else you will have to unlearn,
then," the boy said. "But understand the beads and
you'll be getting close, Wallie Smith. Here, grand-
mother."

He pulled the string through his other hand and then
tossed it to her, but somehow the beads had subtly
changed. They gleamed and they certainly were no
longer clay. "Let's go!" he snapped, and plunged off
along the alley with Wallie striding behind him, trying to
remember just what had been done to those beads and
how the boy had escaped from his grip, and trying to
understand what all the blarney had meant.

They crossed another street and entered another
alley, squeezed past a parked wagon, then huddled into a
doorway as an oxcart went by, pulled by something that
looked more believable than the camel-faced, long-
bodied horses.

Finally they emerged at the edge of an open space,
wide enough to admit the sunlight. The boy stopped.

"Ah! Fresh air!" Wallie said. "Comparatively."

The boy was studying the far side of the court, a wall
like a cliff. Two enormous gates made of timbers thicker
than a man hung crookedly on massive iron hinges,
flanking an arched entrance. But the gates were spread
wide and looked as though they could not be closed

without falling apart. On either side of them, buildings huddled right up to the wall. Beyond the arch, sunlight shone on bright green grass and tall trees. Small groups of people were walking across the square from the various alleys that emptied into it and passing through the gates.

"The way into the temple?" Wallie asked.

The boy nodded. "The guards will not notice you."

Wallie had not noticed the guards. There were two of them on each side, young swordsmen, three yellows and an orange. Two were leaning against the wall and the other two slouched with thumbs in their harnesses—a very unimpressive display of military style. They were eyeing the pilgrims in a bored fashion, periodically making comments, usually about the women.

The boy glanced disapprovingly at Wallie. "Your sword is crooked!" he snapped.

"It's top-heavy," Wallie complained, adjusting it back to vertical.

"Yes, but there's a knack for keeping it right. Only Firsts go around straightening all the time." He sounded annoyed.

"Well, I'm only a beginner!"

The boy stamped his foot. "You don't need to look it."

Wallie had not asked to go mad. "Let's cancel the whole planet, and I'll go back to chemistry."

The boy shook his head. "You can live here or die here. The sooner you accept that, the better. Well, follow the next group of pilgrims in, and the guards won't see you."

That was absurd, for the groups seldom numbered more than a dozen and Wallie had seen no one as tall as himself. "The hell they won't," he said.

"Does it matter?" the boy asked triumphantly.

Wallie glared at him. Did it? For a delusion, this world was incredibly detailed, from the cold filth coating his toes up to the insects that buzzed around his head.

And the sunlight reflected most realistically off the hilts of the swords on the guards' backs.

"It wouldn't matter anyway," the boy said. "They would salute you. When you didn't return the salute, they ought to challenge—but they wouldn't dare. Not a Seventh."

"Four of them wouldn't dare?"

"But which one goes first?" The boy chuckled. "Come on! Let's go."

Wallie stepped in behind a group of eight pilgrims, six men and two women—one Fifth, four Fourths, and three Thirds. They ambled across the square, while he watched the guards carefully out of the corners of his eyes and tried to ignore prickles of apprehension. As they reached the arch the guards looked over the pilgrims and one made a vulgar comment about one of the women being pregnant; but their eyes never seemed to touch Wallie, and he walked unchallenged into the temple grounds.

"You were right, Shorty," he said. Then he looked around in surprise. The boy had vanished. He was on his own.

††† † †††

Wallie followed the pilgrims' leisurely stroll along a smoothly paved road. He marveled at the change from the squalid huddle of the town to a parkland of velvet lawns and precise beds of flowers, under high, soothing shade trees.

Like the horses, the vegetation seemed almost Earthlike but not quite. He was no botanist and could not find the exact wrongness in anything. Bushes like bougainvillaea flamed in orange and purple next to scarlet hibiscus. Palms like pillars soared to fondle the indigo sky. There were formidable buildings hidden in the distance behind acacias and eucalyptus trees; a couple of them looked like dormitories, but some were marble-faced houses. Here were the elite of the temple, flaunting their power next to the town's poverty, and cosseted by their slaves, for he could see many little brown men in black breech-clouts grubbing at the roots of things, scything grass, and carrying bundles. He was nauseated at the injustice, finding that he was having more and more trouble re-membering that this was all a figment of his own subcon-scious.

Two elderly women in blue silk gowns were standing in conversation and they looked up in surprise at the sight of him. He placed his fist on his heart as he went by, but that seemed only to increase their surprise. Al-most certainly they would be priestesses, and he was obviously not invisible to them. The word would be out, then, that a swordsman of the Seventh had arrived. *Does it matter?* Uneasily he was reacting as though it did. He speeded up and went striding forward to overtake the pilgrims, hearing them exclaim in alarm as he went by.

His road was clear, winding ahead through the trees and around buildings and across lawns; the intersecting roads were obviously minor, and there were blobs of pil-grims strung out in front of him. The temple grounds were much larger than the town, the noise of the falls louder.

Then the road turned a corner, and he had arrived.

Ahead was a great courtyard like an airport runway. To his right it was flanked by a few trees and a wide, still pool, almost a small lake. On his left was the temple. His head went back as he looked up at it, and it was breath-taking. A high flight of steps ran the full width of the front, topped by seven huge arches, and above that were gold spires. He thought it was probably bigger than any church or cathedral on Earth, a set of seven blimp hangars side by side. The pilgrims ahead were wending their way up the steps, spreading out along the top like bubbles rising in a glass.

He marched straight ahead along the courtyard until he was level with the center arch, then he swung around and started up the steps, not sure if he was doing this because he was a Seventh and that felt right for a Seventh, or because this was his personal illusion and therefore he should exert his uniqueness.

As he climbed, he noticed that the huddled pilgrims at the top were all kneeling, facing into the temple. He decided that he was not going to kneel, but he was not sure what he *was* going to do. Grab a priest and ask to speak to Mr. Honakura, perhaps. Then what? The little boy had warned him that he was going into a trap. Yet he certainly ought to be safe from sudden death within the temple itself, oughtn't he?

He was almost at the top when a bell began to toll, deep and menacing and louder than the rumble of the falls. The pilgrims rose at once and turned around. More people came drifting out of the temple to stand beside them. At first he thought they were all looking at him, and that was comforting because it was the sort of impossible thing that happened in dreams, but soon he saw that he was not the attraction—arms were pointing.

He stopped and turned around also. The view was spectacular: the court, the lake, and straight up the canyon to the white wall of the falls, framed in rainbow. He thought momentarily how thrilled Neddy would be to see that—Neddy liked waterfalls.

He wished that he had a camera. All his life Wallie Smith had worn glasses, but now he could see every detail of this view. That also was typical of dreams. What was the big excitement about, though? Was someone going over the falls in a barrel, perhaps?

Not quite.

Halfway up the face of the falls a lip of rock protruded from the face of the cliff to make a green-coated shelf, and his startlingly sharp vision could see people on it. As he watched, one of them floated out into space; at first slowly, then gradually gathering speed until it vanished into the spray below.

Human sacrifice?

The bell continued to toll.

Down by the water's edge stood a small group of men and a few women. Another body sailed out from the rock. The River would bring it down into the pool, for now he could see the swirl of the current. And there came the first one already, drifting face downward and turning slowly. The watchers on the beach ran along the shingle with long poles, apparently reluctant to get their feet wet. The body eluded them, swung around out of reach, and was carried away by the River, past the end of the courtyard and off behind the temple. The second came closer. It was pulled in for examination, but then pushed out again, obviously dead.

In all there were five murders while Wallie watched, and none of the victims survived. All five bodies were removed by the River. The remaining figures on the green lip formed up and marched away out of sight, so they were undoubtedly swordsmen. A nice profession you chose, Walter Smith! He was disgusted. First slavery and now human sacrifice! Could he not have fantasized a better world than this? Yet his dilemma remained—if this world was real, then there was no explaining how he came here, not in his terms, nor in the terms of this world itself, for Honakura and Jja had been as puzzled as he. Human sacrifice or not, he could only continue to believe that it was all taking place inside his own fevered and infected brain.

He started up the steps as fast as he could walk. The pilgrims were back on their knees and facing away from him. Soon he could see the roof of the temple, an incredible maze of fan vaulting. There were no interior pillars. It was a single span, which was structurally unbelievable and did much to confirm his disbelief. As he neared the top he saw the idol at the end. There was his destination, then! He would go and talk to this goddess about her world and arrange a few improvements.

He stepped between the knots of kneeling pilgrims. Two brown-kilted swordsmen jerked to startled attention at the sight of him and pulled out their swords to salute. He ignored them, marching through the arch and into the nave, striding purposefully toward the idol at the far end, and marveling at the sheer enormity of the place. The great stained-glass windows were bright with complicated arabesques of flowers and plants and animals and birds and fish in vibrant reds and blues and greens. Take all the greatest churches and temples and mosques of earth and roll them into one . . .

Sauntering priests and pilgrims stared in outrage at his progress as he swept by. The word would certainly be out, and he would see who answered it—little old Honakura or the dark presence of the ill-famed Hardduju.

The size of the temple had been dictated by the size of the idol. But it wasn't an idol. It was a natural rock formation, a conical pillar of some sort of bluish rock, metamorphic he supposed, although he knew little more geology than botany. While it suggested a seated and robed woman, a blank face toward the falls, no human tools had shaped it. It lacked symmetry. So the sacrificial victims died to honor an outcrop, did they? Five per day—if today was typical and if the show was a daily event — times twenty-seven thousand years . . . he needed a pocket calculator . . . how many days in a year on this world?

He reached the silver dais around the idol and stopped. Worshipers on their knees looked up uneasily at him and priests frowned. Wavy lines were the symbol for priests.

The idol was an impressive lump of rock, but the dais was obscene. Around its edge were golden bowls holding coins—some gold or silver, but mainly copper—presumably offerings. Those he could understand and forgive, but behind the bowls was a heap of other treasures: goblets, jewelry, cauldrons, carvings, daggers, and even swords, all kinds of precious things, in a blaze of gleaming metal and shiny faceted gems, in ivory and leather, polished wood and bright fabrics. Back from the front they aged. First the copper and bronze turned green, then the silver black and the ivory yellow, until at the base of idol itself the cloths and leather and woods had rotted away, and even the gold and crystal were hidden in dust. The wealth of centuries was piled there like a heap of garbage.

Wallie stared at this outrageous display in rank disbelief. All the riches of the pharaohs and the shahs and the rajahs and the sons of heaven could not have equaled this. Atahualpa's ransom was small change... First that orgy last night and now this immeasurable hoard! If you must hallucinate, hallucinate BIG!

And he thought of the penury of the town, the hunger and suffering that could be alleviated by a tiny fraction of this...

He must have stood there in shock for some time. When he glanced around he had been encapsulated— sealed off and quarantined by a semicircle of priests and priestesses, young and old, ranging from Thirds to Sevenths; silent, menacing, and resentful. Others were coming up behind to thicken the cordon, and there was not a friendly eye in the crowd. What was he going to do? *Did it matter?*

Then the barricade opened to admit the tiny form of Honakura, out of breath and troubled, minuscule in his blue satin gown, his intricately wrinkled face contrasting with the smooth brown baldness above it. His eyes searched Wallie's, no doubt seeking to discover who had come: Shonsu or Walliesmith?

"You must kneel, my lord," he said.

That broke the spell.

"Kneel?" Wallie roared. "I am not going to kneel to any lump of rock! I saw what was going on out by that waterfall. You are a murdering little monster, and your goddess is a fraud!"

The crowd hissed like snakes and made waving hand gestures. Honakura recoiled with dismay in his face.

Wallie opened his mouth to say something else and stopped. It wasn't going to work. Whatever he tried, he was not about to start a religious revolution, at least not here.

Then the crowd parted once more, this time to admit the temple guard.

The fat man in the front with the rubies and fancy blue kilt had to be Hardduju. His coarse, dissipated face was regarding Wallie with amused and satisfied contempt. Behind him came three brawny Fourths in orange, smiling grimly. The priests backed away, widening the cordon, while the reeve smirked and waited expectantly. Evidently it was Wallie's obligation to speak first.

He did not know what to say, so he said nothing.

His sword hilt had slid to somewhere behind his left shoulder.

Hardduju's satisfaction increased. Then he flashed out his sword with impressive speed and dexterously zipped it around in a complicated routine.

"I am Hardduju, swordsman of the seventh rank, reeve of the temple of the Goddess at Hann, and I give thanks to the Most High for granting me this opportunity to assure your beneficence that your prosperity and happiness will always be my desire and the subject of my prayers."

He shot the sword back into its scabbard and waited.

Before Wallie could think of anything to reply, little Honakura stepped forward and pointed a frail arm at him. "My lord reeve!" he snapped. "Remove this blasphemer!"

Hardduju glanced down at Honakura and laughed gloatingly. "I shall do better, holy one." He waved his men forward. "I denounce this man as an imposter. Arrest him."

Wallie backed up to put the dais behind him, knowing it was no real protection. The three young toughs grinned in anticipation, and then advanced warily, spreading out to come at him from different angles. Probably none was any younger or tougher than he was, but they could count.

If he drew his sword he was dead, he was sure, and it seemed that they were not going to draw unless he did. They wanted him alive, so perhaps dead would be better.

He fumbled for his sword, and they pounced, simultaneously and irresistibly.

He parried one blow with his left hand, felt his right arm grabbed in two hands, took a savage punch to the side of his head, and then the infallible, age-old clincher of a boot in the groin.

And that did matter. It mattered very much.

BOOK TWO:

HOW THE SWORDSMAN
RECEIVED THE SWORD

†

The temple jail was long, narrow, and very, very damp. It seemed to Wallie, once he had recovered his wits enough to study it, like a cross between an open sewer and an empty swimming pool. The timber roof had mostly rotted away, leaving a furry trellis from which long strands of moss hung dark against the blue brightness. The stones of both floor and walls were covered with brown and yellow-green slime. There were rusty grilles at both ends, but the stairs were unbarred. An agile man could have clambered out through the roof.

He did not comprehend much of his own arrival, but he watched the procedure when others were brought in later. If the prisoner was neither unconscious nor sufficiently docile, he was adjusted to one state or the other, then stripped and laid on the floor. A large stone slab was then stood on edge across his legs, pinning his ankles within notches cut in its base.

And that was that.

It took him some hours to recover sufficiently to sit up, bruised, swollen, and aching all over, coated with vomit and dried blood both inside and out. He would have exchanged all the treasure in the temple for a glass of water and he thought he was going to lose about six teeth. Through half-closed eyes, he peered groggily at the line of sitting men, all rooted to the low wall of slabs that ran down the middle of the room. There were five of them, apart from himself, and he was at the end of the line.

His neighbor smiled at him nervously and then attempted the greeting to a superior as well as he could in a sitting position, naming himself as Innulari, healer of the Fifth.

Wallie took a few minutes to gather his thoughts. "I am Shonsu, swordsman of the Seventh, my lord," he said. "I regret that I cannot give you a formal reply, but I am so confused that I do not recall the words."

The healer was a short and pudgy man, his flabbiness displayed by his nudity. He had limp, almost feminine, breasts and a globular belly. The top of his head was bald and the hair at the sides was plastered in all directions. He looked disgusting, but then they all did, and Wallie perhaps worst of all.

The healer simpered. "Oh, you must not address me as 'lord,' my lord. 'Master' is the correct address to a Fifth."

Five teeth for certain, Wallie concluded glumly. "My apologies, Master Innulari. I wish I could engage your professional services, but I regret that I seem to be out of funds at the moment."

The fat little man was regarding him with interest. "Do this," he said, moving an arm. "Now this . . ."

Wallie obeyed, moving as much of himself as he could with his legs pinned to the ground, and every twitch hurt.

"A few broken ribs, perhaps," the healer decided with satisfaction. "You didn't pass much blood, so the internal damage may not be too severe. Obviously the work of experts, for when I saw you I expected worse."

Wallie thought back to Hardduju's instructions to his goons before the punishment had started. "They were told not to reduce my value too much," he explained. "The reeve expects to get five golds for me."

"A denunciation?" Innulari asked, shocked. "Oh, I beg pardon, my lord; none of my business."

Wearily Wallie explained, as well as he could, that he had received a blow on the head the previous day and had lost his memory. He had, therefore, failed to return the correct reply to the reeve's greeting.

"So he thought you were an imposter!" The little man looked shocked and sympathetic. Apparently he was so honored to be sitting next to a Seventh that he was reluctant to make the same assumption. "That is a serious abomination, of course. As he was the one to denounce you, then he gets the slave, you understand."

Wallie nodded and then wished he hadn't. "What do they do about my facemarks?"

"Branding iron," Innulari explained cheerfully. "They'll probably use it to add your slavestripe, too, and save the cost of having it done professionally."

Great.

At that moment the two men next in line to Innulari started to fight, flailing sideways and one-handed at each other, yelling obscenities. After a few minutes a boyish-looking swordsman of the Second came trotting down the stairs. He walked along the other side of the slabs to them. The men screamed, one after the other, and fell silent. The swordsman walked briskly out again.

"How did he do that?" Wallie asked in surprise.

"Kicked their feet. It's very effective." Innulari glanced around the jail with approval. "The whole system is most efficient. Don't try to move the slab. You can probably push it over, but then it will fall on your feet and crush them."

Wallie lay down again, the only other position available to him, and wondered why the floor was so very wet. The smell was even worse than the stink of the town. He thought of the mysterious Shorty and his remark about a sample of hell ... In some ways the little boy had seemed to make more sense than anyone or anything else in this insanity, but in other ways he had been even less believable. That trick with the beads, now...

The healer lay down also. He was obviously a natural chatterbox, Wallie concluded, and therefore one more pain to add to the others, but he might also be a valuable source of information.

"Your blow to the head is very interesting, my lord. I have never met the symptoms before, but they are mentioned in one of our sutras." He frowned disapprovingly. "I am surprised that they did not allow the priests to attempt an exorcism, for that is the treatment of choice. Clearly a demon has gained admittance."

"That seems to have been the problem in the first place." Wallie sighed, and explained. He was trying to remember the argument that had taken place after he had been dragged from the nave of the temple into a back room, with Hardduju claiming the imposter as a slave, Honakura insisting that he was a blasphemer, and others —priests, he thought—talking demons. He had gained the impression that there had been a power struggle going on over his gasping, retching self. He tried to explain that also.

The healer seized on this as an important piece of temple gossip. If the holy Honakura's exorcism had failed, then the old man had been repudiated by the Goddess and had lost face. It might signify an important shift in influence, he said.

Great again.

"Well, at least they didn't try to call in a healer," Innulari said. "I know that I would not take your case— with respect, my lord."

"Why not?" Wallie asked, curious in spite of his pains.

"Because the prognosis is discouraging, of course." He waved a plump hand at the skeleton roof above them and the slimy walls. "That was what brought me here. I refused a case, but the family had money and kept raising the offer. Finally I got greedy, may She forgive me!"

Gingerly Wallie turned his head. "You mean a healer who loses a patient goes to jail?"

"If the relatives have influence." Innulari sighed. "I

was avaricious. But it was my wife's idea, so she must
cope now as best she can."

"How long are you in for, then?"

The fat little man shivered in spite of the steamy heat.
"Oh, I expect to go tomorrow. I've been here three days.
The temple court usually decides faster than that."

Go where? To the Judgment, of course. Wallie levered himself up once more and looked at the line of
naked men. Not a beautiful virgin among them. Not
human sacrifices, then, but executions. Those had been
criminals he had seen thrown into the falls, had they?
Mostly, the healer said. Or slaves no longer useful, of
course. And sometimes citizens went voluntarily to the
Goddess—the very sick or the old.

"How many return alive?" Wallie asked thoughtfully.

"About one in fifty, I suppose," the healer said. "Once
every two or three weeks. Most She chastises severely."

Further questions established that the chastisement
consisted of being battered and maimed on the rocks—it
was very rare indeed for anyone to return unscathed.
Nevertheless, the healer seemed quite cheerful about his
prospects, convinced that his lapse into avarice was a
minor sin that his Goddess would forgive. Wallie could
not decide if the little man was putting up a brave front
or really had such faith. It seemed like a very long shot
to Wallie.

Later in the day, a young slave was brought in and
pinned under the next slab. He regarded Wallie's facemarks with dread and would not speak. Wallie eventually decided that he was a congenital idiot.

The day dragged on in pain and heat and ever-
increasing stink, as the inmates fouled themselves and
the sun turned the damp cell into a sauna. The pudgy
Innulari chattered aimlessly, thrilled at meeting a Seventh, insistent on recounting his life story and describing
his children. Eventually he returned to the subject of the
temple court. The accused person did not appear before
it—he thought that an extraordinary idea—and usually

learned of the verdict only when he was taken away to execution. Acquittals did happen, he admitted.

"Of course you can hardly expect one in your case, my lord," he said, "because several of the members of the court, like the most holy Honakura, were present to witness your crime." He paused and then added thoughtfully, "It will be interesting to hear the decision, though: demon, imposter, or blasphemer?"

"I can hardly wait," Wallie said. Yet had he a choice, he would go for another exorcism—if they had exorcised him into this madhouse, perhaps they could exorcise him out. But a little later he learned from some remark of Innulari's that a second exorcism was very unlikely. Obstinate demons were usually referred to the Goddess.

A woman was brought in by the guards. She stripped and sat down obediently, and was pinned in the stocks next to the slack-jawed slave boy. She was middle-aged, graying, flabby, and loose-skinned, but the boy twisted round to stare at her and remained in that position for the rest of the day.

That certainly was not Wallie's problem—maybe never again. He pondered further about the sample of hell that the little boy had mentioned. Had that been a threat, a prophecy, or a lucky guess? If heaven was to be defined crudely as sexual ecstasy in a man's groin, then his hell had started appropriately with unbearable agony in the same place.

First postulate: All this pain was real. Sex he might fantasize, but not this.

Corollary: This world was real.

There were, he concluded, three possible explanations. The first was Wallie Smith's encephalitis, meaning that the World was all delirium. Somehow that was seeming less and less convincing as time went on.

A second was Shonsu's head injury—he was Shonsu, and Wallie Smith was the illusion. He lay on the hard wet stone and pondered that idea for a long time, with his swollen eyes shut against the sun's glare. He could not convince himself. Wallie Smith's life was too detailed in his memory. He could remember thousands of technical terms, for example, although when he tried to pronounce them he produced nothing but grunts. He could remember his childhood and his friends and his education. Politics. Music. Sports. Earth refused to die for him.

That left the third explanation: both worlds were real —and he was in the wrong one.

Sunset arrived, and a sudden rattling noise from the grille at one end of the cell.

"Clean-out time!" Innulari announced, sounding pleased. "And that drink you wanted, my lord."

Water began to flow along the cell, surging rapidly deeper. It had passed five men by the time it reached Wallie, and its filth made him retch—with agonizing consequences for his bruised abdominal muscles—but soon it ran deeper and relatively clean and gratifyingly cool. The inmates lay back in it and splashed and laughed . . . and drank. The twice-daily clean-out was the only water he would get in the jail, Innulari assured him.

The court sentences you to a week's amoebic dysentery and two weeks' probationary septicemia. It will try your case shortly.

When the water had drained through the other grille, the evening meal was passed along in a basket—leftovers, mostly moldy fruit with a few stale crusts and scraps of meat that Wallie would not have touched even if his teeth had felt firm in his head. Anything better had gone before the basket reached him. A week in this cell would be a death sentence.

Then the sun vanished with tropical swiftness; the cello chorus of the flies yielded to massed violins from the mosquitoes. Innulari's determined optimism seemed to fade also, and he began to brood. Wallie steered him around to the details of his faith and heard the same simple reincarnation belief that he had heard from the slave girl.

"Surely it is evident?" asked the healer, sounding as

if he were trying to convince himself as much as Wallie. "The River is the Goddess. As the River flows from city to city, so our souls flow from life to life."

Wallie was skeptical. "You can't remember previous lives, can you? What is a soul, then, if it is not your mind?"

"Quite different," the little man insisted. "The cities are lives and the River is the soul. It is an allegory to guide us. Or like beads on a string."

"Oh, hell!" Wallie said quietly. He fell silent. You could not move a city on a river, but you could untie a string, move beads around, and then retie the string.

The light faded and the incredible beauty of the rings filled the sky above him, thin ribbons of silver that would make a mere moon seem as uninspiring as a light bulb. He thought of the glory of the waterfall they called the Judgment. This was a very beautiful world.

Even without the pains of his injuries he could have slept little. Leg cramps were common to all the inmates; there were more groans than snores in the jail. The ring system, which the slave woman had called the Dream God, made a good timepiece. The dark gap that marked the shadow of the planet rose in the east soon after sunset and moved across the sky. At midnight he saw it mark off two exactly equal arcs, and he saw it fade at dawn.

Another day came, and he had not yet awakened to reality.

†††

Morning dawned fair, promising to be as hot as the day before. The healer Innulari seemed disappointed and eventually confessed that on very rainy days, when the Goddess could not see the Judgment, there were no executions.

Clean-out came and went. The inmates fretted in uneasy quiet, whispering nervously.

Then two priests, three swordsmen, four slaves came clattering down the stairs, pulling faces at the stench.

"Innulari, healer of the Fifth, for negligence..."

"Kinaragu, carpenter of the Third, for theft..."

"Narrin, slave, for recalcitrance."

As a priest called each name, a swordsman pointed. Slaves levered up the block and pulled out the victim. Each screamed at the pain when his stiffened legs were bent, each in turn was dragged away. Thus Wallie's immediate neighbors and another man farther along the line were taken away for execution, and the Death Squad departed. Then the fruit basket was passed again.

Wallie realized that he was going to miss the talkative Innulari. An hour or two later he heard the bell tolling. He wondered if he should say a prayer to the healer's goddess for him, but he did not.

In the middle of the morning, another five men were brought in. Although there was space beyond for many more, the place seemed suddenly crowded. Wallie acquired two new neighbors, who were delighted to see a swordsman of the Seventh in jail. They jeered at him and replied with obscenities when he tried to make conversation. He was exhausted by pain and lack of sleep, but if he seemed to nod off they would reach over and punch him from spite.

There was a sudden quiet. Wallie had perhaps been dozing, for he looked up to see the reeve regarding him with satisfied contempt from the safe side of the wall of slabs. He was holding a bamboo rod in both hands, flexing it thoughtfully, and there was no doubt as to his intended victim. Wallie's first decision was that he must show no fear. That would not be difficult, for his face was so swollen that probably no expression at all could show on it. Should he attempt to explain or should he remain silent? He was still debating that when the questioning began.

"What is the first sutra?" Hardduju demanded.

"I don't know," Wallie said calmly—he hoped calmly. "I—"

Before he could say more, the reeve slashed the bamboo across the sole of Wallie's left foot. It was bad . . . the pain itself, as well as the reflex that jerked the top of his foot against the stone and skinned his ankle. Hardduju studied his reaction carefully and seemed to approve of it.

"What is the second sutra?" That was the right foot.

Back to the left foot for the third sutra. How many could there be? After the sixth sutra, though, the sadist stopped asking and just continued beating, watching Wallie's agony with a growing smile and obvious excitement, his face becoming red and shiny. He switched from one foot to the other at random and sometimes faked a stroke to see the foot yank back against the stone in anticipation.

Wallie tried to explain and was given no hearing. He tried remaining silent until blood from his bitten tongue filled his mouth. He tried screaming. He tried begging. He wept.

He must have fainted, for he had no clear memory of the monster's departure. He probably went into shock, too, because the rest of the day was a confusion—a long, shivery, disjointed hell. Perhaps it was good that he could not see his ruined feet lying in the furnace beyond the stone slab. The sun moved, the shadows of the lattice roof crawled over him, and the flies came to inspect his wounds. But his neighbors punched and jeered no more.

The evening basket had been passed down the line, and he had sent it on without eating or caring. The sun had set. The sky was rapidly growing dim when Wallie felt himself snap out of his shocked lethargy. He heaved himself up to a sitting position and glanced around. All the other inmates seemed to have become curiously listless and were lying down in silence. The slimy room was hushed, steaming from its latest inundation, shadowy in the fading light.

The little brown boy was leaning against the slab that held Wallie's ankles, watching him. He was still naked, still as skinny as a bundle of sticks, still holding a leafy twig in one hand. His face was expressionless.

"Well, does it matter?" he asked.

"Yes, it does," Wallie said. Those were the first words he had spoken since Hardduju departed. His feet were balls of screaming agony that drowned out all the other pains and bruises.

The little boy did not speak for a while, studying the prisoner, but eventually he said, "The temple court is in session, Mr. Smith, considering your case. What verdict will you have it reach?"

"Me?" Wallie said. "How can I influence its verdict?" He felt drained of all emotion, too battered even to feel resentment.

The boy raised an eyebrow. "All this is happening inside your head—it is all your illusion. You said so. Can't you dictate the verdict?"

"I don't think that I can influence the temple court," Wallie said, "... but I think that you could."

"Ah!" the boy said. "Maybe we're getting somewhere." He put his hands on the slab behind him and sprang up to sit on it, his legs dangling.

"Who are you?" the man demanded.

"Shorty." The boy did not smile.

"I'm sorry!" Wallie shouted. "I didn't know!" He glanced both ways along the line of prisoners. No one stirred.

"They won't notice," the boy said. "Just you. All right, let's get back to faith, shall we?"

Wallie took a moment to gather his thoughts. He had to get this right, or he was going to die. Or worse.

"I believe that this world is real. But Earth was real, too."

The boy nodded and waited.

"It was the horses," Wallie said. "They're like horses but not quite. I always believed in evolution, not creationism, but the People are...people. They don't belong to any Earthly race, but they're human. Two worlds couldn't both produce real people by convergent evolution. Something similar for a similar ecological niche, perhaps, but not so similar. I mean, birds and bats both fly, but they're not the same. Noses and earlobes? They're not necessary, but the People have them, too. So in spite of what all the science fiction stories said, another world would not have an intelligent biped that was indistinguishable from *Homo sapiens*..."

The boy yawned.

"Gods!" Wallie said quickly. "It has to be gods, hasn't it? Purpose! Direction! That was what you meant with the beads, wasn't it? 'Every one is the same yet slightly different,' you said. Many worlds, variations on a theme. Copies of an ideal world, perhaps."

"Very good!" The boy nodded approvingly. "Go on."

"So the goddess is...is the Goddess. She brought me here."

"And who are you?"

That was the big question and now Wallie thought he knew. "I'm Wallie Smith and I am Shonsu...Wallie Smith's memories and Shonsu's body. Soul...I don't know about souls."

"Then don't worry about them," the boy said. "And Hardduju? How do you feel about capital punishment now, Mr. Smith?"

"I didn't say that I didn't believe in—"

"But you thought it!"

"Yes," Wallie confessed. "Get me out of here and let me kill that bastard, and I'll do anything you want—anything at all."

"Well, well! Will you?" The boy shook his head. "Revenge? Not good enough!"

"But I believe in the Goddess now!" Wallie protested, his voice breaking. "I will repent. I'll pray. I will serve Her, if She will allow it. I'll be a swordsman if that is what She wants. Anything!"

"My!" the boy muttered mockingly. "Such unexpected devotion!" He fell silent, staring fixedly, and Wallie had the strangest fancy that he was being skimmed, perused—read as an accountant might run his eye down a balance sheet to the bottom line. "It's a very small faith, Mr. Smith."

"It's all I've got," Wallie said. It was almost a sob.

"It's a sort of chink of doubt in your disbelief. You will have to prove it."

He had been afraid of that. "The Judgment?"

The boy pulled a face. "You don't want to be Hardduju's slave, do you? He wouldn't sell you in the end—it would be too much fun to have a Seventh chained in the cellar. He has many other entertainments to try! So you'd rather go to the Judgment, wouldn't you?" He grinned his gap-toothed grin for the first time. "The trick is this: if you resist, they bang you on the head and drop you over the edge. Then you land on the rocks. But if you run and jump far out, then you come down in deep water. It is a test of faith."

"I can't run on those feet," Wallie said. "Is there anything left of them?"

The boy twisted around briefly to look down at Wallie's feet and then shrugged. "There is a shrine at the Place of Mercy. Pray for the strength to run." He was becoming indistinct as the light faded. "I told you that this was important. It is a rare opportunity for a mortal."

"I haven't had much practice at praying," Wallie said humbly, "but I will do my best. I thought of praying for Innulari. Would it have helped?"

The boy gave him an odd look. "It wouldn't have helped him, but it would have helped you." He paused and said, "The gods must not provide faith in the first place, Mr. Smith. I could have given you belief, but then you would have been a tool, not an agent. A mortal's

service is of no value to the gods unless it is freely given
—free will may not be dictated. Do you see? But once
you have faith, the gods can increase it. You have found
a spark. I can blow on a spark. I will do this much for
you, in return for your kind thought about the healer."

He pulled a leaf off his twig. At once the raging fires
in Wallie's feet seemed to be plunged into ice water. The
pain died away, and all the other pains also.

"Until dawn," the boy said.

Wallie started to gabble thanks, stuttering in his relief.
"I don't even know what to call you," he said.

"Call me Shorty for now," the boy said, and his gap-
tooth grin was just visible in the growing light of the
Dream God. "It's been a long time since a mortal was so
impudent. You amuse me." His eyes seemed to shine in
the shadow. "Once you played a game called chess—
you know what happens when a pawn reaches the end of
its file?"

The mockery was obvious, but Wallie quickly re-
pressed his resentment. "Sir, it can be converted to any
other piece except a king."

The boy chuckled. "So you have reached the end of
your file and you have been converted. Simple, isn't it?
Remember, jump as hard as you can tomorrow, and we
shall meet again."

Then the slab was empty.

Thus, on his second night in the jail, Wallie slept
soundly, but toward morning he found himself sitting at a
table. It was a memory, a scene from his youth being
played back to him so vividly that he could smell the
cigarette butts and hear distant jazz from a radio in another room . . . green baize in darkness with a light shining down on it; playing cards, ashtrays, and glasses. Bill
sat on his left, Justin on his right, and Jack had gone to
the john.

He was declarer in a game of bridge, doubled and
drunk and vulnerable in a crazy contract, in one of those

crazy deals where the cards were distributed in bunches. Clubs were trumps, and he still held the last one, the deuce. Bill led a spade to Wallie's solitary ace on the table, then obligingly moved the ace forward for him. Justin followed suit. That would force Wallie to lead from dummy, and they were waiting for him.

He trumped his own ace, and a voice said "Barf!" Then he could lead out seven good hearts from his hand. The defenders were squeezed—whatever they discarded, he could keep. He heard himself yell in triumph ...slam, bid, made, doubled, redoubled, vulnerable, game, and rubber. He reached for the scorepad. He felt it between his fingers. Then it was gone, he was back in the jail, and the first glimmer of dawn was starting to brighten the eastern sky.

Believing in gods, he discovered, led one to believe in sendings. Who had made a bad lead? Chess and bridge ...did the gods play games with humanity to while away eternity? The spades of a bridge deck were descended from the swords of tarot—had the Goddess trumped Her own ace of swords, Shonsu, with Wallie Smith, the deuce of clubs, the smallest card in the deck?

As the light grew, the pains returned. But that was as the little boy had predicted, and he could believe that today he would be taken from the jail.

A god had said so.

†††

The temple court had been busy. The Death Squad took six of the prisoners that day, and the first name on the list was: "Shonsu, swordsman of the Seventh, possessed of a demon." If Innulari's interpretation was correct, then old Honakura had lost out in the power struggle.

Wallie was dragged roughly up the steps, through a guard room, and allowed to fall limply on hard, hot paving under the blistering sun. He had not screamed. He lay for a moment, fighting down nausea from the pain in his joints and his bruises, screwing up his eyes against the glare. Then he struggled to sit up as the others were hauled out and dropped beside him, whimpering or yelling. After one glance at his feet, he tried not to look at them any more.

He was at the edge of a wide court, like a parade ground, and the heat danced within it in ripples. Behind him was the jail, and he could hear the River chattering happily behind that. Two sides of the yard were flanked by massive buildings, with the great spires of the temple rising in the distance. The fourth side lay open to a heaven of parkland and greenery.

The priests departed, their job done. A bored-looking swordsman of the Fourth seemed to be in charge now. Efficient and shiny-smart, he was tapping a whip against his boot, looking over the victims.

"Ten minutes to get your legs back," he announced. "Then you walk across the square and back. Or crawl, as you please." He cracked the whip loudly.

A yellow-kilted, fresh-faced Second came around, tossing each condemned man a black cloth to wear. When he came to Wallie he frowned and looked at his superior.

"Better get a cart for that one," the Fourth said.

Wallie said loudly, "I am a swordsman. I shall walk." He took the loincloth and ripped it in half, started to bandage one foot.

"You're a filthy imposter," the Fourth snarled.

Wallie tore a small strip from the other cloth and tied his hair back so that his facemarks were visible. "Not according to the temple court, swordsman." That was probably the wrong form of address, because the man flushed and raised his whip threateningly.

"Go ahead," Wallie said. "Just like your boss."

The man stared at him for a moment, then grabbed another cloth from the Second and tossed it to Wallie to wear.

Wallie wasn't sure that he was being very smart, but

he was required to prove his faith, and the only way he could see to do that was to prove his courage. Whether he proved it to the gods or the swordsmen or himself hardly seemed to matter. When the time came to cross the square, a couple of the men began by crawling and got whipped. Wallie walked. He walked very slowly, and as he put down each foot he gasped with the pain, but he lurched all the way across and back. And he held his head up.

Then the six were chained together to be led along the riverbank, past buildings he could not see for tears, past the busy, noisy waters, which in a short while might be carrying his mangled carcass, round to the steps of the temple. There they had to stand for a while until a priestess came out and gabbled a blessing over them.

The guard consisted of nine swordsmen and four hulking slaves. Wallie had been given the place of honor in the front, the chain from his neck held by one of the Seconds.

Every step was a torment. How much of the water in his eyes was sweat running in, and how much tears running out, he did not know or care. He was only vaguely aware of the long road through the park and the big gate, but the chain gang was not far into the slums and alleys of the town when he heard a child's voice cry, "Hey! They got a swordsman!"

He knuckled his eyes clear to look, and there was an instant crowd. It had not occurred to him to wonder what the townsfolk thought of the daily death march. Innulari had told him that a majority of the condemned were slaves or criminals sent in by nearby cities, this being a meritorious service to the Goddess for some obscure and ancient reason, but some of the victims must be from the town and perhaps there might sometimes be attempts at rescue. That might explain the size of the guard, for nine to shepherd six in chains seemed excessive.

But this was no rescue attempt. The crowd was jeering, running along ahead, and following behind—chil-

dren and adolescents and young adults. A swordsman of
the Seventh going to the Judgment was great sport. The
noise and confusion in the narrow passageway grew rapidly, heads popped out of windows and doors, and the
curious flocked in from side streets. The guard grew nervous and angry and increased the pace, jerking at the
chain. Wallie kept his head up and his teeth clenched,
and staggered along.

A soft lump of filth struck him, and then more, not so
soft. The shouting was being directed only at him, the
noble lord, the valorous swordsman. Did you lose a battle then? Where's your sword, swordsman? Have this
one for me, my lord . . .

The Fourth in charge drew his sword, and it seemed
for a few moments as if there might be bloodshed, with a
riot sure to follow. But one of the slaves had been sent
for help. Another troop of swordsmen arrived at the double, and the crowd was roughly dispersed. Wallie was in
too much pain to be frightened, but he could read the
message—swordsmen of the Seventh were not popular.
With Hardduju as the local standard, that was easy to
understand.

The jail had not been hell at all, barely purgatory, for
the journey was worse. A million times he cursed himself
for not accepting the cart, however undignified that
might have been, or rough on his bruises. He saw nothing of how he left the town or of the scenery beyond,
noticing only that the path was climbing steeply. He was
terrified that he might faint, for then he would either be
dragged along to his destination or swiftly run through
with a sword and dropped into the water. The rags on his
feet were blood-soaked and chafing on raw flesh, the
pain and heat unendurable. Every muscle and joint
seemed to scream.

A blast of cold air revived him when they had
rounded a corner of rock and were approaching the falls,
on a path flanked by a sheer drop on one side and over-
hanging cliff on the other. The ground trembled, the wind

swirled a mist of cold droplets, and the roar hammered at his ears. The falls hung like a wall ahead. When he peered over the edge of the path, he saw white fury and rocks and churning tree trunks far below. His frail new faith faltered—could anyone at all ever come through that alive? Even if he managed to do so, would he not end up in the temple again, still not knowing the first sutra? But then the pain drove away the doubts, for deep inside he was raging, raging at the injustice and gratuitous cruelty, slobbering with his desire for revenge on the sadistic Hardduju—and just possibly raging against the little boy, the miracle-working mystery boy who found Wallie Smith amusing. Wallie was going to show them all, and every flame tempered his resolve.

Now the pain in his feet was subsiding into numbness as if they had died, but that might have been the effect of the cooling spray, or partial loss of consciousness, or even because he was now so terrified at the ordeal ahead that he was mumbling a continuous stream of prayer. It was inarticulate and confused and made very little sense even to him, but perhaps it was being heard.

The path ended suddenly, emerging from a gully onto the gentle grassy slope at the top of the jutting rocky spine. The prisoners were shoved forward, unchained, and allowed to collapse on the grass. A slave went around to collect the loincloths.

Two guards with drawn swords remained by the gully, but the rest seemed unconcerned, so clearly that gully was the only way down. No—the only *safe* way down. Wallie fought off waves of nausea. He tried not to think of the future, to think instead how well he had done to arrive here at all. The little boy should be pleased with him.

At the highest point of the slope stood the shrine, a blue stone baldachin over a small replica of the statue in the temple. Behind that was the shiny bare rock of the cliff. The lower edge of the meadow ended in empty air, the far wall of the canyon obscured by billowing clouds of mist. The falls were magnificent—terrifyingly close, a vertical river rushing from the heavens far above to hell far below, shaking the earth in fury, unforgettable, merciless white death.

He turned his back on them and sat quietly, looking down the canyon toward the temple, still astonishingly large, even at this distance. Set like a jewel within its enameled park, it was a truly beautiful building and an astonishing tribute to the deity it honored. Somewhere down there was Hardduju. He owed Hardduju something.

The town was not visible, but he could see the road angling up the valley wall and even make out the minute specks that were the pilgrim cottages. He thought of that sweet slave girl. Crushed at the bottom of the social structure, without status or freedom or possessions of any sort, condemned to whore for others' gain, she had offered him solace and kindness, the only person in the World who had yet done so. If he survived and by the intervention of the gods was given freedom to act, then there was another debt he had to repay.

For some time nothing happened. The naked prisoners, the guards, and the slaves all sat around in the sunshine as if they were having a cigarette break. The wind played coyly around them, bringing one moment the icy touch of death from the falls and next the warm scents of damp earth and tropical flowers. Nobody looked at anybody else. The boom of the falls would have made conversation almost impossible anyway.

The Fourth in charge had been keeping an eye on the temple and must have caught a signal, for he suddenly yelled that it was time. Apparently the honor of marching first in the chain gang was matched by the honor of dying last. Wallie felt no great urge to argue this precedence. The first man squealed and tried to shrink into the grass as the guards approached him. They shouted at him and kicked him until he rose, ran to the shrine, and wrapped himself around the Goddess. After about thirty seconds, a guard hit him with a wooden club, and he went limp. The slaves carried him over to the edge and swung, and if the bell tolled for him in the temple, then the roar of the falls drowned it out.

The prisoners were trying to inch themselves away from the guards, clinging desperately to an extra few moments of terrified life. It made no difference. One by one they went over the edge. Then it was Wallie's turn.

The Fourth came himself and alone. He had to stoop and shout to make himself heard. "You did walk, my lord, like a swordsman. Will you also jump?" His eyes said that courage could be admired in anyone, imposter or not. He was only a soldier doing his duty; Wallie managed to smile at him.

"I shall jump," Wallie said. "I wish to pray first, but tell me when my time is up. I do not wish to be thrown." He hoped that his voice sounded calmer to the swordsman than it did to him.

He limped up to the statue in the shrine and knelt down. Feeling very self-conscious, he prayed aloud to the idol for the physical strength to be able to run, and for the mental strength to want to.

There was no reply, and there was nothing else to say. He was very much aware of the sun on his bare skin, the blue sky with white clouds, the temple at the bottom of the valley, the spectacular wall of water on the other side, and birds wheeling freely in the air around. The World was very beautiful and life was sweet . . . and why did this have to happen to him?

"Time," said the guard with the club.

Wallie rose and turned. He started to hobble down the slope. Amazingly, his legs and feet supported him. He increased speed to a run. There were a few cheers behind him. He reached the edge almost before he expected it, threw out his arms, and sailed off into space in a ragged dive. There was a great wind, and spray in his face, and then nothing.

†† ††

Tumult and madness in the heart of thunder...

Darkness...

He was hung over a beam like a towel, head down and feet down. The noise was calamitous, beating at his head and swinging him around by sheer force of sound, in darkness with just enough glimmer to show the beam wedged in a wall of jagged rocks, with a monstrous wave sweeping along it, rising. He grabbed his knees and hung on grimly as the water engulfed him, lifted him, and spun him over like a hoop on a stick. It sucked at him voraciously and then dropped him again with a sickening impact, until the next one could arrive.

Gasping and desperate, he clambered onto the top of the beam as the water began rising again. He lunged from the beam to the rocks in which it was jammed, found a handhold, pulled himself higher, and grabbed a rock with both hands and his knees. The next wave surged waist-deep around him. His fingers had started to slip before it sank back.

Darkness and terrible noise.

There was no hope of being heard, but he would not be able to withstand another wave. He tried to shout, but managed only an urgent croak: *"Shorty! Help Me!"*

Sudden silence. Peace. The waves had stopped.

He thought he had gone deaf, or died. The pain in his chest was killing him. He had lost half his hide on the rocks.

Light began to creep in around him. He blinked, then made out the shape of the rocks and the beam below and then more rocks, a steep slope of jumbled talus, boulders as big as houses or small as a desk, plastered with debris like the beam—which was obviously a piece of a ship's mast—and planks and tree trunks and branches, heaped and piled in steep chaos. It was a hillside, a giant's junk pile, with him clinging on it like a fly.

His chest was bursting. He breathed in small gasps, every one a death.

There was no source for the light, but it blazed up brighter and brighter like a winter sun. All the rocks glittered with it, and the lumber shone like mirrors. The roof was a jutting ledge of rock. The space below was enclosed in brilliant draperies of crystal and silver, frozen white splendor—iridescent jagged ice curtains. And downward, almost directly below his feet, the monstrous waves churned by the waterfall were stilled into immobile chasms of dark blue-green obsidian, encrusted with timbers and other deadly flotsam, grading to indigo and black in their depths. The air shimmered with myriads of brilliant specks, a mist of airborne diamonds. This was a space behind the falls, frozen by miracle.

He was in no state to appreciate a miracle. He saw a flat rock, pulled himself onto it, and collapsed. Torrents of water gushed from his lungs in spasms of pain. He retched and puked and then lay still, breathing once more in huge, rasping lungfuls.

At length his mind cleared. The pain subsided enough for him to raise his head and look around at this silent crystal-and-stone cathedral, this glacier cave shining whitely like the palace of the Snow Queen. The rugged drop below his rock perch was horrifying. The petrified waves were enormous—angry giants momentarily balked of their prey.

"You have arrived, then," said the voice of the little boy, "safe if not quite sound?" He was sitting cross-legged on a nearby rock, higher, flatter, and more comfortable-looking than Wallie's. He held his leafy twig. He was showing his tooth gap in a mocking grin.

"I think I'm dying," Wallie said weakly. He no longer cared. Every man must have a limit, and he had passed his. The gods could play with someone else.

"Well, we can fix that," the boy said. "Stand up."

Wallie hesitated and then obeyed, staggering to his

bloody and pulped feet, unable to straighten, swaying dangerously.

"My! You are a mess!" the boy said. He looked Wallie over and then pulled a leaf from his twig.

Wallie felt himself heal. A wave of healing pouring through him. It started at the pounding pain in his head, washing that away. His vision cleared, then his loose teeth seemed to grip tightly into his skull, his ribs knitted, his sprains soothed, cuts closed, bruises eased, and his swollen testicles shrank back to normal size. The miracle reached his feet and died out.

He looked himself over, sat down, and inspected his feet. They were better than before, but a long way from being cured. His eyes remained puffed and swollen, his bruises visible, if no longer very painful. The insides of him no longer felt too bad, but the outside was still an obvious catastrophe, and walking on those feet would still be hell.

"Give me another shot!" he demanded. "You ran out of juice about halfway."

The boy frowned warningly. "Hell does much more for you than heaven, Mr. Smith. I'll leave you a few reminders."

There was no way to argue with such power. Wallie looked anew at the strangely vitrified waterfall. It had taken a miracle to bring him here alive. It would certainly take another to get him out. He wondered where the light was coming from. But he was still in pain, angry, and resentful.

"You proved your faith," the boy said. He leaned his reedy forearms on pointed knees, staring thoughtfully down at Wallie. "You told me that faith was an attempt to explain suffering by postulating a higher meaning. Does that help?"

"I thought it amused you," Wallie said, still bitter.

This time there was menace in the frown. "Be careful!"

"Sorry," Wallie mumbled, not feeling sorry. "You've been testing me?"

"Proving you. You proved yourself. That is a tough body, but being tough is more than muscles and bone." He chuckled. "The Goddess does not need a swordsman who will sit down and convene a committee at every emergency. You displayed great courage and persistence."

"And I suppose that I wasn't capable of that three days ago?" Wallie squirmed on the rock, trying to find a smooth spot to kneel on. He assumed he should be kneeling.

"Of course you were," the god said, "but you didn't know it. Now you do. Enough of that! You proved your faith and you have agreed to undertake the task, right? The rewards can be whatever you want—power, riches, physical prowess, long life, happiness...your prayers will be answered. If you succeed. The alternative is death, or worse."

Wallie shivered, although he was not cold. "The carrot and the stick?"

"Certainly. And now you know both. But from now on you must earn your rewards."

"Who are you?"

The boy smiled and jumped to his feet. He bowed, sweeping his twig over the rock as a courtier might have swung a plumed cap over a palace floor. But he was only a skinny, naked little boy. "I am a demigod, a minor deity, an archangel—whichever you wish. You may call me 'Master' as it is forbidden for you to know my name." He dropped back to his seat. "I choose this shape because it amuses me and will not alarm you."

Wallie was not impressed. "Why play games with me? I could have believed in you sooner if you had chosen a more godlike form—even a halo . . . ."

He had gone too far. The boy pouted in anger. "As you wish," he said, "just a small one."

Wallie screamed and covered his eyes, but too late.

The cave had been brilliant before. Now it blazed with glory like the face of a star. The boy remained a boy, but some small part of his divinity gleamed through for an instant, and that was enough to reduce a mortal to abject terror.

In that flicker of majesty, Wallie was shown age beyond imagining, enduring since before the galaxies and continuing long after such transient fireworks would have faded; mind that would register an IQ in the trillions and could know every thought of every being in the universe; power that could snuff out a planet as easily as clean a fingernail; a nobility and purity that made all mankind seem bestial and worthless; cold, marble purpose that could not be withstood by anything; compassion beyond human conception that knew the sufferings of mortals and why they suffered, yet could not prevent those sufferings without destroying the very mortal essence that made their sufferings inevitable. He also sensed something deeper and more terrible than all of those, a presence for which there were no words, but which in a mortal might have been boredom or resignation, and was the dark side of immortality, the burden of omniscience and of having no limit to the future, no surprises in store, no end even beyond the end of time, forever and ever and ever...

He became aware that he was groveling and writhing on the rock, gibbering with terror and contrition, wetting himself, howling, begging for mercy and forgiveness. His limbs shook uncontrollably. He wanted to hide, to die, to bury himself in the ground. He would have run all the way back to the jail, had that been a way to escape from that memory of glory.

It took him a long time to regain control. When his eyes cleared and he could rise to his knees, the little boy was still sitting in the same place, but had turned his attention to the curtain of coruscating crystal that had once been a waterfall. He was pointing a finger at it and fragments moved at his bidding, building themselves into a tall lattice of mind-warping multidimensional complexity. Divine sculpture...even a glimpse at it was enough to make Wallie giddy. He looked away quickly.

"Master?" he whispered.

"Ah!" The skinny little boy turned back to him with a satisfied and gap-toothed smile. He did not wait for any attempt at apology. "You have recovered! I see you have scraped some more skin off. Well, now that we have straightened out your soul, more or less cured your body, and improved your attitude, perhaps we can get down to business?"

"Yes?"

"Yes, *what*?"

"Yes, Master," Wallie said as humbly as he could. Obviously gods did not take kindly to smart-aleck mortals.

The boy put an elbow on a knee and wagged a finger in the air, as though telling a story. "Now—Shonsu was a very great swordsman. There is perhaps no greater in the World at the moment." He paused for a moment, considering. "Possibly one about equal. Hard to say—we shall see." He grinned mischievously. "Shonsu had a mission, a task. He failed, and the penalty was death."

Wallie opened his mouth, and the little boy said, *"You must not question the justice of the gods!"* in a voice that stopped anything Wallie might have been about to say.

"No. Master."

"The Goddess requires you to bring about what Shonsu could not."

How far dare he question? "Master, why me? How and why was I brought here? How can I succeed where the greatest—"

The boy held up a hand and snapped, "You expect an explanation? You could not even understand the politics of the temple, let alone what all this is about. I have stopped time so that we may talk, but I haven't stopped it for you, and if I tried to explain the whole thing, then you would die of old age before you got out of here." He sighed.

"Truth is like a fine jewel, Mr. Smith, with a million facets. If I show you one facet of this jewel, will you be content, but remember that it is only one and that there are many others?"

"I shall try, Master," Wallie said. He squirmed some more on his rock and eventually sat on the edge and dangled his legs over the abyss.

The boy eyed him thoughtfully. "After all," he said, "you believe that life is worth living, yet you know that death is inevitable. You believe that an electron is a particle and a wave at the same time, don't you? You know that love and lust are the finest and most base of human motives, and yet are frequently almost inseparable. You do have some capacity for reconciling incompatible truths?"

Wallie nodded and waited.

"Well, then . . . I gave you a couple of hints."

"Chess and bridge? The gods play games?" Wallie did not want to believe that; all human history merely a game to amuse the gods?

That is one facet of the jewel," the boy said. "Think of it as an allegory. And somebody made a bad lead, as your dream showed you. There is no rule against profiting from a bad lead! In the affairs of gods, you see, there is no coincidence and no unexpected, but sometimes there is the unusual. You were unusual. It explains why you were available. That is all I can tell you."

He gave Wallie a disgusted look. "And don't go rushing off to found a religion over this—that is a hazard for mortals who are told things by gods. You see, whereas that one facet means that certain . . . powers . . . are opponents, on other facets of the jewel, they are partners. Confusing, isn't it?"

Wallie nodded. Confusing was not half of it.

"And on many other facets there is no game at all. So don't think my parable means that you are unimportant. In your former world, when the tin-chested, square-jawed warriors gathered to play war games, were they playing games?"

Wallie smiled. "Yes and no, Master."

The boy looked relieved. "All right, then. Let's go on, and not worry about explanations. You have shown that you have courage. You have Shonsu's body and his language and you can be given his skill. Are you worthy?"

Wallie thought that this had to be the strangest job interview in the history of the galaxy—whatever galaxy this was. A small naked boy interviewing a large naked man on the side of a cliff behind an immobilized waterfall?

"I am a better man than Hardduju. He is the only standard I have to judge by."

The boy snarled something inaudible about Hardduju. "All the crafts have their sutras," he said, "and in most cases the first one contains a code. When a boy becomes a swordsman he swears to follow the code of the swordsmen. Listen!"

He reeled off a long string of promises. Wallie listened with growing dismay and skepticism. The swordsmen, apparently, were something between Knights Templar and Boy Scouts. No mortal could ever live to such a standard . . . at least, not Wallie Smith.

#1   THE CODE

I will be evermore true to
        the will of the Goddess,
        the sutras of the swordsmen,
        and the laws of the People.
I will be mighty against the mighty,
        gentle to the weak,
        generous to the poor,
        and merciless to the rapacious.
I will do nothing of which I may be ashamed,
        but avoid no honor.
I will give no less than justice to others,
        and seek no more for myself.
I will be valiant in adversity,
        and humble in prosperity.
I will live with joy.
I will die bravely.

"I will swear it," he said cautiously. "And I hope I will keep it as well as any man may, but it is more a code for gods than mere humans."

"The swordsmen are addicted to fearsome oaths," the

boy said ominously and stared at him for a time, until he trembled. "Yes," he said at last, "I think you will try quite hard. You are starting at the top, as a Seventh, and you will not have the advantage of a long apprenticeship to teach you the proper attitudes. Your past life has hardly been a suitable training. You need to understand that the battle against evil may require harsh measures, and that sweet reason is not enough."

"Well, I have some idea," Wallie protested. "My father was a policeman."

The little god leaned back on his pipe-stem arms and laughed a long and childishly shrill laugh, for which Wallie could see no cause at all. The crystal echoed it back until the ice cave rang.

"You are learning, Mr. Smith! Very well, then. The first thing you have to do is to go back to the temple and kill Hardduju. That is not your task! It is your duty to the Goddess, and a favor from Her to you. He is insufferable. Obviously the Goddess could dispose of him—a heart attack or a poisoned finger—but he is so bad that he must be made an example. She could throw a lightning bolt at him, but that would be a very crude miracle. Miracles should be subtle and unobtrusive. There is justice in having a better swordsman come along and execute him in public. Can you do that?"

"It will be a pleasure," Wallie said, surprising himself, but remembering that fat, red face sweating with joy in the jail. "I shall need a weapon, preferably napalm."

The boy smiled slightly and shook his head. "You may use this weapon," he announced. He pulled another leaf from his twig.

A sword and harness appeared on the rock beside Wallie.

The hilt was silver, trimmed with gold, and the guard was shaped like some heraldic beast, so finely wrought that every muscle, every hair was visible. Held between the beak and the tiny claws of the forelegs, forming the top of the hilt, an enormous stone shone like a blue sun. The artistry was superb.

Reverently Wallie raised it and drew it from the scabbard. The blade was a ribbon of winter moonlight, chased with scenes of battles between heroes and monsters. It flashed and shone more brightly than anything else in the shiny crystal cave. It was a Rembrandt, a da Vinci of swords. No, a Cellini: it belonged with the crown jewels of a world empire.

Wallie was not sure which impressed him more—the artistic beauty or the sheer monetary value of such a marvel. He looked up at the boy and said wonderingly, "It's magnificent! I've never seen anything so beautiful."

The demigod sneered. "You may find that it comes at a heavy price. Every alley thief will sharpen his knife as you go by. Every swordsman in the World will be ready to challenge you to get it."

That was a disturbing thought, if the swordsmen were the police.

"I can guess," Wallie said apprehensively. What would the god do to him if he let the sword be stolen? "And the first one up is going to get it. I can handle a pool cue better than this. I'm just not a swordsman, Master."

The boy said, "I promised you Shonsu's skill." Another leaf fell.

Wallie felt nothing in himself, but the sword was transformed in his hand. It was still a masterpiece of art, but now he could see that it was also a masterpiece of the swordmaker's craft—a da Vinci, but also a Stradivarius. It was no longer heavy, it was amazingly light. He jumped to his feet and swung it.

Guard at quarte...

Lunge...

Parry...

Riposte quinte!

The balance was perfect, the grip firm. Now he could see the superb combination of flexibility for strength and rigidity for sharpness. He could have shaved with it, had he any need now to shave. It was an incredible triumph of metallurgy and design and beauty, and a fingerlength longer than most swords, to balance the ornate hilt. Yet the metal was so fine that he need not fear that the extra length would weaken the weapon. With his long arms he could draw such a sword—and he would have a fearsome advantage in reach. Instinctively he quoted from the fourth sutra, "On the Care of Swords:" *"The sword is the life of the swordsman and the death of his foe."*

Then he stopped and stared in astonishment at the cross-legged boy on the rock. There were eleven hundred and forty-four sutras. He could have recited any of them. Together they gave him all he needed to know...

He was a swordsman of the seventh rank.

"Truly, you do a great miracle, Master."

The child giggled like a child. "One rarely gets the chance. But be warned—that is a mortal sword. It has no magic powers. It can be lost or broken, and you are a mortal. I have given you the skill and knowledge of Shonsu, that is all. You can be defeated."

Wallie picked up the harness, slipped it on, and slid the sword expertly into the scabbard. He fastened the buckles, and the fit was perfect. Faith and confidence poured through his veins, and now, suddenly, he could revel in this unfamiliar but wonderful youth and strength and ability that he had been given. His terror of the god had faded to a wary respect. For the first time since he had awakened in the pilgrim cottage he could look forward to the future. He discovered that he even had some idea of what those seven swords on his face meant—in medieval earthly terms he was roughly a royal duke. The World was his to enjoy. Small wonder that the god had questioned his ability to handle such absolute authority. *All power corrupts!* The townsfolk had shown their feelings toward swordsmen of the Seventh.

"May I swear that oath to you now, Master?" he said, taking a firm grip on his excitement.

"That oath is not sworn to me!" the boy snapped. He sprang up. "But I will witness it for you. Go ahead."

So Wallie drew the sword again. He raised it to the oath position and swore to follow the code of the swordsmen. The ancient words filled him with reverence, and he felt very satisfied as he sheathed the blade once more. Now he need not worry about keeping it straight on his back—Shonsu's reflexes would handle that for him.

"What is my task, Master?" he asked.

The boy has resumed his seat on the rock, now dangling his legs over the edge. He pondered for a moment, studying Wallie.

Then he said:

> "First your brother you must chain.
>   And from another wisdom gain.
>   When the mighty has been spurned,
>   An army earned, a circle turned,
>   So the lesson may be learned.
>   Finally return that sword
>   And to its destiny accord."

Pause.

"But . . ." Wallie said and stopped.

The boy laughed. "You expected to be told to go and kill a dragon, or put down a revolution or something, didn't you? Your task is much more important than anything like that."

"But, Master, I don't understand!"

"Of course not! I am being Delphic—it is a tradition amongst gods."

Wallie lowered his eyes, standing on his rocky perch, his recent euphoria withered away. Why give a man a task and then not tell him what it is? He could think of only one reason—the demigod did not trust him. What did he not trust—Wallie's courage or his honesty? Then his neck muscles jerked, so that his head came up to face the grinning boy on the higher rock.

"It is like the faith thing," the boy said gently. "You will have to make your own choices. A great deed done of your own will is more pleasing to the gods than one done to order."

That sounded to Wallie suspiciously like a rule in a game. The god seemed to read the thought and he frowned, then laughed.

"Go and be a swordsman, Shonsu! Be honorable and valorous. And enjoy yourself, for the World is yours to savor. Your task will be revealed to you. You will understand my riddle at the right time."

"Am I to be reeve of the temple, as the priest wanted?"

The boy snorted. "Why not use the temple to store onions? The temple doesn't need a Shonsu." He gave Wallie one of his intensely penetrating glances and said, "As well make Napoleon Bonaparte king of Elba."

"But this brother?" Wallie protested. "You have given me language and skill, Master, but what about all the other memories? Home and family? I don't know where to start or what my brother looks like. I'm going to be making mistakes all the time, things like table manners—"

Once more the child screamed with laughter. "Who will complain about a Seventh's table manners? If I gave you all of Shonsu's memories then you would be Shonsu and make the same mistakes he made. You don't think like Shonsu, and that pleases me. You will be guided."

Wallie was relieved. "Then there will be more miracles?"

"Remember what I said about miracles," the boy warned, frowning. "The gods do miracles when they choose, rarely upon request, and never on demand. Honakura is a good man—him you may trust. Get him to tell you the anecdote from the seventeenth sutra. It fits your case rather well." He smiled at some private joke, and

Wallie wondered if the sutra had just been changed by a miracle. He was not about to ask.

"Yes, Master."

The boy frowned again, looking him over. "You still don't look like a hero, more like one of his victims. The sword came from the Goddess, but here is a present from me."

He scooped up a fragment of the crystal and tossed it down. Wallie caught it. In his hand glittered a silver hairclip bearing another giant sapphire, a twin to the jewel on the sword, blue light flickering and flaming within it. He could hear those knives being sharpened behind his back again, but he thanked the god, scooped up his hair, and clipped it.

"Better!" the boy said. "You did not approve of the World when we walked through the town. What do you think of it now?"

"I know better now, Master," Wallie said, hastily but sincerely. "There was poverty like that on Earth, and I did nothing about it there. It is not so long since thieves were put to death there also, or prisoners tortured. They still are, in many places. I shall not presume any more to tell the Goddess how to run Her world."

The boy nodded. "You seem to be improving. And you do look more like a swordsman. Now—expenses." He pulled off another leaf. Nothing at all happened, so far as Wallie could see. The demigod gave Wallie a long stare. "The beast on the hilt of that sword is a griffon: the body of a lion and the head of an eagle. Appropriate, would you say?"

"The body, certainly," Wallie said. "I shall try to think like an eagle."

The god did not smile. "Eagles can see farther than lions," he said. "The griffon is a symbol much affected by the petty kings. To the People it means *Power wisely used*. Remember that, Shonsu, and you will not fail!"

Wallie shivered at the implications.

The boy rose. "And now it is time for time itself to start again. Less than one heartbeat has passed since you came in here. The priests are still waiting by the pool." He pointed down to the icy blue mountains of glass below. "Go and do your duty, Lord Shonsu. Jump!"

Wallie glanced down at that dark and jagged chaos far below him. He turned to stare in horror at the little boy. He received a mocking smile—another test of courage and faith, obviously. He drew the sword and made the salute to a god. Then he sheathed the sword, stepped to the edge of the rock, took a couple of deep breaths, and closed his eyes.

And jumped.

†† † ††

There was no question of swimming—he was whirled around like a berry in a blender, dragged down in darkness until he thought his head would burst, flung up again into foam and lifesaving air. His journey down the canyon was much faster than the journey up. Then the current slackened, and he had reached the temple pool.

The harness was no impediment. Using a butterfly stroke, making all the speed he could, he headed straight for the mighty façade of the temple, marveling at the power he could summon from his new shoulders.

When he dropped his feet, they reminded him that they were still badly battered, but he limped up out of the water onto hot shingle beneath the glare of the tropical sun, hardly aware of his nakedness, feeling like Columbus wading ashore in a new world. He was a swordsman! No more jails and maltreatment for him! Yet Hardduju was still a threat and must be the first order of business, before clothes or food or anything else.

All his new swordsman knowledge was bright and sharp in his mind. He could tell what was needed as easily as he could have pulled a book from a shelf, back in his previous life. As the god had told him, he need only challenge. No swordsman could refuse a formal challenge. But a duelist ought to have a second—not essential, but advisable. Even before his feet had left the water, therefore, Wallie was scanning the group waiting on the beach.

A dozen or so people there were staring at him in amazement. For a man to return from the Judgment unharmed was rare enough and to return bearing a sword must certainly be unique. The watchers did not know whether to cheer or run. Most were elderly priests and priestesses, but there were a couple of healers—and one swordsman.

Wallie had hoped for a Third or higher, and this swordsman was merely a lanky and bony adolescent of the Second, but he would have to do. He had a light skin and unusually red hair, almost copper. He looked as startled as the rest of the bystanders, but while they were retreating he was standing his ground, which was a good sign. Wallie hobbled over the shingle to him and stood, panting.

The kid gulped, looked at those Shonsu facemarks. The apparition from the River might be wearing nothing but a sword and a sapphire, but the facemarks were what counted. He drew. With eyes wide, and in a soft tenor voice, he made the salute to a superior: "I am Nnanji, swordsman of the second rank, and it is my deepest and most humble wish that the Goddess Herself will see fit to grant you long life and happiness and to induce you to accept my modest and willing service in any way in which I may advance any of your noble purposes."

His sword was a travesty of a weapon, pig iron, not fit to stop a charging rabbit, but he had wielded it surely. Wallie drew his miracle blade in reply.

"I am Shonsu, swordsman of the seventh rank, and am honored to accept your gracious service."

The swords were sheathed, and the priests were coming forward, beaming, with hands raised to start their greetings.

Wallie made the sign of challenge to a Second.

The boy flinched and paled as much as one of his skin color could pale. Mortal challenge from a Seventh to a Second would be an execution, not a fight. Hastily he made the sign of obeisance.

None of this was apparent to the happily smiling onlookers—only a swordsman of second or higher rank would have understood the signals. Thus might challenge be given and averted without loss of face. The senior priest was attempting to catch Wallie's eye so that he could start his own salutes. Ignoring him, Wallie continued to face the young swordsman.

"The first oath," he said.

The youth's eyes flickered again to Wallie's sword hilt. Reluctantly he drew his own again. "I, Nnanji, swordsman of the Second, do swear to obey your commands and to be faithful, saving only mine honor. In the name of the Goddess."

The onlookers fell silent; something was not right.

Now Wallie realized that the first oath was too frail for his needs; it was used mainly to impress civilians, as when a small-town mayor might hire a mercenary to clean up a nest of brigands. In this context it was little more than a public acknowledgment of Wallie's higher rank. It reserved the oath-taker's honor, and that could mean anything.

"And the second oath also."

That was much more serious, the oath of tutelage. Young Nnanji's eyes bulged, then seemed to count the intruder's facemarks once more. Slowly he sank to his knees, offering his sword in both hands. He lowered it with a worried frown.

"I am already sworn, my lord."

Of course he was, and for Wallie to demand his oath

was mortal insult to Nnanji's present mentor, whatever his rank, and that must lead to bloodshed. For Nnanji to swear to another mentor, moreover, was technically betrayal, although few would have argued the point with a Seventh.

Wallie put what he hoped was a stern expression on Shonsu's face—uneasily aware that it was probably a terrifying grimace. "What rank is your mentor?"

"A Fourth, my lord."

Wallie drew his sword, and a loud rattle of shingle announced that the priests and healers were leaving.

"He can't even avenge you. Swear!"

The lad started to proffer his sword again, then again he lowered it. He stared up at Wallie with tortured eyes. His sword was junk, his yellow kilt had been washed to a threadbare beige, and he had patches on his boots, but he set his jaw in hopeless defiance.

Wallie was baffled. All he needed was a junior to second him in a duel and here he had run into a death-before-dishonor idealist. A mere Second talking back to a Seventh? The rank stupidity of such obstinacy suddenly infuriated him. He felt a blaze of anger. He heard an angry snarl . . . his arm moved . . .

He stopped it just in time—his sword an inch from Nnanji's neck. Nnanji had closed his eyes, waiting for it.

Wallie was horrified. What had happened there? He had very nearly—*very* nearly—lopped off the kid's head. Just for displaying courage? He moved the blade away, to a safe distance. Nnanji, evidently discovering that he was still alive, opened his eyes again warily.

But it was still a stand-off. Even that narrow escape had not wiped the sullen obstinacy off the lad's face, and Lord Shonsu of the Seventh obviously could not withdraw his demand. Being a highrank swordsman was not quite as simple as the demigod had made out. Hastily Wallie began to rummage through his new knowledge of the swordsmen's craft and he found an escape.

"Very well!" He gave the command for battle: *"Blood needs be shed: declare your allegiance."*

The kid's eyes bulged. "The *third* oath, my lord?"

"Do you know the words?"

Nnanji nodded vigorously. He did not ask for details, although in theory he could have done so. It was a life-saving solution to his scruples. "Yes, my lord," he said eagerly. Laying his sword at Wallie's feet, he prostrated himself totally on the shingle.

"I, Nnanji, do swear by my immortal soul and with no reservation to be true in all things to you, Shonsu, my liege lord, to serve your cause, to obey your commands, to shed my blood at your word, to die at your side, to bear all pain, and to be faithful to you alone for ever, in the names of all the gods."

Then he kissed Wallie's foot.

If that wasn't slavery, Wallie thought, then what was? The god had spoken true when he said that the swords-men were addicted to fearsome oaths. He gave the reply: "I take you, Nnanji, as my vassal and liegeman in the names of all the gods."

Nnanji uttered a loud gasp of relief and scrambled to his knees. He picked up his sword in both hands and looked up expectantly. "Now you can *order* me to swear the second oath, my lord!"

Wallie almost laughed. Here he was trying to start a mortal combat, and this kid was tying him up in Jesuitic quibbling. Still, there had better be no ambiguous loyal-ties. "Vassal," he said solemnly, "swear to me the second oath."

Keeping pale eyes firmly fixed upon Wallie's, the lad swore: "I, Nnanji, swordsman of the Second, do take you, Shonsu, swordsman of the Seventh, as my master and mentor and do swear to be faithful, obedient, and humble, to live upon your word, to learn by your exam-ple, and to be mindful of your honor, in the name of the Goddess."

Wallie touched the sword and gave the formal reply: "I, Shonsu, swordsman of the Seventh, do accept you,

Nnanji, swordsman of the Second, as my protégé and pupil, to cherish, protect, and guide in the ways of honor and the mysteries of our craft, in the name of the Goddess.

"Well done," he added cheerfully and helped him rise. Now he had a protégé as well as a sword. With a few clothes, he could even start to look the part.

All the onlookers had gone, except for two brawny slaves who were watching the scene with carefully impassive faces. Slaves, being property, would never be in personal danger.

"Thank you, my lor . . . my liege." Nnanji looked like a man who had jumped out of bed and found himself knee-deep in snakes. He slipped his pathetic sword into its scabbard, blinked, and straightened his shoulders. Obviously he was making some mental adjustments. He had just changed mentors, which was no small matter in itself, and he had also just become a vassal—a dramatic event for a swordsman of any rank. The third oath was very rare, given only on the eve of battle and hence never required of a Second. A mere apprentice would not be expected to fight in such things. Perhaps it had never been sworn within the temple grounds before.

He stared at Wallie doubtfully. He had gone from dull routine to the brink of death—or so he must believe—and then into high adventure. And this highly dangerous opponent was now, if his facemarks were true, a formidable protector. "My liege," he repeated, tasting the unfamiliar word.

Wallie gave him a moment to collect himself, then said, "Right! Now, Nnanji, there is going to be bloodshed. You will second me. Under no circumstances will you draw your sword. If you are attacked you will make obeisance instead. I waive onus of vengeance." There would be no point in having both of them die if things did not go according to the book. "You know the duties of a second?"

Nnanji beamed, excited. "Yes, my liege!"

That was lucky—they came from a sutra much higher in the list than the minimum required for second rank.

"You will make no offers, nor accept any."

Nnanji's eyes grew wide at that, but he said yes again. Wallie nodded, satisfied. "Now, where is the reeve?"

"My liege, I think he is in the temple. He was watching the Time of Judgment."

Of course! He would. Wallie raised his eyes to look across the heat-blurred courtyard to the great steps. The top was crowded with multicolored spectators watching this unexpected drama. Somewhere in there Hardduju must be thinking hard.

He paused to plan his challenge.

"What ranks would you expect to be with him, apprentice?"

Nnanji wrinkled his snub nose. "I saw him earlier, my liege, with Honorable Tarru and two Fifths."

"Go to him now," Wallie said. *"Do not salute!* Then say, 'Lord Shonsu sent me with this message.' Keep your right arm at your side with the fist closed, your right foot forward, and your left hand flat on your chest. Show me."

Nnanji did as he had been instructed, frowning with concentration. The lack of salute was the insult, of course, but the other was the sign of challenge to a Fifth. Nnanji might guess what it meant, but he must not be told its meaning, nor what rank it addressed.

Wallie nodded. "That's it. Remember—no salute! If you find him alone, then go and get a highrank witness first. And don't answer any questions. He may say that he is coming, but that's all."

Nnanji nodded solemnly, his lips moving in silence. Then, unexpectedly, he grinned a huge and juvenile grin —he understood.

"Off you go, then!" Wallie gave him a cheer-up smile.

"Yes, my...at once, my liege!" Nnanji shot off across the shingle with his long legs flailing.

Wallie watched him for a moment. It would be unfortunate, but understandable, if the kid just kept on going through the temple grounds, through the town, up the hill, and over the horizon.

Then Wallie turned to stare at the two slaves slouching under the meager shade of an acacia. They flinched slightly. He chose the larger.

"Strip!" he said. The man jumped in alarm, ripped off his black loincloth, and kicked off his filthy sandals. "Scram!" Wallie said, and both men scrammed. He dressed with relief, tired of wearing nothing but bloodstains. The hot sun had already dried him.

He crunched up the beach to step onto the fiery flags of the courtyard. He had forgotten how very large it was—a city block wide and at least twice that in length. The priests and healers from the beach were strung out across it in order of age, with the youngest and fittest halfway up the steps beyond. Nnanji was still going, past the sixties and fifties, closing in on the forties. Pilgrims and priests were lined up four or five deep along the top, their backs now to the Goddess, studying the drama unfolding at the water's edge. Those vast steps looked like one side of a stadium. That seemed very appropriate under the circumstances— a pity that he could not sell tickets.

Then he identified Harduju, starting down from the temple arches. With him were four other swordsmen. Nnanji had reached the steps and was angling up toward them.

Wallie recalled with guilt his first impressions of the temple. He had thought then of megalomania, a rapacious priesthood aggrandizing itself from an impoverished peasantry, but that had been when he was an unbeliever. Today he had talked with a god, and now the temple seemed a magnificent tribute raised by generations of faithful worshipers. Magnificent it certainly was, although its architectural style was alien to him; the columns perhaps from Karnak, with Corinthian capitals supporting Gothic arches and, above those, baroque windows and, ultimately, reaching for the very sky itself,

Islamic minarets of gold. Undoubtedly the builders' plans must have been changed and revised many times over centuries of construction, yet the disparate elements had aged into one harmonious, splendid, and reverent monument of mossy, weathered stone.

Nnanji and Hardduju had met. Wallie wondered if the lad would have enough breath left to give his message. Apparently so, for he turned and started bounding down the steps again, returning to his liege. Please don't break a leg, young Nnanji! Now, would the reeve accept the invitation to a challenge, or summon reinforcements, or advance with his present force? Good—he was coming down with a single Fourth. The other three were following more slowly. The shoot-out was about to begin.

Nnanji was down to the courtyard again, running back through the waves of heat that now danced above it. Somewhere in Wallie a small voice of conscience was complaining that thou shalt not kill, being told that a god had commanded this killing, grumbling back that at least thou shouldst not be looking forward to it. For Wallie was very conscious that his pulse was speeding up and he was relishing the coming fight. *Bastinado? I'll show the bastard!* It helped when a god had told you that you were going to win.

Spectators were still spilling from the temple and spreading over the top of the steps like mold. Anxiously Wallie scanned the courtyard, wondering when the rest of the guard would start arriving.

Nnanji was back, shining all over and barely able to speak.

"He is coming, my liege," he panted.

"Well done, vassal!" Wallie said. "Next time I'll find you a horse." The boy grinned and kept on panting.

Hardduju was following at a leisurely pace. He must be a very puzzled man—how had the prisoner obtained a sword? The most obvious answer would be treachery in the guard—the condemned man had not been taken to the Judgment at all. Was this stranger an imposter as he had appeared, or a swordsman? The signal that Nnanji

had given him must have come from a highrank swordsman, therefore Shonsu. If he was not an imposter, then
why had he behaved like one in the temple? Yes, Hardduju must be very puzzled. Of course he might suspect
something close to the truth, a miracle. Now Wallie
could see why the demigod had only partly cured his
wounds—Hardduju had seen him just the previous day,
and a visibly miraculous cure would be a clear sign that
there was divine intervention at work.

Wallie stood his ground and let the reeve advance to
normal conversation distance. The florid face was redder
than ever in the heat. The beefy belly was as sweaty as
Nnanji's ribs. The man was out of condition, and his
weight would slow him. But some of the sweat running
down his face must be from fear, and Wallie found that
idea very pleasant.

Nnanji moved to Wallie's left, the Fourth to the other
side. Wallie smiled, paused a moment for the tension to
grow. Now he knew the rituals. As the younger and the
visitor, he was expected to salute first. Then he drew. He
spoke the flowery and hypocritical words, flashing his
wonderful sword in the gestures. He sheathed it and
waited.

Yes, there was fear. The reeve's eyes flickered around
too much. He was delaying his response, knowing what
must follow as soon as the preliminaries were over.

Wallie went ahead anyway and made the sign of challenge—not challenge to a Seventh, but public challenge.

"Just a moment!" Hardduju said. "You were under
sentence of the court. You didn't get that sword at the
Place of Mercy. Until I'm satisfied that the sentence has
been carried out, I do not recognize your standing."

Wallie made the sign a second time. A third time
would not require an answer.

Hardduju glanced behind him, then looked at his second. "Go and fetch some guardsmen," he barked. "A
prisoner has escaped." The Fourth gaped at him.

He had brought the wrong henchman, thought Wallie;
he had not worked out a strategy in time. Nevertheless,

he must not be allowed to delay this contest any longer, or he might manage to evade it somehow.

"Go!" Hardduju shouted at the Fourth.

"Stay!" Wallie barked. "Lord Hardduju, will you return my salute in the ways of honor? For if not, I shall denounce you and draw anyway."

"Very well," the reeve snapped. "But then you will explain that sword to me."

He drew and began the response—and then lunged. He would have fooled Wallie, and probably nine out of ten swordsmen, even Sevenths, but Shonsu was the tenth. His instincts had been watching Hardduju's left shoulder. When it started to swing away from him, he threw back his own left foot and drew, the superb blade bending like a bow to give him a few precious milliseconds. He parried quinte, but he was off balance, and his riposte failed. Yet it was Hardduju who backed off.

He stared narrowly at Wallie for a moment; this was no imposter. Then he lunged again. Parry, riposte, parry—for a few seconds the metal rang, and again it was Hardduju who recovered, but he guarded quarte, too low for Wallie's advantage in reach and height. One mistake is enough. Wallie cut at the outside of the wrist. It was an unusual move. Had it been parried successfully, it could have left him open. It was not parried. Hardduju's sword clanged to the ground, and he clutched at his wounded arm.

"Yield!" shouted the Fourth, although he should have waited for an offer from Nnanji. Nnanji had remained silent as instructed, so the yield was invalid.

Wallie saw the horror in his victim's eyes, and his resolution wavered. Then he remembered the power of the little god as it had been revealed to him. With more fear than hate he carried out his orders, ramming the god's sword into Hardduju's chest. It slid free easily as the body crumpled.

The fight had taken about half a minute.

Wallie Smith was now a killer.

††† †††

The clashing of swords was succeeded by Hardduju's death rattle, a brief drumming of heels on flagstones—and then silence, broken by a shrill whoop from Nnanji. He started to come forward, then froze when no one else moved. Wallie, not daring to take his eyes off the Fourth, made the acknowledgment of an inferior. The Fourth swallowed a few times, looking back and forth from the dead man to this nemesis from the River. For a few more seconds the issue hung in the balance—would he accept this as a fair challenge under the rules, or shout for the guard and die? There were grounds for dispute, for the rules had not been perfectly observed, but the errors had not been Wallie's, and the man knew it. He drew his sword and made the salute. Wallie responded. It was to be peace—for the moment.

Now Nnanji could stalk forward to pick up the dead man's sword. In proper form he dropped to one knee and proffered it to Wallie, marring the solemnity of the ritual with an ear-to-ear grin. To be dragooned into service by a naked unknown intruder was one thing; to be suddenly on the winning side in a notable passage of arms was something else entirely.

Wallie hardly glanced at the sword being offered to him. It was a gaudy weapon with too much elaborate filigree on the hilt to be properly balanced, but it was now his and would be worth a great deal of money. It would also be a much better sword than Nnanji's, and by custom the winner in a duel gave an honorarium to his second.

"You can keep that," he said. "And see that that thing on your back is returned to the kitchen where it belongs."

"*Devilspit!*" Nnanji said, astounded. "I mean *thank you*, my liege!"

Wallie wiped his sword on the dead man's kilt in the traditional sign of contempt. "We're not done yet," he said. "Who were Lord Hardduju's deputies?"

"Only Tarru, my liege, of the Sixth."

"Honorable Tarru to you, spot. Can you lead me to him?"

"He's coming now, my liege." And Nnanji pointed to the three men Hardduju had left on the steps. One green kilt and two reds—a Sixth and two Fifths. They were halfway across the court. More swordsmen were streaming down the temple steps, and others into the court from both ends.

"Then let's go!" Wallie led the way, leaving the Fourth to dispose of the body, one of the duties of a second. There could be more trouble. Tarru might seek to avenge Hardduju. As acting reeve, he might even be justified in using the whole temple guard against an intruder, although that was unlikely under the code of the craft. Reaction had set in, and Wallie was feeling incredibly weary.

They met and stopped in silence. Tarru was a scarred and gray-haired veteran, but his slight body was wiry and his eyes were sharp. His green kilt was clean and smart—he sported no jewels or finery as Hardduju had done. Deeply etched lines on his face made him appear weathered and seasoned. He might be a rank lower than Wallie, but he would be no pushover and he was in much better trim than his superior had been.

He raised his sword in salute, and Wallie responded.

The two of them studied each other for a long moment, and those sharp eyes flickered to the sword hilt with the sapphire and then down to the blood-soaked sandals. There was no call of honor if Hardduju's second had accepted the duel as a fair fight, but the lure of that sword was too great, just as the demigod had predicted. Kill a cripple and win a fortune—it must seem like a good gamble.

Greed won; Tarru made the sign of challenge.

"Now!" Wallie roared, and the swords flashed out.

Nnanji and one of the Fifths sprang into position as seconds.

Tarru cut at sexte, and Wallie parried—and then pulled his riposte just before he killed his opponent. Again that blaze of fury? Tarru parried much too late and tried a lunge, a very slow lunge. Wallie turned it without difficulty. Seeing that he was in no danger, he relaxed and kept parrying those incredibly obvious strokes, directing the next wherever he wanted, making no effort to riposte.

Tarru danced forward and back. Wallie rotated slowly to face him, the seconds edged around like planets. A crowd was gathering, and the other Fifth kept shouting to keep them back.

Boots slapped on the stones and raised dust. Metal rang. Cut . . . parry . . . lunge . . . Tarru's breathing became loud below the furnace sky, and his face grew fiery also.

Wallie was discovering how it felt to be the greatest swordsman in the World: it was fine sport. He need hardly move his battered feet, and his arm could keep this up all day. Tarru was a fair Sixth—so Shonsu's eye told him—but there was no upper limit on Seventh rank, and Shonsu might well be an eight or nine on the same scale. He utterly outclassed the older man. He dare not look away, but he knew that there were swordsmen among the gathering spectators and he wondered how Tarru was feeling. The effort was telling on him, his breath starting to rasp. He had been the challenger—by not being able to get close he was appearing ridiculous. What emotion had succeeded his greed—anger? Fear? Humiliation?

At last Tarru backed off and stood gasping, obviously beaten, eyes wide and almost glazed. Wallie pretended to smother a yawn. A few sniggers and one very faint boo emerged from somewhere in the crowd.

"Draw?" called Tarru's second. A nice try, but he could not have much hope.

By the rules, Wallie should not speak and he dared

not move his eyes from his opponent, but he made a quick nod.

There was a pause. Nnanji had been given fatally explicit instructions. For mortal challenge not to lead to blood was almost unthinkable. Would the lad understand?

"Draw accepted!" Nnanji's voice was squeaky with excitement.

Wallie sighed with relief, flashed his second a smile of approval, and sheathed his sword. For a moment Tarru was too winded to move, then he came forward for the ritual embrace.

He made no apology, offered no congratulations, and hid any shame he might—and should—be feeling in the formalities of introducing his second.

"May I have the honor of presenting to the valiant Lord Shonsu my protégé, Master Trasingji of the Fifth?"

Wallie accepted his salute and said innocently, "I believe you may have already met my second, Honorable Tarru? Apprentice Nnanji of the Second, my liegeman."

Tarru glowered, and Trasingji choked. A Second bound by the blood oath? Nnanji swelled visibly and saluted.

They could probably spend all day on this sun-blasted griddle, mouthing meaningless formalities like a convention of Chinese mandarins, but Wallie was exhausted and finding these rituals absurd. "You will see that the remains of the noble Hardduju are attended with all due respect?" he asked, and Tarru bowed. "I am somewhat in need of the attentions of a healer myself. Could it please you to direct me to some place where I may rest?"

Tarru bowed again, still panting. "The barracks of our temple guard provide but the most humble quarters for a so distinguished warrior, but if your lordship could graciously deign to accept our poor hospitality, we should be most honored."

Wallie retrieved the sutra "On Hospitality" from his new mental databank and saw that the lions' den might indeed be the safest place to be. "You are most kind. I must summarily attend upon the Goddess and then I shall come at once."

Tarru gestured. Wallie became aware for the first time that the crowd was composed entirely of swordsmen. There were at least thirty of them. He sighed. There would have to be more formalities.

Tarru presented another protégé. Then that protégé and Trasingji presented theirs in a sort of iron-age chain letter. Two other Fifths appeared and had to be presented and present their juniors. Wallie went through the gestures on automatic, that names sliding past him in a blur. He was vaguely aware that he was a celebrity. If Hardduju had ever inspired loyalty, it had now dissolved in professional admiration. They were genuinely respectful.

And of course they all assumed that he was about to become the new reeve. He had not thought to deny it. Should he do so or wait until later? He was too weary to solve such convoluted problems.

Then his wanderings were interrupted, the routine broken. The Fourth standing in front of him was not admiring—he was terrified, his sword visibly trembling. Wallie forced his eyes to focus. The man's face was familiar. He was one of the three who had beaten him up before he was taken to the jail. He searched back a few moments for the name . . . Meliu.

Revenge!

A third time he felt sudden rage. Red fringes flickered in his vision.

Meliu was beefy, about Shonsu's age, and did not look too smart, although it was hard to tell in his present condition. What would Shonsu have done? Answer: Shonsu would never have allowed himself to get into the sort of mess that Wallie had. Yet Shonsu's reaction had expressed itself in that now-familiar blaze of anger—challenge and kill this hoodlum for having had the temerity to strike a Seventh. Wallie Smith's inclination was to forgive, for the man had been acting under orders, and he who had given the orders had now paid the penalty. But to act like Wallie Smith was to risk trouble. He must stay in character. A sheep in wolf's clothing should not bleat within the pack.

Compromise, then. Forcing down his fury, he ignored the salute and turned to the Fifth who had made the introduction.

"Who's next?"

It was a crushing insult. The crowd waited to see what Meliu would do. He had the option of suicide—he could challenge. Instead he turned and fled. Believing Shonsu to be the next reeve, he would probably be gone from the temple before dark. Satisfactory!

Eventually they reached the end, the last stammering Third. All those Seconds and Firsts at the rear, thank the Goddess, did not count.

Tarru bowed slightly. "If I might make so bold, my lord, as to ask what dispositions you wish to make for the temple guard?"

This was it, then. He decided to procrastinate, some uneasy instinct telling him that he should not explain their mistake.

"Until the priests see fit to appoint a replacement reeve, I am sure that you will do whatever is best, Honorable Tarru."

"Lord Shonsu is most gracious...and Apprentice Nnanji of the Second? He is, er, detached from duty with the guard?"

Wallie turned to look at young Nnanji, who was attempting to stand at attention, but could not help sending Wallie an agonized plea out of the corners of his eyes.

"I shall retain Apprentice Nnanji in my personal service for the time being."

Apprentice Nnanji relaxed.

Tarru bowed again. Wallie was feeling more tired by the minute and was frightened his fatigue might make him start to tremble. He made a curt farewell. Forty swords flashed out in salute as he started toward the steps, his liegeman strutting proudly beside him.

††† † †††

As soon as Lord Shonsu's destination became clear, a tornado of activity developed within the multitude at the top of the great staircase. Wallie climbed slowly, being gentle to his throbbing feet, and halfway up he stopped altogether so that the priests could complete whatever they were organizing. He turned to admire the view. The Judgment looked much better from a distance than it did close to.

The guard had been formed up and was being marched away, arms swinging and heads high to impress the newcomer. A dust of pigeons was settling on the great courtyard behind them. Two slaves scrubbed the flags where the reeve had died.

Life was sweet—on any world. Wallie felt satisfied. The unpleasant matter of Hardduju he had disposed of easily, and even the knowledge that he was now a killer distressed him little. He was safe under the aegis of the swordsmen's ways of honor. The only wrinkle in his comfort blanket was the memory of those sudden flashes of rage that had surged up every time his prickly Seventh's status had been invoked—by Nnanji's defiance, by Tarru's impudent challenge, and by the chance to level scores with Meliu. That fury had not come from Wallie Smith, and he suspected that Shonsu, had he been there in his place, would have left four bleeding corpses behind, not one. Anger was fueled by adrenaline. Adrenaline came from somewhere near the kidneys. He had not been given Shonsu's personality, but he did have his glands, and he must take care in future that his Wallie Smith mind stayed in firm control of his Shonsu body.

He would be a swordsman, not a butcher.

Then he glanced at Nnanji and encountered a glazed smile of high-octane hero worship that annoyed him at once.

"Well done, vassal," he said. "You were a great second."

Nnanji at once blushed scarlet with pleasure.

"You did very well to interpret my signal about the draw," Wallie added. "I should have given you more careful instructions beforehand."

"You were up his left armpit, my liege!"

Wallie discovered his memory transplant included swordsman slang, but he could have worked that one out—a left armpit was an impossible target in a right-handed opponent. There was a suggestion in Nnanji's manner, though, that Wallie should have gone for a kill. Bloodthirsty young devil!

The hero worship grew more irritating the longer Wallie thought about it. The honor for a superbly trained body and virtuoso skill belonged to the late Lord Shonsu, not to him. But that distinction he could hardly hope to explain. This youngster obviously had the instant adhesive loyalty of a puppy, and Wallie would have to find some gentle method of detaching him.

He glanced up at the arches. The pilgrims had been herded into two wedges at the sides, leaving the center free for his entrance. "I think we've given them enough time to fix their hair," he said. "Let's go."

Let's go...he had acquired that phrase from the demigod.

The guards at the center arch were now two of the Fifths he had just met, still puffing slightly from their run to get there before him. They saluted as he stepped into the cool shadow of the arch, receiving an acknowledgment from Wallie and an impudent smirk from Nnanji.

So Lord Shonsu entered the great nave for the third time, Wallie Smith for the second. Its cool vastness was still overpowering, the blaze of lights from the windows still resplendent. There was no priest there to conduct him, and he strode straight forward as well as he could on his blood-soaked sandals. Halfway along the nave he came to the beginning of the priesthood, a double line stretching from there all the way to the altar. Priests on one side, priestesses on the other, Firsts in their white at the front, yellow Seconds after them.

As he passed, each one knelt down, making him feel like a storm blowing through a forest—it was embarrassing and horrible to him. He felt unworthy and phony. He wanted to shout at them to stop it, but all he could do was hurry on as fast as he could and not watch.

Nnanji gulped when the kneeling started and whispered, "Should I wait, my liege?" in an urgent tone.

"You stick to me like rust!" Wallie commanded in the same sort of whisper, and the two of them made the royal procession along the nave together, liege in a slave's dirty rag and liegeman in a threadbare yellow kilt. Only Wallie's sword and hairclip were in the right company.

Then, several hundred priests and priestesses later, they reached the end, and their way was blocked by a group of incredibly ancient women in blue, toothless and wrinkled in the extreme, some of them in carrying chairs. They, too, began to kneel.

"The Holy Mothers!" Nnanji said in an awed voice.

"Do not kneel to me, ladies," Wallie protested. "I am but a simple swordsman come to do homage to the Goddess."

They knelt anyway.

Red-faced and angry, Wallie stepped through a small gap in the middle of the line and over to the edge of the dais. And there stood the minute figure of Lord Honakura, smiling proudly at him. Wallie gave him a quick nod. Then in silence he dropped to his knees and made his obeisance to the Goddess. All the proper swordsman prayers and ritual were there in his head—he begged forgiveness, he pledged his sword to Her service, he vowed obedience. He waited, but there was no reply, and he had not expected one. His real dedication had been done elsewhere; this performance was not for the Goddess, it was for the spectators, and perhaps for him. Frightened that he might go to sleep on the floor, he scrambled up, followed again by Nnanji.

He took a farewell glance at the wealth of centuries glittering on the dais. Nothing he saw there would compare with his sword, yet what had once seemed to him a shameful jackdaws' hoard of extortion now struck him as a magnificent tribute. Worshipers for thousands of years had brought their most beautiful possessions, their greatest treasures, to lay before their beloved Goddess. Who was he to question their purpose? Strange how what one saw depended on how one looked.

He turned to Honakura. *Him you may trust,* the god had said, implying that others might not be trustworthy. Before Wallie could speak, however, the priest beat him to it.

"The council is prepared to induct you as reeve at once, my lord," he said, beaming, "although we should prefer to arrange something more formal for tomorrow, or the day after." He glanced sympathetically at Wallie's feet and the bloodstains they had left on the floor where he had knelt.

There was no one else within earshot. "I shall not be accepting the office of reeve," Wallie replied quietly.

That was a shock, and for a moment the tiny old man was at a loss for words. Then he blurted out, "But, my lord, we talked of this . . ."

Wallie fought down a devilish temptation to say, "You made that deal with Shonsu, and I am Wallie Smith." He resisted it, but only just. "My regrets, holy one."

Honakura was looking astonished, worried, and even betrayed. Wallie recalled the god's snide remark about temple politics.

"I have been forbidden to accept," he said simply.

"Forbidden?"

A swordsman of the Seventh? Then understanding dawned, and the old man's eyes went to the sword hilt.

Wallie nodded. "Today I talked with a god," he explained gently. "He gave me this sword and told me to kill Hardduju. But he also forbade me to remain in the temple. I have been given a task to perform for the Goddess, a matter of greater importance to Her, and I must go hence."

There was certainly no appealing that authority. Honakura bowed. "That is the greatest honor that could be given a mortal, my lord. I count myself fortunate even to have met you." It was flowery politeness, but there might be some sincerity in it.

"I shall go to the barracks now," Wallie said. *My feet are killing me!* "Perhaps we may talk tomorrow, holy one?"

"Of course, my lord." The old man dropped his voice to a whisper. "Beware of treachery, Lord Shonsu!"

Wallie nodded again and turned to find his vassal. Nnanji was in position, immediately behind his left shoulder. And staring at him.

Nnanji had heard it all.

Apprentice Nnanji was in grave danger of having his eyeballs fall right out of their sockets.

Wallie hobbled, barely able to keep up as his storklegged vassal stalked ahead of him, leading the way through a serpentine rear exit. The glances Nnanji was sneaking back toward his liege now were so full of wonder and admiration that they almost burned.

Wallie's exhausted mind could easily visualize a comic-strip balloon coming out of Nnanji's head. It read something like, "First Harduju, then Tarru, then the Holy Mothers, and he talks with gods! Zounds! What a boss!"

Hopefully there would be no more dueling, so Wallie no longer needed him; but how did one dispose of such a follower without insult and hurt?

They trailed along corridors, down staircases, through more passages, and eventually emerged into the glare at the back of the temple. There were several great houses there, with slaves pandering flower beds, polishing velvet lawns with scythes, and dragging watercarts. They reached the edge of a place that Wallie knew—the parade ground he had crossed and recrossed that morning.

"Hold it!" he croaked. He limped over to a low wall around the last of the flowery gardens. He flopped down on the wall under a shade tree and let himself melt. Heavy blossoms sent him a murmur of bees and a soporific scent. He must have been on his feet for hours, for the sun was already stooping and the shadows starting to stretch. He put his head in his hands for a while. Exhaustion, lack of food, emotional reaction...

In a little while he looked up and saw a deathly worried expression on his vassal's face.

"I'm all right," Wallie said. "I've had a busy day." He got an uncertain nod. "I said I talked with gods, dammit, not that I am one!" That produced a very weak smile. "Sit down, Nnanji. Tell me why no one is mourning Hardduju."

Nnanji folded his stringy form down on the wall beside his liege. Caution and contempt chased each other over his face until contempt won. "He was despicable, my liege, untrue to his oaths. He *took bribes*."

Wallie nodded. No mention of sadism?

Then Nnanji plunged ahead. "My liege? Why would the priests have ever appointed such a man to be reeve? He was a disgrace to our noble craft!"

"Perhaps he was a good man when they appointed him?"

Nnanji looked blank. "My liege?"

"Power corrupts, Nnanji!" It was a problem much on his mind that day, but obviously a new idea to Nnanji, so Wallie explained, telling how he had been jeered by the crowd.

"Thank you, my liege," said his vassal solemnly. "I shall remember that when I attain high rank." Nnanji was, of course, an idealist, and hence a romantic.

Wallie said hopefully, "Nnanji, the trouble seems to be over. Do you want me to release you from your oaths?"

Nnanji's expression indicated that he would rather be

ground up in a corn mill or fed to vampire moths. "*No,
my liege!*"

"Not even the third? That's a pretty horrible oath,
apprentice. I can order you to do anything at all—
crimes, perversions, even abominations."

Nnanji just grinned—his hero would do no such a
thing. "I am honored to be bound by it, my liege." He
was probably happier than he had ever been in his life,
shining in his own eyes by reflected glory.

"All right," Wallie said reluctantly. "But any time you
want to be released from that oath, you just ask! The
sutra says that it must be annulled when the immediate
need is past."

Nnanji opened his mouth, closed it, looked at Wallie,
then at his feet; then decided to risk it.

"You have a task for the Goddess, my liege," he said
quietly. He had not made it a question, but he was obviously tortured by curiosity.

So Nnanji thought he was in on that, did he? Wallie
sighed. He would have to find a few good swordsmen to
guard his back and the fortune he bore on it, but the last
thing he would choose on a quest would be to have a
lubberly adolescent underfoot. A mere apprentice would
be no protection, more nuisance than use. Again his fatigue brought on absurdity: Nnanji, just run up to the
cave and ask the dragon to step outside? Nnanji, trot
over to the castle and warn them to start boiling the
oil . . .

Then he remembered that there might be treachery
afoot. How would he find swordsmen whom he could
trust, who would truly guard his back and not stick a
knife in it? He would have to find loyalty, and there it
was, glowing at him. Moreover, Nnanji could advise him
on who else in the guard would be safe to recruit. He
heard his own voice, Shonsu's voice, quoting: "*It's a
poor road that doesn't run two ways.*"

Nnanji produced his enormous grin. "Second sutra,"
he said. "'On Protégés.'"

Wallie stared at him for a moment—shabby dress;

lanky and ungainly, but a good reach, red hair, snub nose, invisible eyelashes, and every bone showing; inexperienced as a newlaid egg, but as willing as it was possible to be. Already he had shown courage to the point of insanity, talking back to a naked sword. Nnanji was indeed entitled to consider himself in on the god's task, for Wallie also had sworn an oath that day, to cherish, protect, and guide. In a preliterate world, he had signed a contract. He could hardly just vanish and abandon the lad to the vengeance of Harrduju's friends. Like it or not, he was stuck with this Nnanji.

"You are familiar with the sutra 'On Secrecy'?" he asked carefully.

Nnanji beamed. "Yes, my liege." And before Wallie could stop him, he gabbled it off at high speed.

#175   ON SECRECY

The Epitome
A protégé shall not discuss his mentor, his mentor's business, his mentor's orders, his mentor's allies, nor any report that he himself may have made to his mentor.

The Episode
When Fandarrasu was put to the torment he did not speak, but his breath smelled of garlic. Thus Kungi learned that supplies had reached the besieged city.

The Epigram
The tongue is mightier than the sword, for a single word may destroy a whole army.

"Right," Wallie said, amused at his eagerness—if nothing else, this Nnanji was going to provide entertainment! "Everyone is assuming that I'm going to be reeve —let's leave it at that for the moment. As to the task, I know nothing about it. All the god told me was that . . . a certain very great swordsman . . . had tried and failed, and I'm next. It is important to the Goddess . . ."

Nnanji was silently nodding, looking awed.

"I was told to go out in the World and be an honorable and valorous swordsman. The task will be revealed to me. It will mean leaving here and traveling. I suppose danger. Possibly honor."

He paused then, relishing the sight of Nnanji's wide eyes and open mouth. "I don't suppose...would you like to come along as my protégé?"

Obviously it was a silly question. Protégé to a Seventh? On a mission for the gods? It was an offer Nnanji could not have equaled in his wildest fantasies. His reply was blurted out in more of the barracks slang: "And keep my baubles, too?"

Wallie laughed, feeling better for his rest. "I hope so," he said. "I certainly plan to keep mine! But listen, vassal, I know that I'm a good swordsman, and some strange things have been happening to me. I shall try to be a good mentor to you, but I'm not a superman. I'm not one of those heroes you find in epics."

"No, my liege," Nnanji replied politely.

That was the only thing Wallie could have said that he would not believe.

BOOK THREE:

HOW THE SWORD WAS NAMED

†

The barracks was a massive marble block with balconies and arched windows, somewhat like a medieval Moorish palace. Tarru had sent word, and the visitor was greeted by a deputation of the staff, ancient or crippled swordsmen who had put away their swords. The commissary had all his limbs, but he was old and so bowed that his gray head stuck out like a turtle's, and his hand gestures were hidden beneath him when he presented himself as Coningu of the Fifth. He appraised Wallie's condition with a practiced eye, terminated any further formalities, and asked what his lordship required.

"Hot bath, bandages, food, bed?"

Coningu nodded to a subordinate, then led the way up a marble staircase wide enough to have carried a two-lane highway. Apparently everything associated with the temple was built on the same titanic scale, and the ceilings were all so high that it took three flights for the staircase to mount each story. Wallie dared not look back in case he was leaving bloody marks on every step for slaves to clean. At last they reached the top floor and went along a passage of matching dimensions until Coningu opened a door and stepped aside.

Wallie was impressed. The room was huge and airy—floor of glassy wood with gaudy rugs on it, cool marble walls hung with bright tapestries, and an incredibly high plaster ceiling with faded frescoes that might have come from the Sistine Chapel. There were four beds and numerous other pieces of furniture, but the room was so big that they did not crowd it in the least. Then he saw that Coningu was advancing to another door—this was merely the antechamber.

The main guest room was three times as big, with a bed as large as a swimming pool. Shaded windows at both ends led to balconies and allowed a cool breeze to float across. The rugs and hangings were works of art, the woodwork everywhere blazed with polish. From the expression on Nnanji's face, he had never seen this part of the barracks and was overwhelmed.

"What do you think?" Wallie muttered, hoping that Coningu could not hear. "Will this do, or should we look for a better place down the road?"

Nnanji stared at him in bewilderment. Coningu did hear, and smiled a sideways glance that said nothing.

"It's magnificent," Wallie assured him hurriedly. "Fit for a king."

"It's probably seen many of those, my lord," replied the commissary, mollified.

Wallie could not resist teasing him. "How about jailbirds? You know where I slept last night?"

Coningu flashed a cynical smile. "Those, too, my lord, I expect. The temple court has been overruled before."

Sore feet momentarily forgotten, Wallie browsed around. He found the bellrope and a weighty keg-sized bronze receptacle embellished with nymphs and flowers in bas relief. He decided that it must be the chamber pot. The ornate wall lamps seemed to be real gold. A massive carved chest was full of foils, fencing masks, and barbells—everything a vacationing swordsman could want. He paced off some of the rugs and decided that they were silk, as were the wall hangings. Seeing thick iron bolts on the inside of the door, he confirmed that the outer door was similarly fitted, and then limped out on a balcony to inspect the security there.

The shadowing overhang was wide and the flanking walls smooth. Any burglar trying to enter would need wings. Below him stretched the picturebook park, and beyond that the high wall, the tenements and slums of the town, then the valley wall with its steep road and the row of pilgrim cottages... and finally the indigo tropic sky. The other balcony probably faced the jail. Wallie frowned at the town, recalling the squalor and how he had reacted to it two days earlier. He could hear the messages he was being given: *The Goddess rewards Her servants well. Do not question the justice of the gods.*

He found a full-length silver mirror. There again was the Shonsu illusion he had seen in his delirium, except that the vision had been naked, not wrapped in slaves' sackcloth, and now the face and body were bruised and scraped and swollen all over, eyes puffed and purple, the black hair half in a pony tail and half loose. He grimaced at himself, and the overall effect was terrifying. How could Nnanji have balked at an order from such a horror?

Voices and clatter announced the arrival of slaves with a huge copper bathtub and steaming buckets. A one-legged swordsman snapped orders. Another of the cripples led in more slaves, with towels and boxes. The room began to fill up. Now Wallie realized that he was expected to perform his toilet in public, like Louis XIV, but he was too weary to argue. Nnanji unbuckled Wallie's harness and took his sword and scabbard, evidently one of the duties of a protégé. Slaves poured water and ran for more. Wallie sighed a sigh for a whirlpool tub with some good soap, then accepted the royal treatment.

The slaves slaved, Wallie soaked sensuously in the tub, and the old swordsmen quietly clustered around Nnanji. There were half a dozen of them there, for Wallie was perhaps the most exciting thing to happen for a century or two. Any excuse was good enough to attend and enjoy the drama.

"May I draw it, my liege?" Nnanji asked.

It was the sword that was attracting the swordsmen— they were gathered about it like boys around a foreign sports car.

"Sure," Wallie said sleepily. He heard the murmurs of wonder as the group admired the blade itself. Then Nnanji suddenly declaimed, in a curious chant:

> "A griffon crouched upon the hilt
> In silver white and sapphire blue,
> With ruby eye and talons gilt
> And blade of steel of starlight hue.
> The seventh sword he wrought at last,
> And all the others it surpassed."

"What in the World is that?" asked Wallie, waking up suddenly and hurling bathwater over slaves and floor.

"A minstrel jingle, my liege." Nnanji was staring at him, nervous at the reaction. "About the seven swords of Chioxin. I can tell you all about the first six, if you wish, but it is rather a long poem."

"Chioxin! *Chioxin?*" A picture floated into Wallie's mind—a piece of a sword blade fastened to a wall, a blade old and damaged, broken at both ends, yet inscribed with figures of men and monsters. He reached for more, and there was nothing. It was a Shonsu memory, a fragment on the border between the professional memories he had been given and the personal memories denied him. The sensation made him uneasy. Where or what was Chioxin?

"It sounds like that sword, doesn't it?" he said. "Griffon and sapphire? What else do you know about it?"

Nnanji looked suddenly embarrassed. "I never heard the rest, my liege. It was my first night in the barracks, when I was a scratcher." He grinned at the memory of his younger self. "Looking back now, I don't think he was a very good minstrel, but then I thought he was

marvelous. He sang the ballad about the seven swords of
Chioxin, and I wanted to hear all of it. But he just got to
the last part, about the seventh sword, and then . . . then
I had to leave, my liege."

"Wild Ani, I bet," said one of the others. They all
shrieked and cackled with laughter, and Nnanji turned a
furious red.

Coningu, hovering on the edge of the group like a
wind-bent cypress on a beach, was staring at the
sword. He sensed Wallie's eye, glanced at him, and
then turned quickly away. Coningu had heard that ballad, all of it, and he knew what it had told of the
seventh sword. Old cynic that he was, he looked impressed by something.

Wallie hauled himself out of the tub to provide a diversion. Soon he was dried and being offered a choice of
blue kilts from some barracks store. He chose the plain-
est, although even that was of finest lawn. Nnanji buck-
led on his harness for him—and then stripped and
plopped into his mentor's discarded bathwater. A protégé's privilege, obviously.

Two healers, a Sixth and a Third, bowed before Wallie and nodded approvingly at a patient so spectacularly
battered, but still basically healthy. Reluctantly he allowed them to smear salve on his scrapes. Then they
prepared to bandage his feet.

"Stop!" he barked. "What are those?"

"These are bandages, my lord," the Sixth said, surprised. "They are very good bandages. They were
blessed for me in the temple many years ago and have
healed a great many patients."

They looked like a pile of old garage rags.

"What happened to the last two patients?" Wallie demanded, and his answer was a look of discomfiture. "Get
some new ones, healer. You have worn out the blessings
in those. For now you may use towels."

The healer started to protest.

Wallie was too tired to argue. "Vassal?" he said, and

Nnanji, who had just finished dressing, smiled and drew his sword.

Wallie's feet were bundled in towels, like a terminal case of gout.

A table of food had been laid out, and that was all he needed. He thanked them and ordered them away— commissary, slaves, swordsmen, healers, and bathtub— refusing offers of table service or musicians or female company ... Nnanji looked a little disappointed at that. Then he slid the bolts on the door to the corridor. Peace!

Nnanji lifted the silver covers off the food. Wallie's mouth watered so hard that it hurt. Soups, baked fish, roast fowl and a savory meat pie, something curried, vegetables, desserts, hot breads, cheeses, six flasks of wine, cakes, and fruits. No, not the fruit, thank you.

"There seems to be enough here for twenty men," Wallie said, sitting down. "So I may be able to spare you a little, vassal. What do you fancy to start?"

"After you, my liege." Nnanji's eyes were bright, but he was expecting to wait.

Wallie ordered him to a seat and for some time they gorged in silence. Wallie was astounded at how much he ate, but he was a big man now and had starved for days. Nnanji, as the model adolescent, matched him bite for bite; there were advantages to being vassal to a Seventh. By the time they slowed down and started up a conversation, there was not much left.

"That's a little better than the jail."

"And a lot better than the juniors' mess!"

They laughed together, and Wallie rose.

"I am going to sleep until morning," he announced, "but whether tomorrow morning or the day after, I am not sure. At least one of those doors must stay bolted, because my little god might be a bit annoyed if I let his sword get stolen. If you like, I can let you out now, and you can go and prowl somewhere, then sleep in the outer room. Please yourself."

It was early yet for sleep, but Nnanji could not bring

himself to leave. Perhaps he was frightened Wallie would disappear like a dream.

Wallie laid his sword on the bed, piled up some pillows, and lay back, sinking into the mattress.

"Feather bed! Softer than the jail floor!" Then, because he wanted his companion to do the talking, he said, "Tell me about Wild Ani?"

Nnanji blushed again. "One of the barracks women, my liege. A slave. She's huge and ugly and tough as an old ox. Boobs like meal sacks, one eye gone. She makes bets that no man can rape her, no holds barred, and claims a perfect record." He giggled. "They say that some men lost more than they thought they were betting."

"The girl of my dreams," Wallie said sleepily. "And the scratchers?"

"It's a tradition. We...the Seconds tell them that they have to prove their manhood. Every scratcher spends his first night with Wild Ani." He giggled again. "That was why I didn't hear the rest of the ballad."

"You don't need to tell me."

"It's all right," Nnanji said unashamedly. "She's a great woman, really. You want a she-dragon, she'll be a she-dragon, rough as you like. But with a scratcher she's patient and sympathetic...and helpful. Well, I mean, I didn't know where to...I mean, what to..." He grinned as the memories came back. Then he saw that his liege lord was already asleep.

††

On one side of the sword seven swordsmen fought with seven mythical beasts; on the other the same beasts were being fed, ridden, or comforted by seven maidens. No pose was repeated exactly, and even the expressions on the faces were distinct. Wallie could not guess how lines

of such delicacy and artistry could have been inscribed
in so hard a material.

The barracks was silent yet, and dawn was still drawing breath in the east, preparing to proclaim the day with
fanfares of light. An anonymous blanket bundle lying
across the doorway showed how a certain vassal's romantic ideas of duty had outweighed the attractions of a
bed. A hank of red hair protruded at one end.

Wallie was lying in the vast feather bed, examining
the god's sword at leisure and periodically wriggling lux-
uriously. His bruises had faded to the sort of pleasurable
ache that can come from too much exercise; the throbbing in his feet was a mere whisper of what it had been.
The World was his to enjoy as the demigod had told him.
A few days to complete his healing and enlist a couple of
good middlerank protégés, then he could be on his way
to explore that World, to be valorous and honorable, and
to await the revelation of his task. Yesterday he had
awakened on slimy stone, facing sentence of death;
today he floated in luxury and reveled in power and freedom.

Not a care in the World?

He turned then to the harness he had been given. The
leather was embossed with scenes taken from the sword
itself, although the artistry could hardly be so impressive. The left pocket was empty. Traditionally that held a
whetstone, so there was another message: the sword
came from the gods, but he must see to its sharpness. In
the right pocket he discovered a treasure of sparkling
blue gems. Then he understood the god's remark about
expenses—he was not merely powerful, he was rich.

His eyes wandered to the distant ceiling. The frescoes
above the bed were explicitly erotic. This was a very
lusty body he had been given—he would need more than
swordsman companionship. He turned his head and
looked through the far window, to the tiny line of pilgrim
cottages along the hillside road. He had another debt to
repay, but that was a different matter altógether. If she
chose . . . but it must be a free decision. To own a concu-

bine, a slave, would be rape by Wallie Smith's standards. He was not going to compromise on that. Honorable and valorous, and especially honorable.

A distant bugle sounded. The mummy by the door exploded in a whirl of blanket and long limbs, and there was Nnanji, sitting cross-legged, bright-eyed, and wearing nothing but his incredible ear-swallowing grin, ready to go anywhere and do anything.

"Good morning, vassal."

"The Goddess be with you, my liege."

"And you," Wallie replied. "I trust they serve breakfast in this inn? I'm so hungry again I could eat a horse."

"They usually do serve horse at breakfast," Nnanji said happily, looking as though he meant it.

Wallie placed his bundled feet carefully on the floor and winced. "Today I plan to do almost nothing," he said. "Is there anything that you want to do?"

"Learn to fight like you," Nnanji said shyly.

"Oh!" Wallie pondered. "That might take more than one day. But we'll try a lesson or two."

Nnanji grinned ecstatically.

They performed the morning dedication together and prepared to leave. Nnanji picked up Hardduju's sword and regarded it doubtfully.

"You really mean me to have this, my liege?" he asked, looking unbelievingly at the gold and rubies. When Wallie agreed, he seemed even more puzzled. "I shall have to sell it?"

It took Wallie a moment to understand, and then the thought was so bloodcurdling that he passed it off quickly with a joke. "Or else I shall have to avenge you, of course—every time."

Nnanji smiled obediently.

"Let's have a look at it," Wallie said, and soon showed Nnanji the poor balance and unnecessary weight. Then he let Nnanji try the god's sword, and there was no comparison. Hardduju's was for show, not for fighting. It would buy a first-class blade with enough left over for a dozen more, but for a junior it would be a death sentence.

Nnanji looked relieved, although still surprised by a Seventh who would stoop to joking with a Second and so lightly give him a fortune. "Thank you, my liege," he said. He left the sword under Wallie's bed and bore his own to breakfast.

Their way led back to ground level and through to the working part of the barracks, which was still on a monumental scale, but in sandstone instead of marble. The mess was as large as the guest room and even loftier, its windows set high, and the lower parts of the walls hung with banners. Wallie appraised these skeptically and decided they were the product of an interior designer's imagination and not genuine battle relics.

The big room was half full of swordsmen, sitting at long plank tables, eating from bowls, and chattering, but they fell quiet as he paused in the doorway, and for a few moments the only sound was the snuffling of fat dogs as they scavenged busily in the litter on the floor. Wallie glanced around the available spaces and then strode over to his choice without thinking.

"No, you first," he said to Nnanji, and they both sat down. Swordsmen sat on stools of course, leaving room for scabbards.

"Why, my liege?" Nnanji asked, puzzled.

"Why what?"

"Why did you come across to this seat and why have me sit first?"

Wallie dug into Shonsu's memories. "Backs to the wall where we can see the door, best sword arm on the right," he said.

"Thank you, my liege," Nnanji said solemnly.

"You're welcome," Wallie replied. "That was lesson one." For both of them.

Conversation had picked up cautiously, but the newcomers were being studied with many sidelong glances, which Wallie ignored. A peg-legged waiter delivered two bowls of stew, two black loaves of steaming rye bread, and two tankards of ale. If the stew was horse, it smelled delicious, making Shonsu's mouth water, and there was enough ale to douse a three-alarm fire. He soon found that the ale was necessary, for the stew was fiery with spice in the usual tropical treatment of yesterday's meat; but it was good.

Wallie's feet were throbbing again in their bandages. He put them up on a stool in front of him, aware that they looked absurd, not especially caring. He had complained to the demigod that he did not know the table manners of the World, but if Nnanji were to be his example, the main requirements seemed to be enthusiasm and speed. For a few moments they spooned and drank in silence. Men were coming and going freely, both entering and leaving, and also picking up their food and moving to other tables. As he studied the activity, he noticed that the end of a meal was marked by laying the bowl down for the dogs to lick. He started eating less and watching more.

His first impression of the swordsmen, when the demigod had led him to the temple gate, had been that they were a scruffy lot. Looking round the mess hall, he saw few there to change that opinion. A Seventh would be expected to dress his protégés in good style, but the donation of Harduju's sword would take care of that expense, and Nnanji was at least clean and well combed. Many of the other juniors were not. Which of these swordsmen should he try to enlist as his bodyguard?

Then he saw a Fourth openly staring at him—a man of around thirty, well built, and conspicuously neater and cleaner-looking than most. He knew that man.

"Vassal?" he asked quietly. "Who is that Fourth over there, sitting with a Third? He was in charge of the Death Squad yesterday."

Nnanji glanced over and then away quickly.

"Adept Briu, my liege," he said. He dropped his eyes to his stew bowl and seemed to lose his appetite.

Yesterday Briu had performed a disgusting task with dignity. He had kept his head when the crowd began to turn vicious and he had refrained from using his whip when Wallie provoked him. Briu might be a useful recruit.

"Do you suppose that he might be willing to join our mission?" Wallie asked.

Nnanji gave him a momentary smile at the "our," but then shook his head. "His wife is due to hatch soon, my liege."

Pity, Wallie thought. "But he is a man of honor?"

"Of course, my liege."

That answer had been a fraction slow.

"How about Adept Gorramini?" Wallie asked suspiciously.

Nnanji bit his lip, squirmed, and said, "Of course, my liege," once more.

Tear up plan one! Clearly there was another part of the swordsmen's code, which the demigod had not told him: "I shall not squeal." Loyal vassal or not, Nnanji was not going to rat on anyone—admit to one foul bird and you label the whole hen house, including yourself for roosting in it. And if that rule was generally observed, the lad would not likely know who was up to what, anyway. Gorramini had been another of Hardduju's three gorillas and certainly no man of honor in Wallie's estimation. He had not shown up with Meliu on the courtyard, though, and did not seem to be present now in the hall.

Nnanji took another look at Briu. Then he pushed away his bowl and tankard, folded his arms, and sat staring straight ahead with a tense expression. Wallie regarded him curiously.

"Something wrong?" he asked.

Nnanji showed a flash of misery and then went wooden again. "It was too good to be true, my liege," he said cryptically.

Wallie looked around warily. Firsts, Seconds, Thirds, Fourths . . . no Fifths. There had been at least four red kilts in the hall when he came in. Almost everyone was sitting facing toward him. The hall was growing steadily quieter. Something was certainly afoot, and the focus of it was Briu and his friend. Wallie pushed his bowl and tankard aside also.

Briu and the Third rose, and conversation stopped altogether. The waiters and cooks had gathered in a line along the wall beside the door to the kitchen. Even Nnanji seemed to know what was pending, damn it! Wallie took his feet off the stool and stood up, prepared to repel boarders.

Briu arrived at the far side of the table and made the salute to a superior. Wallie gave the reply.

"Lord Shonsu," the Fourth said in a voice aimed at the audience, "will you graciously waive hospitality upon a matter of honor?"

So that was how they were going to do it? In theory Wallie could refuse, but not in practice. He could not guess what the matter of honor might be, unless his actions yesterday had in some way compromised this Briu. Perhaps all that was required was a declaration from Lord Shonsu that he had not received that inexplicable sword from him.

"Honor must always take precedence," Wallie said, equally loudly. Briu was tense, but certainly did not look as worried as he should be if he were planning to fight a Seventh.

He inclined his head slightly in agreement. "Then be so kind as to present to me your protégé, my lord."

Damn! Nnanji's former mentor, of course. But why was Briu not looking more worried? Wallie turned to glance at Nnanji, standing stiffly at his left, and Nnanji's face bore the same drawn look it had shown the day before, when Wallie's sword had been at his throat.

Wallie was about to start arguing, then decided that the formalities had better come first. "Adept Briu, may I have the honor . . ."

Nnanji made the salute.

Briu's acknowledgment ran straight into the sign of challenge.

"*Stop!*" Wallie said. "I forbid you to answer that."

Nnanji's mouth had already opened and for a moment it stayed that way. His face went as red as his hair, and he turned to stare at his liege in outrage.

"I wish to explore this matter of honor," Wallie said, still loud. "You may not be aware, Adept Briu, that Apprentice Nnanji refused to swear the second oath to me—at swordpoint—on the grounds that he was already sworn to you. I trust that you are worthy of such loyalty?"

Briu colored. "That was his duty, my lord."

"And your burden. You should also know that Apprentice Nnanji swore the second oath to me only when ordered to do so, when he was already my vassal and could refuse me nothing."

The audience had to wait a moment for Briu's reply.

"So I was informed by the witnesses, my lord."

Tarru and the others on the steps—they would have known from the actions which oaths were being sworn.

"Then the fault was mine as his liege," Wallie said. *Go ahead and challenge!*

Briu was keeping his face expressionless, but he shook his head slightly. "As the third oath impinged upon the honor of his mentor, it should not have been sworn without permission, my lord."

Wallie had not thought of that, and the spectators rustled slightly, as if it was causing some surprise among them, also. Had his Shonsu memory failed him? To give himself time to think he raised an eyebrow and inquired, "Indeed? In which sutra is that stipulated?"

Briu hesitated. "In no sutra that I am aware of, my lord, and of course I yield to your superior knowledge of the sutras. It is an interpretation."

There was one way out, then. As senior swordsman in the valley, Wallie could simply tell him that his interpretation was wrong and Wallie's opinion would prevail. That would be a humiliating solution, although it might be all that was expected.

"I confess that I have not heard of the matter ever being discussed," Wallie said, meaning Shonsu had not.

"The fact that the sutras do not provide explicit directions would confirm that it is an extremely rare occurrence. A good topic for a cold beer on a hot day, perhaps. This is your own interpretation?"

Now Briu did not meet his eye. "I have discussed it with swordsmen of higher rank, my lord, and their opinion agreed with my own."

Tarru, of course! He had set this up or at least known of it. Obviously Briu would have referred the question to the highest rank he could find, and only Tarru could have stipulated that all the Fifths would leave the room. Insolence! Obviously, then, the situation called for a small show of strength and—almost as a conscious act like pressing a switch—Wallie turned control over to Shonsu.

His voice rose threateningly. "So you challenge a Second to mortal combat over an interpretation, do you, Adept Briu? I think that is despicable, the act of *a coward*!"

Briu rocked back on his heels and went pale with shock, and the whole roomful of swordsmen seemed to draw breath at the same time.

Wallie raised a mocking eyebrow.

Woodenly, reluctantly—in the manner of a man going to his doom—Briu moved his hand in the sign of challenge.

"*Now!*" Wallie roared, and drew.

†††

Adept Briu's hand stopped halfway to his sword hilt.

The point of Lord Shonsu's sword was at his heart.

One of the dogs at the other side of the room was scratching a flea, and the steady beat of its leg on the floor was the only sound in the hall. There was no movement except the slow rippling of banners in a draft from the windows.

Wallie was leaning forward slightly with his left hand on the table, to leave room behind him for his elbow. There were stools and another table behind Briu, and he probably was not certain where. If he tried to move backward, that sword could advance the whole length of Wallie's arm in an instant. Wallie could feel sorry for him, for he was obviously a proud professional in his smartly pleated kilt and shiny-oiled harness, yet now he was exposed to both danger and utter ridicule. The pause was probably only a few seconds, but it seemed an hour before the man on whom the drama waited suddenly awoke to take up his cue.

"Er . . . yield?" Nnanji said in a croak.

The Third was staring unbelievingly at Briu and the deadly length of steel that had appeared from nowhere. "Yield," he agreed at once, looking as shocked as his principal.

Briu's arm seemed to melt, and his hand sank down. The sword was still at his heart, and now he was Wallie's, even to the ritual of abasement, if that was what the victor demanded. He must obey, or be put to death. His eyes showed horror and shame.

"Tell me, Adept Briu," Wallie said, still speaking loudly enough for the audience to hear, "when you instructed your protégé in the second and third oaths, did you explain that the third must not be sworn without mentor's permission?"

Of course Briu could say yes, but no one would believe him—the point was too hypothetical and abstruse. "No, my lord." His voice was hoarse.

"Then the fault—if there was one—did not lie with Apprentice Nnanji, but with the inferior instruction he had received from his mentor?"

Briu's lips moved and no sound came. Then he swallowed twice and said, "It would seem so, my lord."

Wallie pulled the sword back slightly. "I don't think everyone heard that. Proclaim your error."

"Lord Shonsu," Briu said, more loudly, "I see that I omitted to instruct my former protégé, Apprentice

Nnanji, in the proper precautions for swearing the third oath, and if there was any flaw in his actions yesterday, then the fault was mine, and he acted in good faith."

"Then you have no further grievance against either Apprentice Nnanji or myself in the matter?"

"No, my lord."

Wallie sheathed his sword to show his acceptance. "I withdraw any allegation of cowardice, Adept Briu. You displayed exemplary courage in challenging a Seventh. I shall congratulate your mentor the next time I see him."

"Thank you, my lord," said the humiliated Fourth.

"Now perhaps, *as guests*, we may finish our breakfast?"

Wallie sat down and pulled his stew bowl back toward him, paying no further attention to the rest of the room. Nnanji reluctantly did the same. Briu's companion put an arm on his shoulders and led him away.

However, the matter was not closed for Wallie. He had known that the theft of a protégé must be followed by challenge, but he had truly expected that the challenge would be directed at him, for that seemed only fair. Obviously he had misjudged the swordsmen's view. The sutras did not recognize duress as an excuse—a forced oath was binding, no danger ever excused reneging. So they blamed Nnanji, not him. A merciless creed, but he should have known.

The problem lay in that shadowy region between his Shonsu self and his Wallie self. *You do not think like Shonsu, and that pleases me*, the demigod had said. But when his sword was in his hand, he must think like Shonsu. It was a divided rule, strategy from Wallie and tactics from Shonsu, and a bothersome and potentially serious problem if he were to make errors of judgment like that very often. There was more to being a swordsman than manual skill and a list of sutras—values, for example.

Much whispered argument was going on all over the room. Nnanji was toying with his stew and frowning furiously at it.

"What's wrong?" Wallie demanded. Nnanji did not look like a man who had just escaped maiming.

"I should have refused that oath to you, my liege."

"And died?"

"Yes," Nnanji said bitterly.

"I should not have killed you," Wallie said and got an astonished look. "I rarely kill unless I must." He hoped he was keeping a straight face.

"Well, what would you have done if I had refused?" asked Nnanji, amazed and perhaps resentful.

Wallie was wondering the same. "I'm not sure. I suppose I'd have asked you to go and bring me a coward. I'm very glad you didn't. Do you want me to release you?"

Nnanji could not find an answer to that.

His mentor resisted an impulse to pick him up and shake him. Obviously Nnanji's standards were totally unrealistic and might therefore become a serious nuisance some time in the future. However, now that he had time to think, Wallie could see that a Seventh, with more than eleven hundred sutras available to him, could justify almost anything.

"I certainly would not want a man of doubtful honor along on my mission," he said—and Nnanji paled. "And you did make an error." Nnanji blanched.

"You ought to have asked," Wallie continued, "*why* blood need be shed. I should have told you, of course, that I had a mission from the Goddess . . ."

Nnanji's eyes widened, perhaps at the thought of cross-examining a Seventh.

"And of course loyalty to the Goddess takes precedence over everything, even duty to a mentor."

Nnanji gasped. Relief and gratitude flooded over his astonishingly legible face. "I am a man of honor, my liege . . . I think."

"So do I," Wallie said firmly. "And the matter is now closed! However, we have just had lesson two. What did you learn from the duel, if I may call it that?"

At the mention of swordsmanship, Nnanji recovered

his good spirits and snickered. "He had his thumb up his nose, my liege."

"True," Wallie said with a smile. "But why? A Fourth shouldn't be that easy, even for me."

Nnanji thought, counting on his fingers, then said, "You insulted him so that he must challenge, and that gave you the choice of time and place, right? Then he had seen your bandages and probably he thought you would want to put it off for a day or two. Three: dueling isn't allowed inside the barracks. He forgot that you wouldn't know that rule, or be bound by it." He laughed aloud. "And who ever heard of anyone trying to fight a duel across a table?" He grinned happily.

"Very good!" Wallie said. He thought it over himself for a minute. "I wouldn't recommend that technique for everyday, though. If he'd been a fraction quicker, he'd have nailed me back against the wall." Shonsu might be the fastest draw in the World, but swords were not pistols. This was not Dodge City.

Unobtrusively, a couple of Fifths slipped back into the room, and other men departed on their duties. After a short interval—just long enough to suggest that he had not been waiting nearby—Honorable Tarru came hurrying in, overflowing with remorse. Wallie rose for the formal greetings. Nnanji moved as though to leave, but Wallie waved him back to his place.

Tarru apologized profusely for the breach of hospitality, which of course would not have occurred had there been any seniors around, and which would certainly not happen again.

"Good," Wallie said, with what he hoped was menace.

Tarru was probably younger than he looked, he decided—prematurely gray, and weathered rather than wrinkled—and possibly about as trustworthy as a starving leopard with rabies. During the ensuing polite exchange of pleasantries, inquiries about healing and other trivia, his eyes wandered frequently to the hilt of Wallie's sword.

Nnanji waved for a second bowl of stew. Tarru accepted a tankard of ale and Wallie refused one, although it was small beer and relatively harmless. Wallie suspected that as soon as the conversational froth had settled, Tarru would start inquiring about his guest's plans, so he forestalled him with some business of his own.

"There is a small matter that concerns me," he said. "The priests' attempt at exorcism three days ago left me unconscious. I awoke in a sort of hut, up on the canyon road."

"Pilgrim huts," Tarru said. "They are run by a dragon of a priestess."

"I saw no dragon. But the slave girl who looked after me . . . her name was Jja. I took a fancy to her."

Tarru was contemptuous. "Faugh! Nothing but sluts, my lord. They clean floors by day and clean out pilgrims by night—for Kikarani's benefit, of course—horse traders, pot throwers, and common sailors. Now, we have a very fine stable of wenches here in the barracks . . ."

Wallie heard a strange noise and was astonished to realize that he was grinding his teeth. His fists were clenched, and his heart was pounding in fury. Tarru had paled and stopped in midsentence.

"A slut could be bought at a reasonable price?" Wallie whispered. He reached two fingers into his money pouch and dropped a glittering blue stone on the table. "That would be enough for a slut, I expect?"

Tarru gasped audibly. "My lord! That would buy all of Kikarani's slaves and the dragon herself!"

"I happen to be out of change," Wallie said. He knew he was being unreasonable and he didn't give a damn. "Nnanji, do you know this Kikarani?"

"Yes, my liege," Nnanji said, his eyes wide.

"Then go directly to her now. Offer her this stone in return for outright ownership of the slave Jja. Bring the girl back here, with whatever belongings she may have. Any questions?"

"She will assume that the stone is stolen, my liege."

Wallie gave him a glare that caused him to grab up the jewel and turn quickly toward the door. But after a few steps he wheeled round and headed instead for the far exit. It let him walk the whole length of the room, head high, enjoying the eyes that followed him.

"His father is a rugmaker," Tarru said with infinite contempt. "You may never see either gem or girl, my lord."

"I would rather lose a gem than trust my back to a thief." Wallie's blood pressure was still high.

"True," said Tarru diplomatically—but he could not leave well alone. "A smaller temptation might have been more prudent. I would wager at least that the stone is turned into cash before Kikarani ever sees it, and you will get no change."

The thought of Nnanji being dishonest was utterly ludicrous. "Done!" Another sapphire dropped on the table, and Tarru's eyes widened. "I assume that the temple guard has a few inconspicuous agents? Follow my liegeman. If he cashes the gem or flees with it, then you win this."

He had known of Tarru's greed. The man was hypnotized by the blue star on the table. His hands reached for it and then stopped. "I have nothing of equal value to set against your wager, my lord."

Wallie pondered for a moment. "If I win I shall require a small favor only, nothing that impairs your honor. Here, you hold the stakes." Tarru picked up the gem and stared at it. He was suspicious, but the blue fire was burning his palm. He rose and hurried from the room.

Wallie downed some more ale and waited for his fury to subside. This time Shonsu's glands had won. In a relaxed social context, with swordsmanship not evident, he had let down his guard, and that lightning temper had slashed through before he knew it was coming. It had made him appear as an irresponsible spendthrift and gambler, caused him to throw away his expense money on personal whims when he did not even know the purpose for which the gems had been given him—an inauspicious beginning to his quest. Then he realized that he might also have signed his vassal's death warrant. He half rose and then sank back. It was too late now to stop the bet or recall the gem. Miserably he told himself that Tarru, as the only witness, could not order the jewel stolen without incriminating himself.

So he hoped, but his early-morning joke about avenging Nnanji no longer seemed funny at all.

Then Tarru was back, now accompanied by a tall and heavily built Seventh whose facemarks were swords, but inverted. The man's azure robe was spotless, and his thin white hair neatly combed, yet his hands were horny and blackened, and even the ruddy skin of his face seemed to be ingrained with tiny black specks. He was older than Shonsu, but not a swordsman, so it was he who was presented and made the salute—Athinalani, armorer of the Seventh.

He hardly gave Wallie time to respond and he had no small talk. "It must be!" he said. "The seventh sword of Chioxin! My lord, I beg of you to let me see."

Wallie laid the sword on the table. Athinalani peered at it closely, every tiny line and mark. Tarru and Wallie drank while the examination continued. Athinalani turned the sword over and eagerly scanned the other side in the same detail. When he had finished, he looked deeply moved.

"It is the sapphire sword of Chioxin," he said. "There can be no doubt. The griffon forming the guard . . . the figures on the blade . . . the quality. No one else but Chioxin! When I heard the rumors I was sure it would be a forgery, but seeing it, I am convinced. My lord, may I pick it up?"

His big hands gripped it lovingly, testing the stiffness and the weight and the balance. Here, clearly, was an expert. Then he laid it down and looked inquiringly at its owner.

Wallie shrugged. "Tell me."

Athinalani was tactfully astonished at his ignorance. "Chioxin," he said, "was the greatest swordmaker of all time. Many of his weapons are still in use, after seven hundred years, and greatly prized. His skill was equaled only by his art. His swords were not only the best, they were the most beautiful. The lines of these figures . . . see here, and here?

"Now, tradition tells us that he made seven great masterpiece swords when he was very old. The minstrels claim that he bought seven more years of life from the Goddess on the promise of making these weapons. Perhaps so. But each sword had a different heraldic beast forming the guard and each had a great jewel on the hilt . . . pearl, beryl, agate, topaz, ruby, emerald, and sapphire. Each sword has its own history. I am no minstrel, my lord, so I shall not attempt to sing for you, but the emerald sword, for example, was wielded by the great hero Xinimi when he slew the monster of Vinhanugoo, and then it came into the possession of Darijuki, who won the battle of Haur with it—or so they say. The minstrels can go on all night about them."

At last he noticed the tankard waiting for him and took a long draft. Tarru was looking skeptical. Wallie was waiting to hear of some dreadful curse or other— such stories usually had a curse or two in them. The dining room was emptying as the guard went about its business, the attendants retrieving the bowls the dogs had cleaned.

The armorer wiped froth and plunged ahead with his lecture. "And I have seen the pearl sword! Or part of it, anyway. The hilt and a fragment of the blade are owned by the King of Kalna, and he showed me it when I was a young apprentice. It is said that the city of Dis Marin owns the beryl, and there is a piece of another blade in the lodge at Casr. The hilt has been lost, but is thought to have been the ruby."

Again the whisper of memory: *Casr?* "And the sapphire sword?" Wallie asked.

"Ah! There is no history of the sapphire. Only the six are known. According to the minstrels, Chioxin gave the seventh to the Goddess Herself."

There was a significant pause. That explained the expression on old Coningu's face last night. The unasked question hung in the air, but one did not ask such questions of a Seventh.

"No curses?" Wallie inquired. "No magic powers?"

"Oh, the minstrels...they will tell you that a man wielding one of these blades could never be beaten. But I am a craftsman. I know no recipe for putting magic into a sword."

"This one has so far recorded two wins and one draw," Wallie said blandly.

Tarru managed to blush. "It is in remarkable condition for a weapon of that age."

"The Goddess would have taken good care of it, I suppose," Wallie said, playing with them. He smiled at Tarru. "You saw me come out of the water. I assume that you have questioned the swordsmen who saw me go in?"

"Yes, my lord," Tarru said grimly. "Very closely." Like his former superior, he was not a man to believe in miracles.

"My lord," Athinalani said. "Would you graciously consent to let me have an artist draw this? I should be eternally in your debt."

"Of course. I presume that you have swords for sale? My liegeman will be coming to see you to sell one of some value. He will also wish to purchase a more serviceable, everyday sort of sword."

It was shortly after this that the bent old commissary, Coningu, came shuffling in. He hovered politely at them until Tarru raised an eyebrow.

"A messenger from the temple, my lords. To see Lord Shonsu." Then he added, "A green." And rolled his eyes to see Tarru's reaction—a Sixth as messenger? Tarru scowled.

The conversation broke up, although Athinalani would obviously have been willing to sit all day and just stare at the seventh sword of Chioxin. As they made their way to the door Tarru asked in a low voice, "Did

you give Lord Hardduju's sword to Apprentice Nnanji,
my lord?"

"Yes," Wallie said, and Tarru flashed teeth like a
shark. "Is that funny?"

"Nnanji is but the son of a tradesman. There were
several recruits at about the same time who came from
such artisan families, although I know that there were
many candidates more suitable, swordsmen's sons. It
was about that time that Lord Hardduju acquired that
sword."

Tarru might or might not have been a partner in more
serious crimes, but that petty graft would have been for
the reeve's personal benefit only. Which perhaps explained Tarru's obvious dislike of Nnanji.

"You think that Nnanji's family paid for it?"

Tarru sneered as he held the door for his guest. "Only
a small part, I am sure, my lord. It would buy several rug
shops. But, as I say, there were others. I find it ironic
that the sword has done him so little good, and that now
it should belong to one of those apprentices."

He smiled in satisfaction. Tarru was not a kindly man.

Nor, if he had failed to act upon his suspicions, an
honorable swordsman.

†† ††

"Pray honor me with your distinguished opinion on this
humble wine, my lord," the old priest bleated in his qua-
vering, toothless voice.

"It is a memorable vintage, reverend one," the
swordsman rumbled, several octaves lower.

Honakura was packaged in a great wicker chair
shaped like a sousaphone, smiling his gums and playing
host and talking trivial nonsense while his sharp eyes
missed nothing. Wallie sat opposite on a stool. The table
between them bore rich cakes and wine and crystal goblets; and everything was enveloped in a steamy green

shade below trees whose trunks even Shonsu's arms could not have spanned. Planted to decorate the courtyard, the three giants had colonized it, filled it, and roofed it. The crumbling old paving stones rose to lap around their massive roots and dipped away into the triangular space between them, where the men sat. In a way that nothing else had yet done, the trees' sheer immensity emphasized to Wallie the antiquity of the temple, and thus of the culture that had built it.

It was a private place, this jungle courtyard. The walls were cushioned in vivid moss and hung with showy bougainvillaea. Behind them the River giggled and clattered, covering conversation as effectively as the canopy of branches shut out the overpowering sun or any unwanted eyes. Insects hurried around on business, but otherwise the two men sat undisturbed in the humid shadows. The wine was certainly memorable—harsh and metallic, the worst Wallie could ever remember tasting.

At last Honakura ended the pleasantries. "That was a meritorious deed of arms you performed yesterday, my lord, a fealty to the Goddess. Although you had no formal contract with the council, I have been authorized to offer you recompense; either the office of reeve"— he smiled —"or a suitable emolument."

Blood money? Wallie found himself frowning, although he was also curious to know how much a Seventh charged for a sword job. All he said was, "It was my pleasure, holy one. As I told you, I cannot accept the office, and I have no need of your fee. My master is generous."

Honakura's invisible eyebrows rose. He lowered his voice and said, "I think I hear a nightingale."

The only birds Wallie could hear were drowsy pigeons in the distance.

The old man chuckled at his blank expression. "An old tradition, my lord. It is said that long ago two rulers met in a forest to discuss some important matter, and a nightingale was singing so beautifully in the tree above them that each man listened only to the birdsong. So neither was able to report what had been said, because he hadn't heard any of it."

Wallie smiled. "It is melodious, that nightingale."

The priest smiled back and waited.

"Yesterday," Wallie said cheerfully, "an odd thing happened to me—I talked with a god. Now, it is rather a long story, and I should not want to bore you . . ."

Evidently he was out of character for Lord Shonsu, for he received a look of astonishment, followed by a polite but bewildered smile.

"Pardon me, holy one," he said. "I should not joke on sacred matters. It gets me into trouble. But I did talk with a god, and one of the things he said to me was *Honakura is a good man—him you may trust*. So I wish to tell you the whole story, if I may, and receive your wise counsel."

The old man stared back in silence and suddenly tears were trickling down his cheeks. It was several minutes before he noticed them, then he wiped his eyes with his sleeve. "I beg pardon, my lord," he mumbled. "It is many years since I received praise from a superior and I have forgotten how to handle it. Pray forgive me."

Now feeling an utter heel, Wallie said, "Let me tell you it all, then."

He wondered briefly how ancient the priest really was—at least three times Shonsu's age. Yet there was nothing senile about Honakura. He was a needle-sharp old rascal, obviously a power in the temple, and probably unscrupulous in whatever he might choose to regard as a good cause. Now he snuggled down into his great chair like a bee crawling into a trumpet blossom. Wallie told him the whole story, including the first two talks with the god. Honakura studied him unblinkingly, only small movements of his mouth showing that he was alive at all. At the end he closed his eyes and seemed to mutter a prayer, then he sniffled a little and said, "I am in your debt, Lord Shonsu . . . or Walliesmith. Your tale is more wonderful to my ears than I can tell you. Always I have hoped to witness a miracle—a real, carved-in-stone miracle. And now, after all these years!"

"There is one other thing," Wallie said hastily. "When I asked the god about miracles, he told me that I could trust you, and to ask you to tell me the anecdote from the seventeenth sutra."

Honakura had listened to the whole extraordinary tale without expression, but that remark produced a twitch of surprise . . . then a quickly suppressed frown. Wallie remembered how the god had smiled mysteriously when he gave the order.

"Ah!" the priest said. "Well . . . I expect that your swordsmen sutras are much like ours—most contain a little story to help fix them in the memory. The episode in our seventeenth concerns Ikondorina. Under the circumstances, of course, I shall tell it to you.

"Ikondorina was a great hero, who went to the Goddess and gave Her his sword and swore that he would rather trust to Her miracles than his mortal strength. So his enemies pursued him up some high rocks and the Goddess turned him into a bird. Then his enemies pursued him to the River and the Goddess turned him into a fish. A third time his enemies strove against him, but this time they slew him, and when his soul came before the Goddess, he asked Her why She had not saved him the third time. And She gave him back his sword and told him to go and do his own miracles. So he returned to the world and butchered his enemies and was a great hero again. You see how well the story fits your own case?" He smiled hopefully.

Wallie did not. "That is all?"

"That is the whole anecdote," Honakura replied carefully.

"What else can you tell me about this Ikondorina, then?"

The old man's expression was very guarded. "He is mentioned by name in a couple of other sutras, but there are no other tales about him." He knew something that he wasn't saying. The god had sent him a message that Wallie was not to share.

Irritated but helpless, Wallie said, "May I ask if there is a moral attached to the story?"

"Certainly. *Great deeds honor the gods.*"

He thought that over. "And great deeds are done by mortals?"

"Of course. And miracles are done by gods, but being easy for them, bring no honor."

Wallie wished that he, too, could lean back in a comfortable chair. "So the message for me is that I am to expect no help from the gods?"

"Not quite that, I shouldn't think." Honakura frowned. "But whatever it is that the Goddess requires, She wishes it to be done by mortals—by you. She may help you, but you must not expect Her to do the work."

"The god mentioned that I would be guided. But he also told me that this sword could be lost or broken, and that the gods do not do miracles upon demand. Do I have it right, do you think?"

Honakura nodded, the folds on his neck flapping. "And whatever your task may be, my lord, it is obviously very important. Your reward will be great."

"If I succeed," Wallie said grimly. He wished that the demigod had given him a few rainchecks for miracles.

"The first problem, then," the priest said thoughtfully, "is to get you out of here alive. But I forget my duties ...do try these cakes, Lord Shonsu. Those with pistachios are delicious, I recall, although beyond my own abilities these days." He held out the cake plate without brushing off the insects.

Wallie declined. "Why should staying alive be a problem? I am protected by the code of the swordsmen as their guest. Who can harm me?"

The little man shook his head sadly. "I wish I could advise you more exactly, my lord. There is only one way out, and it involves a long trail, much of it through jungle, and a ferry crossing of the River to Hann. It is sure that several highrank swordsmen, who might have been a threat to Hardduju, started out from Hann and never arrived. I do not know if the culprits were renegade swordsmen or assassins in his pay."

Assassins were any civilians who killed swordsmen—and the worst criminals of all in the swordsmen's eyes.

"How..." Wallie began and then answered his own question. "Archery?" Bows were an especial abhorrence to swordsmen.

The priest nodded, nibbling cake. "I expect so. Or sheer weight of numbers. There have been many pilgrims waylaid on the trail over the centuries. It is the guard's duty to patrol it and keep it safe, but I fear that the dogs have been running with the wolves of late. There is a horse post maintained at the ferry, so that news of important arrivals can be brought quickly to the temple. We suspect that the messages have been going to the wrong persons, and the richest offerings have not arrived."

Wallie had been expecting a discussion of his unknown task, and of the god's mysterious riddle, not of imminent danger. "But why me?" he asked. "I am leaving, not coming. Would these creatures of darkness seek to avenge Hardduju's death?"

"Oh, I doubt that." Honakura poured more wine inattentively. "Their association was commercial, not sentimental. But you have told me what sword you bear; may I see it?"

Wallie drew the seventh sword and held it out for the priest to study. Unlike the armorer and the swordsmen, he was little interested in the blade, but he fingered the hilt and murmured his appreciation. He touched the great sapphire and glanced up at his guest's hairclip.

"Yes," he said at last, "I think that sword may possibly be the most valuable movable piece of property in the World."

Wallie choked on a mouthful of the rank wine. "Who could afford to buy it?" he demanded. "Who would want it?"

"The griffon is a royal symbol," Honakura said contemptuously. "There are dozens or hundreds of cities ruled by kings. Any of them would buy it, for almost any price—which they would plan to recover afterward, of course." His face darkened. "Certainly the temple would buy it, were it for sale. Some of my colleagues would feel very strongly that Her sword belongs here...And you must carry it along that trail."

Wallie did not need to consult the sutras to know that here was a very nasty tactical situation. Air freight, he thought, would be a good solution. "Then I should request an escort from the guard?"

Honakura's face became unreadable. "You could ask Honorable Tarru, certainly."

Wallie raised a skeptical eyebrow, and the priest breathed an audible sigh of relief. Obviously they shared the same opinion of Tarru, but courtesy demanded that it not be spoken.

"Who else would you suggest?" Wallie asked, and Honakura shook his head in frustration.

"I wish I knew, my lord! Swordsmen will not discuss other swordsmen, for obvious reasons. Most, I am sure, are men of probity, at worst reluctant accomplices. They obeyed orders, so long as those orders were not too blatantly evil, assigning any breaches of honor to the account of the reeve. And what else could they do? For example, there are stories of condemned prisoners who did not reach the Place of Mercy."

"Ransomed?" Wallie said, working it out. This tale of wholesale corruption was unnerving to him, and he could feel his Shonsu nature raging on some deep level. "But you can count the executions from the temple steps and you know how many..."

"Bags of rocks, we believe," Honakura said patiently. "Not all bodies return to the pool. But some of the swordsmen must have been deeply implicated, and those are your danger now."

"Guilty consciences?" Wallie said. "They will greatly fear a new reeve, a new broom. Past sins beget future crimes?"

Honakura nodded and smiled, perhaps relieved—or even surprised—that this swordsman was not going to start blustering about the honor of his craft and throw caution to the wolves.

The waters gabbled and bees hummed uninterrupted for a while...

"The first question, then," Wallie said, "is timing." He glanced at his bandaged feet. "And that depends on when I become mobile again. At least a week and probably two—I would be crazy to leave before I am healed. The second question: do I announce that I am leaving, or do I let them think that I am Hardduju's successor?" He paused to consider. "I doubt that we could keep up such a pretense for very long, and I should prefer not to."

The priest nodded. "It would not be honorable, my lord."

Wallie shrugged. "Then we shall be honest. As a mere visitor I shall be less of a threat, and hence in less danger. That will come when I try to leave, will it not? So my best plan is to hobble around, being as lame as possible for as long as possible, to try to determine who among the guard may be trusted—and then perhaps to vanish overnight and without warning."

The old man was beaming, a Cheshire bird in a wicker cage.

"Meanwhile, I suppose," Wallie continued, "I keep my back to the wall, stay out of dark alleys, refrain from eating in private, and sleep with the door locked?"

Honakura rubbed his hands in glee. "Excellent, my lord!" Obviously he had been regarding Wallie as a mere slab of muscle with quick reflexes and was pleased to see that this swordsman did not regard caution as cowardice. "It is just over two weeks until Swordsmen's Day. I should have hoped to have augmented the normal observance to induct you as reeve. As that may not be, perhaps we should announce a special service of blessing on your mission? That should keep you safe until then—as you say, the danger will come when you try to leave."

He hesitated and then added, "If you will pardon my

presumption, Lord Shonsu, it is a pleasure to meet a swordsman who does not mind being unconventional. I do not know what opponent the Goddess has in mind for you, but I think he may be very surprised." He chuckled.

Wallie had been using common sense and a smattering of sutras—mostly common sense—and tactics were supposed to be his business, so he found the priest's surprise somewhat insulting, yet also amusing. *You do not think like Shonsu . . .*

"I have a nephew who is a healer," Honakura said, "and can be relied upon for discretion. He will extend your convalescence as long as possible."

"I shall pay him by the day," Wallie assured him solemnly and was rewarded with a noisy view of the old man's gums. "But, tell me, holy one, if the Goddess has gone to all this trouble over me, will She not stand by me when I am in danger?"

Instantly the priest's joviality vanished. He shook a finger at the swordsman. "You have not comprehended the lesson on miracles, then! As a senior swordsman you are supposed to understand strategy. Put yourself in Her place. You have sent in your best man, and he has failed—disastrously, you said. What does that mean?"

Wallie suppressed an angry retort. "Not knowing the task, I can't guess. Perhaps Shonsu lost an army? Or lost ground to the enemy—whoever or whatever the enemy is."

"In either case," the priest said, "it is not something you wish to happen very often, is it? So what do you do? You send in your next man and if he fails then the next one? Then the next? Of course the gods have infinite resources . . ."

"You are right, holy one," Wallie said repentantly. He should have seen that. "You pick the next man—and then you train him so that he is better than the first."

"Or at least you test him," the priest agreed. "And if he can't even escape from the temple . . ."

He did not need to finish the thought.

"And even if he can," Wallie said glumly, "there may be other tests in store in the future? I see now—no miracles."

Miracles, he decided, were readily addictive.

Honakura again held out the plate of cakes and offered to top up Wallie's glass. Wallie refused both, fearing that much of this rich living would fatten him like Hardduju. He must remember to think of himself now as a professional athlete and stay in training, for his life would depend on it.

"And your first task is obviously to pick some followers," Honakura said, settling back in his chair to enjoy a cream roll.

Wallie chuckled. "Well, I found one. You saw him yesterday." He told of Nnanji, his courage and absurdly romantic ideas of duty and honor, and he described the scene with Briu that morning.

The shrewd old eyes twinkled. "That may be the way you are to be guided, my lord."

"A miracle? That boy?" Wallie said, scoffing.

"That is just the way She works miracles—unobtrusively! You found him near the water—the powers of the Goddess are always most evident near the River, and this is a branch of the River. I am not surprised to hear that he is an unusual young man."

Wallie was courteously doubtful. "I shall have to test his swordsmanship, then," he said.

"His swordsmanship is bad, but he has a very good memory," Honakura said, concentrating on a last fragment of cake. After a moment he glanced up to study the effect he had produced.

"He is the only redhead in the guard?" Wallie was not sure whether he was reacting as Wallie, amused, or Shonsu, furious.

The priest nodded. "You do not take offense? That also is unusual of you, Lord Shonsu."

Wallie ignored the needling. "What else did you learn about Nnanji?"

"I know nothing about his honesty. His former mentor

raged about his swordsmanship, but could not seem to do much to improve it. He was not going to be promoted to Third until it did improve. He is not very popular with the other men—although that may be to his credit, of course."

The old man was looking smug. Swordsmen did not talk about one another, and the barracks staff seemed to be all retired swordsmen, likely bound by the same rule, although perhaps not as strongly. That meant that Honakura's spies gained their information from another source.

"Is he popular with the women, then?" Wallie asked and saw a flash of appreciation to indicate that he had scored.

"They give him high marks for enthusiasm and persistence, low marks for finesse," the priest retorted, eyes shining with amusement.

"Just like his table manners!" Wallie said. Mention of women reminded him of Jja. "Holy one, you recall the slave woman who attended me in the cottage?"

Honakura's smile vanished at once. "Ah, yes. I have been meaning to do something about that girl—she deserves better—but I have been too busy to get around to it. Do you want her?"

So he had thrown away a precious sapphire buying a slave he could have had for the asking.

"I think she is already mine," Wallie replied. "I sent Nnanji to buy her this morning." Now he could see that he had been more stupid than he had realized. He had displayed wealth in front of Tarru, who would surely suspect that there were more jewels where those two had come from so readily, and who now knew that Wallie had casually given away Hardduju's valuable sword.

The old priest was studying him thoughtfully. "I hope you did not pay too much," he said.

Wallie was thunderstruck. "Yes, I did," he admitted. "But how did you guess?"

Honakura looked smug. "You told me that your master was generous. I can guess how he pays."

"You can?"

"He is the god of jewels."

"Jewels?" Wallie had not mentioned those.

"Yes indeed." Honakura paused, looking puzzled and oddly uneasy. "He is usually associated with the Fire God, not the Goddess. Now why should that be, I wonder? Jewels are found in the sands of the River."

Wallie said, "In my world, we believed that most jewels were formed by fire and then spread by water."

"Indeed?" The priest found that interesting. "That would explain it, then. He is normally seen in the form of a small boy. A prospector who finds a good gem will say, 'The god has shed a tooth for me.'"

Wallie laughed and emptied his wineglass. "I like that. As I like the nightingale. You are a poetic people, holy one. Explain to me the god's stick with the leaves?"

Honakura snorted and lowered his voice. "Dramatic effect, I should think. Gods have their little vanities, too. I hardly expect that he needed a mnemonic."

"A who?"

Again the old man sighed and shook his head. "You care a babe in arms, my lord! I should not doubt the wisdom of the Goddess, but I cannot see how She expects you to survive here when you seem to know nothing at all! A mnemonic—an aid to memory. Don't you have public speakers in your dream world? They take a twig and make a mark on each leaf to remind them of a point they want to make, then they tear off each leaf as they go. It can be very effective when it is well done. And what else do you use if you want to memorize a long sutra?"

"We have other devices, holy one. But about Jja... how does one go about freeing a slave?"

Honakura was more astonished by that than anything he had heard yet. "*Freeing* a slave? One doesn't."

"You mean that slavery is for life?" asked Wallie, aghast. "There is no escape?"

The priest shook his head. "A slave is marked at birth. If he serves well in this life, he may be born higher on the ladder next time. You were planning to *free* this girl?"

Wallie had confided so much to the old man that he could hardly hold back now. So he told how he had lost his temper.

"If I had any thoughts in my head at all," he said, "then I was thinking that I would buy the girl and free her. She was kind to me," he protested. "And of course she may have saved my life when the priestess came hunting for me."

"She was also a damned good lay?" the priest asked and cackled loudly. "No, do not glare at me, swordsman! I saw her. Were she of free birth, her brideprice might be many gems, but you have bought her, and she is your slave. You can give her away, you can sell her, you can kill her, but you cannot free her. Indeed, if it amuses you to burn her with red-hot irons, no one will stop you, except perhaps the Goddess, or a stronger swordsman if it offends his sense of honor. Which it probably wouldn't. You should realize, Walliesmith, that a swordsman of the Seventh can do almost anything he wants. But he cannot make a slave into a free lady, and he cannot marry her. Not unless he wishes to become a slave himself, of course."

Wallie regarded him glumly. "I suppose you think this is another miracle?"

The priest nodded thoughtfully. "It could be. Her action to protect you in the cottage was very unusual. The Goddess has perhaps chosen some companions for your journey, and that girl may have some small part to play, apart from providing you with enjoyable exercise. Never underestimate joy, it is the wages of mortality!" He was still astonished. "You can *free* slaves in your dream world?"

"Where I come from we have no slaves," Wallie retorted hotly. "We regard the owning of slaves as an abomination."

"Then of course you will send her to the auction

block?" the priest asked, chuckling. "I hardly think that Priestess Kikarani will give you back your gem."

For a moment the Shonsu temper stirred, and Wallie stamped it down. Anger against the gods was futile. He had been tricked.

Honakura was studying him. "May I offer a morsel of advice, my lord? Do you know the secret of success in owning slaves?"

"Tell me," the swordsman growled.

"Work them hard!" Honakura sniggered, and then cackled loudly at his own wit.

†† † ††

In the marble splendor of the barracks entrance Wallie met the old commissary and asked if Nnanji had returned.

"Oh yes, my lord," Coningu said, with a look affirming some secret amusement, too precious to spoil by telling.

Wallie, therefore, must not show undignified haste, so he took his time mounting the great staircase. But he hurried up the second stairs and raced along the passage. Silent on his bandages, he crossed the first room to the door of the second, whence came the sound of laughter.

There were three people there, and they were all on the floor, on a sunlit rug. On the right was Jja, posed like a Copenhagen mermaid, as graceful and desirable as he remembered, and it was she who was doing the laughing. On the left was Nnanji, down on knees and elbows with his scabbard sticking up behind him like a tail, generally resembling a dog trying to dig out a rabbit. He was tickling the belly of the third person, a brown, naked, giggling baby.

For a moment the tableau held, one of those scenes that burn into the mind to become instant memories—in the end, what is a lifetime made of but memories? Then they saw him. Jja rose, crossed to him, and dropped on her knees to kiss his foot in one flowing movement. She did not seem to rush, but she had done it before Nnanji had scrambled to his feet in pop-eyed embarrassment.

He said, "I didn't know if you wanted the baby, too, my liege, so I brought it. You did say belongings. Kikarani says she will take it back if you don't want it."

Wallie cleared his throat. "The baby is fine. Would you offer my respects to Master Coningu and ask if he could spare me a moment?"

Nnanji disentangled himself from the baby now climbing his leg and left quickly. Even the backs of his ears were pink.

Wallie looked down at the girl kneeling at his feet and stooped to raise her. He smiled at her, seeing again the high cheekbones that gave her face such a look of strength, and the wide, dark, almond eyes that had fascinated him before. No slender elf-maiden she: tall and large-boned, deep-breasted and strong, yet graceful in her movements and bright-eyed. She was younger than he had thought, but he saw again the corrosion of slavery—chapped hands, and her black hair roughly hacked short. Given a fair chance she would be a great beauty, and he knew that she could be tender. If a swordsman must have a slave, then this was the woman to choose.

She looked in alarm at his face and then down at his other bruises and marks.

"Welcome, Jja," he said. "I have acquired a few scrapes since we last met. I sent for you because you are so good at caring for damaged swordsmen."

"I was very happy to hear that I am to be your slave, master." Her expression was attentive, yet so guarded that he could not guess at her thoughts.

The baby was crawling rapidly toward the door, following his new friend. "Bring him over here and sit down," Wallie said. "No, on the chair." He sat on a stool and studied her. "What's his name?"

"Vixini, master." The baby had a slavestripe on its face.

"And who is his father?"

She showed no embarrassment. "I don't know, master. My mistress swore to the facemarker that his father was a blacksmith, but she had never sent me to serve under a blacksmith."

"Why? What's special about a blacksmith?"

She obviously thought he should know. "They are supposed to be big and strong, master. A blacksmith fathermark brings a good price."

Wallie thought a few silent oaths and struggled to adjust his thinking. To buy a slave and free her was one thing; to buy her and keep her and use her was something which only that morning he had defined as rape. Yet the sight of her and the memory of their night together was already arousing him. To own her and not use her would insult her, and was probably beyond his self-control... how did one conduct an employee interview with a fixed asset?

He said, "I want you to be my slave, Jja, but I don't want an unhappy slave, because unhappy slaves do bad work. If you would rather stay with Kikarani, then please tell me. I shall not be angry, and I shall return you. I won't ask for the money back, so you won't be in trouble."

She shook her head slightly and looked puzzled. "I shall do the best I can, master. She never had cause to beat me. She charged a higher price for me than for the others. She did not sell me when I conceived."

Wallie decided that she did not understand the question—a slave could not choose between owners, or have a preference.

"You were very good to me when I was sick. And I enjoyed..." He wanted to say "making love," but of course it translated into "making joy," which stopped him. "I enjoyed that night with you more than I have ever enjoyed a night with a woman." He could feel his face burning as he stammered. "I would hope that you would want to share my bed in future."

"Of course, master."

Why else would he want her? What choice did she have?

Wallie was feeling more and more guilty, and consequently getting angry with himself. The sight of that silk-smooth skin and the curve of her hips and breasts . . . He struggled to suppress the guilt and deal with the World on its own terms.

He asked after parents, lovers, and close friends, and she continued to shake her head. That was a relief. He smiled at her as reassuringly as he could. "Then you will be my slave. I shall try to make you happy, Jja, because then you will make me happy. That is your first duty—to make me happy. And your second will be to look after that beautiful baby and make him grow up as big and strong as ever any blacksmith ever seen. But you will make joy with me, and with no one else. There will be no other men."

At last he got a reaction. She looked both astonished and pleased. "Thank you, master."

Another problem: "I shall be leaving here in a few days."

No reaction.

"We may never return."

Still none.

"Yesterday I got Nnanji as my protégé and I gave him a present. What can I give you? Is there anything at all that you want?"

"No, master," she said, but he thought he saw her arms close more tightly around the baby on her lap.

"I shall give you a promise," he said. "I promise never to take Vixini from you."

It was so pathetically easy! She slid to her knees and kissed his foot. Angrily he rose and lifted her and saw that she was weeping.

"You surprise me, though," he said, forcing a smile.

"Surprise you, master?" she asked, wiping her eyes.

"Yes. You are just as beautiful as I remembered and I didn't really think that was possible." The baby was on the floor now, so he could take her in his arms and kiss

her. What had been planned as a friendly greeting became instantly an affair of tongues and clenching arms
and fingers pressing into her flesh. Desire exploded
within him; he burned, then released her quickly and
turned away, ashamed, fighting for control. When he
looked around she had removed her tattered dress and
was sitting on the bed, waiting for him.

"Not now," he said hoarsely. "First we must discover
whether I can keep a slave in these quarters, and we
must find you some better clothes and make arrange-
ments for Vixini."

Vixini was heading out the door again. Wallie strode
over, scooped him up, and on the way back started to
tickle him. Vixini shrieked with glee and sent a warm
wet sensation down Wallie's chest. His first thought was
that he was in the middle of one of those priceless silk
rugs. He scrambled to catch the flow with his spare hand
and get over the woodwork. By the time he had done so
and could hold the baby safely away from him, Vixini
had done a fine job on him. Jja gave a gasp of horror and
Wallie roared with laughter. Vixini grinned as toothlessly
as Honakura.

Jja was staring at Wallie in dismay, and for some reason he found that funny also and laughed harder. She
looked around for a rag or a towel and, not seeing any,
grabbed up her dress and started to wipe his chest.

It was at that moment that Nnanji and Coningu came
in. Wallie tried to explain, pointing to the baby he still
held and the dark stain on his kilt, but the expression
on Nnanji's face was too much for him. He could not
get the words out. Coningu would never be surprised
by anything and was much too respectful to laugh at
a Seventh, but he did turn away to straighten the wall
hangings.

Nnanji had also brought a matronly female servant,
Janu, housekeeper of the women's quarters, and Wallie
was surprised to learn that there would be no problem in
having Vixini cared for. "You have children here, too?"

"Oh yes, my lord," Coningu said. "The women say it

is the swordsmen's fault, but I never heard of a s ords-man having a baby. I shall ring for a fresh garme. for you and some water, my lord."

"Janu," Wallie said. "I sent out to buy a slave and find I have two. As you can see, they are both naked at the moment. Jja's dress was not worth the purpose to which she has just put it. I want her fitted out in suitable style. What would you recommend?" He hoped his credit was good.

"She is for night duty, my lord?" Janu asked, in-specting the naked Jja as a cook might inspect a piece of meat, but not waiting for an answer. She scowled at Jja's feet and looked closely at her hands. "For the baby, a blanket, back sling, and a hood for rainy days. For the woman, two day dresses, sandals, boots for wet weather, and a cloak. I presume at least one gown for evening wear and suitable shoes? We can't do much with her hair until it grows longer, and her finger and toe nails . . . I'll see what we can manage. A few scents and body oils and cosmetics, nothing too elabo-rate."

Wallie looked at Jja. "Anything else you want? Will that do to start with?" She nodded, her eyes wide. "Very well," he said. "I am sure that Janu will advise you and dress you in proper style for my station. I shall settle the purchases later."

He gave Jja what he hoped was an encouraging smile. She went off wrapped in a bedsheet, looking over-whelmed.

Wallie was feeling the same way. He had a nagging suspicion that he also had just been given a present, and his conscience would allow him no peace for even think-ing like that.

By the time Wallie had repaired the effects of Vixini's performance, Nnanji was seeing the funny side. Such courage, he said slyly—to do that all over a Seventh!

Wallie agreed. "This is turning out to be quite a day,"

he said. "And the jewel was acceptable to the formidable Kikarani?"

Nnanji laughed. "I never saw anything vanish faster, my liege."

He had passed the test, for Nnanji attempting to lie would have red warning lights all over his face. Wallie was not going to tell him about it, though. He said, "By the way, the armorer confirms your opinion of my sword —the seventh sword of Chioxin."

Nnanji beamed. "I wish I had heard that part of the ballad, then, my liege."

"Apparently there isn't any more. Chioxin gave it to the Goddess, and no more was heard of it."

Unlike Tarru, Nnanji was willing to believe in miracles. He laughed excitedly. "And now the Goddess has given it to Shonsu!"

"Certainly, although I perversely refused to say so. But I am curious. It was three years ago that you heard that ballad?"

A shy smile slid into Nnanji's eyes. "A little longer, my liege."

Wallie stared at him, then seated himself on the floor and laid down his sword. Nnanji immediately sat in front of him and put his sword across the first. It was the traditional position for the reciting of sutras.

"How far have you got?"

"Five seventeen, my liege, 'On Duels.'"

Coincidence? "Lucky me! Let's hear a few. Eighty-four, 'On Footwear.'"

They chanted in alternation back and forth. The sutras were a revelation to Wallie. He had them all in his memory, but he had never learned them, and each came out fresh, as if he was hearing it for the first time. They were a mixed bag, from crude jingles to lengthy lists. Some short, some long, they covered a myriad of topics: technique, ritual, strategy, professional ethics, tactics, anatomy, first aid, logistics—even personal hygiene. Many were dull and trite, but a few had the barbaric grandeur found in the best of preliterate narrative everywhere. Some were banal, others as obscure as Zen koans. Most contained a law, an anecdote, and a proverb. As Honakura had said, the stories helped the memory, but frequently the association of ideas was subtle and thought-provoking.

Nnanji was word-perfect in every one they tried, so Wallie chanted five eighteen, 'On Hostages.' Nnanji chanted it right back. Surprised, Wallie gave him two more and then had him go back to 'Hostages.' He made no errors. Wallie knew that preliterates could often perform astonishing feats of memory, but Nnanji seemed phenomenal. Honakura had been correct: this was the hand of the Goddess.

His protégé was looking understandably smug. "All right, smarty," Wallie said. "Here's five eighty-two, 'On the Feeding of Horses.'" That was the longest, dullest, and least associative of them all. He stumbled a couple of times himself before he got it right. Nnanji sat and watched his lips. Then he recited it back—without the stumbles.

Wallie Smith had been taught to read and write. He was thus, by Nnanji's standards, a mental cripple. "You win!" he said, and Nnanji grinned. "If I went through all eleven hundred and forty-four of them, just once at one sitting, would you remember them all?"

Nnanji attempted to look humble. "I don't think so, my liege."

Wallie laughed. "Don't lie to me, vassal! You do think so, and I think you may be right, but I'm not man enough to try it. Let's go see about your sword."

The armory was located far from the temple, near the gate, where the noise would not disturb holy matters. Athinalani, free of his formal robe and wearing a leather apron, was banging away at an anvil while a sweating slave worked the bellows on the furnace. The armorer broke off at once and led his visitors into an inner room, where hundreds of swords and foils hung on racks—far more than the guard could ever break or lose. The economics puzzled Wallie, but perhaps one of the blessings of the World was that it had no economists. Yet there was a commercial air about the place that he found comforting and familiar.

Athinalani knew what sword he would be asked to buy. The respect he paid to its owner was clearly a novel and flattering experience for Nnanji. There would be no market for such a thing on this side of the River, said the armorer, but he was willing to offer three hundred golds for it if the valiant apprentice wished to make a quick sale. Nnanji just gasped and said, "Done!"

That suited Wallie—one valuable sword was quite enough to worry about. He produced a sapphire and asked the armorer's advice on how to liquidate that asset. Athinalani welcomed any chance to be of service to the bearer of the seventh sword of Chioxin and agreed to sell the gem in the town for him.

Selecting a new sword took time, with discussion of length and weight and flexibility and edge and bevel and damask. Nnanji listened wide-eyed, soaking up information. Wallie was fascinated by all the knowledge he was unearthing that had not been in his mind two days before—obviously Shonsu had known his theory as well as his practice. Athinalani was overjoyed at having a customer with such interest and expertise.

Then Wallie began to stray. Steel was not his speciality, but a chemical engineer must know something of the behavior of iron and carbon in crystalline matrices, so he started to discuss quenching and forging. The armorer grew suspicious, and his face darkened—a swordsman was trespassing on the sutras and secrets of another craft. So Wallie backed away quickly and conviviality returned.

At last all three were satisfied with a new sword for Nnanji—and Nnanji would not part with his old one. Wallie pointed out its faults at some length. Nnanji admitted them and finally confessed that he had a younger brother, whom he planned to enroll in the guard as soon

as he himself had achieved third rank and could accept a
protégé. That would never happen if Tarru had any say
in the matter, and Nnanji was not going to be here anyway, but it was not Wallie's problem, so he let it rest.

Then there was the matter of foils. A swordsman
needed a dummy weapon with the same feel as his own
sword. Athinalani had foreseen the problem for the
Chioxin and was already at work. His memory for length
and weight was astonishingly accurate. He promised that
the foil would be ready by sundown. As unofficial
banker for the guard, he advanced both his customers
some coins from the leather bag that served as his till.
Wallie purchased a whetstone.

It had all been as much fun as a tourist shopping trip
—which, in a sense, it was for Wallie. He promised himself that he would come back for more chats with the
armorer. The swordsmen stopped at the door while Athinalani went off to burnish Nnanji's new sword—nothing
below perfection would be allowed out of his shop. Wallie established that lunch was eaten in the same place as
breakfast.

"Right," he said. "I'm slower than you, so I'll leave
now. Eat with your friends, and we'll meet afterward. I
need a word with Honorable Tarru."

††† †††

With his old sword on his back and his new sword and
foil in a carrying sheath under his arm, Nnanji went
striding back toward the barracks, chewing over a problem.

A new sword must be given—whom should he ask? It
was an important tradition, although the sutras did not
specifically demand it except in the case of a scratcher.
As Briu had explained to him years ago, the purpose of
that sutra was to make sure that it took at least two
swordsmen to induct a boy into the craft: one to be his

mentor, another to give him his first sword. But the swordsmen had extended the practice to any sword, even one that a man had bought for himself or won with a kill; before he wore it a friend must give it to him. A friend. Not his mentor. Who?

Of course he could ask one of the other Seconds, like Darakaji or Fonddiniji, and normally he would not hesitate, but they had all been sending him black looks at breakfast. Briu had withdrawn his charges, but the bad taste would remain, and they were all jealous of him with his wonderful new mentor. If he asked Darakaji—or Fonddiniji—he might refuse. If one did, then they all would . . . What then?

Still mulling, Nnanji reached one of the back doors of the barracks just as Adept Briu and Swordsman Landinoro came out and down the steps. There was the answer—at least Briu was the only man in the guard who could not now call him a coward in public. It would be a peace offering. Nnanji intercepted them and saluted.

"Adept," Nnanji began, and it was strange not to call Briu "mentor." "I would ask a favor of you."

Briu looked at him coldly, glanced at the sword under his arm, and then turned to Landinoro. "He isn't short of cheek, is he?" he said.

The Third shook his head, frowning.

Briu held out a hand, and Nnanji hopefully passed him the sword. The middleranks looked it over. "Nice bit of metal," Briu said. "What do you think, Lan'o? Should I give Rusty his sword or should I push it down his throat till the guard cracks his teeth?"

Landinoro chuckled. "After this morning's affair, you best have a fast horse saddled if you plan to do that . . . might be worth it, though."

"Your boss buy this for you?" Briu demanded, testing the balance.

"H-he gave me Lord Hardduju's sword, adept," Nnanji stuttered. "And I sold it." Maybe this had not been a good idea.

The older men exchanged glances.

Briu looked hard at Nnanji. "That's a strange mentor you picked up. Brought you a lot of luck, hasn't he, apprentice?"

"Yes, adept."

"'Yes, adept,'" the Fourth echoed. "He hasn't brought me any, though." He was still looking over the sword, thinking. "He has guts, I'll grant you. I never saw a man walk to the Judgment after the fat man had done his feet. And he jumped head first—did you know that?"

"Head first?" Nnanji said. "From the Place of Mercy?" That was incredible—but Shonsu was all incredible.

"I've never seen that, either," Briu admitted. "Spread his arms out—thought he was going to fly away like a motherin' bird. We stayed to watch, saw him walk out of the water. Okay—we were pleased about that, although we all thought the fat man would move on him quick. Then we got back here, and the place was all unstrapped —the fat man dead and the thin man wanting my head in a basket, accusing me of giving the prisoner a sword, saying he couldn't have gone to the Judgment at all." He gave Nnanji a hard look. "Do *you* know where he got that unspeakable sword?"

A protégé shall not discuss his mentor...Nnanji stood at attention and sweated.

Getting no reply, Briu said, "There's odd stories going round about that sword. Do you believe in the legend of Chioxin, apprentice?"

Nnanji considered the question, and then said, "Yes, adept."

Briu pulled a face. "And after that I learned that one of my protégés had..." He paused and added sarcastically, "been insufficiently instructed regarding the third oath."

Nnanji said nothing.

"Not that you had any choice, apprentice. But it left me with a dirty job to do. And then he goes and accuses me of cowardice! Cowardice? What courage does it take for a Seventh to lip a Fourth? I thought I was dead when I gave him the sign."

Shonsu did not kill unless he must—but Nnanji could not say that, either.

Briu glanced at his companion and shrugged. Then he swung back to Nnanji and demanded, "You were going to take my signal this morning, weren't you?"

Landinoro slapped Briu on the shoulder. "I'll tell them you're coming," he said. He gave Nnanji a cryptic glance and tactfully departed. Nnanji wished he could go with him, even if he had to leave his new sword behind.

"Well?" Briu demanded. "You weren't going to roll over, were you?"

Nnanji squirmed. "I was going to ask for the grace, adept. You would have given me that, wouldn't you?"

"Three days?" Briu snorted. "You think this miracle man of yours can turn you into a swordsman in three days?" He shook his head pityingly. "I'd have tried to leave your arm and do your leg, but even that sometimes doesn't heal well enough."

Nnanji squirmed some more. "If I'd made obeisance you'd have demanded the abasement, wouldn't you?"

"So? Swords can be replaced. Hair grows back."

Nnanji was silent. He would rather die, much rather die than do those things.

Briu shrugged, raised the sword to squint along the edge. "And we all know why it was Rusty he ran into on the beach, don't we? Not Fonddiniji, or Ears, but Rusty."

"You always put me on beach duty when you had Death Squad," Nnanji protested.

Briu scowled at him. "You didn't like throwing rocks, did you, apprentice? You know why you were there—because you didn't want to know if we were throwing rocks. And I humored you, gods help me."

Only once had Nnanji seen a buyback. He had refused the silver he had been offered when the payoff came—and nothing had ever been quite the same since then.

"Who's first?" Briu snapped.

"A-adept?" Nnanji stammered, not understanding.

"Who's first? You've got a real live blue of your own now, haven't you? All to yourself. The guard would like to know, apprentice: which one of us does Rusty shout first?"

Why had he been such a fool as to ask Briu to dedicate the sword? Nothing that Darakaji or Fonddiniji could have done or said could have been this bad. He had told Shonsu that Briu was a man of honor, but of course that was a report made by a protégé to a mentor, so he could not tell Briu that, either.

"What do you expect me to do, adept? Dcnounce the whole guard? Do you think he would believe me? I saw no abominations! I witnessed nothing! The abominations were the fat man's. The rest of us followed orders. We're all men of honor when we get the chance."

Briu studied him coldly. "Some are. All of us took the money, all but you, apprentice."

"I don't think he cares!" Nnanji shouted.

The older man's eyes narrowed. "Then he isn't going to be reeve! He's going away?"

Nnanji wished he were somewhere else. Anywhere else. Jail would be fine.

After a moment Briu said, "You've got what you always wanted, then? You're going to be a free sword?"

"Adept . . . one seventy-five!"

Briu sighed. "No, you can't talk about Shonsu. But talk about you, then. You were his second when the thin man challenged. Why did you let him have a draw?"

Because Shonsu had signaled, with a nod. Was a nod an order from a mentor, which must not be discussed? Nnanji sweated some more and then said, "If my principal had wanted blood, he could have drained him on the first pass, adept."

"So I heard. But a second has discretion. Are you proud of your decision, apprentice?"

Silently Nnanji nodded. It was what Shonsu had wanted.

Briu frowned, then shrugged. "Well, I still have to decide what to do with this metal." Nnanji looked up hopefully.

"Open your mouth wide, Rusty," Briu said. Nnanji grinned with relief.

A party of swordsmen came out the door and started down the steps. Nnanji thought Briu would wait until they had gone, but he didn't. He dropped to one knee, held out the sword, and said the words of dedication: "Live by this. Wield it in Her service. Die holding it."

Reverently Nnanji took hold of the hilt and spoke the reply: "It shall be my honor and my pride."

Briu rose, seeming unaware of the surprised glances from the men going by.

"Thank you very much, adept," Nnanji said.

"Good luck, young Nnanji," said Briu. "Maybe you even deserve it."

"Thank you, adept," Nnanji said again.

"You're going to need it, you know."

"Why?"

Briu gave Nnanji a strange look, then said quietly, "One seventy-five!" He turned round and walked away.

Adept Briu was sworn to Master Trasingji.

††† † †††

The banners in the big mess hall hung limp in the noon heat. As he entered, Wallie hobbled conspicuously, more than necessary, for his feet were doing better than he had expected. There was no sign of Tarru. Only a dozen or so men were there, mostly standing and eating at the same time—lunch was evidently an informal snack. He headed for a trio of Fifths at a table and returned their salutes as they bounced up to greet him, then deliberately sat with his back to the room, to display a confidence he no longer felt.

Honorable Tarru had been summoned to a meeting of

some holy ancients' council. So the Fifths had guessed that Lord Shonsu was not to be their new boss. They were relaxed and almost friendly.

"I expect they will ask him to be reeve," Wallie said offhandedly, "at least temporarily." He helped himself to a roll and some soft yellow cheese, and accepted a tankard of the weak ale from a waiter. Then he smiled at his politely silent but obviously curious audience. "I did not accept their offer this morning. I have been ordered elsewhere."

"Ordered?" two of the Fifths echoed in horror.

So Wallie, between munches, gave them an abbreviated version of his story. It would not hurt to wrap his sword and himself in a little divine authority. He could not tell how much they believed.

Then another Fifth arrived and one departed, pausing on the way out to chat with some Fourths. Very soon the story would be everywhere. Tarru returned, accompanied by Trasingji of the Fifth, who seemed to be his closest crony—a large and craggy man with a dark complexion. He had startling white eyebrows and a bald spot that left him only a very wispy ponytail.

Tarru looked extremely pleased with himself and accepted congratulations. Of course it was just a temporary appointment, until a Seventh could be found . . .

And could arrive safely, Wallie thought.

He dawdled over his lunch, waiting for Nnanji, and waiting until he could get Tarru alone, but that turned out to be unnecessary. Tarru had just finished assuring him that he and his liegeman were most welcome to remain as the guests of the barracks for as long as they wanted, when he suddenly leaned across the table. He held out a fist to Wallie and palmed him the jewel. At least it felt like the same one, but Wallie put it in his left pocket so that he could check it later and make sure it had not shrunk.

"Is there anything you need, my lord?" the acting reeve inquired rather sourly. "Any favor we can do to make your stay more enjoyable?"

Payoff time . . . but Tarru had chosen this public forum so that he need not compliment Wallie on Nnanji's honesty.

"There is one thing," Wallie said. He was going to enjoy this. He glanced around at the obviously puzzled Fifths. "As you are all aware, I recently spent a couple of nights as guests of the guard in less salubrious quarters."

They frowned uneasily. Such things were not discussed among gentlemen.

"The prisoners are pinned by both ankles," Wallie said. "After a few hours this becomes extremely painful. Is this torture a recent innovation, or has it always been done that way?"

Whatever Tarru had expected, it was not a discussion of the jail. "It has always been done that way, so far as I know," he said, staring.

"Then if you change it, it will likely always be done the new way in future? And some prisoners are later found to be innocent. If you only pinned one ankle, they would have much more freedom of movement. Does the Goddess demand such torment? Is it just?"

The swordsmen looked at one another in astonishment—a strange idea, indeed! Who cared?

"A strong man could lift the slab if he could get close to it," Tarru suggested, frowning.

"I doubt it," Wallie said. "It takes two slaves, standing upright, to lift one end. Would you like to go over there with me, and I'll try? If I can't, then few could. They are very smooth, slimy chunks of rock."

Tarru seemed to come to a decision. "You have made a very good observation, my lord! I shall make it my first business in my new post—and while I am at it, I shall order a new roof for the jail. It certainly brings the Goddess no honor."

There was a surprisingly generous surrender! Then Wallie realized that Tarru's lost wager was not going to cost Tarru himself anything.

Tarru's eyes still kept wandering to Wallie's sword.

Gradually the others completed their lunch and rose to make their excuses and leave, until only Trasingji and Tarru were left. Then Nnanji came in and detoured around the table to make sure that Wallie saw him and knew he was back—or perhaps just to let as many people see him as possible. His kilt was brilliant yellow linen, with pleats as sharp as his sword. His boots were butter-colored suede, his harness shiny and embossed. A silver hairclip glittered beside the hilt of his new sword. He looked a trifle out of breath, as though he had been running.

Tarru and Trasingji glanced at each other and thereafter avoided Lord Shonsu's eye...which was just as well. Sevenths should maintain a certain dignity in public, and Wallie was turning bright red from suppressed laughter.

The exercise area was a courtyard, partially roofed, three sides open to catch any breeze that might wander in from the parade ground. It was unfurnished, except for a few full-length mirrors, some racks against the wall to hold masks and spare foils, and a small raised gallery for spectators. On that, Wallie stood for a minute to study the place. Nnanji, beside him, was twitching with eagerness to have his first fencing lesson from this superb Seventh.

Over the parade ground the afternoon sun raged. In that suffocating heat, the twenty or so swordsmen present were slouched around in groups, chatting listlessly. Wallie was looking now at the colors of their kilts and—so far as he could see—at their boots. He had done the same when he was leaving the mess hall, for Nnanji's new splendor had emphasized his previous shabbiness—the washed-out drabness of his kilt and the patches on his boots. Wallie was looking to see how many more impoverished swordsmen there were around.

He could see none. Perhaps Nnanji gave all his pay to his parents. Perhaps he spent it all on women.

Or could he be the only honest man in the guard?

Now they had been noticed. In a few moments all the men were masked and paired off, leaping back and forth, stamping up clouds of dust, and clattering foils with terrifying enthusiasm.

"We seem to have inspired some action," Wallie remarked sarcastically.

"They have heard that you are leaving, my liege. They are auditioning."

"The devil they are!" Wallie studied the fencing carefully through Shonsu's eyes. "Are these fairly average, or are they a duffer class sent in for extra practice?"

Nnanji looked surprised. "They are average, my liege." He started to point out some of the men, commenting on those who were thought likely to win promotion soon, a few who were thought to be slipping.

"Remembering that you don't repeat to anyone what I tell you," Wallie said after a while, "I will give you my opinion. They are the worst collection of ducks I ever saw outside a farmyard."

"My liege!"

"I mean it!" Wallie assured him. "I can't see one Third fencing like a Third, one Fourth fencing like a Fourth. Admittedly they're all so eager to show off right now that no one is left to supervise, but I find them disgusting. I'd drop them all one rank at least!"

Nnanji looked worried and said nothing.

Probably few of these swordsmen had ever fought a serious fight in their lives. They herded prisoners and bullied pilgrims and that was all. Most of them looked as though they had never had a proper lesson. Tarru was a good swordsman—did he not care?

"How many Seconds in the guard?" Wallie demanded suddenly, still leaning on the rail and staring in disbelief at this mass incompetence.

"Twelve, my liege, without me."

"How many of those can normally beat you in a best of three?"

"Two, maybe three," Nnanji said uneasily.

Wallie turned his eyes to look at him. He was very pink.

"And how many can you beat?"

Nnanji muttered, "Three."

"What! That doesn't make sense!"

"Briu says that my defense is very good, my liege. They rarely get a hit against me."

Wallie frowned. Unless his Shonsu expertise was starting to fail him, something was wrong there. Then he noticed a curious contraption at the far end of the court and forgot Nnanji's troubles for a moment. It was an edifice of massive beams and straps, and neither he nor Shonsu knew what it was. Long rods like pool cues stood in a barrel beside it.

"What in hell is that?" he asked, pointing, not able to believe what he was starting to guess.

"The whipping post, my liege."

Wallie wheeled to stare at his vassal. "And who gets whipped?"

Nnanji shrugged. "Mostly slaves. Some mentors use it on some protégés."

"And expect to make swordsmen of them?" Wallie looked once more at the whipping post, briefly again at the fencers. "Let's get out of here," he said, "before I lose my lunch."

In sulky silence, Nnanji followed his liege back to the royal suite, obviously assuming that the lesson had been canceled. They marched through the anteroom. "Close the door," Wallie said and kept walking until he was a safe distance into the great room.

"*Draw!*" he shouted, wheeling and drawing. Nnanji jumped and drew.

"Hey! Not bad!" Wallie said. "And with an unfamiliar sword, too!" He laughed at Nnanji's alarm. "Relax! Did you think I was going to start fencing with real blades? I was testing your speed—and you're a lot faster than Briu. A lot faster! Of course you're younger."

Nnanji beamed—he could have had little praise on his fencing for a long time, if he was third from the bottom of thirteen.

The guest chamber was almost as large as the fencing court. It was cooler and shaded and private. Wallie laid the seventh sword carefully on a lacquered table and moved a stool close to a silk-embroidered chair. He sat down with a sigh of pleasure, putting his feet up. Nnanji was grinning again, still clutching his sword.

"Not foils," Wallie said. "You need to learn the feel of that blade anyway. Now, guard at quarte. Show me a lunge."

Nnanji lunged and there was a pause.

"Terrible," said his mentor. "Foot turned in, thumb turned up. Limp wrist . . . elbow. Gods! The attack of the killer earthworm." He pointed at the mirror. "Try again over there. Now—how were you first shown? Use that memory of yours."

Nnanji lunged once more at the mirror, then adjusted his foot, his hand, his arm, his wrist. He tried again, went through the same process, and looked around uneasily.

"You're dead, apprentice," Wallie said quietly. "They're down at the armory selling your sword. Pity, he was a nice kid."

He lunged a dozen times and was wrong every time. Then Wallie had him concentrate on his wrist. He could do that, but when he tried to get his foot right as well, his wrist wavered as before. In half an hour he had gained no ground at all, and both Wallie and Shonsu were totally baffled. He stood up and gripped Nnanji's left hand.

"I'll take your weight," he said. "Try it very, very slowly." Like a slow-motion movie, Nnanji moved his arm, raised his right foot, and inched through the lunge. Wallie held him steady until his right foot came back to the floor. Constantly adjusting his position, Nnanji managed a travesty of a lunge. They tried that for a while, but the least increase in speed put him right back where he was before.

"It's your damned memory!" Wallie roared. "Can't you forget?" But apparently Nnanji could not, although he was almost insane with frustration. His bad habits had soaked in like the sutras. They tried a fresh start with his left hand, but he was no southpaw, and they gave up on that idea.

They tried with a foil. They tried with his old sword. They tried with his eyes shut. If Nnanji's distress had not been so obvious, Wallie would have thought he was playing games and doing as badly as possible on purpose.

"Well, let's try the celebrated defense, then," Wallie sighed. They pulled foils and masks from the massive iron-bound chest and faced off.

His defense was excellent, out of all proportion to the ineptness of his attack.

Wallie threw down the mask, slumped back into the chair, and folded his arms. Nnanji stood and looked at him with despair.

"It beats me," Wallie said. "Your reflexes are fine, and your defense is 'way above any Second I saw downstairs—Third at least, even by my standards. Your coordination is okay, because you make exactly the same mistakes every time. The only thing you can't do is lunge—and that movement is half of all swordsmanship. What you've got is a mental block."

But it did not come out as "mental block"—it translated as "curse," and Nnanji's eyes bulged. Wallie laughed uneasily and said perhaps they had better send for the holy mothers.

He pointed to another of the chintz-covered chairs. "Sit down and relax for a minute," he said. "Let me think about it."

Nnanji sat. He sank into the down filling. But he certainly did not relax. Wallie picked up the seventh sword and pretended to examine it.

"You were surprised at the price you got for your sword," he said quietly. "What do you suppose this one is worth?"

"I don't know, my liege," Nnanji muttered miserably.

"The holy Honakura says that it's priceless. He more or less said that it would fetch whatever you asked, as much as you could carry of anything. I'm told that there are brigands on the ferry trail."

Wallie continued to peer at the blade, and after a moment Nnanji said, "Yes, my liege," a little more attentively.

"I'm worried about our leaving, then," Wallie continued, still speaking to the sword. "You and me and Jja. I shall ask Honorable Tarru to provide us with a guard."

He wished that he dared look at his vassal, to see what expressions were chasing across his so-legible face. Surprise? Worry? Shame? Surely, eventually, Nnanji would work out that a Seventh could not be so naive? The comment came just a fraction sooner than he expected.

"I did swear to die at your side, my liege."

Then Wallie could look round, with a grin. He saw puzzled and rueful embarrassment. "Who would he choose, Nnanji?"

"I don't know, my liege. They didn't trust me."

"That's to your credit, I fear. But certainly I don't trust Honorable Tarru. Is there any other way out of this place?"

"None, my liege."

"What happens if we cross the River?" Wallie waved a hand in the general direction of the temple.

"Cross the River?" Nnanji said in horror.

"Well, if we could?" Wallie replied, puzzled. The River was the Goddess—was there some taboo against crossing? True, there were rapids and the water was wide, but three active young people could get across, even with a baby. "What's on the far bank?"

"Nothing but jungle, my liege. And the cliff . . ."

True, the cliff looked bad. Well, he would scout that

way himself. "Suppose we organized our own escort? Who would you invite? Granted that you tell me that they are all men of honor, which are the most honorable?"

Nnanji wriggled with shame. "I don't know, my liege! I tried not to know those things!" He was having a bad afternoon—first his inept fencing and now this—but Wallie could not afford to be merciful.

He pondered, squinting along the sword blade. The trouble with Nnanji was that he was too honest. What was needed was a little human fallibility, enough to know the ropes and who pulled them. "If we picked one man and asked him to organize a guard for us? Who?"

"Briu," Nnanji said, and then flushed at the surprised look he received. "He gave me my sword, my liege."

"The devil he did!" Wallie said. "Good for him—and good for you for asking! Well, he has no call to love me, but I suppose we could approach him."

Nnanji squirmed some more. "His mentor is Master Trasingji, my liege."

That was as close to an accusation as Nnanji was ever likely to come, and a warning. Even Briu was unsafe.

Wallie groaned. "I did not know that. Then how the hell do we get out? I need your advice, Nnanji. Remember Farranulu?"

Nnanji grinned.

#106   ON ESCAPE

The Epitome
When honor permits, a wise warrior fights on terrain of his own choosing. Whether at home alone or in the field with an army, he will always know of at least two routes of escape, and in most cases will also have prepared a place of concealment.

The Episode
When Farranulu's wife complained that the bedroom was cold with the window open, he instructed her that she would be even colder without him to share the bed.

The Epigram
When Death is present, the wise are absent.

"We could sneak out quietly, board some mules, and just risk it?" suggested Nnanji, whose thinking could never be devious.

"There is a guard on the gate," Wallie said. "He will have issued orders; he will know when we leave. We shall be followed, or else word will be sent ahead. They may already have an ambush prepared. Have you seen how he looks at this sword?

"Is there another gate?" he asked. "Any way around the end of the walls?"

"One gate," Nnanji said glumly. "And the walls end in the River."

Again this curious reluctance to go in the water! The prohibition must be very strong, and yet they used boats. But many Earthly religions allowed bare feet in their temples and prohibited shoes; religions need not be logical.

Nnanji sat and frowned ferociously, but nothing seemed to be coming of it. He was out of his depth.

Wallie had one vague plan he was not mentioning. If he could get Tarru alone, he could force him to swear the blood oath as he had forced Nnanji, for there was no doubt who was the better swordsman. Then he could make the acting reeve call in his protégés, one by one, and order them to swear also. Theoretically he could turn the whole guard into his vassals from the top down, diamonds and dirt together. The crooks would still be crooks and untrustworthy, but the good men would be true to their oath and surely they were in a majority? The disadvantage to that plan was that Wallie was Tarru's guest, so drawing his sword would be an abomination. Nnanji would die of shame if he knew that his hero was even contemplating such a deed.

"Horses," Nnanji said. "There are only a dozen or so

in the valley and they all belong to the guard." He looked at his liege hopefully.

"Brilliant!" Wallie exclaimed. "Bloody-handed brilliant!"

Nnanji tried to look modest and failed.

"Tell me all about them," Wallie demanded.

There was little else to tell. The valley road was so steep that trade goods and farm produce went on ox-carts, passengers on mules. The guard kept a few horses to service the advance post at the ferry, where there was usually a picket of three swordsmen and a priest. The temple stable was close by the gate. There was a guard of three men there, also.

"You can go see it tomorrow, my liege," Nnanji concluded.

"Not likely!" Wallie said. "I shan't go near it, I'm too conspicuous." They could steal the horses. That would be only a crime, not an abomination, and probably no one would question a Seventh's right to help himself to whatever he fancied. The horses must legally belong to the temple itself, so perhaps he could even make a deal with Honakura to buy them ahead of time. But that left the guards...

"I think you have found the answer, vassal," Wallie said. "Horse thieves we shall be. But I don't know if I can handle a guard of three men by myself, not without a massacre, and I'd much rather not have that. Overpower them and tie them up...I need a good swordsman to help me."

Nnanji's private hell fell over him again.

"So you'd better get back to practicing," Wallie said. "I need you. The sword needs you. The Goddess needs you, Nnanji." He pointed at the mirror. "One hundred lunges with a straight foot. Then we'll work upward."

Now that he had money, there were things to do. But his feet were throbbing, and he wanted to emphasize his lameness, so he used the bellrope to summon a slave. Then he sat back like the royal guest he was and had the barracks minions dance attendance on him for the rest of the afternoon, while Nnanji lunged away like a piston in front of the mirror. The tailor brought swatches and measured him. The cobbler traced his feet on leather, although he would have to guess an adjustment for shrinkage when the swellings went down. Whatever Shonsu had been doing for the last couple of months, he had not been getting his hair cut, so its new owner summoned a barber. Coningu had to have a gratuity, and Janu likewise, for she could make Jja's life a misery. Honakura's healer nephew came to change bandages and mutter a few prayers over Wallie's feet.

Wallie ordered his slave sent up at sundown, and a private meal for the same time. That was a breach of the precautions he had listed to Honakura, but for his first night with Jja he was willing to risk poison. He planned to re-create that strange candlelit dinner they had shared in the pilgrim hut, even if his quarters were now a hundred times as large. A cosy dinner, an intimate conversation to build a few dreams and find what common ground linked their vastly disparate heritages in the human experience . . . and then lots of that Olympic-class loving!

The afternoon wore on. He had hot water brought and took a bath, but this time without assistance. He kept an eye on Nnanji as he lunged and lunged and lunged.

He worked his vassal to exhaustion and made no progress at all. Finally, as the sun grew low, Wallie called a halt. Nnanji was ready to weep as he drooped on to a stool like a discarded shirt.

"You have a family in the town?" Wallie asked.

Nnanji colored and straightened up, taut and defensive. "Yes, my liege," he said, almost snapping the words.

Now what had Wallie said? "I wondered if you might want to go and visit them this evening. I shall be busy demonstrating swordsmanship to my slave and I don't need your help for that."

"Thank you, my liege!" Nnanji was clearly astonished at such consideration.

"You'll have a few things to tell them, I expect," Wallie said and got a grin. "And you'd better warn them that you're leaving soon."

But when? And how?

BOOK FOUR:

HOW THE SWORDSMAN WAS ENSNARED

†

"Put on the shoes now," Janu said, and steadied Jja's shoulder as she did so. Then Janu tapped on the door and led her in to her new master.

It had been a strange day. Jja's head was throbbing. She was trying very hard not to tremble. Now she must also try not to break an ankle, for she had not worn shoes since she left Plo, and never shoes with heels like these. She remembered to swing her hips and smile out of the corner of her eyes as Janu had taught her. Lord Shonsu rose to welcome her.

"The cloak!" Janu said.

Jja dropped the cloak and let Lord Shonsu see her dress. It was a very strange dress, all tassels and beads and nothing else. She was quite accustomed to being unclothed in front of men. That was her duty to the temple and the Goddess, and she did it every evening, but somehow she felt more naked than just naked in this dress. She had hoped that it would please Lord Shonsu, but she knew men well enough to see the shock and displeasure in his eyes. Her heart sank.

A very strange day—hot bath water and perfume and being rubbed with oil; the smell of her hair being curled with hot irons; the calluses being pared from her feet; her hands shaking as she was shown how to put the paint on her eyelids and lashes and face; the little sharp pains as they made holes in her earlobes to hang the glittery pendants . . .

The other slaves had told her that Lord Shonsu was going to be reeve and they had repeated all the stories about the last reeve and the horrible things he had done to slaves. But Jja knew most of those already. They had made jokes about how big Lord Shonsu was and how rough he would be, but she knew that he was not rough. They had told her that swordsmen beat slaves with the sides of their swords. She had tried to tell them of the promise Lord Shonsu had made to her about Vixi. They had laughed and said that a promise to a slave meant nothing.

"Thank you, Janu!" Lord Shonsu said. He closed the door loudly. There was a wonderful odor of food in that huge room, coming from under a white cloth laid over dishes on a table. But Jja did not feel hungry. She felt sick. She wanted to please her new master, and he did not like her dress. If she did not please him, he would beat her, or sell her.

Then he was holding her hands and looking at her. She felt her face turning red and she could not meet his eyes. He must be able to feel her shaking. She tried to smile as Janu had taught her to smile.

"Don't do that!" he said gently. "Oh, my poor Jja! What have they done to you?"

Then he hugged her, and she began to sob. When at last she could stop weeping, he fetched the cloth from the table and wiped the rest of the paint off her face, and off his shoulder, too.

"Did you choose that dress?" he asked.

She shook her head.

"What sort of dress would you like to be wearing?" he asked. "You describe it to me, and I'll imagine it."

Between sniffles she said, "Blue silk, master. A long gown. Cut low in the front."

He smiled. "That was what I said in the cottage,

wasn't it? I'd forgotten. I said you would look like a goddess. What did Janu say to that?"

Janu had said that slaves did not wear silk, or blue, and that long dresses were not sexy.

"They can be!" her master said firmly. "We'll show them! Now, take off those horrid things and put this on." He gave her the white cloth from the table, then turned away while she removed all the tassels and beads and glitter and wrapped herself in it.

"That's much better!" he said. "You are a gorgeously beautiful woman, Jja. The most beautiful and exciting woman I have ever met. You do not need vulgar clothes like that . . . that obscenity. Now, come and sit down."

He gave her wine to drink, and then later he wanted her to sit with him at the table and eat. He would not let her serve him. She forced herself to eat, but she still felt sick and wondered if that was because her own body smelled so strongly of musk and flower petals. He asked questions. She tried to talk. The pilgrims had never wanted talk, and she was not good at it.

She told him about faraway Plo and how it was so cold there in the winter that even the children wore clothes. He seemed to believe her, although no one else in Hann did. She told him what little she could remember of her mother—she knew nothing about her father except that obviously he had been a slave also. She told him about the slave farm where she had been reared. She had to explain about slave farms buying baby slaves to train. Talking to him was very difficult, and she knew she was doing it very badly.

"And I was bought by a man from Fex," she told him. "And when we went on the boat, we came to Hann, and the sailors said my master was a Jonah, but he said that I was the Jonah, because he'd been on boats before. He came to ask the Goddess to return him and he gave me to the temple as an offering."

Lord Shonsu looked puzzled, although he was trying not to, and she knew that she was a terrible failure.

Then at last, to her great relief, Lord Shonsu asked her if she would like to go to bed. She could not please him with talk, or with her new dress, but she knew how to please men in bed.

Except that even that did not seem to work properly. He would not let her do some of the things she had thought he would enjoy, things that pilgrims had demanded. She tried as hard as she could. He reacted as men always did, but she had a strange feeling that it was only his body reacting, that he himself was not pleased, as though his joy did not go very deep. And the harder she tried, the worse it seemed to get.

In the morning, as she was putting the cloak around herself, he said, "Didn't you tell me that sewing was one of the things you were taught in that slave farm?"

She nodded. "Yes, master."

He climbed out of the great bed and came over to her. "If we bought some material, could you sew a dress?"

He had already spent so much money on her, and she had not pleased him . . . Without taking time to think she said, "I can try, master."

He smiled. "Then why not try? Will the others help you if it is what I want?"

"I think so." She dropped the cloak. "Show me," she said bravely.

He grinned his little-boy grin and showed her—tight here and lifting her breasts like that and loose there and tight again down here and cut open all the way down here . . . "Why not a slit up here?" he suggested. "Closed when you stand, but when you walk it will show this beautiful thigh?" Suddenly she shivered all over at his touch and discovered that she was returning his smiles. He put his arms around her and kissed her gently. "Tonight we'll try again," he said. "No face paint and just a tiny drop of scent, all right? I'll tell Janu that's how I like my women served up—raw! I prefer you the way you are now, but any dress you make will be better than that thing."

Just when Wallie thought he was starting to make progress, there on a bed in the outer room was Nnanji, with two black eyes, several loose teeth, and a wide selection of pains and bruises. His new yellow kilt lay rumpled and bloodstained on the floor.

"Stay right there!" Wallie ordered as his vassal attempted to rise. "Jja, go and ask Janu to send up a healer." He pulled a stool over to the bed and sat down and glared at the wreck of Nnanji's face. "Who did it?"

The culprits were Gorramini and Ghaniri, two of the three who had beaten up Wallie for Harrduju's amusement. Wallie had thought them gone, but not so. Meliu had left after being snubbed, but the other two were still around, carefully staying out of the Seventh's way. Nnanji had returned from his parents' house and dropped in on the barracks saloon, probably to do a little flaunting and vaunting. Swords were prohibited in the saloon, but fist fights were not, and perhaps even encouraged as a safety valve.

"Well, that does it!" Wallie roared. "I owe them anyway, and now they have broken the laws of hospitality."

"You will challenge?" Nnanji asked nervously, licking his swollen lips.

"Challenge, hell!" his mentor said, almost ready to start grinding his teeth again. "That's an abomination! I shall denounce them and cut off their thumbs... I assume that they threw the first punch?"

Well, no... Nnanji had thrown the first punch.

One of the things Wallie had learned in his disastrous night with Jja was that Shonsu's vocabulary was greatly lacking in terms of endearment. He now discovered that it was rich in oaths, insults, obscenities, and vituperation. He told Nnanji what sort of idiot he was in sixteen carefully selected paraphrases, without repeating a word. Nnanji somehow managed to cringe while lying flat on his back.

"Well, two against one is still bad," Wallie concluded, and then looked suspiciously at his battered liegeman. "It *was* two against one?"

Well, not exactly. Ghaniri had insulted Nnanji. Nnanji had punched him and then been well punished for it. Ghaniri was a powerful fighter, as Wallie already knew —shorter than Nnanji, but much wider and heavier, with the crumpled nose and puffed ears of a bruiser. Then, when Nnanji had managed to get back on his feet again, Gorramini had repeated the insult, and Nnanji had tried to swing at him—and suffered an even larger disaster.

Now Wallie was too furious and astounded even to swear. "So instead of denouncing them, I have to go downstairs and crawl on my belly and apologize to Tarru for *you*? But what in the World could they have said to you that would make you behave so stupidly?" he demanded. "*What* insult is worth two beatings in a row?"

Nnanji turned his face away.

"Tell me, vassal. I order it!" Wallie snapped, suddenly very intrigued.

Nnanji turned his head back and looked up, grief-stricken. Then he closed his right eye and pointed at his eyelid, repeated the gesture with his left eye, and after that just stared in total misery at Wallie, who did not understand at all.

"I said 'tell me!' In words!" he said.

For a moment he thought his vassal would refuse, but he swallowed hard, and then whispered, "My father is a rugmaker and my mother a silversmith." He might have been confessing to incest or drug trafficking.

Fathermarks? Jja had mentioned fathermarks, and Wallie had not dared to ask her what they were. The god's riddle—*First your brother*...Wallie was instantly frantic to run to the mirror and inspect his eyelids—who ever looks at his own eyelids?

"So?" Wallie said. "They are honest? Hard-working? Kind to their children?" Nnanji nodded. "Then honor them! What does it matter what craft your father belongs to, if he is a good man?" The culture gap was staggering. Wallie opened his mouth to say that his father had been a policeman—and stopped just in time. In his mind he heard the shrill laugh of the demigod when he had made that statement to him. That might mean that the god had foreseen this very conversation, for policeman would translate as swordsman, so Wallie must not tell Nnanji.

However, Wallie Smith's father's father had dabbled in a great many fields in the course of a dubious career, including a couple of years in a carpet factory.

"It's an odd coincidence, though, Nnanji—my grandfather was a rugmaker, too."

Nnanji gasped. If hero worship were measured on the Richter scale, then Wallie had just registered nine and a half or ten.

"What does it matter, though? It's you who's my vassal, not your father. He obviously does a good job of making sons. Except for brains, of course, you witless cretin!"

At that moment a healer came bustling in. While he was examining the patient, Wallie slipped back into the main guest room and hobbled as fast as he could across to the mirror. Both his eyelids were blank. So much for that idea.

As he walked back, he thought about Nnanji. This absurd sensitivity about his nonswordsman background would explain his exaggerated ideals of honor and courage; overcompensation, although there was no such term in the World. Obviously a little psychiatry was required. If a hundred-kilogram, smooth-faced hunk of muscle could manage to imitate a cultured, bearded, Viennese doctor, it was time for Sigmund Freud. So, once the healer had reassured the valorous lord that there was no serious damage to his protégé, had accepted his fee, and departed, Wallie told the victim to continue lying where he was and perched himself back on the stool by the bed.

"Let's have a word about your fencing problem," he said. "When did it start? Have you always had it?"

Certainly not, Nnanji said, staring at the ceiling and speaking with difficulty because of his swollen mouth. As a scratcher, Novice Nnanji of the First had been a model recruit. Briu had said that he was the best natural-born swordsman he had ever seen. Briu had said that no one learned sutras faster or more accurately. Briu had told him after *two weeks* that he was ready to try for promotion—except that the guard had a rule requiring Firsts to be Firsts for at least a year. So it was on the anniversary of his induction into the craft that Nnanji had proved his swordsmanship with two matches against Seconds... "Boy, did I make a mess of *them*!" he lamented nostalgically.

Then he had plunged ahead, hoping to make Third in record time, also—and disaster had struck. One morning he had found that he couldn't connect with his foil against anyone, no matter what he did. And he had been that way ever since.

Now, Wallie thought, we are getting somewhere!

"Tell me," he asked, "did anything else important happen about that same time?"

The unbruised corners of Nnanji's face paled, his fists clenched, and his whole body went rigid. "I don't remember!" he said.

"You don't remember? *Nnanji* doesn't remember?"

Either he was lying, or the very act of trying to remember was enough to terrify him. No, he did not remember, he said, and he rolled over and buried his face in the pillow, and that was that.

Wallie was very sure that he could guess what had happened. The new Second had suddenly learned that the guard was not as pure and incorruptible as he had thought in his innocence. He was still idealistic and romantic—how much more so he must have been before that! How he had learned, whether or not he had been intimidated into silence, what he had been expected or forced to do... none of those things mattered. What did matter was that Wallie was no psychiatrist, that the language did not contain the right words, and that any attempt to explain all this to him would almost certainly make things worse instead of better.

"Right," he said, rising. "I can't denounce Gorramini and Ghaniri, and I shall have to crawl to Tarru. But I'm going to get even with them, anyway. With you."

"Me?" said a muffled voice, and Nnanji rolled over again.

"You! In a week or so, I'm going to put you up against them in fencing as part of your promotion to Fourth, and you are going to trash them in public."

"That isn't possible, my liege!" Nnanji protested.

Wallie roared. "Don't you tell me what isn't possible! I'm going to make a Fourth out of you if it kills you."

Nnanji stared, decided that his mentor was serious, and closed his eyes in ecstasy. Nnanji of the Fourth?!

"Now," Wallie said, "you have been incredibly stupid! You have embarrassed me and endangered my mission and delayed me. You are going to be punished."

Nnanji gulped and returned to the real World apprehensively.

"You are to stay in that bed until noon—no food, flat on your back. It is the best treatment for your bruises, too. And while you're there, you can try to remember what it was that happened just before you lost your lunge."

Wallie turned and strode to the door, leaving his vassal openmouthed. Then he remembered Nnanji's dogged willingness and fired a parting shot. "That doesn't mean you have to pee in the bed," he said, and left.

Breakfast was not a fun meal that morning. Tarru was waiting for him, holding court at a table in the center of the big hall with four Fifths flanking him, across from an empty space obviously reserved for Wallie. There were secret smiles all over the room as he entered—this was what happened to swordsmen who chose rugmakers' sons as protégés.

Wallie apologized for his vassal's behavior and assured his host that the man was being suitably punished. Tarru grudgingly accepted the apology and smiled. Why his smile always made Wallie think of sharks was a mystery, for the man's teeth were not pointed. His eyes were embedded in wrinkles like an elephant's, not glassy and smooth like a shark's. Gray hair was not sharklike. Perhaps it was just the way he eyed the seventh sword, giving a mental image of circling and waiting.

"Of course, insulting and provoking a guest is not good behavior for hosts, either," Wallie said as his bowl of stew was laid before him. "Perhaps I should have a word with those gentlemen's mentors. Who are they?"

"Ah!" said the acting reeve, with a curiously unreadable expression on his face. "They are not hosts, my lord, but guests, like yourself. They were protégés of Lord Hardduju. They asked to stay on for a while, and I agreed."

Clever! They had thought that Wallie would take Hardduju's place. If they had sworn to a new mentor within the guard, they would have been vulnerable. So they had obtained privileged status as guests, just as Wallie had done. A guest must behave himself toward another guest, of course, but now the Shonsu emergency was over...

"So they have no mentors?" Wallie asked, sensing something wrong.

"They have not sworn the second oath to anyone," Tarru agreed, face still blank.

Red flags were waving at the back of Wallie's mind, but he did not have time to search them out, for Master Trasingji of the white eyebrows suddenly turned to Tarru and said, "How is the work on the jail progressing, mentor?" in a singsong voice, as though he had been rehearsed.

"Quite well," Tarru replied. "It will go faster when we have more carpenters. Most of them are busy with the new work at the stables."

"I didn't know you had stables," Wallie said. "Is there anything that the temple does not possess?" He wasn't fooling anyone. Tarru had seen that escape hole and was plugging it, fortifying the stables and probably increasing the guard on them.

There was something wrong with the Fifths, too. Yesterday they had thawed out as soon as they learned that Shonsu was not going to replace Hardduju. This morning only Trasingji was meeting his eye.

Then Tarru rose, made his apologies, and departed. The four Fifths went with him like a bodyguard. So he had seen that way out, also—no blood oath was going to be imposed on him.

Wallie had been left alone in the middle of the hall. He sat and ate in solitary misery, feeling as though he were in a zoo, surrounded by secret grins. Ignorant iron-age barbarians! Bloodthirsty prehistoric thugs! He had promised the demigod that he would be a swordsman, but he had not said he would enjoy it. He despised this primitive, ignorant culture and its murderous hoodlums...

As soon as dignity allowed, he stalked from the hall and headed for the women's quarters. There he summoned Janu and gave her money so that his slave could make a dress. Janu's disapproving expression implied that he ought to make up his mind; did he want a whore or a seamstress?

Then he wandered out to the front steps and stood in black anger, glowering across the parade ground. Faint hammerings drifted over from the jail, and that was one small comfort. He was doing a small good there. But Nnanji was a hopeless psychiatric case, and his attempts to reward Jja were only loading her up with feelings of inadequacy and insecurity—perhaps she would have been happier left where she was, tending pilgrims, doing what she could manage. As for Tarru—if that small-time barbarian gang leader thought he was going to outwit Wallie Smith, then...

Revelation like a sheet of lightning!

Wallie uttered an oath that was half a wail. *Trap!*

Injured feet forgotten, he rushed down the steps and hurried off to the temple in search of Honakura.

††

The heat was incredible. Every day seemed to be hotter than the last, and now invisible waves of fire lashed the grounds, seeming to sear Wallie's flesh from his bones whenever his path led him into sunlight. At the temple he was escorted once more through the dim corridors and into the gloomy jungle courtyard, but even that felt like an airless oven. His harness straps were sticking to his skin. In a few minutes the tiny priest hurried in, and his blue gown was patched with sweat, as though to prove its occupant had not been totally mummified.

Today there were no polite pleasantries after the salutes. As the two men settled down on stool and wicker chair, Wallie blurted out, "I wish I had taken the job you offered, even if only temporarily."

"That might be arranged," the priest replied cautiously.

"It is too late," Wallie said. "Tarru has forestalled me. He is swearing the guard to the blood oath."

He explained what had suddenly become so obvious. Ghaniri and Gorramini had not sworn the second oath—they had sworn the third. Nnanji's ordeal had been ordered by Tarru, as a punishment for being honest and winning a bet for his liege.

The attitude of the Fifths had changed because they also had been made into Tarru's vassals, probably at swordpoint. They would resent it and feel guilty. That was why they had been unable to meet the eye of a man they might have to kill in dishonor.

Tarru had not merely seen all Wallie's possible moves and countered them, he had made one of his own—a beauty. Unbeatable! He was probably even then working his way down through the ranks, and when he had sworn every man in the guard, then he would be ready to spring his trap.

"If I make any move now," Wallie concluded, "then he will promote a coup. How many of the guard he has already sworn I cannot tell, but I expect it would be enough. The rest would obey their mentors first. I would be a reeve with no swordsmen."

He scowled. "I can't even kill the bastard now. Vassals are pledged to vengeance. Damn, damn, damn!"

Honakura comprehended at once, as he always did. "He has moved efficiently in his new post, my lord. He is repairing the jail and the stables. He has increased the guard on the gate. I understand the stables, but I admit that the jail puzzles me."

Wallie snorted and explained, although even the priest seemed surprised over his concern for mere prisoners. "So what do you do, my lord?" he asked.

"I don't know," Wallie confessed. "Sit tight and wait for my feet to heal, I think. It is too late now to think of recruiting more followers. Even if I knew the good men, they may have been preempted by the blood oath and ordered to keep silent about it. The damned thing takes precedence over anything."

"Ah!" Honakura said. "Then you will have to find followers who are not swordsmen. You must have six, you know." He stopped as a junior priestess scampered in to place a tray on the table between them, then nervously fluttered away again between the trees like a white butterfly. "Tell me what you think of this wine, my lord—it is a trifle sweeter than the one we had yesterday."

The goblets were silver instead of crystal, the little cakes even richer and creamier, clustered on a silver plate.

"Six? Why, for gods' sakes?" Wallie demanded.

"Seven is the sacred number." Honakura frowned at Wallie's expression. "The god told you to trust me, you said? Then trust me—it must be seven."

"Me and Nnanji and Jja and the baby . . . do you count babies? Do you count slaves?" Religions need not be logical.

The old man leaned back in his wicker cage and surveyed the airy canopy of branches above him for a few moments. "Normally I would not count slaves, but I think you do. So, yes, I think you could say that makes four." He waved the flies off the cakes and offered the plate to Wallie, who declined.

"How is your protégé?" the priest asked. "You tested his swordsmanship?"

"He couldn't fight his way across an empty courtyard!" Wallie sipped politely at wine he did not want. It tasted faintly like diesel oil. "Indeed Nnanji's problem has me baffled, and I would have your advice as an expert on people." Leaving out his theory that some traumatic experience had caused Nnanji's paralysis, he tried to explain the earthly concept of a mental block, finding suitable words only with difficulty.

Honakura nodded. "I have no name for that, but I have met it. I had a protégé once who got similarly tied up in certain sutras. He wasn't stupid, but on that one point he seemed to be totally obtuse."

"That's right! Did you find a cure?"

"Oh, yes. I had him flogged."

Wallie thought of the whipping post and shuddered. "Never! That is no way to make a swordsman."

"And your slave, my lord? Does she perform her duties assiduously?"

Conscious of those penetrating eyes upon him, Wallie smiled blandly. "She needs more practice, and I shall attend to the matter personally."

As well try to smuggle a plump antelope through a cage of lions. The priest studied him thoughtfully and said, "She is only a slave, my lord."

Wallie did not want to discuss his sex life, but he resented something there. "I intend to make her into a friend!"

"A slave? The gods have picked a man of ambition, I see." Honakura sat back with his eyes closed for a while and then smiled. "Have you considered the possibility that this slave girl and this young swordsman have been given to you as a test, my lord?"

Wallie had not. He disliked the idea very much.

"I sacrificed my principles by buying a slave girl," he said. "If the god was behind that, then he tricked me. But I am not going to flog Nnanji! Never, never, never!"

Honakura cackled. "You may be looking at it the wrong way. Perhaps it is a test to see if you are ruthless enough to have him flogged. Or perhaps it is a test to see if you are patient enough not to have him flogged?" Now he had made Wallie thoroughly confused and looked very pleased with himself.

Wallie changed the subject—there was so much to ask. "Tell me about fathermarks, my lord. I see that I have none."

The priest smiled. "I had noticed. That is very unusual; I have never met it before. Right eye shows father's craft and left eye the mother's, of course. Were you not a swordsman, people would ask you about it."

He smiled and let Wallie catch up with him. "But you met Shonsu that first day..."

"And then your eyelids had parentmarks," the priest agreed. "I don't remember them, but their absence is so unusual that I am sure I should have noticed."

"And I am supposed to find my brother! The god removed them?"

"Apparently," Honakura said complacently.

Wallie sat and brooded on his problems for a while and inevitably came back to Tarru.

"The god warned me that I must learn to be more ruthless," he said. "I should have killed him when he challenged me." Shonsu would have done so, probably any Seventh.

"Then you failed," Honakura remarked, "and have made you own job more difficult." He did not seem very worried, but then it was not his blood that was going to wet the sand. "But some of your problems cancel out, my lord."

"How do you mean?"

The priest counted on his fingers. "You were worried about brigands, dishonorable swordsmen in general, and about Tarru. You should also add priests, I regret to say —some of my colleagues believe that the sword of the Goddess belongs here in the temple, if it is indeed Her sword. But if Honorable Tarru is after it, then he will not alert the brigands, nor cooperate with the priests. And he must have his own worries about swordsmen."

That was true. The ungodly might well squabble among themselves over the loot. Unfortunately it was likely to happen after Wallie was dead.

"I suppose," Wallie said thoughtfully, "that the Goddess will eventually provide a new and more suitable reeve for Her temple?"

"Certainly, my lord."

Another Seventh? With another Seventh beside him, Shonsu could turn the whole guard into a plate of cutlets...

"Eventually," he repeated.

"Eventually," Honakura echoed. "We may be wrong, of course, but if you are indeed being tested, my lord, then I should anticipate that the replacement will not arrive until...until you have resolved your problems by yourself."

"Damn!" Wallie said. "I need time! Time to heal! Time to find some friends! I envision him working his way through the whole guard like a cancer, swearing them at swordpoint, one by one. When he has got them all, or nearly all, then he can strike—kill me, take the sword, and leave. If it is a fraction as valuable as you say, then he can throw away everything else and make a new life for himself somewhere. Or he can make himself master of the temple..."

He stopped, following the thought through and then observing the priest's quiet amusement.

"He wouldn't need the sword, then? He could pillage the treasure in the temple itself!" Wallie said. "It has been done? In all those thousands of years some reeve must have tried it?"

The wrinkled old face broke into a broad smile. "At least five times, although not for many centuries now, so

I suppose someone is about due to try again. Of course it does not work! First of all, your blood oath does not take precedence over everything, my lord. Your swordsman code puts the will of the Goddess ahead of the sutras, is that not so?"

"True. So the temple is protected? But I am not!"

"That is so, I'm afraid, but there is another protection—they must leave by boat." The priest chuckled and refilled the silver goblets.

Wallie stared at him blankly. "So?"

"So the boats don't go!" Honakura retorted, surprised by his obtuseness. "The Goddess will not cooperate with those who despoil Her temple!"

"Ah, you mean a miracle?" Wallie said.

No, said the priest, he did not mean a miracle, he meant the Hand of the Goddess. Boats went where She willed on the River, for the River was the Goddess . . .

"And the Goddess is the River," Wallie finished, his deep growl drowning out the toothless mumble of the priest. "Perhaps you had better explain, my lord."

It took a while, for Honakura could not comprehend how ignorant Wallie was of the ways of Rivers. There was only one River—it was everywhere in the World. No, it had no beginning and no end that he knew of. All towns and cities were on the River, like Hann. Usually Fon was downstream from Hann and Opo was upstream, but not always.

At last Wallie began to understand—the geography of the World was variable. Now Jja's story made more sense, and he asked about Jonahs. A Jonah, he was told, was a person whom the Goddess wanted elsewhere. If he or she stepped on a boat, then the boat went to that place. If the Goddess wished you to stay where you were, then your boat would keep returning. No, that wasn't miracle, Honakura insisted. It happened all the time. Wallie's sword, now, that was a miracle.

There were good Jonahs and bad Jonahs, but mostly they were good—which might be why the word translated fuzzily for Wallie. As soon as the Jonah was put ashore, then the boat was normally returned to its usual haunts and often granted good fortune.

The World sounded like a very interesting place. Obviously pillaging the temple treasury would not be a profitable operation, but the demigod had specifically warned Wallie that his sword could be stolen.

"Do not these priests you mention believe in the miracle?" Wallie asked.

Honakura scowled at the paving stones. "I am ashamed to admit that some of the priesthood are displaying a lamentable lack of faith, my lord. There is a group that believes... the legend says that the sword was given to the Goddess. There are those who interpret that to mean that it was given as an offering here, in the temple, that it has been hidden here somewhere, all these centuries." He looked up angrily. "I have been accused of giving it to you, Lord Shonsu!"

That explained Tarru's thinking, then.

Honakura laughed uneasily and again offered the plate, although he had eaten most of the cakes already. "Have faith, my lord! The gods do not choose idiots. You will think of something. But now it is my turn! Tell me about your dream world."

So, for the rest of the morning Wallie slouched limply on his stool in the hot courtyard and told Honakura what he wanted to know about the planet Earth—Jesus and Mohammed and Moses and Buddha, Zeus and Thor and Astarte and all the others. The little man drank it all in and loved it.

That afternoon Wallie made a reconnaissance. Accompanied by an equally shaky Nnanji—the two of them looking like disaster survivors—he made a complete circuit of the temple grounds.

The River might just be fordable in a few places, and the cliff might be climbable in a few others, but nowhere could he find both together. There were bad rapids downstream, so he need not dream of boats or rafts.

Now he knew that the canyon had been designed by the Goddess to protect Her treasures, so he was not surprised.

Both ends of the great wall stood, as Nnanji had said, in the water and in fast, deep, swirling water. There was no way around.

Wallie stood near the gate for a while and watched the pilgrims coming and going, plus a steady stream of artisans and tradesmen, slaves and carts. It was a busy place, the temple entrance, but now there were eight men on the gate, three of them Fourths. Once he had entered there unseen, but miracles were never produced upon demand.

The new work at the stables consisted of massive doors with wickets for the identification of visitors. A Sixth was required to know almost all the sutras, and Tarru was obviously familiar with those concerning fortifications.

The temple enclosure was a very comfortable place. But now, for Lord Shonsu, it was a very comfortable prison. How long would Tarru allow him to enjoy it? How long until he sent his army?

At sundown Nnanji seemed much better. He had even recovered most of his normal high spirits. Wallie informed him that this evening he was to be social secretary and protocol attaché—although in translation all that came out was "herald"—and they went off to the women's quarters to collect Jja.

She paused shyly in the doorway to let him admire her gown. That was not hard for Wallie to do. It would not have passed in Paris and it was still a shamefully sexist way to clothe a woman, but bare chests and harnesses and swords had their own sexual overtones, so perhaps they were evenly matched. She had chosen a pale aquamarine silk, so sheer that it seemed ready to blow away like smoke, and she had made a tight and simple sheath that displayed every detail of her gorgeous figure. The neckline plunged to her waist, her nipples glowed through the filmy material, and Wallie found that effect enormously more exciting than the previous night's tassels and purple paint.

When she started to walk forward, the slit he had suggested opened to reveal the smooth perfection of her leg. Nnanji gasped in astonishment and uttered a low growling sound, probably the local equivalent of a wolf whistle. Then he looked nervously at his liege.

Wallie grinned sideways at him, without being able to take his eyes off his slave as she approached. "As long as you only look," he said, "I will refrain from disemboweling you."

He thought Jja had worked her own private miracle. He kissed her fondly and told her so, and she shone with pleasure at having pleased her master.

Nnanji led the way to the place he called the saloon, the evening social center for the barracks. In the vestibule, an ancient one-armed attendant guarded a rack of swords. Nnanji dutifully drew his and handed it over. Wallie merely raised an eyebrow, not wishing to give Tarru his prize without at least some sort of struggle. The attendant smiled politely and bowed him through.

It was like no saloon that Wallie had ever seen, but there were hints of a bar, a ballroom, a restaurant, a club, a society salon, and a brothel. Most of it lay outdoors, on a rooftop terrace dotted with tables and illuminated by flaming torches along the balustrades. A group of musicians wailed in a strange seven-tone scale while young people pounded and cavorted on a dance floor. Bachelors leaned against a rail, drinking and commenting, laughing and quarreling.

For a society so formal and hierarchal, the nightlife was astonishingly relaxed. True, an upper balcony was reserved for highranks and their guests—Nnanji qualified, being with Wallie—but that seemed to be about the only restriction. The men mixed freely, accompanied by their wives or their slaves or the communal barracks girls, and they ate and drank and talked and danced.

Swordsmen, valuing footwork, were keen dancers and mostly good ones. The food and the drinks and the girls had to be paid for, probably to restrict consumption by high-spirited juniors, but Wallie was politely informed by the waiter that all services were free to guests. He chose a table on the upper level, sat with his left shoulder to the rail, observed the social life, and for quite a while was able to forget his worries.

Of course the highranks had to bring their wives to meet the Seventh, so he was constantly rising and sitting down again. Of course his slave must rise when he did. He noticed with amusement the careful study being given to Jja's dress and the subtle movements she made to display its properties. Long dresses were not sexy— apparently that had been the local creed, for almost all the women wore extremely short and gaudy garments much bedecked with sequins and tassels. Some wore only the tassels, as Jja had. The color coding of ranks seemed to be forgotten for recreational wear, at least here in the barracks, but her long dress was a surprise, and the men's expressions showed that the creed was due to be reconsidered.

After a while Nnanji asked to be excused and trotted down to the lower level. He was visible for a few minutes in a wild dance with one of the scantily dressed girls. Then he vanished. He returned in an astonishingly short while and drained an entire tankard of ale. He repeated the performance three times while they were eating dinner. Wallie decided privately that he must be indulging in inter-course intercourse, but unfortunately the pun would not translate.

The meal was almost over when a disturbance broke out at the far end of the balcony. Wallie came alert at once. Then the cause appeared out of the shadows, and he laid down his goblet to stare in astonishment. She was very large and very hideous, a female version of a sumo wrestler, her near-naked body trimmed with tassels and sparkles that emphasized more than concealed a bloated ugliness. Layers of paint on her face hid neither the wrinkles nor the badly broken and misshapen nose. She was old and scarred, wearing a spangled patch over her left eye. Rolls of fat and varicose veins and . . . "boobs like meal sacks," Nnanji had said. Obviously this must be Wild Ani.

Her arrival was causing consternation. It was a fair guess that a slave was not supposed to be there. Shonsu instincts: when there is a disturbance check around in case it is a diversion. At once Wallie saw the group of Seconds on the lower terrace, grinning and watching. He swung his eyes back to Wild Ani, and she was heading toward him, rolling her way through the tables. That sway came from more than obesity.

A couple of Fifths guessed her destination and sprang up to block her path.

"Shonsu!" she cried, spreading her arms and staggering slightly. Then the Fifths reached her and grabbed, determined that the noble guest not be insulted.

Obviously the juniors had liquored up the old woman and sicked her on to Shonsu for sport. A slave might well get beaten for that.

"ANI!" he boomed in his thunderous voice. He jumped up and held out his arms, while Nnanji gulped in horror. "Ani, my love!"

The Fifths released her and turned round to stare incredulously. Ani blinked, then straightened up with intoxicated concentration. She resumed her progress, weaving between the outraged diners all around the balcony until she reached Wallie, peered curiously with her single bloodshot eye, and repeated, "Shonsu?"

"Ani!" he said, still holding out his arms. She was huge—almost as tall as he, and half as heavy again. She simpered to show brown stumps of teeth, then embraced him fervently. It was like being attacked by a waterbed.

Now Nnanji had seen the plot. Grinning in great delight, he rose to offer his chair. Ani collapsed on it and eyed the noble lord suspiciously. "I don't know you!" she said.

"Of course not," Wallie said. "But we can correct that. Waiter—a flagon of your best for the lady."

The waiter rolled his eyes in horror. Jja was being totally inscrutable, perhaps not understanding. Nnanji was turning purple, suppressing giggles. The highranks and their wives were not sure whether to be disgusted or respectfully tolerant. Down below, the young blades had their mouths open.

Ani was trying to understand. "Do I know you?" she asked in a slurred voice. Then she accepted a large goblet of wine, drained it at a gulp, and belched. She went back to studying Wallie. "No, I don't," she said. "You're not a scratcher, are you? Pity." She held out the goblet for a refill and noticed Nnanji. "Hi, Rusty," she said. "Want your usual later?"

Nnanji almost disappeared below the table.

After the third glass she seemed to sober up for a moment and visibly counted Wallie's facemarks. "I'm sorry, my lord," she muttered. She attempted to rise, but failed.

"It's all right, Ani," Wallie said. "The Seconds put you up to this, didn't they?"

She nodded.

"You going to be in trouble, Ani?"

She nodded again, then brightened, and emptied the goblet once more. "Tomorrow!"

Wallie looked at Nnanji. "If I went off with Ani to wherever you go to, then she wouldn't be in trouble, would she?"

Nnanji agreed, looking outraged, astonished, and intensely amused, all at the same time. "There are more beds through that door, my liege."

"Right!" Wallie said. "Stay and look after Jja for a minute." This would be hard on his feet, but Ani was probably no longer capable of leaving under her own power.

He crouched, slid his arms under her, and—after a suspenseful moment when the issue hung in the balance —lifted her up. He carried her out, and perhaps even

Shonsu himself had never worked those muscles harder. Enthusiastic cheering rolled up from the lower level.

Nnanji had been correct. The door led to a big, dim room with six beds in it. One in the far corner was creaking mightily, but the rest were empty and the light was dim, a single lantern. Wallie deposited his burden as gently as he could and ruefully rubbed his back.

Ani lay and stared up at him, her one eye wide. She was not too drunk to see his fingers slip into his money pouch. "No need, my lord. I'm one of the free ones."

"I'm not buying tonight, Ani," he whispered, "but don't tell the others. Here." He gave her a gold, which vanished instantly into a garment that did not seem capable of hiding anything.

She lay and looked up at him blearily for a while and then, understanding at last, said, "Thank you, my lord."

He sat down on the bed and grinned at her. She smiled back uncertainly. Someone departed from the far corner, boots clacking on the floor. In a few minutes Ani was snoring.

Wallie waited a reasonable time and then went back to the table. He smiled reassuringly at Jja and said, "I didn't."

"Why not, my liege?" Nnanji inquired, with an innocent grin.

"I think I put my back out before I got there." Wallie reached for the wine bottle. He was not entirely joking.

They did not linger long after that. He led his slave across the floor with every eye on them, and slaves bore flames before them to the royal suite.

"Now do you believe in long dresses?" he asked when they were alone.

"Of course, master! But Apprentice Nnanji would not. It is difficult to take off."

"That's part of the fun," Wallie said. "Let me show you."

But none of it was fun for Jja. She was as diligent and hard-working and frantically eager to please as she had been the previous night. The purely physical part of him, the Shonsu part, took its animal pleasure as before, but the Wallie Smith part suffered more agonies of postcoital depression. It was not her fault—he was too ravaged by guilt at being a slave owner to enjoy anything.

In the pilgrim cottage she had offered comfort. In the royal suite she was doing her duty. And that was not the same thing at all.

†††

The next day Jja found the courage to suggest—very tentatively—that her gown might be improved by a little embroidery. She wanted to copy the griffon from the sword. Of course Wallie enthused, so the middle of the morning found Jja sitting in a corner of the great guest chamber sewing, with the seventh sword before her.

Despite his shattered appearance, Nnanji insisted that he was well enough for fencing. In fact, Wallie could now see that his injuries were superficial, as the healer had said. Undoubtedly, then, the real culprit was Tarru. Gorramini and Ghaniri had been obeying orders, but reluctantly. They had concentrated on appearances and avoided doing any real damage at all. And that, in turn, was a lesson in the difference between obedience and loyalty.

Fencing it was, then. Masks came out of the chest, and Wallie selected the shortest foil he could find.

The swordsmen used no protective garments except masks with neck guards, and therefore all lunges and cuts must be carefully pulled to avoid injury. Of course that habit then tended to carry over into real swordwork —and so reduced what would otherwise have been a monstrous mortality rate in the craft. Vulnerable spots, such as collarbones and armpits, were strictly out of bounds. Any swordsman who injured a fencing partner became known as a butcher and soon found himself blacklisted.

"Now," Wallie said. "I shall try to fight like a Second —a real Second, not a temple Second."

He discarded most of his bag of tricks and slowed down to snail pace. He was still too good for Nnanji to hit, but he wasn't hitting, either. "Your defense is great," he announced approvingly. "Wrist! Foot! Damn! If you could only put on an attack to match...watch that thumb!"

He tried everything he could think of, and nothing helped. The killer earthworm was still there. If his patience was being tested, he was about to fail. Nnanji grew madder and madder with himself until he threw down his sword, ripped off his mask, and swore a bucketful of obscenities.

"I'm no damn good!" he shouted. "Why don't you just take me down to the whipping post and beat me?"

Wallie sighed. The man needed a year's psychoanalysis, and there was no time. He had only one idea left to try.

"Would that make you feel better?" he asked.

Nnanji looked surprised, concluded that his courage was being questioned, and defiantly said, "Yes!"

"I don't want you to feel better," Wallie said. "I want you to feel like the useless dumb brat you really are. Now put on that mask."

Nnanji guarded and got a stab in the ribs from the button of Wallie's foil. It raised a red welt.

"Ouch!" he said accusingly.

"I think you're scared to hit me . . ." Wallie struck him brutally across the chest.

"Devilspit!" Nnanji staggered with the force of the blow.

"Because I'm a swordsman . . ." Wallie banged his foil on Nnanji's mask. "And you're only *rugmakers' trash!*" Then Wallie hit him insultingly on the seat of his kilt.

It could easily have failed. With his self-respect in ribbons, now rejected by his hero, Nnanji might readily have collapsed like a wrecked tent and gone back to herding pilgrims for the rest of his life. But the gods did not put red hair on a man as a warning of nothing. His temper exploded again, and this time it was directed outward, at his tormentor. Perhaps it was even Wallie's own rugmaking grandfather who determined that. He screamed in fury at the insult, and the fight was on.

Wallie butchered. He slashed at Nnanji with the foil, he jabbed him with the button end, and he kept up a stream of all the abuse he could think off—show-off brat, brothel hog, pilgrim pusher, throwing his money around in bars, not a friend who would stand up for him ... Every time he got another bruise Nnanji said *devilspit*! But he kept coming, and his attack grew wilder and wilder.

"Cripple! You couldn't hit the side of the temple if you had your nose on it!"

Wallie jeered and called him a weakling, a pretty-boy gelding, an impotent pansy, and a carpet beater. Nnanji's face was invisible, but his oaths grew louder, and even his chest was turning red. His ponytail whirled like a flame. It was hard work for Wallie, for he had to hold himself back to a low standard, avoid doing serious hurt, evaluate Nnanji's moves almost before he made them— and keep up his insults, all at the same time.

"I don't want a half-baked First. I need a fighter. I'd give you back to Briu, except he wouldn't take you."

Nnanji was screeching incoherently through his mask. Failing to connect, he unthinkingly started to experiment, and at last he achieved a lunge that was much better than anything he had done before. Wallie let it through. He staggered under the impact and wondered if it had broken a rib.

"Lucky one!" He sneered. The comment was fair, but it did not sound fair. The next lunge was about the same, so he parried it to a near miss. Then came a wickedly straight cut. That had to be allowed to pass, and then Wallie was bleeding also. He started to ease up on his hits, but now Nnanji was howling like a pack of hyenas and trying everything possible. The bad ones failed, but each time Wallie detected an improvement he let the blow come, and soon he was hurting almost as much as his victim. They battered and yelled and cursed like maniacs.

Finally he knew he had won. The strokes were coming hard and accurate, and so deadly that he was in danger of being maimed. "Hold it!" he yelled, but Nnanji either did not or could not stop now. Wallie cranked up to Seventh again, striking the foil right out of his hand. Then he grabbed him in a bear hug. Nnanji screamed and kicked, and went limp.

"You did it!" Wallie said and let him go. He pulled off the masks. Nnanji's face was almost purple, and his lip was bleeding.

"What?"

Wallie dragged him over to the mirror and thrust his own foil into his hand. "Lunge!" he said.

Angrily Nnanji lunged at the mirror. He did it again. Then he turned to Wallie, understanding at last. "I can do it!" With a banshee yell he started capering around the room, waving his arms in the air.

Wallie felt like Professor Higgins—everyone into the Spanish dance routine. He slapped Nnanji on the back. He laughed and assured him that he had not meant any of those things he had said, and generally tried to calm him. Unbelieving, Nnanji just kept dancing back to lunge at the mirror, and then go whirling around once more. The block was gone.

"I did it! I did it!" Then Nnanji looked at his wounds and at Wallie's, and his face fell. "You did it. Thank you, my liege! Thank you! Thank you!"

Wallie rubbed an arm over his forehead. "You're welcome! Now—quick, before you stiffen up! Run down and do some cooling off exercises, then get in a hot tub. Scat!"

Wallie slammed the door behind him, leaned against it, and closed his eyes. He needed the same treatment himself, but he also needed absolution. He felt soiled, foul, perverted. Who had been tested? Could it have been Nnanji? Or was it a test to see if Wallie could be bloody-minded? He had sworn not to beat the kid and then he had done just that. What price scruples now? He was worse than Hardduju.

He opened his eyes and Jja was standing before him, studying him with those huge, dark, and inscrutable eyes. He had totally forgotten her in her corner. She had seen it all. What must she think of this sadistic horror who owned her?

"Jja!" he said. "Don't be scared, please! I don't usually do that sort of thing."

She took his hands. "I'm not scared, master. I know you don't."

"I've mutilated him!" Wallie said miserably. "He'll ache for weeks. He'll have scars for life!"

She put her arms around him and her head on his shoulder, wet and bloody as he was, but it wasn't sex she was offering—it was solace. He drank it like a man dying of thirst.

"Apprentice Nnanji is a very tough young man," she said. "I think that lesson was a lot harder on Wallie than it was on Nnanji. He won't care."

He grabbed at the thought. "He won't?"

She chuckled into his ear. "They're only bruises, master. He'll wear them like jewels. You've given him back his pride!"

"I have?" Wallie began to relax. "Yes, I have, haven't I?" The test had been passed. He had made his swordsman, and . . . "What did you call me?"

She stiffened in sudden apprehension. "That was the name you used that first night, master. I am sorry."

"Oh, don't be, Jja! You are welcome to call me that." He held her away from him to look at her. "What do you know of Wallie?"

She stared up at him, puzzled and unsure of the words to express her thought. "I think he is hiding inside Lord Shonsu," she said shyly.

He hugged her tight again. "You are so right, my sweet. He is lonely in there, and he needs you. You can call him out anytime you want."

Although he was not to understand in full for some time, that moment was dawn. While Nnanji had been breaking down his mental block, Jja had been building one of her own—a strange discrimination between her owner and her man. Somehow she had made a distinction between them, in a purely emotional way that could never have been put into words and would have driven Honakura mad. Different world or far country were of no interest to Jja. It might even be that this Wallie, being hidden inside her owner, was invisible, and hence had no facemarks. But it was doubtful that her thought process even went that far. It was a matter of feelings. She had seen him weep in the pilgrim hut. Now he was full of sorrow because he had hurt his friend. If he was troubled she could soothe, comfort, lend him her stoic slave's strength to accept what the gods decreed. He would react then as a man, not a master.

And Wallie had found the friend he needed, another lonely soul hidden from the World, hiding inside his slave. The analysis came later, although he would never dare to question very deeply, lest he break the spell by reducing it to logic.

"Wallie?" she said shyly to his shoulder strap, trying the word. "Wallie!" She said it four or five times, each time with a meaning subtly changed. Then she held up her face to be kissed, and the kiss said more than words ever could. She led him over to the bed and showed him again how the smallest god could drive away the god of sorrows.

Wallie jerked his head up and reached for his sword as the door flew open, but it was only Nnanji returning. He had done as he had been told and had now came back to mount a ferocious attack on the mirror, although many of his cuts were still dribbling blood down to his kilt, and any sensible man would have gone in search of a healer. He barely glanced at the two limp, sweat-drenched figures on the bed. The People saw no great significance in nudity, and sex to Nnanji was merely another enjoyable bodily function, like eating. He would have been very surprised had his mentor complained at having his privacy disturbed. Indeed probably Nnanji's only thought on the matter was to hope that Shonsu would hurry up and recover so that they could get back to important work like fencing.

Wallie sank back into the downy softness and studied Jja's face for a moment. A stripe ran down the middle and a tiny vertical bar on each eyelid . . . slave and child of slaves. Her eyes opened, and she smiled at him in drowsy contentment.

His doubts of the previous day had fled. He had been right to take her away from Kikarani. They could make each other happy, be lovers, and even friends.

If Tarru let them . . .

"The god of sorrows has returned, master?" she whispered. "So soon?"

He nodded.

Now it was she who studied him. Then she said, "Honorable Tarru is swearing the swordsmen against you?"

Surprised, he nodded once more.

She guessed his thoughts. "The slaves know everything, master. They told me."

He felt a surge of excitement. Friend! He had been committing the very crime he had denounced in the People, thinking of a woman as a possession, a mere source of physical pleasure.

"Would they help?" he asked. "Would you?"

She seemed surprised that he would ask. "I will do anything. The others will help, also. Because of Ani."

"Ani?"

She nodded solemnly, her face so close to his that it was hard to focus. "Ani would have been beaten, master, had you not accepted her."

So that trivial half kindness, half joke had earned him the friendship of the slaves, had it? There were many slaves around the barracks, he now realized. He had barely registered them. Probably nobody else noticed them at all. They must be privy to all the secrets. Of course his actions with Ani would be known. Ani was a slave herself. Likely there had been another in the corner bed.

He was still pondering the implications of a slave army when Jja said, "If you try to leave with the sword, he will stop you, master? That is what they told me."

"Yes."

"If I carried it out for you?"

He started to smile as the ideas began to flow together.

"No," he said. "I don't think so. The swordsmen know you—you would not even get down the stairs, Jja. You would be stopped if you were carrying a long bundle, a roll, a . . ."

He sat up and yelled, "Nnanji!"

At once Nnanji stopped his lunging and swung round: "My liege?" He was grinning insanely. He, too, would do anything—he would eat hot coals if his mentor asked him.

"You told me you had a brother?" Wallie asked.

Looking surprised, Nnanji walked over, sheathing his sword. "Katanji, my liege."

"How old is he?"

Nnanji turned pink. "He is old enough to shave," he confessed.

Momentarily nonplussed, Wallie raised a hand to his own smooth chin. Then he realized that Nnanji was not thinking of chins—Nnanji meant that his brother ought to be wearing a loincloth. Poor families had trouble finding crafts for their children. Payment to admit Nnanji to the swordsmen had been a bribe, but artisan mentors demanded initiation dues quite openly.

"Is he trustworthy, really trustworthy?" Wallie asked.

Nnanji frowned. "He is a hellion, my liege, but he always seems to talk his way out of trouble."

"Is he loyal to you, then? Would you trust him with your life?"

Now Nnanji was truly astonished, but he nodded.

"And he wants to be a swordsman?"

"Of course, my liege!" Nnanji could not imagine a higher ambition.

"Right," Wallie said—he had no choice that he could see. "Jja will go and find him. I have a job for him. If he performs it faithfully, then he can have any reward that it is in my power to give."

"You would take a scratcher as a protégé?" exclaimed the vassal who had been little more use than a scratcher himself an hour before.

"If that's what he wants." Wallie smiled. "But you're going to be a Fourth next week, remember? We can make you a Third today if you keep lunging the way you were just now. He can swear to you or me, I don't care."

If either of them survived, of course.

Nnanji's battered appearance at lunch provoked much silent hilarity—the Seventh had obviously lost his temper with his notoriously inept protégé. Only the perceptive might have noted that Lord Shonsu had acquired more bruises and cuts himself, or wondered why the apparent victim was grinning so idiotically.

That afternoon Lord Shonsu proved to be a demanding guest. He sent for the tailor again, and the cobbler. Healer Dinartura arrived and saw the need to call in second, third, and fourth opinions on the noble lord's feet; he also carried away a secret message to his uncle. The barracks masseur was summoned. Priests began to call, bearing mysterious packages. Lord Shonsu decided to buy a saddle and sent for the saddler. He demanded music, so musicians came and went all afternoon. He wanted his slave to sew more gowns, and drapers attended with their rolls of silk. Bath water was required —not once, but twice, because of the unrelenting heat.

Finally, toward sunset, even Lord Athinalani came from his armory, accompanied by two juniors bearing carrying cases full of swords. If Tarru was keeping himself informed about all this meaningless activity, the identity of that last visitor might have warned him what was happening. But by then it had already happened.

Just before sunset the heat broke in a spectacular thunderstorm. Rain dropped in layers from a sky of coal. Thickets of lavender lightning jigged above the temple spires. The gold plating would make those spires good lightning rods, and some other divinely inspired accident of design had obviously made them well grounded.

To Wallie and Nnanji, watching from their palace suite, the thunderclaps hit like blows to the head, leaving their ears ringing.

"The gods are angry, my liege," Nnanji said uneasily.

"I don't think so. I think they are laughing their heads off."

The social hour started later than usual, after the rain, but the night was wonderfully cool, and the torches hissed and steamed around the terrace, reflecting up from the wet flagstones. As the noble guest paraded his tiny entourage across the floor, all eyes turned to watch. With carefully concealed amusement Wallie registered the puzzled glances as the swordsmen tried to work out what was different, the dropped jaws and exclamations when they succeeded.

It was not the battered condition of his protégé that elicited surprise, nor the lithe figure of his slave in her blue gown decorated with a silver griffon on the left breast—half the women in the place were this evening wearing similar gowns, now known as "shonsues." No, the attention was directed toward the valorous lord himself, and his empty scabbard.

Lord Shonsu had checked his sword at the door.

Tarru was not present, but three Fifths attempted an inconspicuous stampede out to the vestibule. There the ancient, one-armed retainer exhibited for them the sword that the noble lord had left with them. They probably recognized it—a travesty of a weapon, pig iron, not fit to stop a charging rabbit.

The sword had been checked.

So had the swordsmen.

Your move, Honorable Tarru.

†† ††

Honakura's spy network had been operating efficiently, as usual, and he greeted Wallie and his brand-new sword the next morning with much toothless chuckling and delighted wringing of hands. The shady courtyard was cool and damp, the bougainvillaea sprinkled with diamond dust. The air was fragrant.

"I told you that you should not underestimate the Goddess' champion!" he said, producing an extremely dusty clay bottle. "This, my lord, is the last bottle of a famous vintage, the Plon eighty-nine. I open it in honor of your victory!"

"It's no victory!" Wallie protested, settling once more on the familiar stool. "But I have won the time I wanted."

"A hit, but not yet the match?" Honakura asked with another chuckle. "Do I have that right?" He put the bottle on the little table and stood over it, fussing with a knife to remove the wax seal. "You greatly frightened my nephew—he was convinced that the demon had returned. You also worried me, my lord. When Dinartura told me that you wanted to be visited by priests bearing long packages, I thought you were going to pass the sword to me. I was much exercised to think of a safe hiding place. Then all the packages returned unopened..." He laughed again, spraying spit. "There!" He poured the wine.

Wallie sniffed the wine in its crystal chalice, sipped,

and paid compliments. It wasn't bad at all, not unlike a fair Muscatel.

"They searched your quarters, I understand?" Honakura asked.

"At least four times, from the look of the place," Wallie replied. "I sent for Coningu and raised a typhoon of complaint. The bed was half shredded! There were feathers everywhere."

The old priest almost choked on his drink. "What did Master Coningu have to say?"

"He dropped a broad hint that the culprit was beyond his jurisdiction," Wallie said. The old commissary obviously disapproved of Tarru and might be a valuable ally. "So now the treasure hunt is on, but I had many visitors yesterday. He can't know which one took it."

Honakura nodded with glee. "And who can he trust to search? The honest men, who disapprove, will doubtless be perfunctory in their efforts; the dishonest would move it to another hiding place. He cannot search everywhere himself."

He sipped his wine in silence, savoring Tarru's untenable dilemma, then raised a nonexistent eyebrow. "Would you tell me in general how you did it?"

"With pleasure." Wallie had been waiting for the question. "The trickiest part was smuggling it downstairs and out of the building, for there were watchers, and I am followed wherever I go. The sword would certainly have been noticed. What I did not know was whether Nnanji was also being followed . . ."

So, while Jja had gone in search of Nnanji's brother, Wallie had instructed Nnanji in how to detect a follower. Nnanji had been disappointed to learn that this was not a sutra, but Wallie had merely been quoting the standard practice set forth in spy stories—dodge into doorways, backtrack without warning, and so on. He had even given some advice on losing a tail, although the temple grounds lacked the taxicabs and hotel lobbies recommended by the spy-story writers. Accepting this as a game, Nnanji had headed for the gate to let himself be seen by his brother, Katanji. And Katanji, as instructed, had followed him at a distance back to the barracks.

Honakura's eyes gleamed. "His brother has black hair?"

"Yes," Wallie said. "I couldn't have risked it if . . . How did you know that?"

"A lucky guess," the priest replied, smirking and obviously lying.

Wallie frowned, then continued. "Of course the guards on the gate paid no attention to a naked boy bringing in a rug. He followed Nnanji, and they both slipped into the bushes below the balcony. And I dropped the sword to them."

Honakura was aghast—he knew the height of the barracks. "You *dropped* it? It wasn't smashed?"

Wallie explained parachutes. He had attached a pillowcase to the hilt with four lengths of Jja's thread. It had not been enough to slow the sword's fall very much, but it had made that superbly balanced weapon drop point downward, and Chioxin would have designed it to take impact from that direction. Only a buried rock could have caused damage, and that he had had to chance.

As things had turned out, what the seventh sword had encountered had been a buried tree root. That had proved to be a problem. Katanji had heaved and strained without success—the sword had remained firmly planted, while Wallie had held his breath on the balcony above. It had made him think, in a mildly hysterical way, of Mallory's tale of the boy Arthur: *Whoso pulleth out this sword of this stone and anvil is rightwise King born of all England.* In this case the boy Arthur's lanky older brother had been standing by in the undergrowth and had emerged to try. But Chioxin would not have foreseen tensional stress, and Wallie had been suffering nightmare visions of the hilt coming loose from the tang. In the event it had been the blade that came free from the root, and Sir Kay–Nnanji had fallen flat on his back, while the boy Arthur collapsed in a fit of nervous giggles.

"Of course," Wallie said, "the guards should have investigated a boy carrying a rug *out* of the grounds, but it was so hot yesterday . . . and he has a rugmaker's father-mark, so a story about repairs would have been believed. Jja was watching. She says he walked through without being questioned at all."

The old priest frowned. "That priceless sword is now in the home of a rugmaker?"

"Certainly not!" Wallie snapped. "Much too obvious!"

He sipped wine, enjoying the expression on Honakura's face—had anyone ever before had cause to tell Honakura that he was being too obvious? Then he continued.

"At breakfast this morning—and, by the way, you could tell who was on my side from the grins when I came in . . . not that I can trust even those men any more. Where was I? Yes, Tarru was not there, but Trasingji was . . ."

Wallie and his protégé had finished breakfast in their usual seats. Then their way out had taken them past Trasingji, sitting with two other Fifths. Wallie had stopped to accept their salutes. Only a slight lowering of the feathery white eyebrows had hinted at Trasingji's thoughts, but his companions had been grinning openly at the Seventh.

"Tell your friend this," Wallie had said. "I do not know where it is. Nnanji does not know where it is. Nor do his parents—it is not at their house. In fact it is not in the town at all. All this I swear by my sword. The Goddess be with you, master." And he had stalked out, feeling very pleased with himself. There was nothing more holy to a swordsman than the oath of his craft, so he would probably be believed.

"I see," Honakura said. "I think. So he knows that it is still within the grounds?" The priest was peeved at being mystified by a mere swordsman. He knew that Wallie knew that.

Wallie nodded. "He may well assume that you have

it, holy one. I should have excluded you also; you may be in danger."

"Bah!" Honakura frowned darkly. "I still think you have removed it from the temple altogether. But you would not perjure yourself . . ."

"And Tarru has extra guards on the gate. They will all swear that neither Nnanji nor I went out. They don't know Katanji. They may have seen Jja come and go, for they watch the women, but she was carrying nothing." He sipped his wine and added casually, "Except a blanket, when she returned."

"A blanket?"

Wallie took pity on him. "Her baby misses his blanket. I gave her a copper to buy it from Kikarani. Having smelled it, I can tell how he recognizes it, but not why he would want it."

Now the old man understood and he shook his head in wonder. "So you trusted the sword to a slave and a boy you have never met?"

Wallie nodded, well pleased. If the devious Honakura, who knew that Jja was no ordinary slave, had found his actions incredible, then Tarru would never get close. Tarru was covetous and a gambler, but not a trusting man. Tarru would not even have trusted Nnanji the swordsman with a jewel.

"Katanji carried it up the road in the rug, with Jja following to watch. Then she slipped into an empty cottage and hid it in the thatch. But I do not know which cottage, so I do not know where it is."

"So the blanket was her excuse to be there and absent from the barracks," the priest concluded, smiling and nodding. "And the sword has not only left the temple but is even beyond the town. Oh, yes! You are a most subtle swordsman, my lord!" He could probably pay no higher compliment.

Wallie accepted a cake and more wine. He could admit the cause for celebration. He provoked more mirth by telling how he had checked in Nnanji's old sword the previous evening.

"How is his fencing, then?" Honakura asked. "I heard that you had treated him severely."

Wallie confessed that he had been forced to beat Nnanji, although not in conventional fashion. "His swordsmanship is astonishing. His defense was fine before, and now he has an attack to match. He tried to butcher me this morning, but he will grow out of that."

Nnanji would be an easy Third by temple standards, even by Shonsu's. Almost it seemed as though those years of frustrated practice had been locked up in storage and were now released. Wallie had offered to arrange his promotion that very day. Nnanji had turned coy, and asked if there was any rule against jumping two ranks at once. There wasn't, so Wallie had agreed to let him wait until he was ready to try for Fourth. Nnanji was now his secret weapon.

Honakura huddled back in his wicker chair and twinkled at his guest. "And the slave?"

Unconsciously Wallie yawned. He was not sure whether he had slept at all in the night. He wished that Honakura was literate, to appreciate a joke about a World book of records. But he wasn't, so Wallie merely remarked that there had been a lot more feathers on the floor again in the morning. Shonsu was a tireless performer when encouraged; Jja an enthusiastic partner. Together they had scaled heights of rapture that he would have thought quite unattainable had he not experienced them.

"So now, what do you do?" the priest asked, refilling his chalice.

"Now I have time," Wallie said. "Time to heal, to train Nnanji, to learn about the World from you . . . time to think! Honorable Tarru can carry on taking the temple complex apart, but now he must be seriously considering the possibility of failure, so I think he will be circumspect."

"And this Katanji?"

"Ah," Wallie said. "I have not met him, but I think he must be the fifth. Two more to go."

"You are learning, Walliesmith," said Honakura.

Wallie could not afford to relax, but he no longer felt death stalking closely at his back. Days crept by, and his feet healed with a rapidity that astonished Dinartura, yet the bandages stayed on. Wallie spent most of his time in the guest room—exercising, chanting sutras and fencing with Nnanji, playing with Vixini, making love with Jja. Any time he went out he was certain that he was being followed, and he suspected that the same was now true of Nnanji.

Shonsu was a brilliant instructor, Nnanji an incredible pupil. Shown a knack, trick, or skill, he never forgot it. His swordsmanship grew like a thunderhead on a summer's afternoon, as Wallie could see from the level at which he had to fence to equal him. He should have had more than one partner, but they were both taking pleasure in keeping his progress secret.

The days crept by . . .

One evening, when teacher and pupil had finished bathing and were both feeling the weary contentment that comes from long and hard exertion, Nnanji confessed to feeling frustrated.

"You are a much better instructor than anyone in the guard, my liege," he said. "You show me all this wonderful technique, but I don't seem to be improving very much at all, not since the first day." He threw down his towel angrily.

Wallie laughed. "Yes you are! I keep raising the standard on you!"

"Oh!" Nnanji looked surprised. "You do?"

"I do. Let's go out to the exercise yard."

They stood on the little platform together and watched the action. At that time of day there were only a half-dozen couples fencing, some supervised and others merely practicing. Nnanji stared for a while, then turned to his mentor with an astonished grin.

"They are so *slow!*" he said. "So *obvious!*"

Wallie nodded. "You can't expect to be hit by lightning every day," he said. "It comes gradually. But you are a hundred times better than you were."

"Look at that thumb over there!" Nnanji muttered in contempt.

Then one of the pairs finished their practice. They pulled off their masks and were revealed as Gorramini and Ghaniri. Nnanji yelped, his eyes flashing with delight. "I could beat *them*, my liege!"

"Possibly," said Wallie, who privately agreed. "Let's give it a few more days, though."

Each morning he visited Honakura in his little courtyard and learned more of the World. He also asked about Shonsu and was distressed to discover how little the priest knew about him. He had come a long way, but that did not mean a long journey. The Hand of the Goddess would have brought him, Honakura insisted, and similarly Wallie could be transported to wherever She wished him to be. So all he needed to do was board a boat in Hann, and he might find his task—or his mysterious brother—in the next port.

"There is one thing you should know, my lord," the little man said. He seemed reluctant to continue. "Obviously the demon had been sent by the Goddess, as our exorcism was a failure."

Wallie found this subject confusing, having been the demon in question, and it always reminded him of the demigod's hints of Someone Having Made a Bad Lead. "So?" he asked.

"Your previous occupant..." Honakura said. "That is...the original Lord Shonsu...he thought that the demon had been sent by sorcerers."

"Sorcerers!" Wallie exclaimed in dismay. "I didn't know you had sorcerers in the World."

"Neither did I," the priest replied, surprisingly. "There are old legends of them, but I have never heard them mentioned by any pilgrim. They were supposedly associated with the priests once."

Wallie did not enjoy the idea of sorcerers. How could a swordsman fight sorcerers? But a world of gods and miracles could presumably be a world of magic, also.

"It figures," he muttered, mostly to himself. "Where there are swordsmen there would have to be sorcerers, wouldn't there?"

"I don't see why." Honakura sniffed. "But I can't advise you about them. They were supposed to worship the Fire God. Their facemarks are feathers."

Why feathers? No one knew, and Wallie discovered that no one else knew much about sorcerers either. Nnanji just scowled and complained that there would be no honor in fighting sorcerers. Nnanji's ideals ran to heroic single combat and epics. He probably dreamed of a great epic: *How Nnanji Slew Goliath.*

One day a junior priest, carefully selected by Honakura, carried a message to Nnanji's brother. Next morning the boy knelt at the temple arches with the pilgrims. A youth not apprenticed to a craft was of little interest to the priests, but this one was approached after a very short while and led in to pray . . . and then spirited out through the back. He sat on a stool in Honakura's courtyard with that gentleman and Wallie and ate all the cakes.

He was very unlike Nnanji: short and dark, with curly black hair, and sharp, restless eyes, plus a bubbling impudence that seemed little impressed by the august company of two Sevenths. He did not look much like swordsman material to Wallie, but Wallie had accepted Honakura's belief that the gods were recruiting on his behalf, and if Nnanji wanted his brother as his first protégé, then that was how it would be.

Katanji solemnly swore that he had told no one of his

exploit with the sword. He was reminded how important that was to Nnanji, for if Tarru laid hands on the sword, he must then kill Wallie in self-defense, or from spite. Then he would have to plan on killing Nnanji, also.

Before Katanji left, he was awarded a contract for repairs to the rugs in one of the priests' dormitories. If he was needed for any more conspiring, then he would be informed when he made the deliveries. Honakura seemed perturbed by the price that the lad demanded. He glanced in rueful surprise at Wallie, but agreed that it would be paid. Katanji was skipping as he departed.

When Nnanji later heard the terms he almost exploded.

"Your father will be pleased, then," Wallie said.

Nnanji growled ominously. "If he finds out."

Wallie had made no progress in planning his escape. Tarru had searched the whole barracks and failed to find the sword. He could hardly rummage the entire temple grounds, so he must wait until Wallie tried to leave. He had many guards on the gate. He had placed a roadblock at the foot of the hill and greatly increased the detachment at the ferry port.

All this Wallie learned from the slaves. His intelligence sources were now better even than Honakura's. The slaves knew everything, but normally they formed a self-contained society. They had no interest in, and played no part in, the affairs of the free. For Lord Shonsu they made exception, and Jja was given all the news to pass on to him.

Tarru was stalemated, but he was continuing to swear swordsmen by the blood oath. Unfortunately this was not done in the presence of slaves, and Wallie could not determine who might still be trustworthy—probably not even lowranks now. There must have been some resistance, for three times slaves had been called in to clean up bloodstains. The guard was so large that the absences were not noticeable, and they were not discussed.

Wallie felt horrified and guilty at these needless deaths. Even Nnanji looked bleak when he heard, but he had to assume that the proprieties of challenge had been observed. Such ritual murder was not an abomination, merely an occupational hazard of being an honorable swordsman. Even the retired swordsmen of the barracks staff seemed to have been infected. The old commissary, Coningu, suddenly became bitter, snappish, and uncooperative. Wallie assumed that the old man was hinting that he was now unreliable, but could not openly say so.

So the slaves provided information on the present situation. For long-term strategy Wallie cross-examined Honakura. What happened if you sailed down the River forever? The priest had never thought of that and assumed that you would never stop—how could there be an end to a River? Where would the water go? What happened if you walked away from the River? You would come back to it, for it was everywhere. The only qualification was that there were mountains, and here his knowledge was scanty. There might be other peoples, other customs, other gods, in the mountains.

Politics, it seemed, was rudimentary, each city ruling itself. Wallie had great trouble explaining warfare to the priest, for it was almost unknown. A city that wished to oppress a neighbor would have to hire swordsmen, because only swordsmen might use violence. But then the neighbor would also hire swordsmen, and why should swordsmen hurt or kill members of their own craft for others' benefit? Surely one side must be in the right, and one in the wrong? And honorable swordsmen would not fight for the wrong. It sounded too good to be true, and Nnanji told contrary stories with good guys and bad guys, but clearly the World was a more peaceful place than certain other planets.

Jja's skill with a needle flourished as fast as Nnanji's with a sword, although there Shonsu's expertise was of no help. She had been taught to sew in her childhood, but had never had a chance to use what she had learned. Now she could discover the joy of doing something purely for its own sake. She was astonished at the idea that she could have more than one garment, and even more than one evening gown, but she produced a second in white, and a third in cobalt, and each was better made and more cunningly provoking than the last. She embroidered a white griffon on the hem of Wallie's kilt—and then on Nnanji's, to his great delight.

Now that the sword had been "mislaid," as Wallie put it, he need no longer fear assassination by dagger or poison, and some evenings he ate in private with his slave in the royal suite. On other nights they displayed her gowns in the saloon.

On one such occasion there was entertainment from a wandering minstrel, who sang an epic about the massacre of seven brigands by three valorous free swords. The swordsmen listened more or less politely. At the end they applauded and awarded the minstrel two barracks girls for the night—three was regarded as top dollar.

A tale such as this fell in the shadowy borderlands of Wallie's dual memories. As Shonsu he could regard it as something of interest, not to be taken too seriously—swordsman sports news. As Wallie he found it a worrisome piece of job description, wondering if one day he, also, would find a Homer to record whatever feat he was expected to accomplish for the Goddess.

He had assumed that the event was recent, but next day Nnanji informed him that the same story had come around two years before, and that the first version had been much better told. He demonstrated by reciting verbatim about a hundred lines of the earlier work. To avoid argument, Wallie agreed with this assessment; he could not have quoted one couplet of the poem he had heard the previous night.

So the days went, but the deeper conflict remained unresolved. Sooner or later Wallie must move and he could not see how. Swordsmen's Day was approaching, with Wallie scheduled to play a major part in the observance. How could he do that without the celebrated sword?

Nnanji seemed to have caught up with himself in fencing. He was still progressing, but at a more normal rate.

The Shonsu part of Wallie was feeling guilty about
Nnanji, for now he was a sleeper, a man with ability
above his rank. Sleepers were regarded with disfavor,
and to create one was a sneaky trick.

Nnanji agreed. He would be happy to make his try for
promotion. "I am a Fourth, now, my liege?"

"You're a Fourth by my standards," Wallie said.
"And that means a Fifth by the guard's. Honorable Tarru
could peel and core you, but anyone else I've seen, you
could serve up as cat food."

Nnanji, of course, grinned. "Tomorrow, then?"

"Tomorrow," Wallie agreed.

Tomorrow...

†† † ††

Wallie wore his boots for the first time in public the next
morning, in honor of the expected promotion. Yet, as he
sat at breakfast with his back to the wall as usual, he
looked around the hall uneasily. He had watched almost
all the Fifths fence at one time or another, and not one of
them was any better than Nnanji was now. Tarru was
going to receive a considerable shock when he realized
that he was opposing not only the best swordsman in the
valley, but also possibly the third best. That realization
might spur him to some dangerous rashness. Wallie was
having second thoughts about pulling the covers off his
sleeper.

Then the issue was forced anyway.

"I am Janghiuki, swordsman of the third rank..."
said the caller across the table. He was a young Third, a
contemporary of Nnanji's, short and skinny and eager,
but nervous at introducing himself to a Seventh.

"I am Shonsu, swordsman..." The formalities were a
nuisance in that Wallie never seemed to be able to stay
seated for very long in public, but the guard did not use

them among themselves, so they were also an important reminder that he was a guest, and hence sacrosanct.

"May I have the honor..." Janghiuki said, and presented his companion, a First by the official name of Ephorinzu. Wallie had noticed him before. Nnanji referred to him as Ears, for two obvious reasons, and so, probably, did everyone else. He was a large, resentful-looking man, absurdly old to be a First, probably older than Shonsu, and certainly older than his fresh-faced mentor.

"And may I have the honor..." Now Wallie had to present Nnanji to Janghiuki, who had known him for years.

"My Lord," the Third said, getting down to business, "my protégé is a candidate for promotion to the rank of Second and he has expressed a wish that Apprentice Nnanji might consent to be one of those who examine him in swordsmanship."

Wallie had already guessed. The swordsmen talked fencing like bankers talk money, and Nanji's secret progress must be a great source of curiosity to them. He knew that Nnanji got asked, and made noncommittal replies, but Nnanji's face was as transparent as air.

"Sit down a moment, Swordsman Janghiuki," he said, and seated himself. "Now, I have some advice. If you are truly anxious to see your protégé promoted, then ask elsewhere. It so happens that Apprentice Nnanji is planning to seek advancement himself this morning. If, on the other hand, you have been instructed to seek this match so that his abilities can be assessed by certain other people, then I am sure that he will be happy to oblige Novice Ephorinzu. But I warn you, Nnanji will shred him."

The unfortunate Janghiuki turned crimson and squirmed and did not know what to say. "My protégé is well above average in fencing for his rank, my lord," he managed at last.

If Wallie had still had any doubts that most of the guard was now bound by the third oath, then this incident would have removed them. The kid had his orders. He was being forced to sacrifice his protégé's best interests and he was unhappy about the implications for his own honor.

So Wallie agreed that he would instruct his vassal to meet with the novice after breakfast and sadly watched the two men depart. He turned to the amused Nnanji, who was busy again with his stewed horsemeat and black bread.

"Novice Ears has trouble remembering sutras?"

"On bad days he can't remember his name, either," Nnanji said scornfully, chewing. "He's about a Third with metal, though." He frowned. "This is his ninth attempt, I think, but his last one was on Fletchers' Day last year, so he's not due to try again yet." The famous memory at work.

"No, this is a put-up," Wallie said. "Tarru will be watching, never fear. You've got him worried, vassal!"

Nnanji was flattered. "Shall I play cripple, then, my liege?" he asked.

Wallie shook his head. "You wouldn't fool Tarru. Better to be as quick as you can and not give him time to judge you—a fast win can always be mere luck. But we were going to promote you, too, so it doesn't matter now anyway. Who do you fancy in the duckpond?"

"Them!" Nnanji said firmly, nodding at Gorramini and Ghaniri across the room.

"I don't think you can have them, I'm afraid," Wallie said. "They have no mentors—I should have to ask them personally and I'm damned if I will. They would only refuse. And as a guest you can't challenge another guest. Sorry, Nnanji, but you'll have to pick two other victims."

Grumpily Nnanji suggested two Fourths, then admitted that they were probably the best two of their rank. Most candidates naturally chose easy marks.

"Let's leave it for the moment," Wallie said, having had an idea. "Box Ears as fast as you can, then maybe I can talk Tarru into something for you." Nnanji was not the only one with a score to settle.

Promotions were matters of great interest, and all the swordsmen not on duty had gathered in the fencing area. Mostly they stood in a circle around the match, but some were on the platform, and a couple of Firsts had climbed onto the whipping post. At the far side of the parade ground the morning sacrifices were emerging from the jail, and Wallie hastily turned his back on that activity. The new roof was completed and resplendent, and the victims no longer need be dragged out screaming, crippled by complete immobility, but he still hated the thought of that jail and the primitive culture it represented.

In the center of the ring of swordsmen stood Ears and a very young and worried Second, presumably the worst fencer of his rank. It was almost an insult to be asked to examine, which was why requests were made to mentors whenever possible. This one's ordeal did not last long. Ears won the best of three in two very fast points. The junior slunk away, scalded by hisses from the crowd.

Wallie stayed back, watching easily over the circle of onlookers. Tarru and Trasingji were the judges and now they called for the second examiner. A slim, tall Second stepped forward, foil in hand, a red ponytail waving behind his mask. Tarru's eyes sought out Wallie briefly and then looked away.

"Fence!" said Tarru.

Nnanji lunged. "Hit!" he called.

The judges agreed in surprise.

"Fence!"

"Hit!" Nnanji said again, and turned on his heel. Wallie could not have won faster himself.

Roaring in fury, Ears flung his foil to the ground—another year to wait before he could try again, and he had lost in the fencing, which he must have expected to win, not in the sutra tests that he found difficult.

There were no cheers, no boos. The swordsmen knew how Nnanji of the Second had fenced two weeks ago. They turned to stare at the Seventh who had worked this miracle. Wallie stalked forward, enjoying the sensation he had caused.

"While we are here, Honorable Tarru," he said, "I have a protégé, Apprentice Nnanji, who would also like to try for promotion. He has expressed a choice, but I need an interpretation from you."

Tarru frowned. The onlookers registered surprise, for there was nothing ambiguous about the rules for promotion.

"I defer to your rank on interpretations, my lord," Tarru said cautiously.

"But you are host," Wallie said innocently, "and this concerns a matter between guests." All eyes swung to Ghaniri and Gorramini, standing nearby. "Would you take it as a breach of the rules of hospitality if he were to make the minor challenge to other guests?"

Suspicion floated around Tarru like a swarm of gnats. "Promotions do not need challenges, my lord!"

Wallie smiled disarmingly—he had been practicing with Shonsu's face before a mirror. "No, but he will be jumping two ranks, which is unusual, and he is reluctant to ask the men in question. There is wood on the hearth, you understand."

Tarru understood very well. He seemed to look for a trap and not find one. If he had set up Ears in order to evaluate Nnanji, then here was the opportunity he wanted. He shrugged. "As the minor challenge allows the choice of foils, I do not think that it violates hospitality," he agreed. A jubilant Nnanji marched over to Ghaniri, who happened to be closest.

Ghaniri's bruiser face darkened with anger—a Second challenging a Fourth was asking for as much trouble as the Fourth could deliver. Tarru and Trasingji graciously consented to be judges again.

The two men faced off, then took each other's foils cautiously upon the signal. They lunged and parried a couple of times. Then Ghaniri tried a cut to the head, Nnanji parried, and landed a superb riposte on his opponent's ribs.

"Hit!" he said. The judges agreed.

Now even Tarru sent Wallie a glance that conceded the swordsmanship. Nnanji was making Ghaniri look as easy as Ears.

The second point took much longer, but Wallie saw right away that Nnanji was holding back. Tarru could possibly tell, although he did not know Nnanji's style, but most of the other onlookers were probably deceived. Nnanji, having satisfied himself that he was the better man, was perhaps worried that he might somehow be cheated out of his second victim if he beat the first too easily. Or perhaps he was just enjoying himself. Then, after a few minutes of stamping and clashing metal and sweating and panting, he moved in again.

"Hit!" he said triumphantly, lowering his foil.

"No hit!" Tarru snapped.

It was a flagrant miscall; Ghaniri's fingers were already rubbing the point of impact. Nnanji's face was invisible behind the mask, but he directed it rigidly toward Tarru as though sending him a fierce glare.

"No hit!" Trasingji agreed reluctantly.

"Fence!" Tarru called.

Nnanji streaked. His foil struck the metal rim of Ghaniri's mask with a loud crack. "Hit this time?" he shouted, and even Tarru could not deny that crack.

The spectators broke into loud whoops of applause, which Wallie suspected would be a unique experience for Nnanji and might make him overconfident. He pulled off his mask to wipe his forehead and turned to grin at his mentor.

"You're keeping your guard too high!" Wallie snapped. Nnanji was forgetting that other swordsmen were not as tall as his mentor. He acknowledged the error with a nod and accepted a beaker of water from a considerate First.

But the short break had allowed Tarru to beckon Gorramini over and whisper to him. Wallie noticed and felt a twinge of unease. Then a chant spread around the circle: "Next! Next!" This was a swordsmen gala day.

Grinning happily, Nnanji waved his foil in acceptance and strode over to challenge Gorramini. Gorramini was a tall, well-built, and athletic man, with an arrogant air that suggested he was aware of his appearance and expected admiration for it. He folded his arms and stared contemptuously back at Nnanji for a moment. Then he said: "Swords!"

So many of the spectators drew breath simultaneously that the sound came out as a collective hiss.

"Hold it!" Wallie boomed. He turned to Tarru. "I don't think swords should be allowed between guests, your honor."

"Ah!" Tarru said. *Shark!* "That is a problem, isn't it? But you must remember, my lord, that juniors are always looking for good practice. The minor challenge allows the choice of blades for just that reason. You yourself, as the best swordsman in the valley, would constantly be receiving the minor challenge if you did not have that protection."

You sneaky damn smart-aleck! Wallie thought bitterly. One thing about Tarru—he was no fool. If Wallie insisted on his own interpretation, then Tarru would be free to drive him out of the barracks with an endless string of challenges.

"I think Adept Gorramini should reconsider," Wallie said loudly. "I am sure that he has no lethal intent, but he must remember that Apprentice Nnanji is my liegeman."

And almost certainly Gorramini was Tarru's. If either man died in the bout, then his liege would have to avenge him. Suddenly the possibility of a massacre was hanging over the fencing ground. Wallie gave Tarru what he hoped was a meaningful and threatening stare.

"Then let us agree that it is a naked match," Tarru said at once. That did not mean undressed, it meant that onus of vengeance had been waived. But the curious choice of words—*let us agree*—was an implicit acknowledgment that Gorramini had sworn the blood oath, also. Gorramini was now wearing a startled expression, as though he had not expected things to go that far.

"You will not reconsider, adept?" Wallie asked, addressing him for the first time.

Gorramini glanced momentarily at Tarru, licked his lips, and then said, "No!" firmly.

Everyone waited for Wallie's decision. As a Seventh he could issue a veto, but he knew that it was too late. Nnanji's eyes were staring at him, silently pleading like a spaniel's. He had been sheltered from Briu by his mentor. It would be shameful to be saved that way again, and on his own challenge. Gorramini had his orders and could not disobey. Tarru had worked it very well—he was probably going to lose a follower, for Nnanji had been fighting like a champion, but Tarru could afford a loss. Wallie could not. Many men who were good with foils were paralyzed when faced with an edge and a point. Nnanji would have to prove himself indeed.

"A naked match, then," Wallie said.

Nnanji yelped with delight and hurled his mask in the air. Perhaps it was bravado, perhaps he really felt that way. No one in the crowd spoke, but the faces radiated anger and disapproval.

There was a necessary delay while a First was sent running to bring a healer. Then the two returned together, and the duel could begin.

Now there were no masks, no judges, merely razor steel against flesh. Ghaniri stepped forward to be his friend's second. Wallie likewise moved to Nnanji's left. The two principals faced each other, both grinning confidently. Nnanji sent Wallie a wink.

"We are ready," Wallie said formally.

"Now!" said Gorramini. The two swords hissed from their scabbards and met with a clang. *Clang. Clang. Clang* ... They were toe to toe and whirling their blades, neither willing to back off. Wallie felt sweat prickle on his forehead. Both men were fighting well up in Fourth rank, perhaps inspiring each other. *Clang-clang-clang*

. . . someone had to give, and it was Gorramini. He began
to recover, and then Nnanji drove him without respite,
effortlessly flickering his sword, advancing behind that
murderous silver fog, while onlookers scampered back
out of the way. There was no doubt now who was the
better. All that was needed was some trivial nick to show
blood, then Ghaniri could call for a draw. Wallie had his
acceptance poised on his tongue. Thrust-parry-riposte-
parry-cut-parry . . . Gorramini screamed and fell, clutching his belly—sudden silence.

Nnanji stepped back, panting, and glanced a grin
across at Wallie.

"Healer!" yelled the crowd, milling in around the
fallen man. Wallie lurched forward, hurling two men out
of the way when they tried to move in front of him.
Ghaniri knelt down to help, but Gorramini had been dis-
emboweled and was about to die.

The healer did not even stoop to examine the injury.
"I do not accept this case!" he announced.

Tarru had turned and was walking away.

"TARRU!" Wallie's roar came echoing back across
the parade ground like thunder. For a moment the
wounded man was forgotten. The spectators looked nervously at Wallie and then at Tarru, who spun around to
glare, and snap, "Yes?"

Gorramini was groaning and screaming by turns,
dying in agony.

"You will now examine my protégé in the sutras required for Fourth rank!" Wallie was seething with fury at
the unnecessary death, teeth grinding, fists clenched.
This was Wallie Smith's anger, not Shonsu's. Tarru hesitated, looking equally murderous—and rebellious.

Wallie made the sign of challenge to a Sixth.

The spirits of death leaned very close now, waiting for
Gorramini, and waiting to see who else might need their
services . . .

"I waive the examination!" Tarru growled. "If you
have taught him . . . We all know of your vassal's memory, my lord." He peered around to locate the face-

marker who had been optimistically summoned for Ears' attempt at promotion. "I certify for Adept Nnanji!" Then he looked back narrowly at Wallie. "Anything else?"

Wallie shook his head—secret challenge withdrawn. Tarru turned away once more.

The spectators were fading like smoke. Trasingji nodded his consent to the facemarker and followed them. The courtyard was empty, except for Gorramini whimpering out his last breaths, writhing in a sea of his own blood and spilled bowels, Ghaniri kneeling beside him weeping, and Nnanji standing with his sword still in his hand, seeming unperturbed and satisfied. The facemarker hovered nervously nearby. The healer departed quickly, stiff-backed.

"Congratulations, adept." Wallie could not keep the bitterness out of his voice.

Nnanji beamed. "Thank you, my liege. You do not cut notches in your shoulder strap?"

"No," Wallie said. He thought Gorramini had heard the question.

"Then I shall not." Nnanji was waiting for his victim to die, so that he could claim his sword.

Not a word, thought Wallie—not a single word of regret!

One lonely figure stepped forward to shake the victor's hand. Nnanji grinned with pleasure and accepted Briu's congratulations. Briu glanced impassively at Wallie, made the fist-on-heart salute, and walked away. Everything Wallie did seemed to diminish Briu, even this dramatic transformation of a pupil who had baffled him for years.

The dying man's ordeal came to an end. Ghaniri closed his friend's eyes. As he rose, Nnanji stepped by him to wipe his sword on the body—Lord Shonsu had done that to Hardduju. Then he turned expectantly to his second. Unhappily Wallie bent to pick up Gorramini's blade. He knelt and proffered it to the victor.

Nnanji took it and looked it over approvingly. "Nice bit of metal," he said.

††† †††

Apprentice Nnanji, having received two more face-marks, plus instruction from Wallie in the secret signals of the third and fourth ranks, had now become Adept Nnanji, swordsman of the Fourth. He must therefore dress the part.

The tailor's shop was a dingy, cluttered room at the far end of the barracks. There he purchased an orange kilt and a hairclip with an orange stone. His hero wore a stone, so it was the right thing to do. Orange did not suit his red hair, but the combination made him seem like a young fire god, glowing with immense satisfaction. He stood and preened before a mirror, his bruises and scars still obvious, but in his own eyes a gorgeous Fourth. He had not mentioned Gorramini, even yet.

Wallie regarded him with sadness and doubt. Clad in middlerank garb and filled with a new confidence, Nnanji seemed years older than he had done that first day, on the beach. He even looked bigger and he held himself with assurance. No longer did Wallie think of him as being ungainly. Possibly that illusion had come from his very large hands and feet. When he broadened out, in a few years, Nnanji was going to be big. The awkward adolescent had suddenly become a very dangerous young man.

He finished his admiration session before the mirror and swung around to Wallie.

"I may swear to you again, my liege?"

"Of course." The second oath lapsed upon promotion.

Apparently a tailor's shop was a suitable location for oath-taking—at once Nnanji pulled out his sword, dropped to his knees, and became again protégé to Lord Shonsu. His grin was so persistent that he had trouble removing it for even that solemn act.

"Now," he said, as he rose, "you will be visiting with the holy one, my liege?"

Most days Wallie did call on Honakura at about this time, and today the need was urgent. Somehow he must come up with a plan, and Honakura was the only person who might help. "What do you have in mind?" he asked cautiously.

"I have a sword to sell. The armorer has the rest of my money ready. I want to give it to my parents before we leave." He assumed an expression of great virtue and innocence.

Swordsmen, being athletes, gained rank much faster than other crafts. Most of Nnanji's childhood friends would still be only Seconds, or even Firsts. A swordsman of the Fourth was an important and powerful citizen. His father, as Wallie had learned from some chance remark, was a Third. There were several younger brothers and sisters to impress, also.

So he did have some human emotions!

"Two hours!" Wallie said and was at once alone, feeling as though that Cheshire-cat grin was still hanging there before him, left behind in the rush.

He went off to the temple.

The most holy Honakura was not available.

Fighting a steadily rising apprehension, Wallie took a walk in his unfamiliar boots. He inspected the great wall again, looking for trees that might overhang it, but none was close enough or tall enough. There were a few crumbling old buildings against the wall, but again none was high enough to allow escape without a ladder. He was being followed, he knew, and ladders would not be permitted.

Bitterly he regretted uncovering his sleeper. That had been an error, and it had led Tarru into a worse one. The blood oath was not totally one-sided, for a vassal was owed protection by his liege. Tarru had callously thrown away Gorramini. He must have had morale problems before, and now they would be much worse. He might well be forced into some desperate act.

The only fragment of a plan that Wallie could find was to sneak out the temple gate in disguise. It was a very leaky boat of a plan. Nnanji would be appalled by the dishonor, and it meant going unarmed. It was horribly risky—Shonsu's body was so damned large and conspicuous—but there seemed to be no other solution. Even the suppliers' wagons were searched as they departed, or so the slaves said. And he would still be a long way from the ferry.

And what disguise? A swordsman's ponytail was distinctive and inviolable. The facemarks of the People were sacred. To tamper with them was a major crime. Reluctantly Wallie had concluded that Shonsu of the Seventh would have to become a woman, using his long hair to cover his forehead. The only concealed foreheads he had seen belonged to female slaves and probably were permitted in their case only because the slavestripes ran all the way down their faces.

Beginning to swelter as the sun grew more cruel, still brooding, he headed back toward the barracks. On this side the shrubbery grew right up to the building, and his way led along a paved path that wound and twisted between high bushes, almost a jungle. Frequent cross-paths and branches formed a maze. He was unfamiliar with this area, although he could hardly get seriously lost. For some time he wandered aimlessly, partly mulling over his problems, and partly—as he suddenly realized with amusement—instinctively making himself familiar with the terrain . . . sutra seven seventy-two . . .

He had drawn very close to the rear wall of the barracks, when something came thrashing through the bushes toward him. Wallie stopped, and a slave emerged onto the path ahead. He was a large and blubbery youth, dirty, and wearing only a black cloth. He stood and panted for a moment, staring at Wallie, still clutching a trowel in his hand. That, and his coating of mud, showed that he was one of the gardeners.

"My lord?"

Slaves did not accost Sevenths—trickles of apprehension ran over Wallie. "Yes?"

The youth licked his lips, apparently not sure what to say next. He was either overcome by nervousness, or else merely stupid. Or both. "My lord," he repeated. Then, "Was told to look for you."

Wallie tried to smile encouragingly, as though dealing with a child, but he had never been at ease when dealing with the disabled. He recalled Narrin, the idiot slave in the jail, and wondered if slavery itself produced mental deficiency, or if impaired children were callously sold to the traders. Of course the World had no institutions where they could be conveniently shut up and forgotten.

"Well, you've found me."

"Yes. My lord." Another pause.

"Who told you to look for me?"

"Mother."

Impasse. "What's your mother's name?"

"Ani, my lord."

Ah! "And what's your name?"

"Anasi. My lord."

"Can you take me to her, Anasi?"

The slave nodded. "Yes, my lord." He turned and started to walk along the path. Wallie followed.

Obviously this was trouble, but at once Wallie registered more trouble—a quiet tap of boots behind him. Then a pause . . . then more taps. Of course he was being followed, and of course a tail must stay close in a maze such as this. Had the conversation been overheard? Should he pull off into the shrubbery with Anasi, and let his follower go by?

Before he could decide, the path came to an end. Straight ahead was the wall of the barracks and a small doorway. The public entrances were huge and imposing, so this one was likely for slaves' use. Damn! There were no more side branches to the path. If Wallie vanished now, his follower must surely guess that the slaves were involved.

"Anasi!"

The youth stopped and turned his moon face to Wallie. "My lord?"

"I'll wait here. You tell Ani where I am."

Anasi thought that over, nodded, and disappeared through the door. As quietly as he could manage, Wallie hurried back to the last corner and stepped aside into the bushes.

He had been very stupid. He had allowed Nnanji to leave, dividing his forces. Without Nnanji, he was ten times as vulnerable. And now he might have betrayed his secret relationship with the slave population—Tarru was smart enough to work that out from very few clues. Shonsu was not much help in cloak-and-dagger work of this nature, but Wallie Smith should have known better —much better. Idiot! He cursed himself for incompetence and he could feel his Shonsu self raging at the need for concealment and stealth.

The bootsteps came closer, louder.

A swordsman of the Third passed by, a short and skinny man. He stopped in surprise when he saw the end of the path and the doorway. Wallie stepped out behind him and joyfully swung a fist hard against the place where neck joined shoulder, crumpling his victim to the ground. With a quiet clatter of sword hilt against paving stone, the man rolled over and lay still.

That had felt good! Wallie rubbed his hand and pondered what to do next. The doorway was too close. No matter where the victim woke up, he would remember that slaves' entrance just ahead of him. He would have to be tied up and held prisoner.

Wallie dropped to his knees and looked more closely.

It was young Janghiuki, Ears' mentor.

Knocking men out and tying them up was good spy story behavior, but forbidden behavior for a swordsman. And trickier than it sounded, especially for a man who had recently acquired a new body and did not know his own strength. He had broken Janghiuki's neck. The kid was dead.

#7 ON DUELS BETWEEN SWORDSMEN
The Epitome
The abominations are seven:

> To attack without warning,
> To attack an unarmed man,
> Two against one,
> Any weapon but a sword,
> Anything that is thrown,
> Anything that throws,
> Armor or shield.

The Episode
Fifty-two came against Langaunimi and
twenty-five he slew.
Great is the name of Langaunimi.
Who were the fifty-two?

The Epigram
A kill without honor destroys two swordsmen.

††† † †††

Anasi returned, accompanied not by his mother but by another male slave, one previously unknown to Wallie. He had many more wits about him than Anasi. The noble lord was in danger, he said. Honorable Tarru had set up an ambush in the guest suite, men with clubs and nets. Lord Shonsu must not return to his room.

Then Nnanji must be sent for, Wallie replied, and he needed a place of concealment.

They led him down to the cellars, and anywhere less like his own quarters he could never have imagined.

The roof was so low that he could not stand erect, even between the massive beams that supported the ceiling. It would be a fiendishly impossible place for him to fight. It was low and very long, like a tunnel. Small barred openings dropped puddles of reluctant light on

piles of dirty straw, on cobwebs and filth, and on varie-
gated patches of fungus in the corners, on scraps of broken furniture long since discarded by rightful owners.
Precious hoarded rags dangled from pegs. A couple of
ramshackle partitions had been constructed to make a
pretense of small private areas, but they only made the
whole place darker. It was the male slaves' dormitory, a
human stable reeking of centuries of unwashed bodies.

The wonder was not that old slaves were sent to the
Judgment when no longer useful, the wonder was that
any of them lived that long.

Wallie sat slumped on a wooden chair that had lost its
back and he brooded. Jja had been informed. Anasi had
returned to his gardening duties. Janghiuki had been left
under a bush and was doubtless already attracting attention from insects.

Murder! What he had done would be first-degree
murder on Earth and it was murder in the World. He
could have killed Janghiuki quite legally had he wished.
Challenge, draw, lunge, wipe sword—five seconds'
work for Shonsu, and no one would have raised an eyebrow. But he had tried to be merciful and now he was a
murderer.

Janghiuki of the Third . . . he had done no wrong. He
had been obeying orders—follow Shonsu. Spying on a
guest was not in itself a breach of hospitality, although
poor manners. The lad's only error had been to swear
the blood oath without due cause being shown, and undoubtedly Tarru or Trasingji or one of the other
highranks had been standing by, with sword already
drawn. The kid would have had no real choice. Probably
Tarru had given him a plausible excuse anyway: "Lord
Shonsu has purloined the Goddess' sword, and we must
retrieve it." Believable enough, when disagreement
meant death.

Sooner or later, Tarru was going to realize that
Shonsu was not returning to his room. The hunt would
begin. Janghiuki's body would be found. Then Tarru's
morale problems would be solved at once. Then the
hounds would bay.

Slave owning, idol worship, capital punishment, flogging . . . all were things that would have filled the old Wallie Smith with horror. Now he had added murder. Morals don't change, he had told the little boy that first morning. The demigod had said that was something else he must unlearn. But he couldn't.

Shonsu would have killed Janghiuki without scruple, doing it by the sutra and feeling no guilt afterward. He would have dismissed the hospitality problem by quoting some sutra or other, and no one could have questioned his interpretation. Wallie Smith could never learn to think that way. He had promised to try to be a swordsman, but he was not going to succeed.

The Goddess would have to find another champion.

Something rustled in the straw behind him. He jumped, but whatever it was, it was not human.

He wondered if Honakura had ever seen slave quarters like these, and what he would say to them. Probably he would only gabble about slavery being punishment for misdeeds in a previous life. Tough to be punished for something you could not recall doing! But Wallie had promised not to tell the Goddess how to run Her World.

There were hundreds of slaves. There were hundreds of swords in the armory. As he had done several times before, Wallie toyed with the thought of a slave army. He rejected it as he always did. The sutras allowed a swordsman to arm civilians in an emergency, but the wording specifically excluded slaves. That would be both crime and abomination. More important to Wallie, though, was the certainty that it would be a massacre. Swordsmen would be infinitely more deadly, no matter what the odds, and he would not save himself at the cost of innocent lives. Furthermore, he was certain that the slaves' friendship would not go so far. They would understandably fear retribution. No slave-owning culture could ever tolerate a slave revolt, no matter who organized it. If Shonsu tried to be Spartacus, he would unite the rest of the World against him.

What to do? Wallie struggled to unravel Tarru's thinking. He must be feeling pressured. Forcing men to swear to him for a dishonorable cause was an abomination. Ordering them to keep the third oath secret was another. There were limits to how long he could hope to keep his illicit army together, and how far he could even trust it. So Tarru had felt his hand being forced. He must find the sword soon and depart. His only lead to it was Shonsu, who, even if he truly did not know where it was, must know who did. Nets were an obvious tactic if a Seventh was to be taken alive.

The penalty for failure, the demigod had said, was death . . . or worse. Tarru was planning torture.

The door creaked and Jja slipped in, with Vixini on her back. Wallie rose, unable to straighten, and kissed her, then pulled over another broken chair so that they could sit close.

Jja smiled reassuringly at him and squeezed his hand.

Wallie was astonished at how relieved he was to see her. By not taking Jja hostage, Tarru had overlooked a winning strategy. But no normal swordsman would mortgage his heart to a slave as Wallie had done, so Tarru could not have known.

He tried to explain that to her, and she seemed as surprised as Tarru would have been.

"I am not doing very well, Jja."

She studied him for a while. Was his guilt so obvious? Did he now have *Murderer* written on his brow?

But no. What she said at last was, "Do you know what the gods want of you, master?"

There was the nub.

He nodded. "I do know. And I don't want to do it. You are right, my love. I must learn obedience." He went back to staring at the floor.

"Ani is coming, master. Honorable Tarru and his men are still waiting in the room. Kio has gone to find Adept Nnanji."

"Who is Kio?"

Jja's white teeth showed in the gloom. "His favorite. He could not afford her before, until you gave him so much money. She has taken half the sword already, the women say."

Wallie smiled and was silent. It was hard on Nnanji to drag him back into the shark pool, but that was his duty. In any case, he must be warned, and danger to his liege would surely bring Nnanji running anyway.

What orders had Tarru given? Nnanji might well die at the gate.

Vixini began fussing. Jja untied him and put him down. He set off on a voyage of exploration like an eager brown bug.

The door creaked again, and this time it was Ani, huge in a black muumuu. Only her big ugly face was truly visible, floating just below the ceiling, with the black patch over her left eye like a hole in it. Her hair was pulled back in a bun, and a thin line of silver framed her face, undyed roots from ear to ear. She bobbed respectfully to Wallie, yet she was trying to hide a smirk at the absurdity of a lord of the Seventh cowering in a slaves' cellar. Her son might have little more intelligence than the plants he tended, but Ani had cultivated men. She had a primitive native shrewdness and also a strange aura of authority, as though she were Queen of the Slaves.

"I am grateful to you, Ani," Wallie said.

"And I to you, my lord. You were kind to a fat old woman that evening. Few would not have taken offense."

"I have been drunk myself," he said. "But I may never get another chance, I fear. What word of Tarru?"

With a sideways twitch of her head she spat on the floor. "He has ordered a search, my lord. He will not look here. If he does, we can move you around these cellars. You are safe here."

That would not be true if Tarru ever suspected that the slaves were fighting against him. The damning corpse lay close to a slave entrance, and Tarru was no fool.

Slaves could move the body elsewhere, of course, but only at great risk to themselves. Wallie decided not to mention Janghiuki.

"I need to get word to Lord Honakura," he said. "He is the only one who can help me, I think."

Ani pouted meaty lips. "Not easy, my lord."

Of course. No slave could just walk up to a man like Honakura and start a conversation—not without starting a riot. Wallie reached in his money pouch. "Would this help?"

Ani's eye glinted at the sight of gold. "It might."

Wallie handed over coins and dictated a brief message. Ani parroted it back at him in preliterate fashion, then rolled away to see what could be done.

He sat down and sighed. The cellar was hot and fetid and hateful. "Being my slave gives you plenty of variety, Jja, does it not? The royal guest suite . . . and now this?"

She smiled obediently. "The women's quarters are a little cleaner, master, but much the same."

He thought of the women's quarters and was puzzled. They were not ostentatious, like his own accommodation, but they were airy and comfortable . . .

"What do you mean?" he demanded. "Not the rooms upstairs, where Janu . . ."

She shook her head, smiling slightly. "Only when you came for me, master."

She meant *slave women's* quarters, of course. He had been thoughtless. "You mean that when you weren't with me, you were down in some hole like this?"

She nodded. "Most of the time."

He took her hands in his. "I had not realized!"

She started to say that it did not matter, and he cut her off. "Yes, it does! Jja, if we get out of this mess, I shall keep you by me always. We may find nothing better than this, but we'll find it together." She dropped her eyes before his gaze. "Jja . . . I love you."

He thought she colored, but the light was too dim to be sure. What could such a statement mean, when made to a slave? "I would marry you if I could, Jja."

She looked up then, startled.

"I would give you anything, do anything for you," he said. "I told you that you would make joy with no other men and now I promise you that I . . ."

She put her fingers over his lips and shook her head.

"I mean it!"

She hesitated, reluctant as always to put her thoughts into words. "Wallie is sure. Lord Shonsu will not let him keep such a promise."

He started to protest, and again she stopped him. Then she shivered. "Do anything for me, master?"

"Yes."

"Drive away the god of sorrows?"

Vixini had curled up on some straw and was sleepily sucking his thumb.

It was a tempting prospect—it might be his last chance, ever. "Just being with you is comfort enough, my love. You don't have to drag me into bed to please me. You're much more to me than just that sort of partner."

She dropped her eyes and was silent.

"What's wrong?"

"Forgive me, master."

"Forgive you for what?"

"I was not trying to please you. I was asking you to please me."

Was she being honest? He never could read her thoughts. It did not matter. Two weeks before, she would not have said even that much. Such progress should be rewarded.

"There will be bedbugs," he warned. But she smiled happily and raised her lips to his, and he quickly decided to risk the bedbugs.

The god of sorrows was unusually obstinate. He was driven away several times, and each time he returned in haste. He won by sheer persistence. When Nnanji appeared at last, the two fugitives were clothed once more

and slouched limply on the wobbly wrecks of chairs, hot
and weary in the smelly heat.

Nnanji ducked in under the rafters, looked around
with a scowl, and then beamed at Wallie.

"My liege, may I have the honor of presenting my
protégé, Novice Katanji?"

Courage, Wallie recalled, had been defined as grace
under stress. He rose to accept Katanji's salute, using
hand gestures because of the lack of headroom. The boy
wore a bloody facemark, a brilliant white kilt, and a surprised expression. Nnanji's old hairclip clung grimly in
his short black curls, unable to make a ponytail no matter how hard it tried. He looked absurdly young.

He ought not to be there, of course. Wallie should
have guessed what Nnanji had been plotting, but it was
too late now to stop the oath.

Novice Katanji? Perhaps he was a sign from the gods,
that the expedition was still going ahead. Number five
had just boarded.

"I bought him a new sword instead of my old one,"
Nnanji announced, producing the weapon.

If he had gone up to the room for the old one . . .

But Nnanji had dried up in embarrassment, which
was rare.

"And you want me to give it to him?"

"If you don't mind kneeling to a First . . ." Nnanji
muttered, meaning: *Yes, very much.*

"I shall be honored," Wallie said. "I'll still be taller
than him, anyway."

Novice Katanji grinned at that. His mentor scowled at
him and told him to remember what he had been told and
not to cut off Lord Shonsu's thumbs.

Wallie knelt to offer the sword with the appropriate
words. Katanji took it carefully and made the reply, but
he did not look nearly as solemn or impressed as Nnanji
did. There was a cynical glint in those dark young eyes.

"Nnanji, you were not followed here—you are certain?" Wallie asked, easing back to his chair.

"Quite certain! You told me how, my liege!"

So Nnanji had been using the spy-story sutra.

"In fact," Nnanji said, "Popoluini and Faraskansi were on the gate. They tried to warn me not to come back in." He frowned. "I said it was a matter of honor. Then they promised not to have me followed."

Wallie tried to imagine that conversation and gave up. But it confirmed his belief that the swordsmen were reluctant opponents. They would obey Tarru's orders to the letter and do no more.

Then he noticed a third person, standing in the background. He had assumed that it was Kio, the favorite barracks girl, but it was no woman he had ever seen before. Nnanji grinned and beckoned her forward into the light.

"I bought this, too," he said proudly. "We have all those things to carry—foils and spare clothes—and Jja has the baby . . ."

Wallie was emotionally jangled and physically satiated, yet he felt himself react. She was voluptuous, clad only in a sort of lace wisp to emphasize her attractions, and they were emphatic enough in themselves. On Earth he would have assumed that such stupendous breasts were the work of an unethical plastic surgeon. In the World only a miracle could be holding them up like that. Her bare arms and legs were sensational. Cascades of light-brown wavy hair framed a perfect face—perfectly blank—with rosebud lips locked in a meaningless smile, big eyes dull as pebbles. A moron.

Oh, *hell*! In the excitement of being promoted, Nnanji had run amok. First his brother, and now this. She was incredibly exciting and incredibly wrong, for he would tire of such an imbecile in a couple of days. She belonged in some pampered corner of a rich old man's mansion, not in a swordsman's wandering life. This could never be the preordained sixth member of the team! Never!

"I suppose I should have asked, my liege . . ." Nnanji had noticed the reaction.

"Yes, you should!" Wallie snapped. He sank back on

to his chair in black depression. Everything was coming unraveled. As soon as he thought he had hit bottom, he found another layer. "*What* did you call her?"

"Cowie, my liege," Nnanji said.

He seemed irritated that Lord Shonsu should find that name so inexplicably funny.

Time dragged along. Nnanji wanted to take his new toy off to a convenient pile of straw and play; Wallie spitefully forbade it. He explained about Tarru and his nets, then reluctantly mentioned that he had killed Janghiuki, but without saying how. Nnanji went as black as the cellar itself and hunched on a stool, scowling. Vixini awoke fretting, hungry and bored. Katanji sat on the straw and stared, probably wondering if this was what a swordsman's life ought to be, perhaps scared of this murdering Seventh. Cowie just sat.

How to escape from the barracks, from the temple grounds, from the town, from the island?

Wallie wanted to stand up and pace, but in that squalid hole he could only crouch, so pacing was impossible. He was cornered. Tarru had driven him by inches, like a gangster assimilating a neighborhood, or a Hitler swallowing a continent, relentlessly taking advantage of a peace-lover's reluctance to resort to force.

Shonsu had known what was happening. So had Wallie Smith and he had let it happen. He had told himself he was playing for time, when time had been helping his opponent more than him. His mind squirmed and twitched in its predicament as he tried to think of an escape. He could not find one, except the slim hope that Honakura might yet have some cards in hand.

Nnanji seemed to grow grimmer and grimmer. He might be blaming Tarru for corrupting the guard, or he might be reconsidering the man who had said he did not kill unless he must. A guest slaying one of his hosts? Who had started the abominations? Was preparing a trap an abomination, or did the abomination come only when the trap was sprung? Was following a guest around permissible behavior?

Wallie noted his poisonous expression and wondered if the killer earthworm might now return. Nnanji must be feeling betrayed a second time—first by the guard and now by Shonsu. Tarru was not the only one with morale problems.

At last the door creaked, and Ani's vast shapelessness floated in. She came to a stop in front of Wallie and shook her head sadly.

"Lord Honakura?" the swordsman demanded, but he could tell from her expression that he had fallen to a lower level yet.

"No, my lord," she said. "He is in jail."

BOOK FIVE:

HOW THE SWORDSMAN FOUND HIS BROTHER

†

Murderous noon; the birds were silent in the trees, the gardening slaves moved listlessly, staying out of the light, and even insects were silent. The line of pilgrims kneeling on the temple steps melted and groaned under the lash of a sadistic sun. Only the River continued to move and make noise as the World endured, praying for evening.

The parade ground was deserted and hot as a griddle. Three people came around the corner of the barracks, past the fencing area. With every man in the guard now searching for Lord Shonsu, there was no one there to notice the trio. They marched unseen across the parade ground toward the jail, floating on their shadows in the white glare.

The man in front was a swordsman of the Fourth, resplendent in a very new orange kilt. His ponytail was inky black. So was the expression on his face. He had very nearly mutinied against his sworn liege lord and had spoken not a word since the slaves had smeared his hair with lampblack and grease.

The man at the back was a short, dark-haired First. With awkward gait, sword tilted, facemark swollen, kilt sparkling white, and much-too-short hair, he was an obvious scratcher. Even the stunned look in his dark eyes proclaimed that. He clutched a rope, whose other end

267

was knotted about the neck of the captive being brought in.

She was huge and very ugly for a woman. Her black hair was much too long for a slave's—loosely flopping curls, still smelling of hot iron. Her black, all-enveloping garment might have belonged to the infamous Wild Ani, and it bulged oddly, as though the wearer were deformed.

The heat inside the pillows was incredible. It was dangerous, Wallie knew. Even if he did not collapse from heat prostration, he was weakening steadily. He could hardly see for the sweat running into his eyes and he dared not wipe them, because he must pretend that his hands were tied behind him. No sane swordsman would ever expect Lord Shonsu of the Seventh to dress like that. He had refrained from faking a facemark, partly out of consideration for Nnanji's feelings, but also because if anyone got that close to him, the pretense would be over. Apart from his size, though, he could pass as a slave at a distance. He kept his stride short, he crouched—and he sweltered.

Before the jail had been fitted with a new roof, it might have been possible to rescue a prisoner without the guards' knowing, but now the only entrance was through the door, and that led into the guard room. The door was open. The newcomers marched straight through.

Briu of the Fourth was playing dice at a table with two Seconds. Three slaves were sitting on the floor in a corner, picking lice out of clothes. They looked up and saw swordsmen bringing in a new prisoner.

Katanji, in his so-brief career, had been taught only one piece of swordsmanship. This was a maneuver that no other swordsman had ever been taught. He performed it now, twirling around and kneeling down with his head bent. The female slave pulled the sword from his scabbard, and put the point at Briu's throat before he could draw.

"It would have to be you, wouldn't it?" Wallie said.

"Keep your hands on the table and order your men to do the same."

Briu's impassive face hardly changed expression. He glanced over Wallie, took in Nnanji with a hint of surprise, and then placed his hands on the table. The Seconds followed suit without being ordered; they looked stunned.

"Why is it always you that I damage?" Wallie demanded. "I had no quarrel with you, yet every time I do anything I mess up Adept Briu. You are Tarru's vassal?"

"I refuse to answer that question."

"He's hunting me down. He plans to torture me to make me tell him where the sword is. Do you deny it?"

"No. Nor do I confirm it."

"How does a man of honor feel about this?"

Briu's eyes narrowed. "What makes you think I am a man of honor?"

"Nnanji said so, about two minutes before you challenged him that first morning."

"He was lying."

"I don't think he was."

Briu shrugged. "Any crime committed by a vassal is laid to the account of his liege. If I am Tarru's vassal as you claim, then I am sworn to absolute obedience, and my honor is of no account."

"Why would you swear that oath to such a man?" inquired Nnanji's soft voice from behind Wallie's shoulder. He sounded bitter.

"I might ask you the same question, adept," Briu said.

Nnanji made a choking sound, then said, "You saw Shonsu go into the water. You, better than any, know that his sword was a miracle!"

Briu stared at him stoically. "I did not do a good job of instructing you in the third oath when I was your mentor, adept. Let us see how I did otherwise. If a commander is corrupt, whose duty is it to do something about it?"

After a moment, Nnanji whispered, "His deputy's."

"How? What should he do?"

"Challenge, if he is good enough. Else go and find a

stronger force." It was a quotation. He sounded like Briu as he said it.

Briu nodded. "Yet your Lord Shonsu let Tarru live, when he was obviously guilty."

That, Wallie knew, had been his first error. The god had told him that harsh measures would be necessary. At their very first meeting, he had warned that an honorable swordsman would feel it his duty to kill Hardduju and to restore the honor of the craft. He had even dropped a broad hint when he mentioned Napoleon, for Napoleon *had* been king of Elba, briefly. By sparing Tarru, Wallie had betrayed the honest men in the guard. He should have killed Tarru out of hand, taken charge, and put the Fifths on trial right there, calling for denunciations... but he had not.

"I admit the error," Wallie said. "Nnanji almost pointed it out to me right afterward, on the temple steps. But since then I have been Tarru's guest."

Briu ran contempt over him like a blowtorch. "You had plenty of chances, and excuses. He swore Gorramini and Ghaniri by the third oath, and set them on Nnanji. Then he went to work on the Fifths. Did you not know?"

A Seventh should not take this from a Fourth, but Wallie was feeling too guilty to be assertive. "I suspected."

"So?" Briu demanded. "If you had done something and called for help, do you think the rest of us would have stood idly by? We wanted leadership! We wanted our honor back! None of us was perfect, but..." He paused, and then looked down at the table. "There was one. If the rest of us had been half as honorable as he, we would have mutinied years ago."

Wallie's excuse would never pass a swordsman—he had been trying to prevent bloodshed. He had spared Tarru, one man. When Nnanji had mentioned the stables, he had recoiled from the thought of killing three men. Yet every delay had raised the price. If somehow he could escape now, then the cost in lives must be much higher.

Before he could speak, Briu looked up again, red-faced and glaring. "Even this morning! Gorramini was betrayed! Yet you did *nothing!*"

"I am doing something now," Wallie said firmly.

Briu looked again at the slave costume and spat.

Shonsu's temper flamed. Wallie suppressed it with difficulty. "You have a priest here, and I am going to take him. Then I am leaving." How? "The Goddess will attend to the honor of Her guard. It was not the task She gave me."

Briu shrugged and went back to brooding over his hands on the table.

"Why did you swear the third oath to Tarru?" Nnanji asked again.

"My wife had just given birth to twin sons, adept," Briu said. "She needs to eat, and so do they. When you are older, you will understand."

Swordsmen were addicted to fearsome oaths, but they were human.

"Briu," Wallie said, "my story is too long to explain here. But I admit my error. If I get a chance to correct it, then I shall. I do have a task for the Goddess. I need honest men to help. Is your wife well enough to travel?"

Shonsu, Nnanji, Katanji, plus Briu and his family . . . seven, if one did not count slaves.

"No, my lord. And neither am I."

Wallie told Katanji to take the men's swords.

The new roof made the jail hotter than ever, and smellier. His head swam as soon as he went in, and he wondered how long a frail old man like Honakura could survive in it. There were four prisoners there, all tethered by one ankle only, but Wallie was too bitter now to feel satisfaction at that small improvement. He headed over to one tiny, shriveled form.

Honakura cackled with amusement when he saw his rescuer. Then he slipped his tiny foot out of the stocks and accepted assistance to stand up.

Wallie pulled a black cloth from his padded bosom.

"You will be a Nameless One, my lord. There is a headband in the pocket. Better dress upstairs, it is cooler."

Still chuckling, Honakura tottered toward the steps. Wallie made the slaves pin the swordsmen in the stocks, and then pinned the slaves as well.

"Good-bye, adept," he said to Briu. "We are none of us perfect."

Briu sighed. "No. And I suppose we must keep trying to do better."

Wallie held out a hand. After a pause, Briu took it. "I do hope some man tries to rape you on your journey, my lord."

Still laughing at that unexpected humor, Wallie went back up to the guard room. He handed Katanji back his sword and then had to help him put it in his scabbard. Honakura had dressed himself in the black garment, and Nnanji was tying the headband on for him.

"We are in serious trouble, my...old man," Wallie said. "How we are going to get out of it, I don't know. But we had better get back to the barracks as soon as we can."

"The barracks?" Honakura said innocently. "Why not out into the town?"

"And how do you propose..." Wallie began, then glared at him. "Hell's knuckles! There is a back door, I suppose?"

"Of course," Honakura said. "Did you think the priests would not have a back door? You never asked me."

He cackled in shrill glee.

††

Once away from the jail they rearranged themselves, putting the two swordsmen in front and the two black robes behind. Honakura stumbled along, holding up his too-long gown and hurrying as much as he could. Wallie was not much more agile himself, his half-healed feet starting to chafe at the slave sandals he wore. And a slow pace was advisable anyway; it was too hot to rush. The few people they passed paid no attention to them.

The old man directed Nnanji in asthmatic gasps. They traveled downstream almost to the end of the grounds, then along a wooded trail close to the great wall.

"We shall need a shovel, I suspect," he wheezed at one point, and the gods directed them past a deserted wheelbarrow of tools. Wallie had only to take two steps out of his way to collect a shovel. Then the priest said, "Is it all clear?" and they turned into the bushes.

Well hidden in the undergrowth, an ancient and weathered dovecote stood hard against the perimeter wall, its stones lichen-coated and half-rotted with age. The door was small and decrepit. It yielded easily to Wallie's shoulder, and a great explosion of wings sounded inside.

The interior was gloomy and dark, rank and filthy. Thick piles of guano on the floor crawled with beetles. Curtains of spiderwebs shone in the light filtering through a hole in the roof. Surprised white birds peered down from the pigeonholes that lined the upper walls.

"Unless we were seen," Wallie said, "we are safe here. Obviously no one has been in here for years."

"For generations!" Honakura retorted. "I only hope that the route is still open. It probably has not been used for centuries. Perhaps never before." He sneezed. "The other end may be bricked up."

"Cheerful!" Wallie said. "I think Katanji should go for the others, don't you, Nnanji?"

Nnanji, still gloomy, nodded.

"We need someone to close up behind us," said the priest.

"Then bring Jja, Cowie, and Ani," Wallie ordered. The boy grinned and headed for the door. "Walk slowly! If anyone asks, you're Adept Briu's new protégé, on an errand for him ... you can refuse to discuss what it is. And bring my boots!"

Katanji departed.

Honakura chuckled. "And who might Cowie be?"

"I suppose she's number six," Wallie said in a growl, looking around the fetid obscenity of the dovecote. "Nnanji bought a slave."

"And I make seven."

Wallie turned to him in disbelief. "You? With respect, holy one, it will kill you!"

"I expect so," Honakura said calmly, "if by that you mean that I shall never return. It may also kill you, young man, and you have a great deal more to lose than I have. Moreover, you have a good chance of returning."

"What do you mean?"

"You have to return the sword, remember? I don't know what that means any more than you do. But it could mean that you have to bring it back to where you got it."

The doves purred disapprovingly while Wallie pondered the idea of a man of incredible age, accustomed to luxury and easy living, setting out on an unknown mission of hardship and danger. "I don't want to take you."

The priest snorted and then sneezed several times again. "Ever since you gave me the god's message, I knew I would be coming. Don't you think I shall be useful?"

There was no answer to that. "I still think that you should stay," Wallie said, as gently as he could. He had grown to like the old man and wanted to spare him.

"If I don't come then I shall be sent to the Judgment! Of course I am coming. Seven it is! Now, the exit was said to be in the corner farthest from the temple, so I suppose that one."

Wallie scowled at the heaps of guano and handed the shovel to Nnanji. Nnanji had recovered slightly from his sulks, becoming interested in the adventure side of secret passages. He, also, pouted at the filth for a moment. Then he removed his new orange kilt and handed it to Wallie. He started to dig, immediately raising foul clouds of putrid dust. Wallie and the priest beat a cowardly retreat out to the fresh air. They stood in the bushes, talking in whispers.

"How many priests are aware of this?" Wallie asked.

Honakura shook his head. "I don't know," he said. "There are chains. I was told many, many years ago. When my informant died, I told another. But the first man I approached already knew."

Simple, but it had worked for unknown centuries. Wallie should have guessed that the priests would have an escape route unknown to the swordsmen. There might even be more than one.

Then he asked why the old man had been thrown in jail. The answer confirmed what the demigod had told him—he could not understand temple politics. Part of the problem seemed to be that Honakura, planning to depart with Wallie, had surrendered too much power too quickly. There had also been much conspiring about the Swordsmen's Day festival. Honakura had been trying to introduce an affirmation that Wallie's task was the will of the Goddess, thereby ensnaring all the swordsmen present into accepting that. As the will of the Goddess was paramount, in effect he would have negated Tarru's third oath. Nice try, Wallie thought, but he doubted that swordsmen would have taken such direction from mere priests. Whether Tarru had been involved in his downfall, Honakura did not know.

He did not say so, but Wallie wondered if he himself might have been partly to blame. In the Byzantine power dealings of the priesthood, Honakura must have gambled a large part of his influence and reputation on this cryptic swordsman, who had then neglected to clean up the temple guard. Wallie had failed his supporters among the priests as well as the honest swordsmen.

Where was Katanji? Wallie began to fret as time crawled by. He was putting incredible responsibility on an untested boy.

Stooping through the doorway came Nnanji like the Spirit of Plague, thickly coated in gray dust, striped with brown sweat streaks. His eyes were red and streaming. "Trapdoor," he said between coughs. "Can't move it."

Wallie went in and climbed over the heaps of filth to the clearing Nnanji had made. He found a stone manhole cover with a bronze ring, badly corroded by the nitrates in the guano. He took a firm grip and heaved until his joints creaked. For a moment he thought that even he would not be able to move it, but then it crunched loose and tilted up quite easily on a pivot. He scowled down into darkness, wishing he had told Katanji to bring a light. He went back out into daylight to give time for any bad gases down there to dissipate.

The three men sat on the ground in worried silence. Katanji was quite credible unless he ran into Tarru himself, or unless Briu had been discovered and had told his tale. A new First was believable, Wallie told himself firmly, and then wished that he had warned Katanji to keep his eyes open. Two rugmakers' sons would certainly be too many.

"If there is another trapdoor at the other end, then there may be a house on it by now," Nnanji suggested gloomily.

"We shall find a staircase within the wall leading upward to a dead end," Wallie said, "with another trap in the floor, down to an alcove on the outside."

The priest peered at him. "How do you know?"

Wallie smiled smugly. "I shall tell you that if you tell me how you knew Katanji had black hair." He got no reply. He was guessing, analyzing the design problem. This was a one-way escape route. Traps were the most secure and reliable seals. The demigod had told him that the town burned down every fifty years or so, and he had seen how the buildings went right up to the walls. An alcove would be a useful closet space, and so would be incorporated into each reconstruction. Anything else might end behind a wall or under a floor.

A party of gardener slaves sauntered along the path, and the watchers stayed silent. Then a meditating priest went by, mumbling sutras to himself.

At last Katanji and the others arrived, and Wallie realized just how tense he had become. He welcomed Jja and Vixini with a hug. Cowie looked bewildered when Nnanji put an arm around her. Obviously she was not quite sure who he was. Did not her new owner have red hair?

Ani chuckled as she reported that Honorable Tarru was ready to die of apoplexy, so incensed was he by the disappearance of the fugitives and the lackadaisical performance of his vassals. He had scoured the whole barracks and the main public buildings, and was now about to begin a search of the grounds. Janghiuki's body would turn up soon, then. And then the guard would be after Wallie in earnest, screaming for vengeance on the recreant.

Ani had brought flint, steel, and tapers.

"What made you do that?" Wallie demanded, delighted.

"The scratcher said to, my lord."

Wallie looked at Katanji's twinkling eyes in astonishment and congratulated him, admitting to himself that the Goddess had chosen his companions better than he could have done.

With Nnanji left outside as guard, the others crept into the dovecote and inspected the passage. The taper burned confidently when Wallie lowered it into the hole, so the air was fresh. Katanji was hopping up and down with excitement and he had earned the reward—Wallie sent him in to explore.

He returned in about five minutes.

"There is a staircase, my lord . . ."

Wallie returned Honakura's admiring gaze with much satisfaction.

The passage was very cramped for Wallie. Centuries of ants and other insects had fouled it horribly; fortunately there seemed to be no scorpions.

At the top of the steps was the tiny chamber he had predicted. He could not stand up straight in it, but again his strength was needed to lift the trap in the floor. He had counted the steps and could guess that the underlying alcove must be very low, probably about the size of a dog kennel. He hoped it was not being used for that purpose. Awkwardly, bumping against the walls, he gripped the bronze ring and heaved. Dim light flooded up around him.

He dropped to his knees to put his head through the hole and see where he was.

It was arguable who was more surprised—Wallie or the mule.

†††

Pilgrims mostly traveled in the morning and evening. Noontime was slack time and thus it was the custom of Ponofiti, skinner of the third rank, to stable his string at midday—but without unsaddling them, for he was a lazy man. He had gone home for lunch with his wife, and then to visit his mistress for a siesta. It was early afternoon before he returned to work.

Just an ordinary day in the life of a muleskinner.

Until he unbolted the stable door.

Katanji had squeezed down into the hoard of litter in the alcove—broken chairs and pieces of harness and miscellaneous sacks—and persuaded the hinny to let him move her to a stall without an alcove. Then he had cleared a path for the others.

Jja had explained why mules stood in the dim and smelly stable in the middle of the day.

Jja, also, had located saddler's gear and stitched her master's disguise back together where the pillows were showing. Wallie had found a mirror and confirmed that the dust had turned his hair gray, which was appropriate for the old-woman's dress he wore. If he kept his head down, he might escape much notice in the town.

Nnanji had angrily agreed that a clean orange kilt looked out of place on him in his present condition, and had rubbed it well with stable filth. He had even unfastened his ponytail, growling obscenities, unable to bring himself to look at his disguised leader.

Ani, they assumed, had covered the other trap with guano, closed the dovecote door, and returned to the barracks.

Cowie, having done nothing, had somehow stayed cleaner and fresher than any of them. Wallie intercepted Nnanji leading her to the hayloft and prohibited such evaluation until further notice.

Vixini had expressed a strong desire to mount a mule by climbing its back leg, but his mother had restrained him.

Honakura had found a grain sack to sit on and grin toothlessly.

Now there was nothing left to do but wait for the skinner to return.

Ponofiti was not a large man and he entered the stable much faster than he ever had before, assisted by Wallie's hand in his hair. The door was closed behind him.

The skinner was swarthy, rat-faced, and even ranker than his mules, but he was not entirely stupid. The sight of his own dagger in front of his eyes sufficed to concentrate his attention.

"What is your normal fare from here to the jetty?" asked the huge figure that wore an old slave woman's black dress and spoke with a man's bass voice.

"Three coppers . . . master?" he said.

Wallie lifted his curls to let him count the marks. They had even more effect than the dagger.

"My lord!"

If the brigands had confederates in the guard, it was highly probable that they also controlled the skinners, by graft or by coercion. There could be signals. Wallie reached out to a convenient ledge on the wall and carefully laid down five gold coins. After a moment's thought he added two more.

"That stays here until you return," he said. The man's eyes said it was a fortune. "I shall be riding the mule directly behind you. If we are stopped by brigands or by swordsmen, especially swordsmen"— he hurled the dagger, and it slammed into the wall —"you will not be returning. Any questions?"

Concealing the swords would be difficult. It took all of Wallie's absolute third-oath authority to persuade Nnanji to hand over his sword and harness, and he did so with sullen ill temper. They were wrapped in sacking with Katanji's and strapped on one of the mules under a bag of grain. Wallie's was back in the barracks somewhere. Thus, unarmed except for the dagger hidden in Wallie's ample bosom, the adventurers rode out on the string of mules, heading through the town toward the checkpoint at the foot of the hill.

Except for Cowie, they were all incredibly filthy. Wallie knew that he looked a freak, with muscular male legs hanging below an obese female shape. Nnanji, with his hair a greasy cake of black frizz, was merely a skinny Fourth of indeterminate craft, although unusually young for such a rank. Katanji was only an anonymous First. The others should not attract notice.

The checkpoint was the great danger, for there were eight men there, and Wallie had only a dagger. Had it not been for the feeble Honakura, Wallie would never have dared to try passing the checkpoint—there had to be another way up the hillside somewhere.

The swordsmen were lounging in the shade of an arbutus tree, watching the traffic from a distance, not inspecting closely. Their relaxed attitude proved that the murder victim had not yet been found. They were looking for a swordsman of the Seventh, or possibly his vassal, and most of them would still be thinking of Nnanji as a Second. They had no interest in a group of half a dozen miscellaneous pilgrims. Highranks would not mix with such riffraff, and the idea that a swordsman of the Seventh would disguise himself as a female slave would never occur to them if they lived to be as old as the temple. Wallie kept his face down and sweated even harder than he had been doing before, but in a few minutes the mule train was past the checkpoint and climbing the hill.

Brigands were not likely to bother pilgrims departing. They would prefer to plunder before the priests did, not after. So all that remained for Wallie to do was to retrieve the seventh sword and then shepherd his party safely onto a boat. Sounded simple! If he reached the jetty before news of his crime arrived, then he could hope that the watchers there would be as negligent as the farcical force at the checkpoint—the inefficient reluctant to perform the unpopular. For the first time in many days, Wallie began to feel hopeful. He prayed.

The sword was easy. All mules needed a rest somewhere on the hill, and he shouted to the skinner to stop when they reached the fourteenth cottage. "Mule train. Ferry mule train," the skinner called obediently. Wallie and Jja dismounted.

They slipped through the curtain and found the cottage empty. She had chosen it because it was one of the most dilapidated, and hence rarely used. There was filth all over the floor, no furniture except two rotting mattresses. Apparently the hovel in which he had first met Jja had been one of the luxury suites.

"There, master," she said, pointing, and all Wallie had to do was reach up and pull the seventh sword out of the thatch. It shone in his hand, the sapphire flamed, and his heart leaped once more at the sight of its beauty. He held it up to admire it briefly, and then reluctantly wrapped it in Vixini's blanket.

Jja had turned to go, but the nasty little hut was reminding him of their first night together. He reached out and took her arm. She turned to stare at him questioningly.

"Jja?" he said.

"Master?"

He shook his head. She smiled and whispered, "Wallie?"

He nodded. "This is the second treasure I have found in these huts."

She glanced out the doorway at the steaming mules and frowned slightly. Then she turned back to him. "Show me the World, master?"

"If you will give me a kiss?"

She dropped her eyes demurely. "A good slave only obeys orders."

"Kiss me, slave!"

"Ferry mule train!" the skinner called. He was outside the door, but he sounded far away to Wallie.

Embracing while upholstered like a sofa was lacking in romance, but a moment later Wallie said breathlessly, "Kiss me again, slave."

"Master!" she murmured reproachfully. "We must go!" Yet there was a gaiety and happiness about her that he had not seen before. She was leaving a place that could hold few pleasant memories for her. Slaves were not supposed to have feelings, but whatever these squalid huts meant to Wallie, to Jja they must be a reminder that there she had been included in the rent.

And he knew that she was right. They would have to go, or the unusually long pause might attract attention. "Quickly, then!"

They kissed again, briefly, and then stepped to the door. As always, he wanted her to precede him. As always, she hung back. He insisted; she obeyed.

Then she backed into him, pushing him quickly into the cottage again. "Horses!" she said.

Wallie risked a glance. There were three of them coming up the hill, bearing a red, an orange, and a green —Tarru himself!

"Skinner!" Wallie waved for the train to move on. He

unwrapped the sword and stepped to the window. Keeping well back, he watched as the string went by...

First rode the skinner himself, slumped over in his saddle, bored; Nnanji, hair black as coal, holding Vixini and trying to reassure him that his mother would be back soon; Katanji twisted round to stare down the hill; Honakura hunched on his saddle and already looking exhausted; and Cowie at the end.

Wallie's eyes locked into position. It was the first time he had seen Cowie in full sunlight. And Cowie on a mule! All her spectacular leg was visible, and the net garment had pulled tight to display the rest of that sensational body. Wow! Shonsu's glands went into a crash program of hormone production just looking at her. She was wrong, he was sure, an error. Someone else ought to be on that saddle, almost certainly another swordsman, an older and more experienced man than Nnanji. Another fighter. But Wallie did not know who, and...Oh! what a sight!

Then the sound of hooves grew louder.

Had they been recognized? It did not seem possible. Much more likely was that Tarru had decided to move his strongest force, himself, to the jetty. If he could not find his quarry in the temple grounds, then that was his best strategy, for there he could not be outflanked.

Had the body of the Third been found?

Perhaps. And Briu? The jail guard was changed at noon, and Briu would have been rescued then, if not before. He would have reported that Lord Shonsu had said he was leaving.

Worse, Briu could have warned that Honakura was with the fugitives and wearing black, and that Nnanji now had black hair. Fortunately Nnanji was holding the baby, which would tend to distract attention from him, but Tarru was certain to inspect the mules as he went by. However unwilling some of his followers might be, Tarru at least was motivated, and Tarru was no fool.

Or perhaps...a sudden realization struck Wallie with

horror. Perhaps the checkpoint had been too easy. Perhaps it had been a blind. The men's orders might have been to allow the fugitives through and report back to the temple. Even for Tarru, murder would be better committed outside the town, in the jungle.

Tarru, a Fifth, and a Fourth... they were coming up that gradient much too fast for the good of their mounts. Wallie and Nnanji together could probably handle those three in a straight fight, on level terms. But the three were on horseback, Nnanji was unarmed, and there were eight more men at the bottom of the hill.

Even with the seventh sword of Chioxin, Wallie did not think Shonsu could best three mounted men single-handed.

He pulled back from the window and listened to the hooves, waiting for the sound to falter.

The train had crawled four or five cottages higher when the three horsemen went thudding by the hut where the sword they sought was gripped in a white-knuckled hand. And the beat of the hooves did not change.

Wallie risked sticking his head out the door for a glance after them. He pulled back quickly, for all three men had twisted round in their saddles to look—he glimpsed Tarru, Trasingji, and Ghaniri. Briefly he thought the game was lost, but the horses still did not break stride. In a few minutes the sound died away.

He wiped his brow and looked at Jja. In one spontaneous movement, they threw their arms around each other.

"Cowie!" he said at last.

She looked up at him blankly.

He explained. They started to laugh. They were still laughing as he wrapped the sword in Vixi's blanket again, and still laughing when they ran off hand in hand to catch the train.

Cowie was not a mistake. She was truly one of the seven chosen by the gods. She had brought them safely by the checkpoint also, although he had not realized at the time.

Tarru and Trasingji and Ghaniri had passed within a sword's length of Nnanji, and all they had seen was Cowie.

†† ††

The mules crawled by the last of the huts, and the dusty trail continued to climb the valley wall. The town and temple were spread out far below, with the pillar of spray from the Judgment of the Goddess standing over them like a guardian.

Wallie cursed in silence against the forced inactivity of sitting on a slothful mule. Briefly, from the top of the hill, he had a last glimpse of the whole valley, clasping the great temple to its heart. Then it was gone. Someday, perhaps, he would return the sword . . . or perhaps not.

The road, now no more than a trail, wound through vegetation that became steadily thicker until it was a true tropical forest, a high trellis of treetops arched against the sky and a tangle of ground cover. The shade deepened. Even the far-off rumble of the falls faded away, until the only sound came from the feet of the mules, plodding the stones at their unvarying mulish pace, oblivious of any human urgency or turmoil.

From time to time they passed clearings showing red soil planted with crops that Wallie could not identify, and rarely smaller trails branched off and disappeared mysteriously into the jungle. Few other travelers shared the road at first, only rare pilgrims walking in twos and threes and half a dozen mule trains bringing in those who could afford a ride. But as the day began to age small groups of farm workers appeared, slouching along without a glance at the fugitives.

There was no evidence of brigands, but they would

not advertise, and he could not relax. Certainly the road could have been designed for them; it wound and twisted and rolled. At every bend he half expected to see a line of armed men standing in his path.

He sweated unendingly in his pillows and a fog of flies. His canteen was soon empty. Apparently the stirrup had not yet been invented in the World, and the saddles were a sadistic torment, rubbing folds of wet clothing against his flesh to raise blisters, then rubbing them away again. Heat prostration was becoming a real hazard for him now, and he finally decided that he had better conserve what was left of his fighting strength. He slipped off his mount and stripped back down to his kilt and harness. The relief was unspeakable. Out of his padding came his boots. He put them on, tucked the skinner's dagger in his belt, and ran to catch up with the train.

First he reached Cowie, who looked pitifully confused and miserable. He tried speaking to her, but she merely blinked slowly and did not reply. "Won't be long!" he assured her and could not resist patting her lovely thigh. In a few days Nnanji would likely be honored to lend... He suppressed that lustful thought firmly.

He stepped out again to catch up with Honakura and was shocked by his haggard appearance.

"Are you all right, holy one?"

For a moment there was no reply. Then Honakura peered at him and said, "No. What are you going to do about it?" and closed his eyes once more.

Katanji did not have a grin as huge as his brother's, but he was doing the best he could, obviously enjoying himself greatly. If this was a swordsman's life, then he was obviously in favor, not knowing that he had already found more excitement than he should normally encounter in years.

Wallie called to Nnanji, who jumped off and came back to walk on the other side. He noticed the dagger at once and scowled at it. Katanji was now looking down on a swordsman escort; he seemed to find that more fun than ever.

"Can I have my sword back now?" Not having appeared unarmed in public since he reached adolescence, Nnanji must be feeling horribly naked and vulnerable without his beloved sword.

"Not yet!" Wallie said. "I only stripped because I was cooking like meat in a pie. You saw Tarru go by—I think he'll stay at the jetty, but he might return. There may well be messengers going to and fro. So we won't show our swords yet. If we hear hooves, then it's the bushes for me. Now, tell me about the dock."

Nnanji said, "I was only there once, when I was a First." The grieved expression faded as he stalked along beside the mule, looking blankly ahead, retrieving from his infallible databank.

Wallie could feel very sorry for Nnanji. Only that morning his world had come together just as he might have planned it. He had made his first challenge, proved his courage against a real sword, and made his first kill—all those things would matter greatly to him. He had achieved middlerank, so that he could accept his brother's oath and buy that dream slave. How he must have been relishing the thought of displaying her in the saloon that evening!

Then the world had all come apart again, much worse than before. His hero had proved to have not merely feet of clay, but devils' hooves. Midnight had chimed. Cinderella's coach had turned into a lemon.

"The road ends suddenly," Nnanji said, "in a clearing by the water's edge—about a hundred paces both ways —and there is a paddock in it and only one building, the guardhouse. That's about twenty paces square, I should think. You can only get to the jetty by going through the guardhouse—the road runs right through. Big arch one end and another at the other. Horse stalls on one side, and rooms on the other—a kitchen and dormitory and such. It was messy and not much used when I saw it.

Nothing upstairs but a loft—hay and so on. No windows on the horses' side. That's . . . downstream.''

"Very well done!" Wallie said. "Good report, adept."

Nnanji's smile died stillborn. For a while they walked along beside the mule in silence, flapping hands at flies.

Wallie said, "I'm going to slip away before we reach it, then. As soon as I go, you can put on your sword."

He glanced up at Katanji. "You listen to this, too. I ask you, Nnanji, to get the others safely to Hann. Don't argue! That's the best thing you can do for me, for then I have only myself to worry about. I shall try to get on the boat as it leaves, but don't hold it for me—just go. Wait for me in Hann. We need a rendezvous. You must have heard of some inns in Hann?"

Another recall. "There's The Seven Swords."

"No, I don't want one where swordsmen might stay."

Nnanji looked surprised and thought some more. "The Gold Bell, but the food is bad."

Incredible memory! That must have come from some chance remark, perhaps heard years ago. Wallie was going to miss Nnanji.

"Right! If I'm not on the boat, then please put Jja and Vixi and the old man in The Gold Bell and pay their board for ten days. If there's no word from me by then, I give you Jja. The old man you can trust, but he doesn't look as though he'll live to the jetty, let alone Hann."

"Tarru won't let me through," Nnanji said angrily.

"I think he may, Nnanji, and I'm only asking you to look after Jja, not telling you." Wallie took a deep breath. "I'm going to release you from your oaths."

"NO!" Nnanji shouted, staring in horror across the mule at him. "You must not, my liege!"

"I'm going to. I'd do it now, but I don't want you putting on your sword."

"But . . ." Probably Nnanji had thought that things could not get worse, and now they had.

"But you will have to denounce me," Wallie said, completing the thought. "You have seen abominations. It is your duty to denounce me to a higher rank or stronger force. Tarru's is a stronger force. Go ahead! He'll love it. He'll be so happy that he'll let you go free."

"The second oath can't be annulled unless I agree, too!" Nnanji said triumphantly.

"Then I order you to agree!" Wallie replied, amused at the backward logic of the conversation. "As my vassal you must obey, right?"

It really wasn't fair to tie up Nnanji in such mental knots. He had no answer, his face a wasteland of despair. Now he was torn between his ideals and his duty on one hand and—clearly—personal loyalty on the other. Wallie was touched, but determined.

"You don't trust me!" Nnanji muttered.

There was truth in that. His loyalty was unquestionable, but his subconscious might be resurrecting the killer earthworm.

"I trust your honor and your courage totally, Nnanji, but I think that this is leading to a showdown between me and Tarru. I want Jja taken care of—you will do that for me? For friendship alone?"

"But Tarru committed abominations first," Nnanji said angrily. "How can I denounce you to him?"

That was Wallie's defense, of course. "Did you see those? Do you have any evidence, except what the slaves said? A slave's testimony is not admissible, Nnanji."

Nnanji had no answer.

"He probably doesn't know you know of his misdeeds," Wallie said. "Anyway, I'm going to release you and I'm going to leave you. Now, please, Nnanji my friend, will you look after Jja and Vixini for me, and the old man if he lives?"

Angrily, not looking at him, Nnanji nodded.

"But it is possible that Tarru will detain you and let the rest go," Wallie said, wondering if Tarru would know that Honakura was a fugitive from his jail. "If so, then you, novice, will then have to do what I just told Nnanji. The old man is a Nameless One. Neither he nor the slaves can carry money. If Nnanji is stopped, you are in charge."

The light died from Katanji's youthful face. Wallie rehearsed him, made sure he understood, and gave him money. When he had done, both brothers looked equally worried and unhappy.

"Now cheer up!" Wallie said. "The Goddess is with us, and I'm sure She will see us safely through this. And one last thing—if the worst happens, don't sell Vixini away from Jja! Good luck."

He trotted forward to talk with Jja for a while. She smiled bravely at him, but she was worried about Vixini, who was exhausted and hungry. Wallie could say little to cheer her up. Then he returned to his own mule, the mule that carried the most valuable piece of movable property in the World. He sat and brooded some more.

It was a strategy of desperation. If, by a miracle, Tarru was not at the jetty, then Nnanji and the others might very easily get through unquestioned. If that happened, Wallie was going to swim out to their boat, or another. If Tarru was there, then he might let Nnanji go—unlikely! Or he might detain Nnanji and let the others through—not much more likely. But at least they would distract him while Wallie improvised something. He was not fighting the whole guard, now—maybe ten or a dozen, and half of those would be trash. The odds were getting better.

At long last the trees thinned, the trail reached a cliff edge, and he had his first view of the River. He was astonished at the size of it. He could barely see the far bank, although he was atop a scarp that was almost as high as the wall of the temple valley. In the far distance the evening sun gleamed on roofs and spires, probably temples in Hann, but otherwise only a faint line divided blue sky from a vastness of twinkling water, decorated here and there with sails of various colors and shapes. For the first time he could appreciate how this great navigable flood so dominated the culture of the People that they would worship it as their Goddess.

He prayed that he might win through to sail on it. He wondered where it might take him.

The trail wavered in and out of the woods, giving glimpses of the bank ahead and then a brief view of the port. He saw the solitary wooden building on the water's edge and a jetty of red stonework running out a long way over the pale-blue water. At the end of it a boat was unloading and loading passengers—the River must be very shallow there to need so long a pier. Then it all vanished behind more trees.

His next concern was where to leave the mule train. He got his answer when the trail abruptly plunged back into jungle and started to descend a thickly wooded gully. Soon the trail was almost as dark as night and completely concealed. He could relax and wait until they were almost there. A mule train came by, bringing in another contingent of pilgrims.

Then the slope leveled off. The road ahead began to brighten. He shouted to the skinner to halt, dismounted, and went up to him.

"How far now, skinner?"

"Next bend, my lord," the rat-faced man replied nervously.

"You have done us proudly," Wallie said. "Enjoy your reward when you get back. I need a minute, here."

As he walked back to the apprehensive Nnanji, the mules started to bray angrily, smelling the water ahead.

"Nnanji of the—"

"No! Please, my liege! Don't!" Nnanji was in torment.

Wallie smiled and shook his head. "Nnanji of the Fourth, I release you from your oaths." He did not offer to shake hands, not as a man without honor. "Please don't watch where I go," he said. "The Goddess be with you, friend. You were a great vassal!"

Then he shouted to the skinner to go ahead, pulled the seventh sword from its place on the mule, and stepped into the trees.

†† † ††

Tarru might have set watchers in the woods, but that was unlikely if the situation was as Nnanji had described it. The man was holding a very strong tactical position and he need not divide his forces. He was facing an open meadow and he had horses. He held the only road. Wallie must come to him. He had the numbers.

The jungle canopy was so dense that there was almost no ground cover. Wallie pounded along between the pillars, through the hot green gloom, until he reached a wall of undergrowth flourishing in the sunlight at the edge of the clearing. He could catch glimpses of the guardhouse now, but he turned upstream and ran around, heading for the water, his feet thumping squishily in rotting leaves. The downstream side had no windows, Nnanji had said, so there was more likely to be a sentry there.

Then he was at the bank and he stopped to catch his breath, gasping in the sultry heat. Two or three billion insects discovered him at once and brought their friends. Ignoring them, he peered out through the leaves.

The meadow was, as Nnanji had said, flat, grassy, and open. It ran down very gently to the River, ending in a bank as low as a doorstep. It contained no cover, just a ramshackle corral at the end of the trail. The colors were all as brilliant as a child's painting—grass and jungle in vibrant greens, the water an improbable sparkling blue.

Only the guardhouse was drab, its planks shabby, silvered by weather, and showing many layers of patchings. Larger than he had expected, it straddled the water's edge and the start of the crumbling red stone jetty. The jetty was deserted at the moment, but another boat was coming in. His friends had dismounted and were slowly making their way over the meadow to the building.

There were no guards in sight, no one but his party and the skinner. Trap?

Nnanji and his brother were wearing their swords again. They were supporting Honakura between them, making slow progress. Vixini was wailing loudly in his sling on Jja's back. Cowie was following Nnanji in a seductive hip-swinging saunter.

Wallie waited until they had entered the building, in case they saw him and gave him away to watchers. He counted time to the moment of maximum distraction. They would enter an empty shed, walk forward . . . when the last one was inside, the trap would be sprung behind them. Tarru would accost them. After a moment or two Nnanji would tell them he was no longer Shonsu's vassal . . . surprise and reevaluation . . .

Time to go!

Wallie plunged through the thorns and branches, then sprinted along the edge of the bank. The skinner had taken his mules to the far side of the building and was swinging a bucket on a pole, loading water into a drinking trough. Wallie reached the building and stopped, panting again.

Nothing happened. No alarm, no shouts, no challenge. No one had been posted in the trees, no one at the windows. He had not expected that. Now what?

Two doors opened into the shed, and the landward one would certainly be guarded. He stepped down carefully into the water. It was full of weeds, but it came only halfway up his boots, and the bottom was firm. He waded out along the side of the guardhouse, trying not to splash, gradually going deeper. His boots filled with a cool rush, and then he had trouble keeping them from falling off at every step. When he reached the far end of the building, the water was well above his knees, soaking his kilt, wonderfully welcome and cool.

The red stonework of the jetty was rough, but coated with algae below the waterline. The deck was level with his shoulders. Along the wall of the building, flanking both sides of the doorway arch, lay a litter of broken wheels and scrap lumber, rotted fishing nets and old baskets. He found finger purchase between the cobbles, hauled himself up, and bent his knees to tip water from his boots.

He knelt there for a moment, puzzled. He had outflanked the guard. That seemed to have been suspiciously easy.

Then he heard voices, laughter—the clash of swords.

He crawled on hands and knees around the junk pile to the edge of the doorway and peered in with his head at floor level.

There were ten of the guard there. The closest, with his back turned to Wallie, was the square-hewed figure of Trasingji, blocking any final escape to the jetty.

Farthest away, and just inside the landward doorway, three lowranks were guarding Jja, Katanji, and the rest.

Slightly closer stood a line of five middleranks, Fourths and Fifths, all watching Nnanji and Tarru himself, both with swords drawn. Nnanji lunged, Tarru parried easily, and laughed. Then he waited for his victim's next move, playing cat to Nnanji's mouse.

That morning Nnanji had revealed himself as a first-class swordsman. Tarru was now going to cut him down to size. It would be bloody murder.

Wallie was not going to allow that. He rose, slipped the dagger from his belt with his left hand, and unsheathed the sword of the Goddess.

In an obscure corner of his mind he registered that the next ferry boat had docked behind him, but he paid no attention. The scene was taking on a strange pink tinge. He could hear an ominous noise that he had heard before, a grinding of teeth. He knew what was happening, and this time he let it happen. When the bloodlust was upon him, Shonsu was a berserker.

Shonsu now took over.

With a barbaric scream of fury, he launched himself forward. As he went by Trasingji, he pushed the dagger into his back and then tugged it loose again, without even breaking stride. Out of the corner of his eye, he saw the man begin to crumple, but already he was bearing down on Tarru and Nnanji, howling for blood, his hair standing on end and his eyes red. Tarru started to turn and was cut down from behind with a sideways slash to the base of the rib cage, where there was little chance of a sword being caught between bones. It would not kill at once, but it would put the man out of the fight.

Nnanji's jaw dropped, and his comic charcoal eyebrows shot up. His face was a ludicrous, frozen picture of horror, his sword suspended uselessly in midair, as the monster rushed past him.

Wallie was often to wonder later what would have happened had he stopped there—halted, waved the blood-soaked sword of the Goddess at the middleranks, and told them that it was Her will that he leave the island with the sword. Very likely they would have agreed, and the killing would have been over at that point. That would have been the way of sweet reason, and certainly the choice of the old Wallie Smith. But it might also have been suicide, for surprise was his only advantage. It was not a tactic to appeal to Shonsu when the bloodlust was upon him. Harsh measures, the god had said . . .

The line of five Fourths and Fifths awoke too late to their peril, to the realization that this nemesis was bearing down on them also. They started to draw. He took the middle one as a start. As the man pulled his blade from its scabbard, he was spitted by the seventh sword extended at arm's length. His neighbor to Shonsu's left managed to draw, but before he could reach guard position the attacker's momentum brought them into chest-to-chest contact, and he died on the dagger.

That left two to the right and one to the left, and just for a moment they were delayed by the shock of the deaths, and by the two bodies falling in their path. Shonsu stumbled from the impact, pulled his dagger free, and swung around to lock swords with the first man on his right—Ghaniri, he noted through the red mist. He forced the weapons high, striking once more with the dagger, this time at his opponent's sword arm. It hit bone. Ghaniri yelled and fell back as Shonsu swung around, parrying a lunge from the single man on the left as though he had seen it through the back of his head. But he knew that Ghaniri was still mobile and still behind him, and there was another man also . . .

Then he heard a clang as swords met, and he knew that Nnanji was in the battle, too, and holding that one.

He made riposte, was parried, and heard the blades *clash—clash—clash*, as though measuring precious seconds off his life. Then he was under his opponent's guard and could bury his sword in his chest, but it caught in the ribs as the body fell, and another vital instant went by while he bent to pull it loose. He swung round, bringing up the dagger in the hope of parrying Ghaniri's inevitable attack behind him. Even as he did so, he knew it was too late.

He caught a momentary vision of Ghaniri's ugly, battered face, contorted in hate or rage or fear. With right elbow high, he was bringing his sword down like a toreador in a long straight-and-true lunge, and there was just no time . . . Then that face showed sudden surprise as Nnanji's sword swept down in a slash to sever his wrist, swung back up, and gutted him. Blood in torrents . . .

Still howling, Shonsu whirled right around in a circle and registered a grinning Nnanji on his feet and five bodies on the ground. Then he raced for the juniors. They had already fled, abandoning their captives. Sword high, he ran after them, straight between Jja and the shrieking Cowie.

He caught up with one just beyond the end of the shed and cut him down without missing a step. The other two separated, one fleeing along the road, the other turning to the right and racing across the meadow. Shonsu came screaming after that one, steadily gaining, until without warning the kid wheeled around and fell on his knees. Shonsu's sword stopped an inch from his neck. His head was tilted back, staring up, with eyes white all round the iris, lips curled in a rictus of terror, hands trembling in the sign of obeisance, waiting.

Red fog faded. Yelling stopped. The sword was withdrawn.

The Second fell forward in a dead faint.

More or less conscious again, but still twitching and jigging, chest heaving hugely, Wallie stared down at him. The events of the past few minutes felt like something remembered from long ages past. Had that been him? That screaming, murdering fiend? He flopped on the grass to catch his breath. His throat was sore.

It was over!

Tarru was dead and the last junior was tearing up the trail as though Hell itself were still on his heels.

He had won.

Praise to the Goddess!

Feeling strangely removed from events, like an onlooker, Wallie wiped his sword on the turf. The Second opened his eyes and twitched with renewed terror on seeing him.

"It's all right," said Wallie, smiling. "It's all over." He rose and sheathed his sword, held out a hand to the kid and helped him up. He was shivering like an aspen with ague. "Relax!" Wallie insisted. "Tarru is dead. You're alive and so am I. That's all that matters. Come on."

He put an arm on the Second's shoulders and led the way back to the shed, not quite sure who was supporting whom. Just outside the doorway was the body of another Second, the one he had cut down. That was bad, very bad. That was the worst thing that had happened in the whole horrible day, for the youngster had been no threat. Even Junghiuki had been a threat, but this one had been running away. He had fallen victim to the berserk frenzy that Wallie had not brought under control in time. Almost it made the whole thing seem not worth while if he had done that.

Inside the door were five more bodies, but those Wallie did not mind so much—especially Ghaniri and the other Fourth whom Nnanji had killed, for their deaths meant that Nnanji was all right. The killer earthworm had not returned. And Nnanji had not done that as a vassal, he had done it for his friend Shonsu. That felt good.

He saw Jja and Cowie and the old man sitting on the floor, backs against the wall, and he smiled at them. He got no answering smiles. Honakura had his eyes closed and seemed to be unconscious. Cowie, as usual, was blank. Jja was staring at him with an expression that surely was meant as a warning.

He looked around groggily. He felt mildly surprised that there were so many men standing there, but they were against the light of the far doorway, and for a moment he could not make them out. Then he distinguished Nnanji.

Nnanji was standing between two swordsmen, quite obviously under arrest.

††† †††

"I am Imperkanni, swordsman of the seventh rank, and I give thanks to the Most High for granting me this opportunity to assure your beneficence that your prosperity and happiness will always be my desire and the subject of my prayers."

"I am Shonsu, swordsman of the seventh rank; I am honored by your courtesy and do most humbly extend the same felicitations to your noble self."

He was a big man, broad and masterful, probably in his late forties. Experience and achievement had sculpted the leathery, square-jawed face into a mask of arrogance and authority. He had bushy salt-and-pepper eyebrows, but his hair had been bleached with lime, giving him a magnificent white ponytail, which he wore longer than most. The only other sign of vanity about him was his poverty—his blue kilt was patched and threadbare, his boots scuffed, his harness positively shabby. Poverty was an affectation of the frees, to show their honesty. Yet his sword was bright and shiny, the heavy arms were scarred, and there were at least a dozen notches in his right shoulder strap.

Here was a true swordsman, a veteran, a professional. Compared to this, Tarru had been garbage. Commander of a private army, owing allegiance to no man, guided only by his own conscience and his Goddess, Imperkanni was one of the powers of the World.

His eyes were the palest Wallie had yet seen among the People, even paler than Nnanji's. Those amber eyes observed the seventh sword and the sapphire hairclip and they narrowed in disapproval. They were very cold, no-nonsense eyes.

"May I have the honor of presenting to the noble Lord Shonsu my protégé, Honorable Yoningu of the Sixth?"

Yoningu was a little younger and slighter, with curly brown hair and quick eyes. His face was oddly lopsided, giving the impression that he might be a fun guy at a party. The fun side of him, if there really was one, was being suppressed at the moment, for he looked as hostile as his leader. He was another fighter, scarred like a butcher's block.

Wallie accepted the salute and glanced across at his former vassal, standing with his head down, looking beaten and crushed.

"We have already met Adept Nnanji," Imperkanni said icily. He turned to Yoningu. "You are willing to do this, protégé?"

"I am, mentor," Yoningu said. He glanced briefly at Wallie and then Nnanji, then said loudly, "I also denounce Lord Shonsu for violations of the seventh sutra."

So he had already denounced Nnanji. Imperkanni would be judge, Yoningu prosecutor. It was primitive justice by Wallie's standards, for both men were also witnesses, and they were probably buddies of many years' standing, but it was better than nothing.

These were the passengers who had disembarked from the boat—about a dozen of them, two slaves and ten or so swordsmen ranging in rank from Second to Seventh. They had arrived just in time to see the fight, a company of the free swords of whom Nnanji spoke with such admiration and longing—the enforcers, the peace-keepers—those who supported, regulated, and, if necessary, avenged the swordsmen of garrison and guard.

Imperkanni glanced out at the meadow and called over his shoulder to one of his men. "Kandanni, make sure those mules don't go without us."

A Third trotted quickly out of the shed.

"Good idea," Wallie said. "Perhaps, my lord, you would be kind enough to detain the boat also."

Imperkanni raised a skeptical eyebrow, but he nodded to a Second, who went running along the jetty. He might be convinced already of the accused's guilt, but he was willing to observe the formalities.

Wallie was so weary that his knees were trembling, but if they were not going to sit down, then he was not going to suggest it. The swordsmen had carefully sealed off the entrance to the meadow in case the prisoners tried to escape and, while both prisoners had been allowed to retain their swords, Wallie was quite certain that it was a mere courtesy. These men would not be pushovers like the temple guard. These men were fighters.

He was to be tried, here and now, in the echoing and blood-spattered guardhouse. It was a strange courtroom: a big wooden shed with a wide cobbled floor like a street running through the middle of it. The horse stalls along one side were open to the high timber ceiling, but the opposite wall was solid, pierced by a few ordinary doors. Barn swallows swooped in and out the archways at the ends, soaring upward to their nests in the rafters, twittering angrily at the men below. If it reminded Wallie of anything at all, it was of a theater stage seen from the rear, the beams and bare flats exposed, and all the bodies from the last act of *Hamlet* strewn over the ground.

The skinner and the boat captain were marched in and made to sit, close to Jja and Cowie. Swordsmen pre-

ferred action to argument. Not that any sane civilian
would argue.

Katanji was standing behind his brother, staring at
Wallie with big, scared eyes. The low evening light was
pouring in the River door, floodlighting Trasingji's body.
Horses were chomping behind the stall doors.

"You may begin, Honorable Yoningu," the judge said.

The prosecutor led the way over to Trasingji. Imperkanni and Wallie walked beside him.

"I observed Lord Shonsu strike this man from behind,
and with a dagger."

They paced back to Tarru. Wallie was staggered to
see that he had cut the man almost in half, and that the
cobbles were drenched with blood all around, as though
he had exploded.

"I observed Lord Shonsu attack this man from behind."

Then the group of five corpses, and Yoningu paused
for a moment, to refresh his memory, or to make sure
that he had significant charges to lay. His wry expression
was caused by a scar, pulling the corner of his mouth
up—perhaps he had no sense of humor at all. If his
mentor ruled against Wallie, would Wallie then become
this man's slave? No, these were capital offenses.

"I observed Lord Shonsu attack these men without
formal challenge. I observed Lord Shonsu strike this one
with a dagger, and this one also." He shrugged, implying
that those charges would do for now.

Imperkanni turned to Wallie. "Do you have any defense?"

"A great deal, my lord." Wallie smiled to show that he
was not feeling guilty. "Honorable Yoningu has missed
one, I think." He pointed between the guarding swordsmen to the body of the Second outside. That one *was* a
capital offense in Wallie's eyes, and the only one.

Yoningu glared at him angrily, as though Wallie were
wasting the time of the court with trivialities. "That man
was running away," he said.

A wave of culture shock broke over Wallie, temporarily choking him. By running away, the boy had forfeited his right to be avenged. Yet, after a moment, Wallie found some comfort in that, because the other Second had stopped and made obeisance, and that had been enough to trigger Shonsu's controls and halt the berserker. Not much comfort, but a little. The first kid would still be alive, had he remembered his training.

The court was waiting for him.

"May I hear the charges against Adept Nnanji, please? Then we shall present our defense."

Imperkanni nodded. Nnanji looked up from his study of the floor and gazed bitterly at the proceedings.

Yoningu hesitated over the first man Nnanji had killed, decided to ignore that one, and pointed casually to the body of Ghaniri. "I observed Adept Nnanji strike this man from behind when he was already fighting another."

Nnanji dropped his eyes again.

"Your defense, my lord?" Imperkanni asked Wallie. His manner implied that it had better be good.

"I think Adept Nnanji has some charges to bring against me, also," Wallie said recklessly.

That had a welcome shock effect, but Imperkanni recovered quickly. "Adept Nnanji?"

Nnanji looked up once more. He stared at Wallie with more pain and reproach than seemed humanly bearable. When he began to speak, he was so quiet that he stopped and started again. "I saw Lord Shonsu draw a sword on Adept Briu this morning without warning. I saw Lord Shonsu disguise himself as a female slave."

That had even more of a shock effect. Wallie was looking regretfully at Honakura. A priest of the Seventh would be an unimpeachable witness, but the old man was still sitting like a rag doll. His eyes were partly open, but showing only the whites. He might be dead, he might be dying, but he was in no condition to testify.

"We are waiting, my lord," Imperkanni said threateningly.

"Are you familiar with the legend of Chioxin?" Wallie asked.

"No," Imperkanni said.

Hell!

Then he noticed the Second he had spared. He was cowering beside a post, hunched and still shivering.

"Let's have an independent witness, my lord," Wallie said. "My story is unusual, to say the least, and I should prefer to have it corroborated. You! What's your name?"

The Second rolled his eyes and said nothing. One of the free swords, a Fourth, went over to him and slapped his face. The kid gibbered slightly, and drooled.

Hell and damnation!

"Then I must tell it myself, I suppose," Wallie said. He needed food, drink, and about two nights' sleep. "The reeve of the temple guard, Hardduju of the Seventh, was a very corrupt man. The priests have long prayed that the Goddess would send them a replacement..."

That replacement was obviously Imperkanni, but to mention that would sound like a bribe, or an attempt at flattery. It was ironic that the man whom Wallie had hoped might come to rescue him had instead turned up in time to threaten him with vengeance for winning the battle. This whole thing was infinitely ironic. He hoped that the little god was finding it amusing.

Halfway through the story he had to ask for a drink. Imperkanni was not a consciously cruel man. Now he noted Wallie's fatigue and ordered seats. His men jumped to search the rooms and produced stools. The court continued to meet at the scene of the crime, a circle of four in the midst of carnage. Wallie, Nnanji, Imperkanni, and Yoningu. The other swordsmen moved in to stand around them, alert and impassive.

Finally, hoarse and so weary that he wondered if he still cared, Wallie reached his conclusion. "There were abominations," he said, "but they were begun by Tarru. Once he imprisoned me within the temple grounds, this was no longer an affair of honor."

Imperkanni waited to be sure that that was all, then drew a deep breath. He looked questioningly at Yoningu, as though saying, "Your witness."

"Did you try to leave the grounds, my lord?"

Wallie admitted that he had not.

"You say that you were Honorable Tarru's guest. You were hardly still his guest when you reached here, were you?"

"Well, we hadn't said good-bye and come again!"

Yoningu was persistent. It was only his twisted mouth that made him look as though he were enjoying himself. It must be painful for him to denounce a man who had displayed such swordsmanship, but it had been illegal swordsmanship. "A guest who leaves without farewell does not remain a guest indefinitely. He was no longer your host, so he was within his rights in challenging Adept Nnanji. You interfered in an honorable passage of arms."

That was ridiculous. Wallie was sure that there was an answer to all this somewhere, but even the fear of death seemed insufficient to get his brain working again.

"Nnanji," he croaked. "You talk for a while."

Nnanji looked up sadly. "I admit the charge," he said. Then he leaned his elbows on his knees once more, clasped his oversize hands, and went back to staring across the circle at Yoningu's boots.

"What!"

This time Nnanji did not even raise his head. "I allowed a personal friendship to lead me into an abomination. I am happy that I saved your life, Lord Shonsu, but I was wrong to do so."

"What the hell was I supposed to do?" Wallie demanded, looking at Yoningu and Imperkanni. "We were his guests, and he had prepared a trap in our room. He was swearing his men to the blood oath at swordpoint. That oath needs a specific cause, and the only cause was that he wanted to steal my sword, the Goddess' sword! They did not address him as 'liege.' He was keeping the oath secret—another abomination, as you well know."

"Did you observe this swearing, my lord?"

Wallie sighed. "No. As I told you, it was reported to me by the slaves."

Nnanji looked up and drew back his lips in a grimace. Slaves could not testify. Lord Shonsu had already discredited that defense himself.

"Adept Briu confirmed the third oath!" Wallie shouted. "Also the attack on Adept Nnanji—"

"Then, by admitting it, this Briu was either disobeying his liege or lying to you?"

Wallie wanted to pound his head with his fists. He could not think of an answer to that.

Katanji nudged his brother from behind. Nnanji waved him away without turning.

"Who shed the first blood?" Yoningu demanded.

There it was—death before dishonor. A man was supposed to be honorable at all costs. If his enemy killed him by dishonorable means, then that was too bad, he must be avenged. By their standards Wallie should have tried walking out the gate and let himself be cut down, or just waited until Tarru came for him. He who cast the first stone was the sinner.

Some of the swordsmen had died rather than swear to Tarru . . . but there were no witnesses to that, except the slaves.

"I killed first!" Wallie said. He was thinking of Janghiuki, but they would assume he meant Transingji. Did it matter?

Imperkanni broke the ensuing silence. "Why did you release your vassal and protégé from his oaths, my lord?"

That must seem a very odd decision to him, and perhaps he was looking for some way to spare Nnanji.

"I hoped that he might be allowed through," Wallie said, "with the others."

Imperkanni and Yoningu glanced at his companions and then at each other—two slaves, a boy, a baby, and a beggar? Why bother?

Imperkanni folded his arms and pondered for a moment, studying Nnanji. Yes, he was trying to find some way to acquit the accomplice—Wallie's guilt was obvious. "I am curious as to what happened when you arrived, adept. What was said before Honorable Tarru challenged you?"

Nnanji raised his eyes and returned the Seventh's gaze glumly. "I challenged him, my lord," he said.

Obviously Imperkanni was finding this a difficult case. He frowned. "By the look of your facemarks, adept, you were a Second quite recently."

"This morning, my lord."

A very difficult case; both defendants seemed to be insane. "You were a Second this morning, and this afternoon you challenged a Sixth?"

Nnanji glanced at Wallie and suddenly, for just an instant, grinned. Then his face darkened again. Wallie dearly wanted to punch him. Gorramini and Ghaniri had known how to provoke Nnanji to violence. It must have been common knowledge in the guard. Tarru had only to make some remark about rugmakers.

"He insulted you?" demanded Imperkanni.

Nnanji shrugged. "Yes. He was determined to pick a fight, so I ignored his insults to me, but then he insulted my . . . friend, Lord Shonsu, who was not there to defend himself."

The other men glanced at one another. Wallie could guess what was coming now.

"What did he say?" Imperkanni asked. When Nnanji did not speak he added, "The noble lord is here to defend himself now."

Nnanji looked up angrily. "He said that he was a murderer."

The court looked at Wallie, who was sadly feeling that he was not worthy of Nnanji's friendship. That hurt almost as much as the guilt of the murders, or the prospect of sudden death now looming ahead of him.

"I'm afraid that he was right, Nnanji," he said. "I killed Janghiuki with my fist. I only meant to stun him . . . but his death was not an affair of honor."

Imperkanni demanded to know who Janghiuki might

have been, and Wallie explained, not caring very much any more what was said.

"I add that confession to the list of . . ." Then Yoningu stopped. He and Imperkanni stared at each other for a moment in silence. The Seventh did not seem to move at all, but his white ponytail waved very slightly, as though in a faint draft. Yoningu said quickly, "I withdraw that."

"I will accept that Swordsman Janghiuki's death was accidental, my lord," Imperkanni said. "If you had wanted to kill him, I hardly think you would have used a fist."

Nnanji looked up momentarily in surprise.

Katanji poked his back again. Nnanji ignored him.

Wallie glanced over at Honakura. His eyes were properly open now, but he was panting wheezily and not paying attention. No hope there.

"The will of the Goddess overrides the sutras!" Wallie said. Incredibly, this trial was going against him. He needed witnesses! Old Coningu would do—he had known. Or Briu. But he was certain that the court would not adjourn to the temple if he asked it to. Imperkanni was starting to fidget.

"True," said the court. "We swear to obey the will of the Goddess ahead of the sutras. But who is to determine Her will? We must assume that the sutras represent Her commandments to us unless we receive clear evidence to the contrary . . . a miracle, I suppose. I agree that you have a remarkable sword, Lord Shonsu, but it does not give you the right to commit any atrocity you fancy. There are eight dead men here. Do you have any further defense?"

What was the use of saying more? Wallie had been given a fair hearing, probably a lot more than a man of lesser rank would have received. The gods were punishing him. He had murdered Janghiuki and then he had cut down a Second running away. It could be that he would be punished for the wrong crimes, but crimes there were. Nnanji was right—why not just admit it?

The penalty for failure was death. Decapitation was quick and painless; he might have done worse.

"My lord!" squeaked Katanji, white-faced with terror,

his sword canted at an absurd angle across his back. Imperkanni's face darkened at the presumption. One of the Fourths reached out a large hand to grab the impudent urchin.

"Ask Lord Shonsu how he got his kilt wet!" Katanji screamed as he was dragged away.

"Stop!" Imperkanni barked. "What did you say, novice?"

The Fourth restored Katanji to a vertical position and released him.

"My lord, ask Lord Shonsu how he got his kilt wet." Katanji made a sickly smile and rubbed his ill-treated shoulder.

Imperkanni, Yoningu, and Nnanji all looked down at Wallie's kilt and boots.

Great! Wallie thought. He had broken the taboo against going in the River, but no one had noticed except the smarty-pants kid. Probably there was an automatic and painful death penalty for that—ganching on hot irons for a first offense, perhaps. Thanks, Katanji!

Yoningu jumped from his stool and raced out to the jetty, leaping over Trasingji as he went.

Imperkanni was looking at Wallie with teeth bared in a very strange and unhumorous smile.

Nnanji was also staring, and his eyes were glistening.

Yet under the guano and the road dust and the charcoal smears and the bloodstains...under all those, Nnanji was certainly wearing something like his old grin. Hero worship, force ten.

What the hell was going on here?

Visibly pale, Yoningu strode back in, came to attention beside his stool, and said stiffly, "Mentor, I wish to withdraw the charges against Lord Shonsu."

"Indeed?" Imperkanni said. "Yes, I expect you do! Lord Shonsu, will you graciously permit my protégé to withdraw his charges?" He was openly smiling now, very friendly.

That was how it was done? Wallie recalled the little healer in the jail, Innulari, who had died for losing a patient. So Yoningu was less of a prosecutor than a plaintiff, and if the court decided that he had brought false charges then he would pay the penalty—a good way to prevent frivolous litigation and an excellent means of deterring the proliferation of lawyers. Not that Wallie needed a slave, if that was an option, but a good Sixth would be an invaluable addition to his force, so perhaps there was room to bargain...

Then he saw that his hesitation had caused Imperkanni's smile to dry up, and that there were lowered heads and tightened fists and slitted eyes all the way around him. Whatever the rules said, Yoningu was one of the band. If Wallie demanded his pound of whatever flesh he was entitled to, then he was going to have to fight every last man of them afterward, from Imperkanni himself down to the lowest apprentice.

"The charges against Adept Nnanji are likewise withdrawn?" Wallie asked, not understanding why anything should be withdrawn.

Imperkanni relaxed and restored his smile. "Of course, my lord." He looked for a long moment at Nnanji, and when he returned his smile to Wallie it said quite plainly that Nnanji was a glass box to him. He was a practiced leader of men. In Nnanji he could see the juvenile doubts and hero worship that would fade in the light of experience; the courage, tenacity, and integrity that would shine more brightly.

"As you said, my lord, this was no affair of honor, but a true battle. Adept Nnanji is to be congratulated on a fine start to his career. He was correct to come to your assistance. His honor is without reproach, his courage beyond question, my lord, like your own."

Nnanji gasped, then stammered and thanked him, and sniffled. Then he squared his shoulders and grinned at Wallie.

Imperkanni rose, so the others did. "Indeed, I would seek to recruit him to my troop, but I assume that you will be taking him back as protégé yourself, my lord?" he asked, and his yellow eyes twinkled.

"If he will accept me as mentor," Wallie said, "I will be honored—and very humble."

A look of disbelief and delight spread over Nnanji's filthy face. "My lord! You will let me swear to you after I denounced you?" Cinderella's lemon was a coach again, with all the optionals.

"It was your duty," Wallie said. "If you had not done so, then I should not want you." He could out-Alice their Wonderland any time.

Yoningu had been following the treatment of Nnanji with a smile adding to the lopsidedness of his face. He and Imperkanni, as longtime companions, could probably read each other's thoughts without difficulty. He flickered a wink at Wallie and remarked, "Of course, my lord, the first minstrel we meet will be informed how Shonsu and Nnanji defeated ten swordsmen in a redoubtable feat of arms."

Nnanji had not yet thought of fame. His mouth opened and nothing but a croak emerged. It was the glass slipper—Cinderella could live happily ever after on that alone.

"Not *Shonsu and Nnanji*," Wallie said solemnly, "but *Nnanji and Shonsu*. He started it."

Jja was smiling at him. Cowie was asleep. Even the old man was looking better, sitting up straight and listening. Katanji . . . Katanji was studying Wallie with a puzzled expression. He alone seemed to know that Wallie was winging it, and did not understand his acquittal.

"Indeed, my lord," Imperkanni said thoughtfully, "I do not presume to advise you in your affairs . . . but in this case you might even consider eleven forty-four."

Seniors loved to quote high-number sutras over the heads of juniors—they all did it. Yoningu frowned, for Sixths were usually immune to that game. Nnanji pouted and looked puzzled.

Eleven forty-four? The *last* sutra? Was Imperkanni testing to see if Shonsu was a genuine Seventh?

Then Wallie worked it out, and a great blaze of excitement banished his darkness of guilt and fatigue. He rec-

ognized the favor of the gods. It had not been a test—for
a test he must have failed—but a lesson, and he had
learned as required. He was not a failure, he was still
Her champion. His relief was as great as Nnanji's.

"Of course!" he said. "Why not? A very good idea,
Lord Imperkanni!" Then he threw back his head and
bellowed that vast sepulchral laugh of Shonsu's, lifting
the swallows and frightening the horses, startling the
mules in the meadow, waking the baby, echoing and re-
echoing over the corpses in the guardhouse like the tolling of the temple bell.

TRIUMPH!

#1144 THE FOURTH OATH

Fortunate is he who saves the life of a colleague,
and greatly blessed are two who have saved each
other's. To them only is permitted this oath and it
shall be paramount, absolute, and irrevocable:

> I am your brother,
> My life is your life,
> Your joy is my joy,
> My honor is your honor,
> Your anger is my anger,
> My friends are your friends,
> Your enemies are my enemies,
> My secrets are your secrets,
> Your oaths are my oaths,
> My goods are your goods,
> You are my brother.

††† † †††

The sun was sinking into the horizon like a drop of blood
soaking into sand, pointing an accusing, bloody finger
across the tops of the ripples toward Wallie on the jetty.
Perhaps, suggested Imperkanni, the noble lord should
consider spending the night at the guardhouse and

continue his journey the next day? But despite his sudden mood of jubilation, Wallie wanted nothing more than to get away from the scene of carnage and the holy island as soon as he could. Anywhere else would be better.

He turned to the boat captain, who had been resignedly sitting on the floor through the whole trial and had now been released. "Have you any reservations about traveling by night, sailor?"

"Not with you on board, my lord," said the man, groveling. So whatever it was that had happened, it affected sailors, also.

The suspicion and hostility had vanished. Every man of the free company had been presented to the relentless Lord Shonsu and the inexorable Adept Nnanji and each had humbly congratulated both on their magnificent feat of arms. Nnanji's grin appeared to have become permanent.

Imperkanni had put his efficient organization to work. Food and straw mattresses were being stripped from the guardhouse and carried to the boat, bodies gathered up, horses inspected and tended. A laughing Third produced food to silence the loud Vixini, and a glass of wine for the old man, which affected a dramatic improvement there, also.

"We shall stay here ourselves tonight," the Seventh said. He looked at the skinner. "You can sleep in one of the horse stalls. We shall need some of your mules in the morning. Not many."

The skinner seemed to have had news of a major disaster. His rodent eyes switched plaintively to Wallie, who was puzzled for a moment, and then started to laugh.

"I expect that he will be missed if he does not return to his loved ones, my lord," he said. "Someone will go looking for him. Right, skinner?"

The man nodded meaningfully. "My wife, my lord."

And she would find no husband, no mules, but a fortune in gold coins in the stable.

"I am sure that your men can handle mules, can they not, Lord Imperkanni? Keep what you need and let him go. He was helpful to me."

The white-maned swordsman raised his salt-and-pepper eyebrows in astonishment, but agreed as a favor to Lord Shonsu. Wallie was amused—even mass murderers can be good guys sometimes.

By tacit consent, the two Sevenths began to stroll along the jetty for a private talk.

"You realize that the Goddess has brought you here to be reeve?" Wallie said. "The priests will have you appointed before you can get off your horse."

The older man nodded. "I admit that the idea tempts," he replied. "Yoningu and I have talked much lately of finding the stone scabbard. One grows old, I fear. The cheering becomes more fun than the fighting."

He was silent for a moment and then continued. "This was not the first time that Her hand has moved us, and always thereafter we found noble work for our swords. But Hann was a surprise; we could find no problem that needed us. Then Yoningu persuaded me to make the pilgrimage. He wanted to inquire after his father... and here we are." He chuckled, being jovially patronizing. "When we stepped on the jetty and heard the swords, I thought that you were the problem, my lord. I see now that you were the solution."

He was probably testing Wallie's spark point, but Wallie was in no mood to let him find it. "Tell me about his father, then?" he asked.

Imperkanni shrugged. "He last heard of him years and years ago. At that time he was planning to come here to enlist with the guard. I expect acorns have grown oaks since he died."

"Nnanji may have heard tell of him," Wallie suggested. "What was his name?"

"Coningu of the Fifth."

"Indeed?" Lord Shonsu suddenly seemed to lose interest. "On second thought, perhaps Yoningu's best bet would be to inquire of the old commissary I mentioned. He would know, if anyone would. You will find him co-operative and honorable." He turned to a more delicate subject. "Some of your younger men will find life in the guard very dull, will they not?"

The gold eyes went stony cold, and Wallie had the impression that the white ponytail was twitching by itself. He wondered if Sevenths could ever relax together, two stags discussing their herds.

"I have not yet been offered the position, my lord."

No recruiting!

Wallie sighed and then smiled. "There are reports of brigands fleecing pilgrims on the trail."

Imperkanni chuckled. "Most humbly I pray to the Holiest that they try that tomorrow."

At the end of the quay they turned and started back. There was very little wind. Work on the boat seemed to have been completed. Wallie started looking around for his party—and once more caught the eye of young Katanji.

Katanji nudged his brother, who was standing beside him. He got angrily hushed, but Imperkanni also had intercepted the exchange. He raised an eyebrow at Nnanji.

Nnanji flushed. "Nothing, my lord."

"That protégé of yours is a sharp little dagger," the Seventh remarked. "He noticed what no one else did, and what Lord Shonsu was too proud to mention. I am in his debt. Present him."

"He does not yet know the salutes and responses, my lord," Nnanji protested.

Any swordsmen of the Seventh rank could freeze a man through to his spinal column with one glance. Even the intrepid Adept Nnanji quailed before the look he now received.

"Then let him salute as a civilian," Imperkanni said.

So Katanji was presented and had his chance: "I wondered if I might ask one of your juniors, my lord, to take word to my . . . our parents? Just to tell them where we have gone?" He flashed a glance toward Wallie. "And say that I am in good hands?"

Nnanji squirmed at such sentimentality. Imperkanni exchanged a smile with Wallie. He had noticed the civilian parentmarks. "I shall deliver that message myself," he said. "And I shall tell them that they make fine sons, good swordsmen . . . and that you are in Her hands. Who can direct me to them?"

"A-adept Briu, my lord," stuttered Nnanji, red and awkward.

Wallie said, "I commend Briu to you, my lord. I think he would be grateful for a chance to redeem himself. He is basically an honest man. He could advise you on the others, if nothing else."

Imperkanni thanked him politely, but obviously intended to make his own decisions about the temple guard.

Then the boat was ready and night had seeped into the sky.

"You are quite sure?" Wallie asked.

"Certain!" Honakura snapped, although he was still very shaky. "One mule trip is two too many." He chuckled. "Also I have a professional interest in miracles, and they follow you like flies follow cows."

"We have a sad ceremony to perform before you depart, my lord," Imperkanni told Wallie, nodding to where his men had laid out eight naked bodies on the jetty.

"Mm?" Honakura said. "Perhaps I should be a priest again for just a minute?" He tottered along to the bodies and pulled off his headband.

The expression on Imperkanni's face when he counted the facemarks gave Wallie considerable satisfaction.

Thus Wallie's last deed on the holy island was to attend a funeral. The free swords knew how such things should be done. Not wanting to show his ignorance, he went off to relieve himself, and by the time he returned they were all lined up, and his place was obvious. Twelve swordsmen stood in a line along the edge of the jetty, Katanji the smallest and youngest and most junior at the far end, Imperkanni on Honakura's right in the center. Wallie slipped into place on his left and drew his sword in salute with the rest.

"Honorable Tarru," Nnanji said as the first body was dragged forward by the slaves. Honakura recited the words of farewell:

"Tarru of the sixth rank, we return you now to the Great Mother of us all, for your journey in this world is ended.

"You go to Her, as we all shall, bearing dust and stains from the road, and those She will wash away; bearing hurts and sorrows, and those She will comfort; bearing joys and honors, and these She will welcome.

"You go to Her to be restored and to be cherished until, in Her own time, She sends you forth to travel once more.

"Tell Her, we pray, that we are mindful of Her, and that we also await Her call; for from waters we come, and to the waters must we all return."

The body hit the water with a splash . . . and the water boiled, exploded in a wild eruption that rapidly became a silvery foam, turned crimson and hissed as the air in the lungs surfaced, and then died away to a faint pink stain, drifting slowly downstream. It was all over in moments, but the corpse had vanished. Wallie was so shocked that he almost dropped his sword.

"Master Trasingji . . ."

From then on Wallie was ready for it, but he found that cold shivers ran through him every time and he was hard put to stop himself from trembling visibly. What he had escaped! From the depths of Shonsu's vocabulary came a word ... it floated around and around in his head until at last the translator found an approximate equivalent: piranha.

Now he understood the verdict of the trial. The will of the Goddess took precedence over the sutras, and She had made Her will known. Only Her champion could have reached the jetty alive by that route, so She approved of his actions. No human court would overrule her. Now he understood Nnanji's shocked reaction when he had once suggested crossing the River, he understood why the word for "swim" applied only to fish, why the priests by the pool had been so reluctant to get their feet wet, why the skinner watered his mules at a trough, why it had been so easy to outflank Tarru. Little wonder that he was being regarded with superstitious awe, after an act of such faith and courage.

He stared out over the miles of calm water to the last blush of evening. He thought how wonderfully soothing a swim would be to his jangled nerves, his filthy and weary and saddle-sore body. But there would be no swimming in this lifetime for him.

The gods perform miracles when *they* choose, never on demand.

The ferry was a whaleboat with fore-and-aft rigging. It could have carried perhaps two dozen passengers on its thwarts, but most of those had been removed by the swordsmen. With straw-filled mattresses spread over the gratings there was ample room for seven passengers to sprawl in comfort and chew at the provisions provided —cold fowl, stale bread and cheese, and flagons of warm beer. Eased along by a barely perceptible breeze, the ferry slid through the lazy ripples without a sway. There was enough food to feed a regiment of Nnanjis, so they shared it with the potbellied, obsequious captain and the loutish boy who formed his crew.

The night was warm and silent and glorious, the arc of

the Dream God spectacular among the stars, brighter than a full moon on Earth, painting the boat in silver and gray, on black and silver water.

The rugmaker's sons and Cowie had settled amidships, the crew by the tiller. Wallie sat on the bow thwart with Jja beside him and Honakura cross-legged at his feet. Vixini had been forcefully restrained all day, screaming for freedom to move around. Now he had his chance, so he rolled up in a ball and went to sleep.

As soon as the boat was away from the jetty Wallie turned to Jja and kissed her. She returned the kiss as a well-trained slave should.

A slave, but not a friend. He smiled encouragingly at her and tried not to show the hurt he felt. Yet how else could it be? She had witnessed him in a rampage of slaughter. He could hardly bear to think about it himself, so how could he expect her to forgive, and overlook, and understand? If he had lost her love, then the price of victory had been higher than he had been willing to pay.

He was miserably conscious of the nosy little priest beside him, who would listen to anything he said. He wished he could take her away and talk, yet he did not know how he would put his feelings into words.

Jja almost never tried to put feelings into words, but she returned his look with a long, searching gaze, her expression unreadable, and finally said, "We are both slaves, master."

"What do you mean?"

A very faint hint of a smile crept into her face in the silver dimness. "I must please my master. My master must please the gods."

He tightened his arm around her. "Very true, my love."

"This was what they wanted of you?" she asked softly.

He nodded. "Blood! Ruthlessness. Ferocity."

"Wallie or Shonsu?"

"Wallie!" he snapped. "Shonsu had it already."

She was silent for a while as the boat seemed to pick

up speed. "It is easier for me," she said quietly. "My task is to give you pleasure, and that gives me much joy also."

"Killing will never give me pleasure," he growled.

She shook her head. "But you will obey the gods, master?"

"Yes." He sighed. "I suppose I will. They reward me greatly."

Then she put her arms around him. They kissed with lovers' fervor, and he knew that their love had not been lost, it had been strengthened.

He broke off the embrace before his glands went totally out of control and sat for a minute, breathing hard and feeling much better.

"I was just thinking," Honakura remarked to the night sky, "that boats are greatly superior to mules."

"That was not what you were thinking, old man!"

"Yes, I was," the priest replied with a chuckle. "How could you kiss her on a mule?"

Later, when Wallie had finished his meal, he dropped the scraps overboard, piece by piece, watching in horrified fascination as the piranha swarmed on them. This close to the water he was able to make them out if he watched carefully—momentary flickers of silver in the black water, no larger than a man's little finger, but able to appear instantly in unlimited numbers.

"You did not have piranha in your dream world, my lord?" Honakura asked, leaning back against the gunwale and watching him with quiet amusement. Wallie started guiltily.

"Not normally," he admitted. "If the demigod left me in such ignorance of the World, then he must make himself responsible for guiding me."

The priest smiled. "I suggest that you do not attempt that maneuver again, now that you know."

"I have already made a vow to that effect," Wallie said. "Explain the temple pool to me?"

"Even there, sometimes," said the old man. "But they avoid fast water, it is said, and that may be why the pool is usually safe. I would not walk in it from choice, though."

Wallie wondered what other horrors the World might have in store for him.

Jja lay down beside Vixini and went to sleep at once. Wallie was too jumpy to try yet. The light was brighter than moonlight, but strangely diffuse, throwing double shadows. A mist was forming over the River. It was hard to make out much at a distance, even as close as the vague figures of Cowie, Nnanji, and Katanji amidships.

Nnanji, a few minutes later, came scrambling forward to kneel in front of Wallie and, incidentally, Honakura. He was still licking his fingers, and his face was a blur in the darkness under its coat of grime. He had not removed his sword, which seemed odd, but doubtless he had one of those strange swordsmen reasons for it.

"My lord?" he said. "May I swear the second oath to you now?"

Wallie shook his head. "It can wait until morning, surely? You didn't want a fencing lesson in the boat, did you?"

White teeth showed in a grin. "No, my lord." Then there was a silence . . .

"Let me guess," Wallie said. "You want to know why the gods approved of all those abominations?"

"Yes, my lord." Nnanji sounded relieved.

"Perhaps our venerable friend can explain," Wallie said. "Why should the Goddess have permitted so many abominations? We assume that She does not approve of abominations. Correct, holy one?" He looked down at the tiny, huddled shape beside him.

"I'm not a holy one any longer," Honakura said pettily. "But, yes, that is a fair assumption."

"And I do not approve," Wallie said, "of mentors beating protégés. But I butchered you very thoroughly once, my young friend."

Nnanji's eyes showed gleaming white in the dark. "That was to break my curse, my lord."

Suddenly Wallie became aware that something unexpected was happening amidships. He tried not to stare too openly, but it looked as though Katanji had moved very close to Cowie. Nnanji was kneeling with his back to them.

"I think that the gods were trying to break *my* curse, Nnanji."

"You did not have a curse, my lord!" Nnanji protested loyally.

"Oh, yes I did! I told you, once—I don't like killing people."

Nnanji's mouth opened and then closed.

"The god ordered me to kill Hardduju. I did it—but only because I had been specifically told to do so. The only other order I had been given was to be an honorable and valiant swordsman. An honorable swordsman of the Seventh should not have tolerated Tarru and his sleazy tricks for an instant. I butchered you and taunted you, until you lost your temper and turned on me. The gods forced me into a corner until I started shedding blood and showed that I could be a killer. The same process."

"It's like testing a sword, isn't it?" Nnanji said. "You bend it, to see if it snaps back or breaks?"

"Yes!" said Wallie, surprised. "Very good comparison!"

"But," Nnanji persisted, "even if the gods planned all this . . ."

His conscience was still bothering him.

"We committed no abominations, either of us. The temple guard was a gang of recreants. Imperkanni acquitted us. Do you agree with his verdict, old man?"

"Oh, yes! Obviously you were forced," said Honakura. "The gods chose the two of you and—"

"Two of us?" Nnanji said.

Katanji was making progress. He was getting no cooperation, but neither did he seem to be meeting resistance. In Katanji's world, evidently, all those not opposed were in favor, and obviously this was one scratcher who would not have been in need of Wild Ani's evening classes.

"If you will swear the second oath to me, Adept Nnanji," Wallie said, "and I hope you will, for I shall be proud to have you as a protégé again, then there is another oath that I would swear with you also."

"The blood oath? Of course, my lord," Nnanji said eagerly.

"Never!" Wallie said. "I think that oath is an abomination, even if the Goddess did make the sutras. I have had enough of the third oath to last two lifetimes. No, I speak of the fourth oath."

Nnanji looked wary. "I never heard of any fourth oath!"

Honakura claimed to know nothing about swordsmen's oaths, but he was peering curiously at Wallie in the gloom.

"You could not have done," Wallie said. "First, it is contained in sutra eleven forty-four..."

"Ah!" said Nnanji.

"The last sutra. Only a candidate for Seventh would ever hear of it, unless a Seventh deliberately told him, as I am going to tell you. Secondly, it is restricted..."

"Oh!" said Nnanji.

"But we qualify, you and I. It may only be sworn by those who have saved each other's lives, and that can happen only in battle, not in the ways of honor. I think, friend Nnanji, that that was why the gods sent us into battle today. I saved you from Tarru, and you saved me from Ghaniri. Obviously it is a very rare oath, and I think maybe it is not much talked of, anyway."

Nnanji's eyes were shining in the dark. Secret signs and fearsome oaths were the very essence of the swordsmen's craft, so a secret oath was double pleasure to him.

"Tell me the words, and I will swear," he said.

Katanji's explorations were coming along very well now. He had removed Cowie's wrap and was still progressing. Nnanji was clearly very fond of his young brother, and his attitude to sex was astonishingly casual, but could it possibly be so casual that he would loan his new slave even before he had tried her out himself?

With difficulty, Wallie pulled his eyes away. "Don't be in too much of a hurry, Nnanji," he warned. "In some ways it is even more terrible than the third oath. But it is fair. It binds both parties equally, not like slave and master."

Honakura coughed in the gloom. "Is it, by any chance, an oath of brotherhood, my lord?"

"It is," Wallie said, smiling. "You see, Nnanji, the first thing I have to do, the god told me, is to find my brother, and...and I don't have any brothers that I know of."

"Me?" Nnanji was greatly excited. "The god meant me?"

"I'm sure he did, because he put you on the beach, so that I almost fell over you coming out of the water. You have a part to play in Her task, Nnanji, if you will swear to be my oath brother."

"Give me the words, my lord!"

Time had run out. Katanji's kilt had flopped to the mattress.

"Nnanji," Wallie said. "I hate to interrupt this important conversation, and it is certainly none of my business, but did you give your protégé permission to do what he is just about to do?"

"Do what?" Nnanji asked, turning round. "Arrrrgh!"

He went scrambling rapidly aft, while Honakura smothered sniggers. A sharp cry of pain rang out, followed by thumping noises.

"You didn't mention the part about gaining wisdom," Honakura remarked.

"I suspect that 'another' means another brother," Wallie replied, stretching himself out on the mattress, "and if so, then the man in question just gained a little wisdom for his own account."

"But *chain*, my lord? *Chain* your brother?"

"The fourth oath is irrevocable."

"Indeed? I have never heard of such an oath. That is interesting!"

"But now it is your turn. How did you know about Katanji's black hair? And brotherhood?"

"Mmm, yes," Honakura said. He also lay down and made himself comfortable. "I told you that Ikondorina was mentioned a couple of times in other sutras, my lord. Once there is a reference to 'Ikondorina's red-haired brother,' and once to 'Ikondorina's black-haired brother.' That is all. Red hair is very rare, as you know, and pure black hair is unusual."

Wallie gazed up at the rings and the stars. "Tell me the stories about them, then."

"Maybe one day," Honakura said.

Why was the old man so reluctant? What had he guessed? Wallie had no way of finding out—and perhaps he would be happier not knowing. Yet he was sure that he had now begun his task. He had solved the first part of the god's riddle. Nnanji had a role to play, and almost certainly it was Katanji who would bring wisdom. In fact, he had already done so, for it was he who had turned the trial around. Thus Wallie's laughter and joy in the guardhouse—he was on the right track.

The boat started rocking with a new rhythm, and he sat up to find the cause. The cause lay with Cowie.

He could not sleep. Something was missing, some thought struggling to escape from his subconscious. The events of the day crawled all over his mind and would not let him go. The old man was snoring. There was something sticking in his back . . .

He moved to a new position and tried again, with no more success. The light of the Dream God reminded him of his nights in the jail. Then he tried turning on his side and found himself looking into a pair of big dark eyes not far away. Katanji, also, could not sleep, and that was hardly surprising. If it had been a big day for Wallie, what had it been for him?

"Homesick?" Wallie asked quietly.

"A little, my lord."

Even at Katanji's age, his brother would have pulled out all his toenails rather than admit to that.

"It would be nice to be at home," Katanji whispered, "just for a little while, telling them all about the day I have had."

"You can't expect a day like that very often," Wallie told him.

"But there will be other good days, my lord?"

This had been a good day? Well, perhaps it had, in the end. "I expect so. Good night, Novice Katanji."

"Good night, my lord."

Nnanji started rocking the boat once more.

Then Wallie opened his eyes again, and the boy was still awake.

"Thank you, Katanji. I didn't know about the piranha."

"I thought not, my lord."

Wallie said, "That money I gave you on the trail . . ."

"Oh!" Katanji started to fumble with his unfamiliar harness pouch. "I forgot, my lord."

And eggs could fly! "No," Wallie said. "You keep it."

Katanji thanked him solemnly.

After a pause, the boy whispered again. "My lord? You did not have any parentmarks?"

"Did not?"

"You have a fathermark now, but still no mother-mark."

"I do?" Wallie said aloud, and then dropped his voice again. "You're serious?" He rubbed his right eyelid with a finger and some spit. "Still there?"

Katanji leaned closer to have a look. "Yes, my lord. A sword."

"Thank you, Katanji. Now . . . try to sleep."

"Yes, my lord."

A sword . . . Shonsu's father? Or Detective Inspector Smith? Or just a sign of approval from the demigod, who must be laughing, somewhere. *Thank You, Shorty.* What craft had Shonsu's mother followed? Wallie Smith's mother had been a crime reporter. That would translate as minstrel, he supposed, and chuckled.

He lay and listened to the creak of the ropes and the hiss of water flowing by. He thought of the silvery death that swarmed below him, only inches away.

"My lord?" It was a very soft whisper.

Wallie opened his eyes. "Yes?"

"What happens tomorrow?" Katanji asked.

"Oh, I expect we'll think of something," Wallie said.

That was what had been wrong—he had been brooding on the past day, which was gone and done, washed away forever in the waters of the Goddess, like the bodies. He should be thinking of the future. The struggling thought in his subconscious surfaced, and it was the command of the demigod: *Go and be a swordsman, Shonsu! Be honorable and valorous. And enjoy yourself, for the World is yours to savor.*

Then he slept.

And the Dream God shone among the stars.

What happened the next day
—and on many subsequent days—
is recounted in
THE COMING OF WISDOM,
Book Two of *The Seventh Sword*

THE SWORDSMEN

SHONSU—of the seventh rank, a swordsman of unknown antecedents.

HARDDUJU—of the seventh rank, reeve of the temple guard.

GORRAMINI—of the fourth rank, a henchman.

NNANJI—of the second rank, a sword-carrier in the temple guard, and, later, vassal to Lord Shonsu.

TARRU—of the sixth rank, deputy to Lord Hardduju.

TRASINGJI—of the fifth rank, protégé to Honorable Tarru.

MELIU—of the fourth rank, a henchman.

CONINGU—of the fifth rank, a retired swordsman, commissary of the temple barracks.

BRIU—of the fourth rank, former mentor to Apprentice Nnanji.

LANDINORO—of the third rank, a friend of Briu's.

JANGHIUKI—of the third rank, a swordsman of the guard.

EPHORINZU—of the first rank, known as "Ears," protégé to Swordsman Janghiuki

GHANIRI—of the fourth rank, another henchman.

IMPERKANNI—of the seventh rank, a free sword.

YONINGU—of the sixth rank, protégé to Lord Imperkanni.

ABOUT THE AUTHOR

Dave Duncan was born in Scotland in 1933 and educated at Dundee High School and the University of St. Andrews. He moved to Canada in 1955 and has lived in Calgary ever since. He is married and has three grown-up children.

Unlike most writers, he did not experiment beforehand with a wide variety of careers. Apart from a brief entrepreneurial digression into founding—and then quickly selling—a computerized data-sorting business, he spent thirty years as a petroleum geologist. His recreational interests, however, have included at one time or another astronomy, acting, statistics, history, painting, hiking, model ship building, photography, parakeet breeding, carpentry, tropical plants, classical music, computer programming, chess, genealogy, and stock market speculation.

An attempt to add writing to this list backfired—he met with enough encouragement that he took up writing full-time. Now his hobby is geology.